The
BLACK
NORTH

The
BLACK
NORTH

Nigel McDowell

HOT
KEY
BOOKS

First published in Great Britain in 2014 by Hot Key Books
Northburgh House, 10 Northburgh Street, London EC1V 0AT

A CIP catalogue record for this book is available from the British Library.

ISBN: 978-1-4714-0067-4

1

This book is typeset in 10.5 Berling LT Std using Atomik ePublisher

Printed and bound by Clays Ltd, St Ives Plc

FSC

Hot Key Books supports the Forest Stewardship Council (FSC),
the leading international forest certification organisation, and is
committed to printing only on Greenpeace-approved FSC-certified paper.

www.hotkeybooks.com

Hot Key Books is part of the Bonnier Publishing Group
www.bonnierpublishing.com

For Wendy

History, Stephen said, is a nightmare from which I am trying to awake.

James Joyce, Ulysses

FIRST
OONA AND MORRIS

I

'Would you snap-shut your trap and listen – I can hear something.'

'I hear nothing. Imagining things, so you are.'

'Not. Tell the lads to be ready. They're close now.'

'The lads are ready enough – we all are. Ready to die for the Cause!'

'Not gonna die.'

'Don't be frighted now, sister dearest.'

'Not.'

'Dying in battle isn't a thing to be worried about. Remember – it's how Da and Granda went.'

'I know that. Can't forget, can I?'

'Da and Granda – pair of them would be proud of us now!'

'Give over, would you?'

'I'm sure they're watching down over us, in the company of the Sorrowful Lady Herself!'

'I'm sure they've got better things to be doing, wherever they are. Now *shush*.'

'Don't tell me to –'

'*Quiet*! I can hear something.'

'It's near enough night now anyway – they'll not come. Cowards.'

'Well, you better be ready, brother dearest – this is it. Things are about to begin.'

2

Then Oona cried, *'There they are, lads!'* and Morris cried, *'Attack!'* and blood-red ran the river where the battle broke. The banks of the Torrid were whited by winter then dashed with crimson. Crimson too across many mouths: rags were knotted to hide tell-tale breath, boys of the Cause on bellies and knees behind trees and rushes, all firing, mouths bellowing –

' !'

(Too much gunfire to hear anything but gunfire.)

When Invaders fell on the opposite shore others came rushing to take over. When boys fell on the side of the Cause, no one came to replace.

Oona ordered, *'Keep your heads down!'* and Morris ordered, *'Keep firing, don't give in!'* Not one was thinking surrender.

Morris roared, *'Don't let them cross! Don't let them into Drumbroken!'*

Look closely – Morris was on his front among reeds, small, skinny as a sally-rod and soot-haired, chilled to the soul but with heart blazing. He took aim with his granda's rifle, slowly and carefully and patient. But too slow – the thing jammed and his hearing rang with a long thin note as a shot went out from another rifle. The Invader he'd been eyeing fell.

Look closer – see Oona, the twin sister, on her belly too and only feet from Morris, same coloured head of hair on her.

'That was my shot to take!' Morris told her.

'Not my fault you're too slow,' said Oona. 'Is it my fault that gun's too heavy for your wee hands?'

'*One down doesn't win a war!*' said Morris. (Old bit of preaching from their da's mouth.)

'Thanks for reminding me,' said Oona. She rolled her eyes.

So Morris had to prove: his finger tugged the trigger and there was a blue-white flash and the gun bucked against his collarbone and another Invader fell into the River Torrid.

'Good shot, boy Kavanagh!' one of the Cause boys shouted.

'Notice no one is so quick to thank me,' said Oona.

'Now now,' said Morris, 'none of them bitter words. Very unappealing from a lady.' Oona used words to reply that definitely weren't lady-likely.

'Turf-mouth,' he told her.

'Clod-head,' she told him.

Both kept firing like it was their own private game. But how did they get there, these two? Beside the River Torrid, bickering?

Morris's first meeting with the Cause had gone like this: in a tin hut on the edge of Drumbroken with flags rippling on all walls, whiskey bottles were lined up along the rim of a tin bath and the Cause had said, 'Show how good you are with that gun of your granda's!' He'd done well enough, exploded all of the bottles except one. The boys of the Cause had all cheered and hailed him, 'A legend in the making!' Then they'd waved their crimson flags, sunk enamel cups into the bath, drunk the

8

whiskey that had collected there and all gotten wildly drunk as they sang their anthem, *The Song of the Divided Isle*.

Back by the river and Morris aimed once more. Fired – another Invader down. Again the call of congratulation: 'Good one, boy Kavanagh!'

Oona held her breath and one-two-three quick shots = three Invaders falling.

No one acknowledged.

Oona's first meeting with the Cause: she turned up at the tin hut the night after Morris had, but was told she wasn't wanted. But she wouldn't be told, kept coming back and back every night, and in the end they said that if Oona wanted to try to act like a man and fight then that was her burial, but they wouldn't be there to pick her up or look after her. Then she'd done the same shooting trick as Morris, but destroyed every single bottle on the bath. Nothing was said. The gun Oona had used was one she'd found in a ditch on the way there.

Now Oona ducked low in the reeds by the River Torrid – suddenly so much gunfire was her way, Invaders knowing she'd be a good one to take out.

'Watch yourself there, girl! Shouldn't be here at all, should be at home keeping house!'

This was Davy, near by. Fifteen years old, so only had two years on the twins, but he was their self-appointed leader. But Davy couldn't (Oona thought) have hit a cow in a cattle-mart. She showed him the tip of her tongue. Then she watched Davy's shoulder jerk, saw blood dash his cheek and any scowl slipped from his face. He collapsed.

Oona looked at Morris. They both did a deep swallow, and

continued to fire. But night was determined to darken the scene, and each moment meant it was harder to see what was approaching. And maybe-minutes-maybe-moments and more of the Cause were felled.

Somebody else made a feeble cry, 'They're going to cross into Drumbroken!'

But said too late: Invaders had entered the river and begun to wade across, their uniforms quickly shifting colour from winter-white and blood-red to just blood, matching the colour of the river.

'See!' Morris told Oona. 'It's true they have some North magic to make them blend into things, so they'll not be easy seen!'

'It's just the river staining their clothes,' said Oona. 'We're not winning this. We need to move into the forest – we know the trees and these Invaders don't. We'd be better off.'

Morris said, 'No! You said you weren't frighted.'

Oona nudged him and said, 'Not. Also said I wasn't going to die.'

Morris said, 'You go. I'm staying.'

And then came the call from other boys fleeing: 'Boys of the Cause retreat! Back into the trees! Run for it!'

Said Morris again, 'I'm not going anywhere, sister dearest.'

'Morris,' said Oona, 'I know it's hard for you, but try not to be the usual stubborn eejit!'

Morris didn't speak.

Invaders arrived on the shore and were shouting, 'After them! Pursue into the forest! We need them alive!'

Oona took her brother by the wrist and said only, '*Morris.*'

He swallowed. 'I can't,' he said. 'For Da and Granda, and for the Cause and for our county of Drumbroken, for all the Divided Isle I have to –'

'Don't give me that chat,' said Oona. '"*All the Divided Isle*"? You think they care up North about what you do here? And what about Granny? Going to leave her alone in the Kavanagh cottage and us pair dead in the Torrid? We're Kavanaghs, remember? And what did Da always say? *Kavanaghs don't do as expected.*'

Morris looked at her.

'We run,' she said. 'We live. We fight tomorrow.'

A moment. Then Oona's brother gave her something close to a nod and they were both up and off.

An Invader saw and shouted, 'Get him!'

Just *him?* thought Oona. Am I bloody invisible or just not worth bothering with or –? Morris turned and fired one-two shots and one-two Invaders dropped.

Gunfire was returned but the same Invader cried, 'No! I said don't shoot them. Remember the Captain's orders!'

Oona and Morris hurried on through the trees and deepening dusk, across snow on bare soles, shouts and calls and commands all flying and more boys of the Cause being brought down. Shot down? Not a bit – *dragged down*. Oona heard another shout from one of their own: 'They've got Briar-Witches with them!'

'What chat's this?' said Oona, to herself, and she had to stop to see . . .

A low rise was racing along underground, a hump that moved fast, weaving between trees, burrowing. A rabbit wouldn't do that, Oona thought. Nor a badger neither. Her look went to

11

one of the Cause boys standing: he was backed up to a tree, his gaze on the ground. The boy was Eamon O'Riley. Oona watched. She saw Eamon's last expression: terror and some tears, and then he was gone, pulled into the ground.

Some other in the Cause announced, 'Beware that ground beneath your feet!'

Oona said to Morris, 'Quick – up and climb.'

Oona leapt from the spot she stood on and caught a branch but Morris was too slow . . .

Her brother cried out, swore as he was taken by the ankles and yanked down, falling into the earth to his armpits. Still he held tight his granda's gun, and with the other hand he snatched for what little was there – grass, root, weakened weed, all snow-soaked and slipping.

'Hell's bells,' said Oona.

She returned to the ground and dropped her gun so she could take her brother's hand with both her own. Oona tried to drag him back, but already he was telling her, 'Leave me be. Run on. Go!'

'Shut up,' she told him. 'Stop trying to be a bloody martyr. And let go of that gun, will you?'

'Not a chance,' said Morris.

Then whatever held her brother snapped out at Oona – a rough, clubbed claw flew and a sharp spur like a cockerel's entered her hand at the fatty bulge below her thumb. She had to recoil and Morris slipped further into the ground, almost gone. But Oona Kavanagh wasn't being beaten – from the pocket of her dress she took a kitchen knife she'd brought from their cottage and slashed at the claw. It was quick to retreat.

But still something held Morris and wouldn't relinquish. And Oona wouldn't let go of him either.

'Don't be so bloody stubborn,' said Morris, teeth gritted. 'You're gonna have me in two halves!'

'Stubborn?' said Oona, teeth gritted too. 'You should talk!'

But she knew she was losing him to this creature underground, this Briar-Witch. A call of an Invader: 'Over there! They're having trouble with one!'

'Let me go,' said Morris. 'Like you said – think of Granny, her being alone . . .'

Invader: 'It's only a girl. Do we bother capturing her?'

And this was the thing that made Oona lose strength and lose her brother – *It's only a girl* . . .

Suddenly she had only a hole in the ground to stare into, and nothing in her hands but the crimson rag Morris had shed on his way down. She heard another Invader asking, 'What girl are you talking about? I can't see no one.'

Didn't see because Oona was already gone. She ran alone, the only member of the Cause in Drumbroken left standing.

13

3

Follow Oona – but need to be quick to see her! Fast through forest, up over or under or around any obstacle nature threw. She knew where she was going without needing to think it. And not a soul in Drumbroken could've caught her; no Invader could've laid a hand. Those things underground, though? Oona went on faster.

'By the blazes you're a fast one!' her granda used to tell her, and she always agreed, always liked to hear it said. He'd told her, 'Could run a mile a minute, couldn't you, girl?'

Could, did: Oona ran miles with only her own deep breathing for company and the thump-thump-crunch of her feet across snow. She didn't stop, not till she was almost home and she heard –

'*Morris! Morris, no!*'

A screaming. She ran on faster, the final half-mile conquered in less than half a minute. Then the Kavanagh cottage appeared between trees, a small stone tower with snow a blue-white cap on its hat of thatch. The front door of the cottage was wide. But when the screams came again they didn't sound from inside –

'*Help! Someone help!*'

It was Granny Kavanagh. Oona held tight her knife. What if Invaders were near by, skulking? She remembered: *It's only a girl, do we bother capturing her or . . . ?* And she thought to herself in answer: *By blazes, I'll show them!*

'Help me!'

Her grandmother was standing in just her nightdress in a clearing, arms outstretched and grappling with things unseen, screaming, 'No! Leave me alone! I can take no more of these sights! Leave me be now!'

Oona approached slowly. She settled her hand, gently, on her grandmother's arm.

I'm no good at this kind of thing, she thought. No good at being soft. Morris was better – he knew how to deal with her well, how to bring her back to herself.

'It's all right,' tried Oona. 'I'm here, Granny. I'm back.'

Her grandmother wasn't startled by Oona's sudden appearance. Didn't recoil at all or seem frightened. And this worried Oona more: the look Granny Kavanagh gave Oona was almost uncaring, as though they were scarcely more than strangers passing.

In the trees there was unrest. Oona saw plenty of yellow eyes watching and feet shifting. She looked closer – jackdaws.

'Come on now, Granny,' said Oona. 'It's cold. And not safe either now. Let's go home.' And slowly, she led Granny Kavanagh back towards the cottage.

'Where is he?' her grandmother asked. She had her hands clutched close to her chest like she was holding something safe inside. 'Where's Morris?'

Oona said nothing. She wasn't one for lies.

'He's in trouble,' said Granny Kavanagh, shuffling through snow. 'He's been taken. He's down in the dark with all the other children.'

'How did you know that?' said Oona, before she thought.

'I know,' said her grandmother. 'I know too well. I've seen.'

When they stepped over the threshold into the Kavanagh cottage it was too dark to make much out. No fire had been lit in the hearth so their only light was candlelight – their small shrine for the Sorrowful Lady by the back door, flames like small tongues wagging. Oona heard the soft cluck of the chickens in their corner. Still wary, she went slowly, looking to all shadows. But she found no lurkers.

'Now,' said Oona, and she settled her grandmother in her armchair. 'You'll be all right now, Granny. I'm here.'

'None of us will be all right now,' said Granny Kavanagh. Her breath smelled like milk on the turn. 'They're here, aren't they? Those Invaders. They're going to take everything from us.'

'No,' said Oona. 'I won't let them.' She held her kitchen knife tightest and the wound on her hand, the bite of that thing – Briar-Witch? – screamed and spread its hurt.

'Promises like petals,' said Granny Kavanagh. She swallowed with a sound like a lock. She still kept her hands clasped tight across her chest. 'Promises like petals, like I always say – dead as soon as they're dropped. We've no hope now. Soon the South will be made as Black as the North. They'll come and take this cottage and all in it, us included. And if the boys and men of the Cause can't stop them, then there's not a thing you or I can do about it.'

Soon, Oona's grandmother began to snore.

Oona waited till she was certain of the old woman's slumber and then said, like someone close could hear and care, 'Well you know what Granny? I escaped. I'm the only one of the Cause left in this county, and if any Invader thinks they're gonna come into this house and take me or you, then they had better be ready for a fight.'

4

Oona dreaming: in a cold forest, alone, so quiet. Then perhaps
not alone: there were eyes of crimson watching from the trees.

Oona walked on, and had the deep feeling that she was
searching. She walked further, a little faster, and then knew
who she was looking for – her brother. The trees were becoming
darker as though dying, were almost black as though burnt.
And then she was stopped. A voice she didn't recognise spoke
from the forest itself, a voice like this – not a whisper and not
a shout, but something softly crackling and as slippery-sticky
as sap, and then as smooth as poison. The voice told Oona –

*'My servants – those you call the Invaders – will soon be with
you. Though I am hardly a whole and formed thing yet, though I
am in pieces, I am still worshipped. I am scarcely able to speak,
to move, but still I am obeyed. I am feared.'*

And in dreaming, Oona found she could speak, asking,
'You're an Invader?'

The voice replied, *'I am much more. I am one who will rule.
I have come here from far away, but my roots are old, and deep.
You do not know me, not yet. But soon you will. You shall see
my work. You will see this Isle split and buckle and churn and*

transform, all at my will and word. I will command, and you will be bid. No tree, no stone, no bird nor blind thing beneath the earth shall defy me. Soon, I will own you all.'

Again, Oona asked the only question she could think of: 'What are you?'

A pause, then the voice of the blackening forest replied: *'I am your worst nightmares made real. And I am coming for you.'*

5

'Waken-up now, girl!'

Oona was struck – a quick clout to the back of the head that made her sit up. It was her grandmother, up and shouting, 'We can't lie about, girl! We need to make the preparations and concoctions for protection. We need to keep out those Invaders!'

Oona didn't speak. The voice she'd been hearing in her head remained, like an echo. Was it a dream? It had felt like more – closer, more than something made up. *But no*, Oona told herself. *Wasn't and couldn't be! Need to be sensible now*, she decided.

Oona had fallen asleep at the family table, the kitchen knife settled on the smooth top. And, like gentle disagreement, her first 'sensible' sight was one of her mother's paintings on the opposite wall. It showed a landscape rippled like the sea, but like a meadow too, with the colour of high summer in its greens and yellows and purples, with tall, skinny, silver strokes for trees. And in the distance were a scattering of small stone cottages with wooden roofs. An impossible-seeming place.

'Stop your daydreaming!' said Granny Kavanagh, and the old

woman slapped a hand on the family tabletop. 'Just like your poor mother – a dreamer, so you are! Now up and about – we need to get preparing!'

Oona watched Granny Kavanagh's fingers fussing on the dresser, one hand still holding something tight and the other searching through bottles and pots, saying, 'Ash? Aye. And a bit of that birch. What else for protection? Better a bit of feverwort – no *masterwort*. Where's the devil's shoestring? Plenty of agrimony too – herb of the Kavanagh family. Yes, that'll do . . .'

Oona stood but could scarcely discover enough energy for the effort. The wound on her hand had spread its pain further, wriggling out into everywhere and making her weaker. But so much needed to be done! Sweeping and baking and preparing . . . and the chickens were out already so would need to be fed . . . and still Granny Kavanagh's muttering went on: 'Need winter's bark, larkspur, neckweede . . .'

Oona felt again the lack of Morris to help her. Felt the absence of mother and father and grandfather, whom custom had buried six spadefuls down, beneath her toes. But she needed to try.

'Now Granny, why not sit down in your chair and I'll wet some tay. I'll bake the day's bread too and you can have something to eat.'

'No time now!' her grandmother cried. 'You think we've time for the tay and toast when the county is being overrun! Down from the Black North and over the river and into the forest and down the Eastern slope into the valley – they'll be here soon, wait and see!'

'How do you know that?' asked Oona.

'I know,' said her grandmother. She stilled, voice low. 'I've seen it.'

Then the sound of something approaching – crunch of snow under swift feet. Oona snatched the knife from the family table and waited.

'It's them,' said Granny Kavanagh. 'They're here.' But then the call: 'Oona Kavanagh! You in there?'

Oona returned knife to tabletop as Bridget O'Riley appeared in their doorway, breathless.

'You are here,' said Bridget. She breathed out, then bobbed with a bit of respect to the shrine for the Sorrowful Lady and said all in the same breath: 'Thank Herself you're all right! They've crossed the Torrid, those Invaders. Word's out everywhere. Paddy McGulder said he saw them on the Eastern slope near the Turn-Stump, and Eamon didn't come home.'

Oona knew, so only nodded. She saw again Eamon's final look – terror, tears, then Bridget's brother vanishing into the ground.

'Lots of them,' said Bridget. 'Lots of guns and North magic and they're saying that –'

'Outside we'll chat,' said Oona, and she moved towards the door. She thought there was no sense in adding more worry to the worry already in her grandmother's mind.

'Where you going, girl?' asked Granny Kavanagh. 'You're not to be off gallivanting! You're hardly much use to man or beast at the best of times, but we've got too much to do here! I know what's going on so don't try to be hiding things!'

'Won't be long away, Granny,' said Oona. 'You get on with

22

readying things and I'll be back soon. Don't fret now.'

'Not fretting!' her grandmother called. 'I don't fret! And don't be hanging around with those O'Rileys – they've manners a Sow-Mam would be ashamed of. I blame the mother!'

'*What?*' said Bridget. 'Hold on a minute, my mam is –'

'Come on,' whispered Oona, and she took Bridget by the arm and led her outside.

'Just walk with me. I've got things to tell you that you need to hear.'

6

'So do you think Morris is still living or what?' asked Bridget.

Oona said nothing. Then she became too aware of her silence so said (near-shouted): 'Course he's still living. I'd know if he wasn't.'

'Is that the twins thing?' said Bridget. 'Do you feel it when he gets hurt and things like that? Cos my cousins Veronica and Vera are twins, and when I punch one of them the other one feels it.'

'Don't start punching me,' said Oona. 'Bloody sore enough as it is.'

Bridget smiled, then said, 'Well, if you believe Morris is all right then I believe Eamon is alive, too.'

They had their favourite place to perch, the pair of them. Preferred tree to climb, same branches to sit. Best view! Oona looked Drumbroken over, searching. But the valley was silent, forests pale and unsuspecting. Every sound sounded clear in the stillness: the thud of a hatchet, the crack of ice being broken on the surface of a water-barrel, the snap of a latch being dropped on a front door. Oona saw smoke – the first fires in the first hearths, everyone in the county an early riser. And they've no idea, she thought. But they will soon.

'Here – a bit more food?' asked Bridget, holding out some potato-bread.

'We're supposed to be keeping a look-out, Brid,' said Oona. 'Not filling our faces.'

But old habit, beloved ritual: Oona had brought just herself and Bridget brought plenty of food, and answers –

'Do you know what a Briar-Witch is?' asked Oona.

'I heard of Briar-Witches,' said Bridget. 'Burrow like blazes underground!'

'I saw that,' said Oona. Saw, but something in her still didn't believe.

'And they used to be feared more than anything else in the Isle,' said Bridget.

'"*Used to*"?'

'See – they were all supposed to have died out. Used to live above ground like us, then they became more like animals and went under. Had a nest up North someplace, haven't been seen in the South for a long time. Were driven outta the South by the Sorrowful Lady, along with all the Changelings and Whereabouts Wolves and Giants and the –'

'Brid, nobody believes all that!'

'It's true!'

'Aye! As true as winter's warm and the morning moon's made of lard!'

'Well,' said Bridget, 'those Briar-Witches must've joined up with them Invaders now. And let me tell you what else – my uncle Billy up in Ballyboglin, he sent word down to my granda, said that more and more Invaders are coming over

25

the Divide. Crawling in like lice, trying to destroy Ballyboglin and make it Black as the North! And all the men in Innislone are fighting as hard as they can to keep them back. They're more fishermen than anything else, though. Granda says Billy doesn't hardly know what a gun *is* let alone which end it fires outta. But they're luckier than us in Drumbroken cos Innislone is an island town, and they saw the Invaders coming and could draw up their bridges or whatever. They're fighting and fighting against the Invaders. Calling themselves *the town that won't be drowned*! I'd go and fight too if I was allowed. Uncle Billy, he'd like me there. Says I'm the best with a gun he's ever seen, boy or girl! We're not so lucky in this county, Granda says. He says we can't see the wood for the trees, and we're too busy climbing and planting seeds and growing vegetables and flower arranging to be fighters when things get nasty. What does your granny say about it all?'

'Granny's making her potions,' said Oona. 'She seems to know some things. Then she goes off somewhere else, forgetting. Ranting and worrying.'

'My granda says we'll need to be ready to leave,' said Bridget.

'Leave?' said Oona. 'Leaving Drumbroken?'

'That's what he said,' said Bridget, nodding, and more potato-bread in her mouth.

'Says if the Invaders take over we'll not stand a chance. Apparently lots of people are going South and going to see about boats on the coast. See if they can leave the Isle altogether.'

'Aye, right,' said Oona. 'I'll believe it when I see it. And your granda wouldn't get far on those sticks of his.'

'Think Granda's frighted.' Then, her voice lowering, Bridget said, 'They're talking too about this thing the Invaders are bringing with them – the *Echoes*.'

'Doesn't exist,' said Oona. 'That's just a story to scare.'

'Isn't,' said Bridget, and she had forsaken any food to shuffle closer to Oona, to whisper: 'Isn't just a story, Oona. My uncle Billy sent word about it too – everyone in the North has come down with it. It's like a disease.'

'Well, if it's true, then what is it?'

'That's what makes it so bad – no one knows. Not how to stop it or even how to look for it.'

'That's cos it doesn't exist. More stories, same as the like of Giants and Wolves and whatever else.'

'Like Briar-Witches?'

Oona squirmed, sought something to say and decided on, 'Don't believe it.'

'Always the doubting-Dervla,' said Bridget.

'Always the gullible-Gráinne,' said Oona. Then some silence. Oona felt it like a challenge, and again felt compelled to fill it.

'When's your granda planning to go from Drumbroken if he's going?'

'They're having a meeting tonight,' said Bridget. 'At midnight, all the grandfathers from all families in Drumbroken. Going to decide what to do.'

'Where?' asked Oona.

'At the Tower,' said Bridget. 'But now – don't tell anyone about it. I heard Granda talking to Mammy and he'll kill me if he finds out I said anything to anybody.'

Oona spoke nothing, just took the remaining piece of potato-bread and tore it in two.

'Oona?' said Bridget. 'Do you hear me now? I'll be such bother if he finds out I said. Sorrowful Lady herself won't be able to stop me getting slapped!'

'Oh, calm down woman!' said Oona. 'I hear you well enough. And here – share this last bit of bread with me. I know if I don't give it you'll have the hand eaten off me anyway.'

They had some final moments of sharing, and then Oona saw something. She half-stood, and Bridget half-upped too, and together they watched. Like the opposite of dawn, a shadow was being cast, slipping slowly into the valley.

'What is it?' asked Bridget.

Oona shook her head. 'Like a shadow of something.' And she even looked to the sky, like it might harbour a cloud large enough to cause such dark. She almost shivered.

'Like a *dispell*,' said Bridget.

'What are you on about now?' asked Oona.

'Kind of North magic,' said Bridget. She swallowed, did shiver. 'Now what? Go tell the grandfathers?'

Oona said, 'No. But we can't just sit about here either. We have to do something.'

'"*We*?"' said Bridget.

'I,' said Oona.

28

7

Near enough midnight and Granny Kavanagh was asleep and snoring in her armchair.

'Whether she thinks she needs it or not,' whispered Oona, dropping a blanket over her grandmother. Oona had changed into a fresh dress, one she'd hurried to set the last stitches of that afternoon after doing so much – sweeping, churning butter, turning the heel on a pair of stockings, cracking the neck of Ethel (one of their fatter chickens) and plucking and boiling the bird for soup.

'Sorry for leaving you, Granny,' Oona whispered, 'but there's things important that need doing.'

From under the bed Oona took her mother's old cloak, where it'd been bundled and kept safe – rabbit and hare pelt, warmest they had in the house. What else before setting out? Only other thing: Oona made sure to take her knife. She dropped a few more sods into the hearth to keep it going, gave a swift bob to the Sorrowful Lady, pressed a kiss to her granny's forehead, and then entered the night.

To keep herself warm she kept moving, climbing the Eastern slope of the valley fast. At certain times Oona scrambled quickly up an oak to have a look, and soon the men of Drumbroken appeared: their journey slow, a trail of lanterns rambling up the Eastern slope. And Oona thought, *Do they not know better? Too obvious in the dark! What if the Invaders are watching?*

She returned to the ground and went on in a hurry.

How to get to the Tower – even without the wander of firelight to follow – wasn't difficult. It was a forbidden place for women and children, so it was somewhere of which every child and woman in Drumbroken knew the whereabouts. And Oona knew she could get there well before the men. But a single thing was trying to slow her: the Briar-Witch wound. Each touch to a tree was a sting, whole hand sharp like she'd added needles to it. No time though for pain. Oona kept on climbing.

When she emerged it was under a moon so full it looked overflowing – grey-white spills on a bald rise, snow shrunken up but not gone. A wide circle of birch was the forest's last outpost, the bark peeling like scuffed knuckles. And at the centre of the rise was the stone Tower of Drumbroken. It was stunted, crumbling, with windows as narrow as knife wounds.

The Tower held firelight, and the low grumble and echo of old men.

Oona looked all ways then hurried across the rise to crouch beneath one of the windows. So many voices inside, but all slow, all disagreeing.

'So we'll leave Drumbroken, is that what we've decided?'

'Is that the consensus, to leave? Is that what we've said? I must've missed something . . .'

'Speak up all! I can't hear a damnable word! Did you say something?'

'Are we going to vote on this or what happens? I'm sure that's the routine – a proper vote?'

'How long do I have to stay here? I'm cold to me bones!'

'I said "speak up"!'

'Does anyone have a pencil or chalk or slate? Need to write it all down. I'm sure we should be writing all this down . . . does anyone fancy some tay?'

Oona thought, *Invaders in the county and children being snatched by those Briar-Witches, and these men in there talking about pencils and and tay and* votes?

Then a softer voice she'd not heard before said: 'Has anyone else heard the rumours about these Invaders? Rumours from the river, all about some Briar-Witches and boys being stolen? About children being taken North?'

'Nonsense! Briar-Witches were driven out of the South a long time ago! Long gone and long dead!'

'I know that, too, but I've heard –'

'Rumour and gossip – that's what you've heard and nothing else worth chatting about!'

'And what about these whispers from Ballyboglin?'

'My son lives there!'

Granda O'Riley, thought Oona. *Must be.* He went on with: 'Sent me word of all that's going on. And it's not half-good, I can tell you.'

Then some stronger voice, determined –

'What happens in the next county is none of our concern! Who agrees with me?'

'I do!'

'Aye! Me too!'

31

'It's our concern only about our own county, not the next one over!'

'Sure they've taken the North and made it Black. Why not let them stay up there?'

'I agree – let them keep their land and not bother us! We're only a small county, after all. If they come, we'll just tell them there's nothing here worth bothering with, and they'll be on their way.'

'True! We've had peace in this valley since we got rid of Slopebridge from the Big House!'

'True enough! And we'll stand for no more from anyone – agreed?'

All voices then: 'Agreed.'

Enough, thought Oona. And before she knew what her feet were doing they took her to the doorway, and before she knew what her mouth was doing it was shouting –

'No, it's not agreed!'

Many a weary face looked at her (most cases – looked *for* her). Oona saw the oldest of old men from each Drumbroken family, all sat on raised and low levels, on fragments of rock long-fallen from the Tower. The lanterns they'd carried with them up the slope were still in their hands. Oona saw flowers and herbs of each family arranged in beards and hair – here holly and there thistle, some loosestrife, bit of houndstongue. Oona thought of all that agrimony Granny Kavanagh had scattered throughout the cottage and wished she'd brought some for ceremony's sake.

'Who's there now?' said one of the men, squinting, not seeing. 'Is that one of the Wee Folk or some damnable spirit or what?'

Oona cleared her throat and said, 'I'm no spirit or nothing like it, Mister – I'm Oona from the family Kavanagh. And I wanted to say that we can't make agreements with these Invaders and we can't send them on their way. They're already here. And the rumours of these Briar-Witches are true. I didn't believe in them either, but I saw my brother taken by one and that's no word less than the truth. We were fighting with the Cause me and him and –'

Then there was too much noise to make herself heard at all.

'Girls aren't in the Cause! That's a sin for you, lying like that!'

'The Cause is the noble fight for the men to make!'

'You shouldn't be in here anyway, girl!'

'Aye! A female hasn't stepped foot in Drumbroken Tower for – for – I can't even remember how long!'

'*Never*, that's how long!'

'A sin for you indeed! Do you want to bring an unholy curse down on us all!'

'Go and say your sorries to the Sorrowful Lady and hope she's forgiving tonight!'

But Oona shouted, 'I'll not take anything to the Sorrowful Lady – she's no good to us as far as I can see! And there's no man left in the Kavanagh cottage to come here and talk for us! My da is dead and my granda with him, both killed fighting in the Cause! And my brother was taken, like I told! Snatched by them Briar-Witches!'

But the men barely heard her, too loud and decided on their bloody-minded outrage.

'Such cheek from you, girl!'

'Out this instant!'

'Away home to your bed!'

Oona cried, 'Now listen to me! I'm all there's left of the Kavanagh family and I've a right to have some say! And I'll not go home to my bed when it isn't safe! I won't rest, not with those Briar-Witches about. And if you don't believe me, then look!'

Oona held her hand to the nearest light: the Briar-Witch wound was black, a bruise just as black surrounding it. Oona flexed her fingers and the wound wept something dark.

The Tower found some quiet.

'I don't know how to fix it,' said Oona. Her head was beginning to fizz, the pain in her hand too much. 'I don't know what to do.'

Then a voice said, 'I believe you, child.'

Oona looked. One of the men was moving towards her, a pair of sticks to prop him up: Bridget's grandfather. He had churnstaff, the herb of the O'Riley family, twisted into his thistledown hair.

'I believe you,' he said once more. 'But what are we to do against these Invaders? What else but leave and head South? We know what they did up North; it'll happen here too. And my son in Innislone tells me of more arriving every day, all –'

'– coming across the Divide,' finished Oona. She dropped her hand. She tried to shake some of the pain out of it but failed. 'I know all this, but that doesn't mean we have to run.'

Then she heard running. Heavy footfalls heavy breathing and a shout –

'*Granda!*'

Oona knew who it was before she saw, and for the second

34

time that day: Bridget O'Riley in a doorway, breathless.

'What is it?' said Oona. 'What's happened?'

'It's them,' said Bridget. She swallowed. 'The Invaders, they're –'

A single gunshot and everything shivered, stopped – Bridget fell, slowly, and Oona had to rush to catch her.

8

Out of all silence, a shout –

'We have the place surrounded so you haven't got a hope! You've got to the count of three to make yourselves known! *One –*'

Oona held Bridget. She looked for help – to Bridget's grandfather, who just stared at his grandaughter, eyes brimming with bewilderment.

'*Two –*'

And to the other old men of Drumbroken – none moved, not one of them knowing what to do.

'*Three!*'

So Oona ordered them, 'Get down you bunch of doddering old –!'

The remainder was lost in attack: gunfire, the Tower shaking and shedding more of itself. Oona dragged Bridget from under the doorway as bullet split lintel. A crack, a tumble trailing dust and heavy stone fell across the opening. Oona crouched over her friend and held her. The men all about were on their bellies, Granda O'Riley too, his sticks dropped beside.

Another Invader cry amid gunshots: 'Move in, men! Take

the children alive; do what you like with the rest!'

No, thought Oona. *I'll not be taken so easy.*

'We have to do something!' she told Mr O'Riley. 'Have to try to get out of here!'

But before old O'Riley could reply, an unknown voice cried out, 'Leave him be! Sure he's no good to you in that state anyway! None of them are!'

Oona searched for a source but didn't see any.

Another cry from the voice of, 'Look a bit harder and closer, my girl!' and at the same time a darkness swooped at Oona, plucking at her hand. Oona cursed, and followed the dark: it settled as a large jackdaw in one of the narrow windows. Its eyes were wide and yellow and watchful.

'Aye, it was me who spoke, so quit staring!' said the jackdaw. And it hopped like it stood on something hot, telling Oona, 'Now I'd suggest you be getting a move on or very soon you'll be moving nowhere but six spadefuls down!'

A gunshot made the jackdaw enter the air and screech. (To Oona, it sounded like a sharp *caw* and a swear mixed together.) The bird completed a single bedraggled circle of flight then dropped, landing on a slab as wide as the Kavanagh family table.

'Beneath this is the only way out now!' the bird told Oona. 'Crawl under – there's a big enough gap.'

Oona turned to Mr O'Riley but the jackdaw leapt to her shoulder, telling, 'He'll not fit! So let them be captured – they waited too long without doing anything, it's what they deserve!'

'Get off!' Oona shouted and flung her arm in the jackdaw's direction.

'Bloody cheek!' said the bird, again in the air. 'I'm trying to save you!' Oona looked once more to Bridget – felt her shivering so still living.

'She'll be fine,' said the jackdaw. 'They've hardly any interest in the girls. Follow me!'

Again the bird dropped, but this time it didn't bother reappearing.

Oona heard Bridget whisper, 'Go. Leave me. Escape.' Oona wanted to disagree, but hadn't the will for it. She knew what decision had to be made. She looked to the old Drumbroken men – still unmoving, still unable to act.

'Go on,' said Bridget again. 'The Invaders won't let me die. They need the children. They're taking them all up into the Black North.'

Invaders at the doorway were shoving stone, shouting, 'Push it aside! Move it!'

Oona swallowed, then whispered into Bridget's ear, 'I promise I'll find you. I'll not forget.' And she lowered her friend to the ground. One weight left, another gained – guilt. But Oona crawled towards the place into which the jackdaw had vanished.

Invader: 'None of you move! You're all under arrest by order of the King of the North!'

But Oona was up and over the slab of stone. She stooped and saw an opening and had to slip in: tight squeeze, head-first, feet fumbling and –

'One of them's getting away!'

Oona stuck. One ankle was wedged and then she felt a damp hand on it tugging, an Invader screaming, 'I've got him! Someone help here or he'll get away!'

And Oona kicked out as hard as she could and felt such a flood of pleasure when the ball of her foot met bone. The Invader gave a roar, Oona was released, and she was let slither down into dark.

9

From slip to tumble – rock and earth was toying with Oona to turn her over and over and there was plenty of swearing lost from her lips on the journey down. She was stopped when her backside met the bottom. Surrounded by dark. But something was waiting –

A flutter overhead and the something touched Oona and she was on her feet, kitchen knife whipped from her dress as she demanded, 'Who are you?'

'Oh, calm yourself,' said the voice. Female voice. A soft ruffle and shiver from somewhere – the jackdaw. It said, 'We've no time to waste on much, so let's get your legs moving. Follow!'

'No,' said Oona. 'I'm not going anywhere till I see you proper and I know who you are. *Tell.*'

Sound of such a sigh. Then the jackdaw said: 'I'll tell you what I tell you and you'll take it.'

'Name,' said Oona.

'Evelyn Merrigutt,' said the jackdaw. 'But call me Merrigutt just.'

'Who are you, anyway?' Oona asked.

'I'm telling you no more!' said Merrigutt. 'We've not time!'

There was a scatter of earth from the passage above. Oona looked up; was sure someone was trying to make their way down.

'They'll not take long finding their way, that lot,' said the jackdaw.

The bird was back in the air, then back to perching on a shallow shelf of rock, then saying, 'Them ones have more tricks up their sleeves than a travelling tinker, so consider this thing: above you've got Invaders and around us you've got Briar-Witches. Sure you want to hang about and chat?'

'Briar-Witches,' said Oona, and her voice sent a cold echo. She looked to the walls, worried.

'They won't get you,' said the jackdaw. 'Not any time soon – this stone is too much even for those things to be burrowing through.' Oona heard the tap of beak against rock. 'But eventually,' said the jackdaw, and left it there. 'Now follow on!'

A quiver like thrown silk, and when the bird spoke next its voice was all echoes: 'Moving your feet will help you move forward more than all these questions!'

Oona wanted not to follow. But was there any choice? She went.

'Don't drag your feet!' called the jackdaw. 'Don't dawdle!'

'Not dawdling!' said Oona. 'I can't see anything so don't know where I'm going! Where are you leading me to anyway? *Tell!*'

'Quit yapping and hurry up! Those Invaders won't rest, my girl. So we shouldn't either.'

Oona's thoughts strayed – Drumbroken, the men in their

Tower, Mr O'Riley, Bridget . . .

'What'll happen to those oul Drumbroken men?' asked Oona. 'And to my friend?'

'Who knows,' said the jackdaw. 'Take them North is likely.'

'How do you know?' asked Oona. 'How did you know anyway to come to the Tower?'

'We knew,' said the jackdaw. 'We've been watching. Which is something the people in this valley needed to be doing more of! Too late now, though.'

'We need to tell people,' said Oona. 'Warn them what's going on.' She slipped, reached out for support and swore, her hand stinging. 'Bloody Briar-Witch bite!'

'Here,' said the jackdaw, and the bird returned to her, close. 'Stay still now. I'm not gonna fib – this'll hurt a good bit.'

Oona felt the jackdaw press a careful beak to the wound, into the wound. Oona had to bite down on her other hand and slam one sole to the wall to distract. The pain reached its queasy peak and –

'There now,' said the jackdaw. It sounded like it had something caught, then Oona heard the sound of small falling. 'Creature left a bit of its spur in you,' said the bird. 'Should start to heal up a wee bit now. So – can we continue?'

Oona saw the bird move off. She flexed her fingers, then whole hand, shook it: not all painless, but any pain was slower to rise. She followed and soon saw the jackdaw pausing at a meeting of many ways. She saw its yellow eyes widen to almost human-sized, then fly on – leftways.

Oona went faster after, saying, 'Thing we need to do is warn the people.'

'And I said too late for that,' said the jackdaw.

'Not a bit!' said Oona. 'Never too late.'

'Is that right?' said the jackdaw. 'Well this morning we saw two hundred Invaders cross your River Torrid into sleepy Drumbroken with we don't know how many Briar-Witches beneath. And they've brought such magic with them that it'll soon make this place you've been hiding all your life as unfamiliar as anywhere. So I'd say it's late enough, my girl!'

'I haven't been hiding,' said Oona. 'And I can fight!' Her head met stone – more pain, more cursing.

'I don't doubt it,' said the jackdaw, and Oona thought the bird's tone not quite as scathing.

'But that'll not do much good now. These Invaders have their orders from the King and they'll carry them out as quickly as they can, not caring a bit for anything.'

'What King is this?' asked Oona. 'The Isle looks after itself, we've no King.'

'Really are backward and behind the times in this part of the world,' said the jackdaw, something like sorrow in her voice. 'Things changing around you and you can't even see them.'

'Not bloody backward!' said Oona. She stumbled, staggered on, shouting, 'I'll tell you one thing – they'll not be changing me!'

'You can't help the change,' said the jackdaw. 'You'll have no choice in it.'

'Says you,' replied Oona.

'Just keep up, Oona of the contrary Kavanaghs!' said the jackdaw, all impatience returning.

'You'll soon see just how much Drumbroken has been changed, and how quick.'

10

Some leaking-in moonlight let Oona see more – the pale promise of an outside, an end to the tunnel, and she rushed towards it.

'Stop!' called the jackdaw. 'I told you, it won't be like you left it!'

Oona ignored the bird for blessed cold, a welcome chill to soothe the wound on her hand some more. But when she breathed in, there was no relief: she near retched, sniffing a stench sudden and unfamiliar. Oona stood, looked, and wondered, *was it even Drumbroken she was in?*

Everywhere had the appearance of a place ancient. The forest looked like it had seen the woes of a multitude of ages, and had been slowly beaten and broken open by them. An unkempt web was spun in great tangles between boughs, cruel cat's cradles. Trunks had twisted and split as if they had many mouldering secrets to spill, and roots had wriggled free of their earth to battle with the onset of briars and bitter weeds. A litter of leaves lay over everything, like a floor never swept. Oona walked and the reek rose higher and for a moment she was reminded of the dream she'd had in the cottage – the memory of walking through a blackening forest.

Oona stopped, asking of the frigid air, her breath making cold shapes: 'What's happened?' The jackdaw landed beside her on a branch that bobbed as though it might break.

'The North magic,' said the bird. 'I told you – they've brought it with them. Doing like they did up North when they ruined and made it Black. They –'

Oona had time for no more – the land might've been so changed but still she recognised it, knew that home wasn't far. She ran and didn't stop until the Kavanagh cottage came to sight, but nothing showed her a greater change than home – the place was leaning, thatch rotten and sagging, door open like a desperate mouth with a gasp. Oona ran on – over the threshold with knife in hand and calling, 'Granny!'

The hearth was cold and there was no light from anywhere, not even at the shrine for the Sorrowful Lady. The same smell existed inside as out – sweet, like the rot of things left long alone. Oona stepped forward and many softnesses touched her face. Her fingers moved fast and fumbling to remove them – a web had been woven wild across the one room of the cottage. Briar and creeper and vine had ensnared the family table, claimed dresser and sideboard and encircled the hearth at the centre of the room. Weed and nettle and dock were as high as her knee.

'No,' said Oona, softly. Then again, feeble protest: 'No. Can't be like this. Can't.'

Her home was no longer her own. Oona couldn't discern her memories of the place past the thicket of transformation – no more the comfortable space her mother had tended, nor the busy place that her father and grandfather had worked hard to keep and improve. Not the happy place she'd grown alongside Morris. And if her brother reappeared just then, would he even know that he'd come home?

Oona listened but heard no sound from the chickens in the corner. She took a step to explore but felt something sharp at her ankle.

'Don't move!' said the voice of the jackdaw, somewhere.

Oona saw a thorn as long as her middle finger threatening her ankle. Then she saw more – many longer, most sharper.

'What's happened?' asked Oona. 'Like a hundred years gone by.' She hated the solemn echo her words sent. She had a notion then, a memory of Bridget's words and asked, 'Is this the Echoes they talk about?'

'No,' said Merrigutt. 'Not that. The Echoes aren't as simple as that.'

'Then what?' snapped Oona, and she remembered more of Bridget's words. 'Some *spell* or something? Isn't that what they call it?'

'A *dispell*,' said the jackdaw. 'Takes away, doesn't give. Gets rid of things. I'd say what's lacking and been banished from here is hope.'

Oona said, 'Not no hope – more like what's gone out the door is anything living.'

'Same thing, my girl,' said the jackdaw.

Then there was a slow groan, and words rose from somewhere deep –

'Morris? Is that you, my dear? Have you returned to me now?'

46

Oona went working with her knife, quick to slash at anything that dared touch or come close as she fought her way forward. And any anger – dark confusion too – she let loose, snapping and tearing towards her grandmother. She kept careful though when it came to avoiding the thorns, thinking they were bound to be primed with poison.

And eventually Granny Kavanagh was uncovered – still in her armchair where she'd been left maybe an hour before – and Oona kneeled beside.

'You're all right, Granny,' said Oona. 'I'm here now.'

But her grandmother was so still, as though she'd been so long awaiting and so long disappointed that she couldn't rouse herself to movement. Oona saw that the spell had been busiest on her granny – a shroud had been worked across the woman's face and spiders had spun a delicate fortune on her one open palm, the other still closed tight and clutched to her breast. And the web that hid Granny Kavanagh's face moved only a little, not enough, shifting again with the same question: 'Morris? Is that you, my dear?'

'No,' said Oona. She swallowed. 'It's me, Granny. It's your Oona.'

Oona laid down her knife on bare earth and peeled aside her grandmother's veil. What she saw behind the web? Granny Kavanagh and not Granny Kavanagh. Only a shell – a cold husk like the kind Oona used to like to collect in the forest. Her grandmother's eyes were almost empty of anything, cheeks deep-hollowed like places relentlessly dug, and so much else of her given to shadow. Her face was a testament to what worry and waiting could do – a sad story told in too many broken lines. Oona sought her grandmother's hand and found nails that were long and broken.

'How did this happen so quick?' asked Oona.

'Was the same up North,' said the jackdaw. The bird came to Granny Kavanagh's chair, perching on its back. 'They didn't see it coming either, didn't think things could change so quick around them. But these dispells aren't easy things. Like weeds, they can be kept under control. No North magic comes into a place uninvited. Like I said to you – Drumbroken has been too much asleep, and your grandmother had too much bitterness and weakness and misery in her to fight this. Only pure hopelessness could've allowed a dispell like this in through the door, and then allowed it to thrive so thick.'

A fierce whisper from Oona of, '*Quiet!*' She held her grandmother's hand tighter and said, 'You don't know what you're talking about.'

'Oh, I do,' said the jackdaw. 'I've seen enough to know what I know, and your granny in her own lonely and bitter ways has seen too much.'

'Get away!' said Oona, and again she struck out towards the jackdaw to shoo it.

'Don't make the mistake of thinking she can't help the way she's being,' said the bird, and it settled among the mass and crackle on the family table. 'No matter what she's been seeing in her dreams or nightmares she still has her choice about how to behave and she –'

'What do you mean "*nightmares*"?' said Oona. 'And how'd you know that she –?'

'I know,' said the jackdaw. 'And most of all – I know the

48

ways of old women.'

'Nothing can change this quickly,' said Oona, but it was protest for the sake of protest.

'Is that right?' said the jackdaw. 'Well, let's see, my girl.'

And then something more changed. Something quick, some squirm of the dark – some shiver and flicker and fall, and Oona stared, wanting to see.

'What do you see of me?' said the voice of the jackdaw. 'Describe.'

'I see just –' started Oona. But there was no longer any jackdaw to describe. Oona was looking at an old woman, and she was perched with legs dangling and bare feet flexing on the edge of the Kavanagh family table.

Oona stood so she might see better.

The old woman on their table had hair all hanging – thin, some grey and some black but most white, and all loose like lots of unpicked thread. And her face could've beaten a barrel of off apples in a wrinkliest-thing contest. She was covered in flitters of dark cloth like feather. She smiled, delighting in Oona's looking. Then Merrigutt (jackdaw, now an old woman? thought Oona, still not close enough to believing) plucked an apple from somewhere in the black mass that covered her and removed half of it in a bite. Chin running wet with the dribble of juice she asked, 'Just gonna stare and stare?'

'Who are you?' asked Oona. 'And I don't mean names. You're from the North?'

'I am,' said Merrigutt. 'And why do you think that?'

'Because changing shape,' said Oona, 'that's not a Southern thing – we stay as we are.'

'Very good,' said Merrigutt, and she even gave a small bow.

'Why have you come here, anyway?' said Oona. 'Why now?'

'You know the reason, my girl,' said Merrigutt. There was another crunch of the apple. 'You know that things are on the hinge on the South. The Invaders are coming, and this is the moment it can all change and very fast, as you can see. It can all go downhill in the handcart, or some of you can be saved.'

Oona opened her mouth with so many more questions but there was a distraction – the sound of things, many things, making more sound outside.

'Ah!' said Merrigutt, and she dropped the apple – pips, stalk, all – down her throat. She swallowed, belched, and said, 'That'll be the rest of the ladies now. You best go welcome them, my girl. Because believe me – they aren't the type of creatures to be kept waiting!'

II

'No!' shouted Oona. 'No more bloody jackdaws in here! You can all just hoof it!'

Oona stood herself in the doorway, what remained of the Kavanagh cottage behind her. In front, the Kavanagh clearing was a floor of shifting and fidgeting feather. A mass of jackdaws had gathered and were preening and plucking at themselves and each another, their *caws* such a racket Oona reckoned it could've woke the six-spadefuls-deep.

Old-woman Merrigutt shuffled into the doorway beside Oona to chuckle, and then address these familiars: 'Now good evening to you all, ladies! I'm sure you've been busy and have lots of bits and all else of news! Come in now and make yourselves as comfortable as you can!'

Oona opened her mouth, disagreement ready, but the noise! The fresh fuss and surge of the jackdaws! She had to retreat, returning to protect Granny Kavanagh as birds rushed on in, such a tide of them all ignoring the dispell and breaking on cupboard and bed and dresser and family-table and hearth. With small hops – squirm and spasm and shudder – they transformed, same as Merrigutt had done, landing on dirty

51

soles as ragged old women.

'More bloody Northerners,' whispered Oona.

The women began what looked like a hunt, seeking out and swallowing down anything edible. Any apples Oona had stored in the barrels by the back door were soon made pulp by the uninvited visitors; any bread would be better described as breadcrumbs after they'd been at it; preserves preserved for months were opened and plucked at, and eggs were taken down whole . . . but the dispell had gotten rid of anything like ripeness, and Oona listened to the clamour of complaint from the women –

'Apples too sweet!'

'Bread too tough!'

'Eggs near rotten!'

'What about tay to wash it all down? Boil some water for the sake of sanity!'

Merrigutt called out, 'Now calm your souls, ladies! We've things to discuss!'

But Oona saw that even Merrigutt wasn't for quelling them, and the women's words were –

'The magic is moving down from the Divide, making everything Black!'

'Aye, bringing death and dark to everywhere!'

'And more and more Invaders coming down from the North with it!'

'True! More Invaders by the day and even more by the night!'

'And some of the ones down *here* are for going up *there*!'

'Aye! Going up North to fight, or so they think!'

'Challenge the King? Fools!'

'That's the bloody Cause for you! That's men for you, too – charging in without thinking!'

'Now tay! Where's the tay we were promised!'

'All right,' Oona heard Merrigutt mutter. 'Good for nothing without a drop of tay.'

Oona saw Merrigutt flex her fingers, reach into the dark that clothed her and return with a pinch of scarlet powder. She scattered it slowly among the cold hearth-stones. Moments, and then they had flames – bright, high, like they'd been burning there for hours.

'Bit of reliable old North magic,' Merrigutt told Oona, and she winked. Merrigutt hung the Kavanagh kettle on its hook over the hearth.

Oona straightened. 'Look: you can't just come in here and take over this house. You're as bad as those bloody Invaders, just doing as you like with people's things!' Her voice had climbed into a shout, and all movement in the cottage was stopped.

'As bad as the Invaders?' repeated Merrigutt. 'Is that right?'

Oona nodded. She swallowed and said, 'I'm not leaving here if that's what you're planning. I'll not let those Invaders take this house. This is our home, and has been for longer than anything!' And her hand enclosed the back of her granny's chair.

'She's a stubborn one,' said one of the other old women. 'She's a Kavanagh through and through. Look at that grim look on her face – just like the father!'

'Quiet now!' said Merrigutt. 'You're not to make judgements so easy!'

Silence, and in it the kettle began its grumble, firelight blinking on battered belly.

'Why are you all here anyway?' said Oona. She looked to Merrigutt, who held her gaze. 'Tell me the truth, cos I don't like being lied to. I'm not a child or stupid, so don't think it!'

'All right,' said Merrigutt. 'We're here to escort you South, my girl. We're here now because those Invaders haven't come over the Divide and down South just for the sake of it, not for their own amusement.'

'Not a bit of it!' went one of the women with her mouth full of blue-moulded loaf.

'No, they've been looking and looking for something,' said Merrigutt.

'Children,' said Oona. 'I know that much. I've seen.'

'True!' said one of the women with half of one hand buried in a pot of gooseberry jam.

'But more than that,' said another, fingers around a tendril-sprouting potato. 'They don't want the children just for the sake of having them!'

'They're here now,' said Merrigutt, still focusing on Oona, 'because of their King's orders. And he has no interest in cottages or kettles or anything else.'

'What does he want?' said Oona.

The room was at its quietest, the old women all like they were waiting.

'We don't know everything of what this King wants,' said Merrigutt. She looked away from Oona and focused instead, with sudden intentness, on the painting Oona's mother had done. Its rough rectangle was occluded with so much web, but Oona knew it was the painting of that dreamed-up place: low hills like the softest rise and dip of the sea, the colour of wild

54

meadow and bright blossom. 'All we know,' said Merrigutt, and she turned once again to face Oona, 'is that the Invaders are keen on capturing and not killing those children. Using the Briar-Witches to snatch? Those creatures are more used to just gobbling up whole and thinking about the bones later. No, they're keeping those children for some reason.'

'Information,' said Oona. 'By the Torrid, they were all shouting about keeping the children alive, so –'

'They're looking for something,' said Merrigutt. 'A small thing, but precious enough too that the Invaders and their 'King of the North', as they call him, would happily turn this Isle to dark and rot if it meant getting it.'

'What something?' said Oona.

Some shiver passed through the air. Everything in the cottage shook.

'It is a something,' said Merrigutt, 'that we've been searching for too. And we think we've found it – we think we're right in believing that it is hidden right here in the cottage of the Kavanaghs.'

12

And the ground might've been listening in – could've been waiting readied to hear just these words spoken! – because it began to seethe with something underneath and every old woman was suddenly into the air and all transformed in the same hop-spasm-shudder back to jackdaws, with Merrigutt crying, 'Oona, quick! Quick, onto the table!'

Quick but not quick enough –

Oona was grabbed by the ankles and pulled down into the earth all the way to the waist before her hands snatched and closed around a table leg. She looked for her knife – where was it to slice with once more? She dropped, was pulled down further, and no help came from the jackdaws as they whirled in a frenzy, but then someone not expected: her grandmother rose suddenly rushing from her chair, trailing web, unhooking and heaving the pot of boiling water and pouring it into the hole. Such a scream from below! And at the first hint of release Oona was kicking and crawling away, finding her knife for protection. But the screaming from beneath didn't stop – the Kavanagh cottage shook with it, the Briar-Witch racing underground, sending cracks across walls, the whole place already broken enough by the dispell but beginning to lean, the whole home folding in like a fist.

Merrigutt shouted, 'Out! Get out before the whole place comes down!'

The jackdaws left in as fast a flood as they'd come out through the door. But Oona stayed. Her granny Kavanagh was on the floor and Oona took her by the hand and said, 'We have to go, Granny! Quick now, we have to leave!'

But the old woman wouldn't budge. She was just as still and near-silent as she'd been in her armchair a minute before, one hand still held tight to her breast.

'Leave now, my girl!' said Merrigutt, landing on Oona's shoulder. 'Out! We've no time for waiting!'

'I won't go anywhere without her,' said Oona, and then she tried to lift her grandmother, but still no movement. Oona decided: *I won't leave if she won't. If this world falls in then this is where I'm supposed to be. Mammy died here, so it's where I'll die too, if I have to.*

'Oona,' said Merrigutt, 'we have to escape!'

'Go, child.'

It was her grandmother's voice then, and it had no edge, no spite. Instead only a special gentleness Oona hadn't heard for so long. Granny Kavanagh said again, 'Go, child. But take this – you must have it . . . it's your turn now . . .'

And finally her grandmother released what she'd held so tight: Oona felt something pressed into her own hands, a small knot of material with something small and round and hard at its heart. Oona hadn't time (or much care) to open or examine and she said just, 'Granny, please, you have to come with me or –'

'No,' said her grandmother, 'not *have to* any more. It was too much for me, child. It's a burden, but I know you can bear it. And this is the most important thing – don't lose sight of the light. Keep looking for it. Just do as I should've done and didn't – don't let the light go. Don't just look for the dark.'

The roof began to fall in fragments and night sky to show through –

'Oona!' cried Merrigutt. 'Now or not at all!'

Granny Kavanagh pushed Oona from her. And Oona went, the gift that her grandmother had given safe in her hands.

13

'Keep going now! Don't hang about!'

The jackdaw was on Oona's shoulder, telling. Oona didn't wish to but had to move. The bundle her grandmother had pressed on her in one hand, knife in the other, she fought on into the travesty of former forest. And any time Oona tried to look behind to see what had become of the Kavanagh cottage Merrigutt scolded, 'No! Don't look back! Briar-Witches never move on their own so you can bet last Tuesday's washing that if there's one about then there'll be many! Keep going on now, we'll head for the –'

The jackdaw stopped, like she'd been struck dumb.

'What?' asked Oona. 'What is it?'

The bird's head tilted, slowly like she was listening, her yellow eyes growing. And then Merrigutt said, 'It's the Coach-A-Bower.' A pause from the jackdaw, and then a panicked, '*Run!*'

Oona tried to move faster, but a hush was settling over her senses, a softening, the world holding itself still. Only one sound existed then, and it was the faint rattle of cheap metal against cheaper. By the time Oona realised that she was running towards the sound, Merrigutt told her, 'Get down!'

On the fringe of a wide clearing they stopped. Oona tried to make herself small, hiding behind what remained of a once-noble Drumbroken oak. In front of her were a dozen or more Invaders, their faces the only thing seeable, the rest of their uniforms blending without seam into surrounding night. They were on guard, keeping watch over a convoy of twelve dark stallion-drawn carriages. Oona noticed what the strange rattle had been – many coins held together with fine thread, hanging from the front of each carriage. They continued their rattle even without movement, without a single snatch of wind. Dark figures sat at the reins of each stallion.

'Quiet,' said Merrigutt. 'Quiet, or you'll end up caught too.'

Behind bars, in each carriage, Oona saw many faces: *children*. They were packed close, stacked like all that was left of them were heads. All pale and wide-eyed, thin fingers closing tightly around the bars. But when Oona looked too long at them, the hush that pressed on her hearing became stronger, heavier. She began to rise from where she was crouched, half-led without knowing it, whispering to herself, 'Bridget? Maybe Morris?'

'*Stop!*' said Merrigutt. 'You can't run out there or you'll get caught too, and then what good are you to anyone? And especially not with what your granny has just given you.'

Oona stayed where she was, half-stooped. If she went on without any weapon but her kitchen knife – against Invaders with a couple of guns each – then the old jackdaw was right: she'd be caught quick, and then what? She sank a little, and listened. And what she heard from the Invaders had to press through the hush, words just vague whisperings when they reached Oona's ears –

'Said we had to collect them all.'

'We have done!'

'What about the one from that falling Tower?'

'They'll turn up, those Witches will find them. They can sniff out a child from twenty miles off!'

'We'll need to get these supplies shifted off soon.'

'Don't worry. These children'll be going nowhere any time soon. Or any time at all! Ain't that right, Coachman! Eh?'

The Invader's call brought a slow stirring from the front of one of the carriages. From the seat stepped one of the dark figures – a someone see-through, shaped like a man but with no flesh or blood or bone. He was hardly more than shadow. And like the carriages and horses, the figure summoned no sound. He dragged a whip with a pale handle that looked to Oona like a rough bone. The rasp of the whip across broken ground made all of Oona shiver. When the Coachman reached the bars of the carriage the children tried to recoil but their movement was slow, without much strength. The dark, transparent figure extended one dark, transparent hand to them, like an invitation into comfort. None of the children took it.

'They'd take it if they knew what was good for them!' shouted an Invader, and he thumped the side of the carriage with the butt of his rifle. The Coachman's dark head snapped around to face the Invader, who looked enough humbled (or frightened?) to take a step-and-a-half back.

'What are they?' whispered Oona.

'More forces that have sided with the Invaders,' said Merrigutt. 'The Coach-A-Bower.'

'The Funeral-Makers?' said Oona. She remembered

61

something, some trace. Or some story?

'Up North we called them just the Coach,' said Merrigutt. 'They come to collect the dead on the night they are due to die. To take the souls, accompany them to –'

'On to the end of the world,' said Oona, remembering whispered words, prayers spoke for the Sorrowful Lady. She said what she recalled: '*The Coachman will come and, if you pay him the proper price, he will extend his hand to the soul that needs guiding into the next world and make them as much shadow as he is himself. And then he will take them with care and gentleness to the place beyond all places, to the place neither above nor beneath – on into the final silence.*'

'True enough,' said Merrigutt.

The Invaders were joined then by others, maybe twelve more all jogging into sight.

One of the arriving lot nodded to one of those already gathered, then said, 'The last cottage has been destroyed, sir.'

'Good man,' said the Invader who was being addressed. 'And whoever was inside, what happened to them?'

Oona listened, waiting to hear of Granny Kavanagh's end, but the conversation was interrupted by movement, by the upset of earth – what could only be to Oona's eyes the swift burrowing of a Briar-Witch. It stopped in the centre of things, and Oona saw all the Invaders take many steps backwards, their faces repulsed by something Oona couldn't see. A voice with no more shape or depth to it than a growl spoke from the ground –

'*There was one within the cottage, but it escaped me.*'

'What?' said the Invader in charge. 'You let one of them

escape? The order was to catch *every single child*!'

'*We cannot catch all. We have been dormant for many seasons, and –*'

'Excuses!' said the Invader. 'You think my Captain will listen to excuses? Do you think the Faceless will take any of this nonsense? And what about the King himself?' At these last words, Oona heard worry creeping into the Invader's own voice.

'*We have gifted you many things,*' said the voice of the Briar-Witch. '*Not least the skins of the Acre-Changeling – countless of them have been slaughtered and stripped, their coverings stolen and given to you so that you can match the look of the land you wish to conquer. And our Mother has given the greatest power to your King – to be able to reshape the land itself. We work tirelessly to assist you, and still we have had no reward.*'

'You made the Oath,' said the Invader. 'You know the deal – when all the children in this Isle are in our custody, when we find what the King is looking for, then you creatures will get what you want. All girls go North to the Witches, and all boys go North to the King.' He took a breath, and looked to those Invaders looking at him, waiting. Then he faced again the ground, and told the Briar-Witch, 'Tell no one of the loss of this or any other escaped child, but I want you to continue looking for them. Go!'

Dirt flew into the air, the Briar-Witch making a fresh path underground, leaving the clearing as the Invader shouted, 'Coachmen – take these children North!'

'They're looking for you, my girl,' Merrigutt told Oona. They know you've something important, otherwise they wouldn't be bothered with *every single child*. You can't reveal yourself.'

'I know,' said Oona. 'Stop pestering me. So now what if we don't do something?'

'We go to the White Road,' said the jackdaw. 'You won't be the only one trying to escape from here. South is the only safe place now. Let's go.'

But Oona didn't move. She waited – knife in one hand, her grandmother's gift in the other. She saw all the Coachmen raise dark arms, their whips all poised, and as one they struck their stallions, the crack they sounded bringing everyone in earshot lower. She felt a cold wind shake the clearing, deep hush became a dark rush and the dozen carriages were gone, chased like unwanted children off into the night.

14

Oona walked herself sore. Jackdaw on her shoulder, she wandered a dispelled Drumbroken until the world lost some of its stubborn dark and what she took for morning arrived. But it was a sky to match her mood – the colour of damp stone and screwed down tight, any glimpse of the dawn hidden behind. Then the ending forest finally ended and Oona stopped and saw the extent of shadow – she and Bridget had seen it seeping into Drumbroken, and it had seized the entire valley, a pitiless stain that wouldn't be shifted. And just below Oona, at the bottom of a slope, was the only thing white: a wide trail of chalk, the White Road, wandering off on its way South and towards the coast. But to safety? Oona doubted that idea.

'See now,' said Merrigutt, speaking at last. 'Told you that you wouldn't be alone, didn't I?' Oona said nothing, just watched the creep of dark along White: a slow mass of people with possessions all strapped to their backs and across shoulders and wrapped around arms and legs and heads and anywhere at all that could take weight, or leading carts stacked high as hillocks with chairs and sawed-short-scrubbed-down tables and clothes flapping limp farewell, pots and pongers and kettles and coal scuttles and spoons and griddle plates all rattling like the grimmest band at a Nip-Winter Fair. And everywhere Oona could see the small porcelain shrines for the Sorrowful Lady, stuffed wherever they could fit.

'So quiet,' said Oona, and all of her shivered. Apart from the scuff of bare feet and crackle of cartwheels and the sometimes sniff and whimper, there was no sound.

'You'll be fine now,' said Merrigutt. 'You'll be safe with so many.'

Sounds like she's trying to convince herself, thought Oona.

'And looks like you're not the only child either,' said Merrigutt.

And Oona could've counted the number of children without needing both hands – all of them were seated high, as much distance between them and the White Road as could be managed.

The jackdaw swapped Oona's shoulder for a branch, the first hint that she was about to leave. 'Don't stop,' Merrigutt told her, 'not for anything.' The jackdaw's eyes went to Oona's cloak – the bird had ordered Oona to hide Granny Kavanagh's gift there, alongside the kitchen knife. 'And if anyone tries to take anything from you – fight like you've never fought yet and run and don't slow till you the see the sea!'

'Where will you be?' asked Oona.

'I'll need to round up the other women,' said Merrigutt. 'We've things of our own to do, plenty of watching that needs to be done. But we'll be checking on you all, when we can find any time.' The jackdaw's head was flick-flick-twitching all the time, its gaze going everywhere, watching, appraising.

Then its look rested once more on Oona's cloak. 'Take care of yourself now,' said Merrigutt.

Off, away high, the jackdaw's wing-beats left only the faintest ruffle on such stillness, and Oona was left alone on the edge of the White Road.

15

Oona allowed herself a few moments, and then was down the slope and accepted into the exodus without welcome or question or hello. There was nothing to do but walk. Oona would've liked to scream just to see what it did. She didn't – she behaved, and walked on without words, just like the rest. But she watched.

Oona saw a pair of boys a bit younger than herself go by. Both were pale-haired, pale-skinned, noses scattered with a trowelful of freckles. Their appearance said to Oona – *twins*. They were standing at the top of a cart, arms out stiff to keep balance. Oona knew that if one went to fall the other would grab and she recognised the game she and Morris had played in the high reaches of the forest around the Kavanagh cottage: private, quiet, something just for them two. An ancient mare was dragging their cart, pulling their world along on big, wheezing wheels with their mother walking alongside, head lowered.

Oona let her gaze fall to her feet: her toes were already white. She knew each step was taking her South, was taking her from everything. Maybe to safety, but most important of all to her, the thought of which she couldn't let go: each step was taking her further from her brother. *I would know if Morris was dead*, Oona told herself. *Somehow, don't know how, but I'd know it if he were gone. I'd know if I was alone.*

Then things changed –

No screams, but things shifting. Was there a tremble against Oona's soles? In her bones? Oona stopped and turned to see.

Carts were being tossed high, toppling, everything tumbling –

The pair of pale-haired, pale-skinned boys began to cry with a mewling like newborn kittens, 'Mammy, what's happening? Mammy?'

But Oona knew what would happen.

A ripple that raced, things underground rushing to tip – the twins were falling, the mother thrown aside. The boys struck ground and cried out and their looks went anywhere, to everywhere, to anybody that might help or explain or save. Last of all, to Oona. But she couldn't have helped – not even time for a final word and the twins were gone. Tugged down into the earth.

And everywhere the same. All along the road was the crying, the pleading, the vanishing –

There was nothing Oona could do but save herself. She ran, leaping places where the ground had sunken and was being shifted as she heard voices shouting –

'No one move! You're all under arrest in the name of the King!'

A quick glance back – rifles appearing, then Invaders, their uniforms a perfect blending-in of what surrounded. Mostly, Oona saw mouths emptying words –

'Get down!'

'Hands in the air!'

'Stop crying!'

'Get away from that hole, you can't help him now!'

Oona reached the same slope she'd descended minutes before and fought her way up, eyes on the forest. It might be a corruption of its former self but still she saw the trees of Drumbroken as sanctuary. She hoped herself unnoticed. But always, there was one –

'There, someone's escaping! Stop her!'

Oona dragged herself on hands and knees and fingers, soon scrambling, but the earth was too loose beneath and too keen to send her sliding back to waiting rifles and waiting White Road seething with waiting Briar-Witches. And when Oona next looked up it was a rifle that met her. A mouth behind it promised, 'Move an inch and I'll blow your barbaric little brains out!'

Oona half-stood, half-raised her hands, some instinct making her. She thought of her knife in her cloak but knew she couldn't be quick enough to retrieve it.

'That's a good girl,' said the Invader. Oona still didn't see all of him, his uniform coloured the same kind of decay as the forest behind. But she saw his grin, his mouth shivering a little with laughter.

Then another stronger instinct crept over Oona – defiance. She let her hands fall.

'I said keep them up!' the Invader told her.

'No,' said Oona. 'Shoot me if you want.'

'I'll do worse,' said the Invader. 'We'll take you North with all the other children and then you'll wish you'd done as I said!'

His eyes wandered, going to the White Road behind Oona. 'But he's not too keen on the girls, the King of the North, so I'll just let those creatures underneath have you, eh?'

The Invader jammed his rifle into Oona's belly. She slipped, then slid all the way down and stopped herself just on the edge of the White Road.

The Invader was at her back with his rifle saying, 'Walk! Go!'

Oona could only be forced on, no choice. Her toes touched white and claws exploded from the ground –

Instinct: Oona turned and swung a fist and caught the Invader's cheek. He swore, spat, aimed at her and –

A flash of feather-claw-beak –

Jackdaws fell like they'd had forgotten flight and attacked – the birds took to the Invader's hands and legs, covered him, pinning him to the ground. One jackdaw took his tongue in its beak to keep him quiet. A familiar weight fell on Oona's shoulder with a familiar voice of disapproval: 'I left you not five minutes ago and already look at the trouble you're in!'

'Not my fault,' said Oona. 'I was walking like you said and –'

But the Invader smothered in jackdaws managed to shout, 'Help! Help me!'

'Go!' Merrigutt told Oona. 'Keep to the trees and we'll draw them off!' Merrigutt took to the air and Oona to the slope.

Then Oona stopped, turned. And made her decision. She went back into the valley of Drumbroken – only moments alone before Merrigutt returned to chide, 'What in blazes are you doing? You're going the wrong way! I said to follow the Road South!'

'Nowhere's safe now,' said Oona, running.

'What?' said Merrigutt. 'South is the only way and –'

'– North is the way they've taken Bridget and my brother and everyone else!' said Oona. She ran faster – the fire of an idea made her fleet. 'Morris is still alive, I know it. And King or no King and Black North or not, I'm going to follow, and I'm going to find him!'

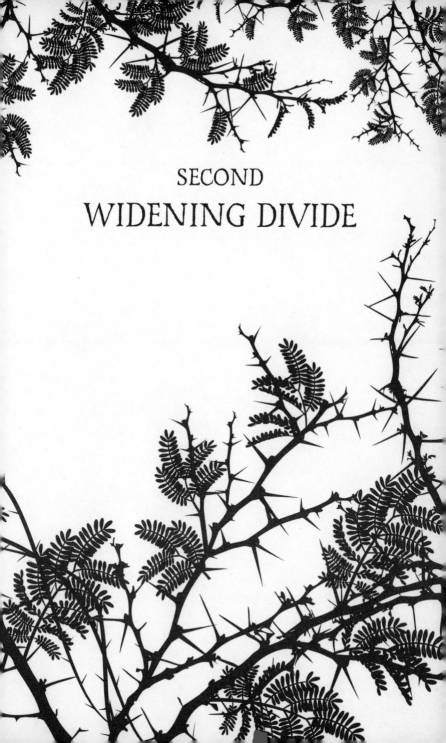

SECOND
WIDENING DIVIDE

16

'– and I hope you know what you're getting yourself into, my girl! But I'd place a farmer's bet that you don't!' Merrigutt, badgering and flapping. Oona didn't know where the jackdaw found the energy to keep on at her. 'And just off on a whim! Just like a Kavanagh: no stopping nor thinking it out first!'

Oona had no breath left to tell the jackdaw to give it a rest. And if she'd discovered a breath it wouldn't have been wasted on words: there was too much climbing to be done, too much stepping over and slipping and squeezing through the tangle and disintegration of the dispell. But Merrigutt with plenty of breath said: 'Where in blazes are we going anyway? Top of this slope and then where? Tell me that!'

Oona thought but didn't bother saying – top of the Western slope, then up and along the ridge, then on down. Then where, though? Follow the River Torrid? The next county North was Ballyboglin, but how safe was it there? Not safe at all, if Bridget's words were to be relied on – *Crawling in like lice, trying to destroy Ballyboglin, make it Black as the North*! And like her own nagging doubt flying beside, Merrigutt still kept on with, 'You're just going to dander on into the Black North to find this twin brother of yours? A brother that even if he's somehow still living is probably on his way to see the King of the North! And what then? If we're planning on coming face to face with the King then what –'

'Oh hell's bells, would you ever shut up, woman!' shouted Oona. She had to slow – she hardly had energy left to stand, exhaustion making a mess of her as she staggered and sniffed and gasped.

Merrigutt said, 'The cheek of you to talk to me like that! And after I helped you!'

'Quiet,' said Oona. 'I'm thinking of things.'

'What things?' asked Merrigutt. The jackdaw flew on ahead, stopping on a branch so she could perch and preach without interruption. 'I hope these thoughts are for how you're going to survive in the Black North, how to not get yourself captured. Or is it how to find food not befouled or water not polluted, or air not feeling like glass when you breathe it in? And keep this in your mind – that's even if we manage to cross the Divide itself!'

'Oh, give it a bloody rest,' said Oona. She didn't shout: couldn't. She slowed, and then stopped: the slope too sheer. 'A wee minute,' said Oona, sinking. 'Rest a minute here.'

'Why?' asked Merrigutt. 'Oh, I see – planning on some prayer for your answers, are we?'

Oona half-turned, looked – the jackdaw was perched on a tree relieved of its limbs, the trunk cut short and worked into a shape. Oona blinked: it was the shape of a woman, the shape of the Sorrowful Lady. But it was such a rough likeness, as though someone had just hacked and hacked at the oak and discovered something like the image of the Lady cowering inside. Always she was cowering – Oona had never seen the Lady any way else. Even so, the sight gave Oona some pause, and stirred something in her. Though she didn't often bother with believing, she felt something close enough to hope.

The Sorrowful Lady's heart glowed: a rough cavity had been cut to contain candles, some looking new and others with hardly any height left, but all scarlet, wax bleeding free and solidifying around offerings of winter flowers, woodcarvings the size of children's noses, and some things that looked to Oona edible.

'I wouldn't take anything from there,' said Merrigutt. 'Looks and smells rotten to me.'

Oona ignored the jackdaw.

She did her duty before she took, kneeling at the Lady's roots, closing her eyes and recalling whatever pieces of prayer she could. It took some forcing herself, but Oona begged help, guidance, strength, sustenance . . . *Oh Sorrowful Lady, please aid me in my humble need! Please watch over and protect me with your warmth and light! Please provide for me!*

That should be enough, thought Oona.

She opened her eyes and stood and took: from the Sorrowful Lady's chest she plucked blackberries and hearth-bread, a shrunken yellow apple with a faint red blush and a vial of what Oona knew was whiskey. She ate and drank all, and knew that Merrigutt was watching everything.

'I didn't think the people of the South put faith in Sorrowful Ladies or Good Women or Merciful Maids,' said the jackdaw. 'You got rid of all your Worshipping Houses, did you not?

Invaders have been doing the same up North – dragging all into the marsh and dumping them there, leaving them to sink.'

'Well,' said Oona, pressing fingertips to lips, licking up every drip and crumb, 'the way you talk about the Black North, I'd say we'll be needing any and all the help we can get. Doesn't matter to me as long as it keeps me fed and watered for another while. Not agree?'

Merrigutt said nothing, which to Oona meant the jackdaw agreed but didn't want to say.

'We need to keep on going,' said Merrigutt then.

'Not far to the ridge,' said Oona.

'I'd say a few hours of climbing, at least. And we'd need to think about disguising you before we go on. Maybe cut your hair or something.'

'You're not cutting my hair!' said Oona. 'I'll look like some boy!'

'You'll have to learn how to change,' said Merrigutt. 'You'll not stay out of the hands of the Invaders if you can't be quick to adapt.'

'Is that why you switch between bird and old woman?' said Oona. Merrigutt said nothing.

'Why not just stay one or the other?' asked Oona.

'Who made the rule saying we had to stay the same?' said Merrigutt. 'Now – you stay put. I'm off for a look.'

'A look for what?' said Oona.

'Oh, just the usual sights,' said Merrigutt. 'My fellow ladies who might've come to some horrific end because of your careless ways. Or else Invaders who might be on the way to shoot us dead. Or Briar-Witches to tear out our insides and –'

'Go then,' said Oona. 'Give me two minutes' peace from your moaning.'

'Just try,' said Merrigutt, 'not to use those two minutes to find trouble.' As soon as the jackdaw went, Oona sank to the ground once more.

'Rest a wee minute,' she told herself, lying on her back, finding a flattish stone for a pillow and shutting her eyes. 'Only a wee minute or two and she'll back anyway to wake me. Bloody grumpy old bird.'

17

'*Now, Oona Kavanagh – let me show you such nightmares.*'

Dreams in Drumbroken remained unbroken. No such thing there as nightmares: peaceful place, so peaceful slumber. But as Oona dreamed – as she found herself once more in a forest with its trees blackened – she saw not the usual whimsy or warm thoughts. Instead, she was invited by the same voice she'd heard once before. It enticed: '*Follow my voice, Oona Kavanagh. Follow, and you shall see flame. You shall see what shadows haunt this valley, and what sin. Your eyes will see what they would rather not. Follow, follow . . .*'

And Oona was led, walking through a ruined forest until she heard a sound like ripping and splitting, screaming. This was not dreaming, she decided. She was afraid, but fear didn't stop curiosity.

She discovered a sight of falling stars, or were they rising sparks? Then she saw a house burning. Flames were wicked behind windows and there were onlookers all cheering and feeding the flames with whatever they could find, tearing up forest and tossing it to feed the appetite of the inferno and screaming –

82

'*There you are, Slopebridge! Not as powerless as you thought, are we?*'

'*You think we'd lie down in the ditch and let you take our land?*'

'*Coward!*'

'*Thief!*'

'*Liar!*'

Oona watched, and then asked aloud (though no one near heard or seemed to see her): 'What is this?'

And the voice of these dreams answered: '*Slopebridge Manor.*'

'Slopebridge?' said Oona. 'Owner of the Big House?'

'*Yes. Slopebridge was Master. Was, until he was burned out by the men of Drumbroken.*'

'Why?' asked Oona, watching the figures moving fast and looking intent on their fury.

But then the screaming came again from those determined to burn the Big House, sentences that might've been questions but sounded more to Oona like grim statements –

'*Don't you know we'll drive you out! Same as is happening all over the Blessed Isle!*'

'*Think you can drive our rents sky-high for no good reason and take what you like!*'

'*Think you're safe in there with all your riches and ill-gotten wealth! All your blood money!*'

Then things changed: Oona saw the onlookers not onlooking but hurrying, moving fast towards the blaze, and she was sure they were all men. They were throwing themselves into the flames. And then such screaming – everyone who was

83

gathered around the house began to shriek as parts of the Big House began to fall and inside were such roars of agony as flame went taller and wilder, and with a scream of her own Oona Kavanagh tore herself free of sleep.

18

Oona found herself upright with hands outstretched and groping for things unseen. She was shaking. She faced night: cold stars were out but they looked shrunken, desperate like they were drowning in surrounding dark. Hidden almost behind cloud was the faint face of the moon, a chalk-smear on black. And there was no sight of Merrigutt, jackdaw or old woman.

Oona breathed. Her throat was raw. So had she been shouting, or screaming? She closed her eyes like it might allow relief, but behind was waiting the vision of the Big House, its burning, and men drawn in towards flame . . . how had she seen these things? Must be imagined, she decided, but where had these notions come from? And the voice – those same commanding and beckoning and burning words?

Oona opened her eyes again, needing to be up, and not thinking. But when she shifted she felt a hard hot weight against her side. It took more moments for her to remember, to recall more words: '*Keep it with you. It's a burden, but I know you can bear it.*'

Somewhere close something howled.

Oona returned to the ground. She pulled her mother's cloak

closer, fingers finding the bound bundle she'd been given as a final thing before leaving the Kavanagh cottage, and decided: it's about time I saw what exactly Granny Kavanagh has given me.

19

Oona's trembling fingers tried for many minutes to unpick the knots of the cloth, and in the end she got her teeth involved to bite and tear and rip. And with a bit of scattered swearing, eventually the rags fell aside.

Inside was a stone the size of a plum, and not far off the same colour – a bruised-looking thing, crimson dark. She let it slip into her palm and it was like holding a stone not long out of the hearth, warmed to only just holdable heat. Oona brought it closer. In its depths lived some slow, solemn flicker of light – not a reflection of anything, the moon too faint and stars too small. And when Oona tried to examine the light more closely it squirmed away from seeing. The longer Oona looked, the heavier the stone became in her hands. And the more she sought that small sliver of light that was finer than a single fair hair, the more it retreated, and the more something shook and trembled inside her.

Her grandmother's words returned: '*And this is the most important thing – don't lose sight of the light. Keep looking for it.*'

Like some second heart suddenly awoken, something inside Oona fluttered, frightened. Like some unbidden voice burning in her mind, she felt addressed. And for more unknowable moments, Oona was shown again the sight of the burning Big House and heard screaming and saw men rushing towards death and –

She shut her eyes and dropped the stone.

But all that made up Oona Kavanagh – thoughts, feelings, senses – were like leaves upset by a gale, or hard earth being broken open. She stood and took a step backwards from her grandmother's gift. Breathed in. She wondered again about her grandmother's words: '*It's a burden, but I know you can bear it.*' Breathed out.

Then a step forwards and Oona tried to be definite in it, feeling as though this stone was something that needed showing who was in control. She kneeled and took it up, and then looked again –

The small shred of light brightened to a blaze, widening as slow as a fish-eye, and Oona was shown a single image – a wooden shrine for the Sorrowful Lady . . .

Oona lifted her gaze – the same Sorrowful Lady stood before her, the same shrine.

'So the house I saw is close?' said Oona. The stone grew warmer in her hand, as if in agreement. 'It's close,' she said. And not knowing what force was leading her or why, she decided: 'It's near. And there's something in that Big House that I need to see.'

Still no sight (or more likely *sound*) of the jackdaw, and Oona started uphill. The stone her grandmother had given held in her hands like an offering, Oona once more was climbing – out of the valley, out of Drumbroken, and feeling led into she didn't know what dark.

20

Knowledge made Oona bold: she had the stone and her knife too, and she knew the Big House wasn't far, though barely knew how she knew it. Something dreamed? Surely an imagined thing, but stronger – like something that clung close to memory, like an echo. But Oona didn't have time for this or that doubt or to wonder or worry about it all. She'd stopped: sooner than she'd thought, she was there.

Broad and high and blighted by burning, stone scorched and window-frames emptied and roof showing shattered ribs to the sky – the Big House of Drumbroken. As Oona looked, a mounting heat touched her palms, the fresh remembrance of fire – the stone was blazing. And again its warmth felt like an urging, a telling as strong as the voice she'd heard in her head saying, *On. Go.*

Oona looked down: from her feet stretched a stone bridge, fallen in places and about to fall in others, crumbling but still managing to span a depthless dark. From somewhere in the below came the rattle of water over broken rock.

Oona's eyes again went to the Big House. The stone throbbed hot against her palms. She started across.

When she searched for a way in she saw a large doorway – might've been a wide welcome in ordinary days, but it had become an invitation into a deeper dark, a doorway with no door at all. On the wall beside, Oona noticed an oval of oak hanging by a nail, saying –

~~SLOPEBRIDGE MANOR~~
BUT RECLAIMED FROM THE INVADER BY THE MEN OF DRUMBROKEN!

And somewhere in the dark of Slopebridge Manor she sensed a rustling, a shifting like uneasy memories stirred, things shaken that would have rather stayed settled.

Once more, the stone made its order: *On. Go. Go in.*

And Oona had to obey.

21

On into a long, long hall that was rich with remains, so many things Oona had to keep herself from tripping on – torn carpet, toppled tables, a scatter of shattered crockery. On the walls were many frames showing painted landscapes, but all were darkened by the burning – scenes of perpetual dusk. All paintings except one, the largest: a portrait of a uniformed man with too many medals for Oona to count, a cap on his knee and a pistol resting on his lap beneath long fingers. A sculpted scroll at the bottom of the frame told – *Major Arnold Slopebridge*.

On the right appeared another doorway devoid of door. Oona stepped inside.

What little moonlight was admitted sketched a room in dull lines. So much shadow, nothing certain of itself. But Oona saw the throat of a large fireplace, heard it breathing with winter. She walked on and more detail was added: the coil and curl of candle brackets on walls, a darkened heap of an old sofa, a fallen cabinet with contents fleeing in fragments across a naked floor and –

Oona swore and stopped just in time, just on the brink of a vast dark. The floor had been opened wide. Had been torn up? The stone blushed in Oona's hands to tell her, *Yes*. And she saw for less than an instant this image: fingers tearing furious at wood, a determined ripping of floor by desperate hands. The unease of rustling and shifting rose all around and Oona looked to the walls. She could hear two voices in hushed yet fervent dialogue –

'Is that him? Has he returned to his house?'

'Don't be daft! Why would he come back here, you eejit? He wouldn't dare!'

Oona turned and turned, seeking the source of the voices. She saw walls scorched in swathes and – like some new trick of her imagination – she thought some portions were almost human shaped. Then those voices spoke again, and there was no trick in them: Oona knew they were not merely imagined.

'I still reckon it could be him. Who else would come? Everyone else is too scared. This one doesn't look scared.'

'Not him.'

A new, third voice. One deeper, slower –

'It's not a "he" anyway, it's a she. Only a little girl.'

Oona waited. She found herself craving response from either of the first two voices. Found herself holding her grandmother's stone tight to her chest, a deep need in her for warmth. Then the deep, slow voice ordered, *'Go, my friends – explore, find out for yourselves.'*

And suddenly things were plucking at Oona – like a teasing breeze they tugged on her dress and cloak and tossed her hair and again she turned and turned on the same creaking spot of floor, trying to catch sight of something. She thought of her knife and whether showing it would do any good. Again, she looked to the walls – the black there, had it shifted?

'Who are you?' she demanded. 'And why are you hiding?'

A chorus of voices then, countless echoes –

'*Not hiding!*'

'*How dare you!*'

'*Bloody cheek!*'

'*Coming in here and invading this place!*'

'*It's our own – we fought for it and you've no right to set a foot in it!*'

Their tone sounded to Oona like the old men of Drumbroken when she'd stepped into the Tower – disgruntled, more put out than anything. But then from the walls came that deep, slow voice, the one that seemed most keen to command:

'*She doesn't seem at all worried, my friends. Well, let's see how long she stays not scared.*'

Then such a rush through the room as the scorching stormed – dark squall! – and the sight itself sent Oona twirling on her toes. She staggered, threw out a hand and found a candle bracket to cling to stop herself falling, but dropped the stone. Had it fallen into that larger dark in the floor? Oona wanted to fall to her knees and seek but she stayed, gripping the bracket as the men's voices spoke again, this time with plenty of wheedling words and a lot of low laughter –

'*She's as scared as any, look!*'

'*Who is she, that's what I want to know? Coming here to thieve?*'

The return of the deep, slow voice –

'*Why else would she come?*'

On the chimney breast, Oona saw shadow shaping itself: surely an arm, surely a hand, then without a sliver of doubt she saw a single, scolding finger . . . and then a face that told her –

'This girl has heard about the gold and riches hidden beneath these boards. Heard of the treasure behind these walls stored by Slopebridge that we came to claim. She's come to steal it from us, to take what belongs to no one but us!'

Oona cried out, 'No! Look: I don't want any bloody treasure or whatever you're talking about, so you can get that idea out of your head!'

But the voice from the chimney breast told her cold –

'Enough. We are men of honour, of dignity, and we tell nothing but the truth. And I tell you one thing for true: as sure as I'm a man of Drumbroken, as surely as I drove that fool and coward Slopebridge from this place, you won't be leaving here alive with our treasure. Get her!'

22

'No!'

Oona screamed and abandoned the candle bracket: fleeing and just leaving the stone wherever it lay was all she thought of. But again she was spun by whirling dark and this time fell – her skull met stone, spine met broken floor, and her fingers met something else. Something warming? At Oona's touch, the stone Granny Kavanagh had given glowed and gave enough light for Oona to rise, to feel she could fight. She stood and brandished it like it might be a weapon. Then words as well as images crowded her, a deep knowing –

'You all burned here because you were too selfish to leave it all when it was going up in flames!' she told the walls. 'Too bloody stupid to go back to your families, too greedy! You came here to get rid of Slopebridge and then stayed to tear up floorboards looking for what he took, and you didn't care whether you died or not!'

The walls calmed, a little: looked like they were breathing, trembling. And what remained of the men said –

'How dare you come and judge what we did so harshly!'

'We should be heroes for what we did that night for the

sake of Drumbroken!'

'Aye! We drove out Slopebridge!'

'He would've had us all in an early grave if he'd kept on the way he was going!'

'Working us day and night, putting the rents up and up and up!'

'We needed to act or else –'

'Else what?' said Oona. She stepped forwards and stood on the brink of black. 'He put you in your graves anyway!'

As the words left Oona's mouth she saw violent past and dark present together: figures at her feet tearing, men with as much burning in their hearts as there was in the Big House, flames edging in . . . Oona shook her head. She swallowed and said, 'I know what you did. I know you shouldn't have stayed and burned, it only let Slopebridge win. And he got away, didn't he? He lived on and all of you died.'

'Chased out of this Blessed Isle, he was!'

'Aye! I can still see the look on his face, the big bulging eyes on him!'

'And how he tripped and wept like a child, begging us to spare him!'

'Some things are more important than staying living!'

'What's the point in a life led without pride or honour or cause?'

'We got rid of him and that's that!'

But, Oona thought, were the voices weaker, more unsure? And the deepest and slowest of them all – that voice was staying silent.

'Aye,' said Oona, 'you got rid is right. But then what happened? He went across the sea and told those over the water what we were like. Must've told them what barbarians and all we were, and then, not long after, the Invaders came. Blessed Isle became Divided Isle.'

Oona didn't know how she knew this, but knew she spoke the truth.

There was no answer for her, no other word from the walls. And in Oona's hands there was a sudden chill – the stone was cooling, had (for the moment) given all its secrets, felt fragile. And then the voice that had been silent spoke, deepest and slowest –

'You say these things, child, but it is a knowledge gained without learning.'

Oona opened her mouth to answer but was interrupted.

'No disagreement, girl. I know you're fond of it, but this you cannot argue with. You do not know what you carry, but I do. It was something given you, a something you don't yet understand.'

'What is it then?' asked Oona. 'If you know so much – *tell.*'

Voice: *'It is a something more powerful and dangerous than you have ever dreamed of.'*

Oona didn't speak then. She held the stone closer, like someone might reach out, snatch.

'Tell me your name,' said the voice.

Oona said, proud as she ever was of herself, 'I'm of the family Kavanagh. My mam gave me the name Oona. It means "Unity".'

A softest sigh from this someone unseen. The deep and slow (and now soft) voice replied –

'Kavanagh? Thought as much. Now – do you know my name?'

'I do,' Oona found herself saying. She waited. And the stone passed her truth: 'You're a Kavanagh too. You're my great-grandfather.'

'I am. I was given the name Aedan. It means "Born of Fire".'

'How did I know all this?' asked Oona, hearing a helplessness in her own voice that she couldn't hide. 'What is this stone? Where did it come from?'

The walls shivered, shadows shrinking.

'*Where has it come from?*' repeated the voice of her great-grandfather. '*It comes from the ages, from the blood and broken bones of history itself – from the nightmare of the past. What is it called? Has been called many a thing in its time: the Knowing Stone, the Darkness and the Seeing, the Nightmare Stone. But the name my wife always gave it before she handed it down to your grandmother was this: the Loam Stone.*'

Oona looked – the Loam Stone's light was low, a slither and flicker, but at the same time so very fierce. It might have been small but the ardency of its convictions were great, and too much to be looked at. Oona had to turn her gaze.

'Your wife?' she asked.

'*It is an object that has been passed down through generations of Kavanagh women,*' said her great-grandfather. '*An object that allows you to know the most painful of things. Allows you to see all darkness, all nightmares. And through such dark – all truth.*'

'I woke and I'd been dreaming,' said Oona. 'But not like normal dreaming. I saw the burning, the screaming here in this Big House . . .'

'*When you are dreaming,*' said Aedan Kavanagh, in a voice only just above a whisper, '*you are defenceless, and that is when it likes to take hold. For years, whichever of the Kavanagh women had it in their custody would sleep with it under their pillow. And during the night it would feed on all pain and discomfort, all anguish of the family. Have you ever, Oona, had a dream like the one that woke you earlier? The one that brought you here? Tell.'*

Oona remembered that voice she'd heard in the Kavanagh cottage – the set of promises, of threats uttered in her mind before her granny had clouted her awake.

'Yes,' she said.

'Only once? Because your grandmother had been burdened with all nightmares for all the years of your life. Same as all the Kavanagh women who came before her and slept with the Loam Stone close – they would wake in the morning and know their family better than they knew themselves, know her husband better than he liked to admit. The women of the house would know all, and endure all pain and nightmares for the sake of the family.'

Oona remembered her granny Kavanagh – confused, plagued. She felt closer to understanding. 'My granny,' she said, 'could see things that were happening elsewhere. She knew things.'

'Over time the power of the Stone can stretch,' said her great-grandfather. *'It can sense the nightmares and fears of the family even when they are not at home.'* Another slow sigh. *'It is a terrible thing to bear, Oona. A burden that my wife, in the end . . .'* The voice of Aedan Kavanagh went silent.

'Then I should get rid of it,' said Oona. 'I don't want it. Don't want to know these things.'

'I would agree if we were in more peaceful times. But that object is something you cannot surrender, not to anyone.'

'The Invaders are looking for it,' said Oona. 'They're taking the boys and asking them for information about it.'

'In their foolishness,' said Aedan, *'they think that something so powerful must be kept among men, passed from father to son.*

99

It gives you an advantage, for the time being.'

'Not much chance of that seeing as she's planning on carrying it up with her into the Black North!'

Oona turned: a jackdaw was perched in an empty window-frame.

'I thought I told you to stay put!' said Merrigutt. In one swoop she was in front of Oona and no longer a bird but back to an old woman, pointing, nagging: 'If we're going to survive then you'll have to start doing as I bid! You've no self-control in you at all!'

'Now don't be so harsh on her, Evelyn,' said Aedan Kavanagh. *'She's already learned the trick of resisting the Stone, was able to pull herself away from it and able to pull out what knowledge she liked. More importantly – she wasn't driven mad by it, and there's been many's a Kavanagh woman who has seen that sad fate. I would say that shows some self-control, wouldn't you?'*

Merrigutt said nothing.

Oona said to the old woman, 'You knew I had this or knew it was in the Kavanagh family – that's why you came to the Tower and took such an interest, isn't it?'

'I needed to make sure,' said Merrigutt, not looking at Oona, 'for the good of us all, that the Stone didn't drop into the hands of the Invaders. But like I say – some chance of that now!'

'You should've not lied and just told me,' said Oona.

'You were supposed to be taking it South and to safety!' said Merrigutt.

'There's no safety now, Evelyn,' said Oona's great-grandfather.

'I told her that too!' said Oona.

'We've heard whispers from the forest, from the many Invaders

passing by – they are moving across the Divide in vast numbers, bringing with them all magic they can summon, all creatures they can recruit. Soon the South will be as Black as the North.'

Then another of the men spoke from the walls –

'You plan to go North, into the Black?'

'We do,' said Merrigutt. 'Apparently.' She gave Oona such a look, could've curdled milk.

'My brother Morris is there,' said Oona. She looked to the shape of her great-grandfather that haunted the chimney-breast. 'That's why I'm going. He was captured and I want him back. I'll not lie – he's a pain in the arse most times, but he's all I've got now.'

Oona heard the same long, slow sigh from Aedan Kavanagh. Then he said: *'Tis a foolish folly indeed, heading into the Black.'*

'Exactly!' said Merrigutt.

'And I don't have the heart to tell you what awaits you beyond the Divide.'

'Are you listening, my girl?' said Merrigutt, giving Oona a sharp nudge.

'But.' A pause. *'I can think of no greater reason to do such a foolish thing than for family, and no greater fool to do it than a Kavanagh.'*

Oona smiled the kind of smile she hadn't smiled for too long a time. Merrigutt muttered, 'Heavens-and-the-Sorrowful-Lady-herself help us!'

Then other words entered the room, which sent shivers everywhere. The sound of outside voices –

'She came up the slope here, I can see tracks. Search the house from top to bottom, every room and crack and cupboard!'

The walls all whispered: '*Invaders! Invaders! They're coming!*'

'A way out, Aedan,' said Merrigutt, and she was once more a jackdaw, again on Oona's shoulder with claws closing tight. 'Fast as you could would be appreciated.'

Another pause, then the echo of Oona's great-grandfather breathed, '*Into the fireplace. Hurry.*'

Oona had to edge around the opening in the floor, the men on all walls cowering, their darkness slipping low to the skirting-boards, skulking. Then the voice of an Invader, inside the Big House, too close: 'You three go upstairs, the rest search this level and anything below.'

'Aedan,' said Merrigutt, 'is that him? The Faceless?'

Oona whispered, 'Who are you talking about?'

Voice from the hall: 'I sense something close. This way . . .'

Then Merrigutt and her great-grandfather both: '*Quick!*'

Oona found the fireplace, ducked down and crouched in its emptiness. She felt like a child seeking not to be seen and futile in her effort.

Then a voice: 'There she is.'

Oona saw a figure in the doorway. And she wanted to believe that the dark was confusing her: what she saw was a figure with arms hanging almost to the floor and wearing an Invader uniform, on its shoulder a small bird with crimson eyes. And surely some trick, some devilry in the dark air – the figure had no face, wore only grey-white blankness for an expression, like a grubby page awaiting scrawl.

A voice coming from somewhere near this faceless Invader said again: 'There she is.'

And long-armed and long-legged, the Invader moved in two

strides to clear the chasm with hands outstretched, reaching for Oona –

Then, all in the same moment –

Cry of Merrigutt: 'Protect the Stone!'

Screech of the bird on the faceless Invader's shoulder: 'Grab her!'

Cry of Aedan Kavanagh: '*Now, Evelyn!*'

Merrigutt leapt to a candle bracket and then to Oona's shoulder, and the back of the fireplace opened and shut like a trap and Oona was swallowed, the hands of the faceless creature and the screech of the crimson-eyed bird left on the other side.

23

Oona demanded, 'What the hell was what thing?'

But her great-grandfather's voice was keen to urge, '*Hurry! Down the steps and don't stop for nothing!*'

'But –' began Oona, but beginning to move too.

Merrigutt said, 'Just move like you're told or we might as well say our Farewell Prayers to Her Sorrowful Self! And keep that Stone close!'

So Oona moved, on bare feet down cold stone steps.

'*Quicker if you can,*' said her great-grandfather.

The Loam Stone gave some light to see by, the littlest; felt smaller in Oona's hand, seemed shrunken. Like it's been frighted, thought Oona. But even if there'd been more light from the Stone it would've had nothing to show: walls to left and right of Oona were blackened, same as above. Alongside her she had the sense of something moving, of her great-grandfather keeping close. He said, '*Don't spend time looking for me. Just concentrate – quickly down. Few more steps just.*'

Oona felt laden with questions, but she waited till the end of the staircase and her feet fell on flatter ground and then she let words escape: 'Now tell me what that was. Or who?

Was it a who or a what?'

'A *creature*,' said Merrigutt, still on Oona's shoulder. The jackdaw sounded almost breathless, like she'd been flying ceaselessly for a long, hard season and had landed only that instant. 'A *thing*. And something I wasn't expecting to see.'

'*Must've come South to lead the Invaders,*' said Aedan Kavanagh. '*He is the King's most trusted advisor. His Captain.*'

'He –' began Oona. She wasn't sure how to say it except to just say it: 'He didn't have a face.'

'We should be thankful he didn't,' said Merrigutt. 'Thankful he wasn't wearing some other face he'd stolen to fool us!'

'*He can take on the appearance of any he likes,*' said Great-grandfather Kavanagh.

'How'd he get like that?' asked Oona. 'Some North magic, is it?'

'Some darkness,' said Merrigutt. She shook her feathers. 'Some seed that the King planted, fed with blood and poison and up popped that creature. Was tugged out like a weed by the bird he carries on his shoulder – a Carrion Changeling. And since then the two of them can't be separated, some rotten bond between. The bird does the talking, the thinking, all things – the bird is the thing you need to worry about.'

Oona said nothing. She drew her mother's cloak closer.

'Is this tunnel even safe, Aedan?' asked Merrigutt. 'Will they not have it covered at the other end?'

'*Let's hope and give prayers that they don't. This is the tunnel Slopebridge used to escape, and I don't think many know about it. It'll take you all the way into the next county – to Ballyboglin and the island town of Innislone. It's the best choice you have.*'

From there, it's not far to the Divide.'

Oona had more questions but had to concentrate – on into the lowest stone tunnel, stooping, her head held so low all of her soon hurt, neck and spine and scalp. Merrigutt had to swap Oona's shoulder for the ground to hop ahead. And still Oona couldn't help checking for her great-grandfather, wanting to see him fully, this remainder of a Kavanagh she'd not ever known. She watched, and saw something like a shadow of her own shadow travelling keen, fast-moving, and always a little ahead. And then she lost him. His whisper said, *'This is as far as I can take you. Only as far as the fire touched.'*

Oona looked and saw some end to the burning, some stone untouched.

'So you're trapped in that Big House?' said Oona. 'Forever?'

'And ever more,' said her great-grandfather. *'It is where I died, where my body rotted and bones burned. I died, as you said so rightly, in a shameful way – in search of wealth. And so here I must remain.'*

'But what happens if the house just crumbles away to nothing?' asked Oona. 'What'll you do then?'

'I do not know,' said her great-grandfather.

'Or can you not try some other way to get out maybe?' asked Oona. 'Are you some kind of spirit now or . . . ?'

'I do not know what I am. Perhaps only little more than an echo.'

Oona opened her mouth with more but found that she couldn't follow such fine words.

'Listen,' said Great-grandfather Kavanagh. Behind them, following: fast footsteps. Ahead: an uncertain light. *'Go now!'*

But Oona didn't want to leave. He might only be darkness

and uncertainty – whisper and shadow – but she had found some comfort in the presence of her great-grandfather. And before she went, for a silent moment she settled one hand to the stone, to where she imagined his dark lingering. Then Oona heard Aedan's voice once more, a final murmur for her only –

'Be careful with that Stone. Be so very careful. Its echoes have destroyed so many in our family. In the end, everyone has lost sight of its light and fallen into nightmares.'

Oona said, 'I won't let that happen to me. I'll be different. I promise it.'

Then the sound of footsteps still approaching, and faster –

'I'll distract them as best I can,' said Oona's great-grandfather. *'Good luck.'*

'Go!' said Merrigutt, always there to will on, to command.

But already Oona was running, eyes on the end of the tunnel, on a light that flickered and fell in scraps and made doubles and triples of her juddering shadow.

'Firelight?' said Oona.

Merrigutt said, 'Aye. It's Innislone.'

Then Oona remembered Bridget's words, and said to herself aloud: *'The town that won't be drowned.'*

24

Suddenly Oona was walking through water, a soup of sucking and squelching beneath her feet.

'Ballyboglin,' said Merrigutt. 'Dampest and dankest county in the whole Divided Isle.'

So walking (near wading) onwards, Oona lifted her cloak and dress and was thankful just then for the firelight to see by . . .

Noise reached her ears first – a crackling-crunching, loud as a whole forest being taken by flame. Noise, then heat, and Oona lifted herself from the passage and looked down: fire was tearing at night-sky, the town of Innislone under attack.

'Well hell's bloody bells,' breathed Oona.

'Look out!' said Merrigutt.

Oona ducked down and half-ran, finding a bedraggled birch – web-choked and rotten and broken by the same dispell that had crept into Drumbroken – to hide behind as a trio of Invaders appeared from the tunnel. They looked about a bit, but were more drawn by the sight of Innislone. They ran on and down, joining Invaders who were streaming in across the bogland from all sides, all flowing into the hollow towards blaze and battle.

Oona edged up for another look, a squint.

Firelight was reflected far – a mirror made by the lough the town was built on. Oona thought it must've given Innislone some protection, the surrounding water. And hadn't Bridget mentioned something about bridges? Oona couldn't see any, but couldn't see much. What she did see was fire being kindled by Invaders and launched on the end of long arms, hurled by a snapping mechanism and then falling on the buildings closest to the edge of the town. The flames took quickly, chewed-up and spat out whatever they fed on, fragments of Innislone ending life in the lough in a final gasp of steam.

'How the hell have they even survived this long?' asked Oona.

'Sometimes sheer stubbornness can work wonders,' said Merrigutt, landing on Oona's shoulder. 'But they'll not hold for much longer.' They watched more flame leap across the lough and land. They saw more houses collapse. 'Till dawn,' whispered Merrigutt. 'By sun-up, Innislone will be at the bottom of that lough.'

Oona couldn't disagree.

'Is there some other way to get to the Divide from here?' asked Oona.

'If you're still set on this,' said Merrigutt, 'then across the lough is the quickest way. Over to the far shore, then only a bit farther on. But if we hadn't gotten ourselves into this situation, if you hadn't gone to that Big House then –'

'But I did and there's nothing I can do about it,' said Oona. 'We can't go back. We're here now, so how are we gonna get by this mess?'

'All up to me now, is it?' said Merrigutt.

'Yes,' said Oona. 'It's about time you showed some of this North magic that I've heard so much about. Or is at all just talk?'

She felt the jackdaw stiffen.

'You'd better get ready to run like blue blazes, my girl!' said Merrigutt. 'You want North magic – then keep your eyes wide and watch.'

25

Oona caught Merrigutt's transformation more clearly than she'd done any other time, but still it was too quick: just jackdaw-then-old-woman in a blink-quick glimpse. The old woman Merrigutt shook herself, and then started a rifling with one long-fingered hand through the black that covered her, eventually finding another pinch of scarlet powder. She gave Oona a wink, and then began a slow stroll down the slope.

'Where are you going, woman?' said Oona. 'They'll see you!'

Merrigutt didn't answer. She looked to be letting the powder leave her hand slowly, at the same time back-walking and muttering, changing direction like it was precise. Backing and backing until she was back by Oona, who stood and looked out over the broad scarlet pattern dropped on bogland: it had been laid out in the shape of a man.

'Suppose it's impressive enough,' said Oona. 'But how does a nice pattern help us to –?' The bog began to twitch and churn.

'Better step back a wee bit there,' said Merrigutt. She was smiling.

Within the shape Merrigutt had drawn, all grass and earth and bush and falling bog-water was lifting, tearing itself up, was lifting to stand massive. Oona herself stepped back and back. She lifted her gaze to look and couldn't look high enough, the figure of the bog-made man towering tall. And she wasn't the only one watching – a new urgency could be heard in the voices of the Invaders attacking Innislone, shouts and callings as they stopped their attack on the town to watch.

'They mightn't be unused to the sight,' said Merrigutt, 'but unlike their Muddgloggs, this is our own solitary soldier. He's a man, but one that'll at least do as he's told.'

Oona was still watching: felt dumb in her gaping but she could do little else. The bog-soldier's head was a dark eclipse across moon, and Oona saw a pair of rough openings like eyes that allowed moonlight through. And did he look to Merrigutt then, wanting orders? She saw the old woman nod, and the bog-man nod back in reply. Then he began to stalk down the slope, into the hollow, towards Innislone.

'Now follow,' said Merrigutt. A twitch and small hop and again she was a jackdaw, again onto Oona's shoulder. 'Now run!'

Oona had to swerve to avoid the place where the bog-soldier had lain before being summoned: a deep pit in his image, new scar on the South. She stayed close in his shadow though, hoping to remain unseen. But as the bog-man walked he lost pieces of himself, great clumps of sog and clay and damp dark falling to the ground.

'He won't hold together long,' said Merrigutt. 'Hurry!' It was a command for Oona and the bog-soldier both –

In only two or three strides he reached the lough and the army of Invaders were sent scattering. Oona reached the shore less than a minute later and saw a single currach bobbing, abandoned, a single oar resting across. She ran to the boat and leapt in. Oona had never rowed a boat but didn't dwell – she'd have to give it a go – what else could she do? She pushed off from the shore and began to beat her way towards Innislone.

Merrigutt told her, 'I'll fly ahead and warn the Lough-Master that you're crossing, otherwise they might shoot. Don't have long of our soldier left by the looks of him.'

The jackdaw left, and Oona half-turned, looking up – true enough, their bog-man was returning to the earth, one vast limb at a time. His arms were easing away from his body, falling and sending more Invaders scampering. And still Oona smashed at the water, trying to move herself on. Then Merrigutt was back, perching on the rim of the boat and saying, 'All right, they say they're gonna open a bridge for you. Row faster!'

Oona had no breath to spare for speech. She worked hard towards the wooden platform she saw being lowered, a section of the wooden wall that enclosed the town being opened in one of the few parts of Innislone not crawling with flame. Then a shout from behind her –

'There! Look! Someone's crossing!'

Oona swore as the surface around her was broken by gunfire.

'Look out, my girl!' called Merrigutt.

Oona turned to watch: body sinking, the final piece of the bog-soldier was falling, the massive dark of its head tumbling and –

'Damn,' said Merrigutt. 'Hold on.'

Oona dropped the oar and clamped hands around the rim of the currach as the bog-man's head hit water and a wave sprang high. No more rowing was needed – the boat was rushed towards the wall of Innislone, was flipped and Merrigutt was lost to the air as Oona fell into the water. The lough was so cold it stole her breath. A fast runner, quick climber, but not a strong swimmer – Oona surfaced and straight away shouted for help.

'Here, girl!'

A man of Innislone was at the wooden platform. He swung and flung a line to her. It landed beside her hand and she took it as gunfire cracked wood and water and the Innislone man reeled Oona in as fast as you would a limp fish. At the platform he took her under the arms and lifted, shouting, 'Close it up now!', Oona's feet and hands just avoiding being taken off as the bridge snapped shut behind.

26

The man who'd removed Oona from the lough dropped her on her feet and threw orders to others: 'Barricade that bridge up, best you can do! Don't let anything get in!'

Oona watched boards stacked and held, nailed like it might do some good against the siege, all men and all hands working to try to keep Innislone secure. Everything around was wood – flat-roofed houses, encircling wall, boards underfoot. And everywhere too was the keenness of encroaching fire. One thing not seen though – Merrigutt.

The man who'd saved Oona continued with his orders: 'You lot – keep watch to the North for more Invaders! You three – keep water going to the houses at the edges, keep them as damp as dishcloths!'

Oona saw a system near by being pumped, water from the lough sucked up and splashing out into a small reservoir, the surface steaming in the climbing heat. Buckets went in and the men lugged them away.

'Faster!' the man called. 'Quickly, fellas!'

This Innislone man wasn't like any Oona had seen in Drumbroken: he was all muscle and agitation, wide chest working fast to fill him with breath, all of him sharp-edged, hair and clothes singed short, blades all along his belt going from the long to the small, from smoothest to serrated. Both his arms were tattooed with fish scales.

'We won't give in!' he was hollering. 'Remember, fellas: this is the town that won't be drowned!' He saw Oona doing so much watching, then kneeled down as though in deference, laid two huge hands on her shoulders and demanded with sudden anger, 'What the hell do you think you're at, coming here now? You think we've time to fish wee girls out of the lough? Where are you from, anyway? Everyone's supposed to be going South, I've been spreading that word as far as I can! Are you Drumbroken?'

Oona nodded, then saw around the man's wrist a braid of blackened churnstaff, and then said, 'You're Billy O'Riley.'

'I'm Lough-Master here,' said Billy, nodding once. 'But give me the talk from Drumbroken – did all get out? Are all on the way South? What about the O'Riley family, did they escape? My niece, Bridget, she's about your age – is she safe?'

Oona said nothing.

And suddenly Merrigutt was back on Oona's shoulder to say, 'Never mind all that now – we've ourselves to worry about! I've had a quick look from above and this place doesn't have long, Lough-Master!'

'And why-come you're here?' said Billy O'Riley. He stood. Stood back, letting his arms fold tightly across his chest. 'Why now? Coming here so late with your North magic, why not earlier? Why not when them Invaders were crossing the Divide? What good is it now, your tricks, with them all at our door?'

116

'I don't answer questions,' said Merrigutt. 'You won't be interrogating me like one of your docile wives. I haven't come here to make things right and save you. I'm here because this girl is here, and that's the height of it!'

Oona watched Billy O'Riley. She saw his fingers flex, fists being thought of.

'We're going into the North,' said Oona. 'Into the Black.'

Those who'd been moving so swiftly around them were stilled. Like the tension that follows the dropping of a pot in a crowded room, Oona was at the centre of their shocked attention.

Some moments, and then slowly the Innislone men resumed whatever rushing or hurrying they'd been in the middle of, most shaking their head at the young girl and her ridiculous words.

'Then you're as much for the fire as the rest of us,' said Billy O'Riley. Then an explosion and shouts from someone of, 'Look out!'

More fire came streaking through the air and Oona ran as a whole house was made splinters on impact. Ran to nowhere – no escape.

'They're doing this on purpose,' Oona told Merrigutt. 'The Invaders could've had this place burned down ages ago but they're playing. Like they're trying to torture the people here.'

'Or kill time,' said Merrigutt. 'Keeping the men of Innislone busy while the Invaders move their armies further South. And the people here are falling for it. Fools.'

Oona looked back – O'Riley the Lough-Master hadn't budged. He was as solid in his standing, shouting to his men, 'Bring more water! Put out that fire! We can't let any more flames take hold! We won't be defeated here!'

Did he sound, Oona thought, like he was enjoying it all?

'Faster!' shouted Billy O'Riley. 'Quicker now! We'll not let them get the better of us!'

But no matter what commands the Lough-Master tossed, Oona knew it was only chaos ruling Innislone. Just someone hadn't told Billy O'Riley. So she ran back to the Lough-Master and told him, 'You need to stop this. It won't work. There's no way to stop the fire. We've seen it from farther off, so believe me!'

O'Riley heard, but hardly half-turned to smirk a little and say, 'Is that right? And you've some better ideas mebbe?'

'Your men aren't good with guns,' said Oona, remembering Bridget's words.

'And you are?' said O'Riley.

'Yes,' said Oona. 'I am.'

'Look,' said the Lough-Master, 'I've no time to babysit, and if that creature there on your shoulder can't be helping then I've no more to say to the either of you!'

And Billy moved to leave.

Oona needed him to listen, and she had only one way, so she told him: 'Bridget was taken by the Invaders and we're going to try to rescue her.'

It did the job – the Lough-Master stopped.

'Bridget was my best friend,' said Oona, all concentration on Billy. 'I tried to help her and would've done anything I could but I couldn't do a thing. There was no saving her. But now I'm trying. I'm trying to find my brother and Brid too if I can, and we'll need your help to get us on our way to the Divide.'

Billy O'Riley said nothing, did nothing: just stood in his unshiftable way, breathing shallow. His hands for the first time were loose at his sides, shoulders hunched.

'I thought,' said Billy O'Riley, and from a man so large issued a voice suddenly small. 'I thought, when I saw you running on down into the hollow there, in the shadow of that thing – I thought mebbe it was herself come down to fight, mebbe Bridget. Would've been just like her, doing something so stupid.'

'It would've indeed,' said Oona. 'But I can be just as stupid.'

'You can say that again,' Merrigutt said.

Then another explosion and everything cowered. A curtain of flame was drawn, crossing the wall that surrounded Innislone. And Oona saw in Billy's eyes the same knowledge she had: it wouldn't be stopped, there was no way to save the town.

Billy looked to Oona. His head fell forwards, his mouth grappling with something unpleasant. Then he said, at last: 'All abandon. There's nothing we can do now.' He said to Oona, 'Come with me, quick. There's only one way to escape from all this now.'

27

Oona ran with Merrigutt flying beside and Billy O'Riley a bit ahead. Oona didn't spot a single house untouched by fire. Everything was folding, boards beneath her feet groaning, opening to drop buildings into the lough. Figures were faint in their flitting between places, shrouded by smoke.

Billy O'Riley shouted back to Oona, 'Close! Stay close now!'

'Look out!' called Merrigutt. 'Follow the way I fly, my girl!'

The jackdaw made a swift turn left and Oona followed, only avoiding falling flame by a few steps as a fireball dropped, exploding, spreading itself.

'Almost there now!' the Lough-Master told her.

They arrived at a row of buildings on the edge of town: flat-roofed, small, more like sheds than anything, but with people and more people all piling in.

'Here now,' said Billy, and he opened the door of one for Oona.

Inside, a small window on the far wall showed the lough – it looked alight. But Oona was more struck by smell than seeing and pinched her nose shut. She stood in a storeroom filled with fish: packed into crates, pale bodies stranded among thawing ice or hung from the ceiling, wood-smoked and stiff. On a second wall she saw veg and fruit – carrots and spuds and beans and scallions. And on the third – plenty of bread in all sizes alongside small spheres of cheese and earthen bowls of butter and cream and whey.

Merrigutt went to the small window to watch. She said, 'Lough-Master, whatever's gonna be done you'd better do it fast.'

Billy said, 'First things first, old bird.' And to Oona's shoulder he added a leather satchel, saying, 'Doubt if the Sorrowful Lady lady herself would know when you'll next see food or water if you're going into the Black.' He packed the satchel, filling it with whatever his hands fell on.

'Take this. And then this, too, you'll need it all.' Rushwater in a narrow bottle, corked; the smallest, fattest pair of loaves; a clutch of damp strawberries Billy wrapped in linen; a pear and two rainbow trout . . . the satchel soon hung heavy on Oona's shoulder.

'Not too much,' said Merrigutt. 'She'll be like a dead weight if she falls into the lough.'

'You know what the North is,' said O'Riley, his look askance, to Merrigutt. 'You know well enough.'

'Do indeed,' said the jackdaw. 'Have you been over the Divide yourself?'

'No,' said O'Riley, 'and I've no desire to. No business of ours what goes on up there.'

'Sounds like some fear there to me,' said Merrigutt, then said no more. She seemed somehow satisfied.

Then the loudest explosion yet – the building around them rattled and shook and Oona fell against one of the shelves and was drenched in ice-water.

'You all right?' asked Billy, taking her by the arm.

'I'll live,' said Oona. 'Not the first time I've been soaked this night.'

'Hopefully it'll be the last,' muttered Merrigutt.

'You may as well have this, too,' said Billy, and he kneeled and added something final to Oona's satchel, something wrapped. 'There now. You're all set.' He tightened the buckles and at the final tug came yet another explosion. Their building began to move, drifting.

'What's going on, O'Riley?' asked Merrigutt. 'We're loose from the moorings!'

'Quiet and calm yourself, old bird,' said Billy, and he set a ladder to the ceiling and in a moment was up and out through a hatch onto the roof. Oona had to follow, even with Merrigutt saying, 'I think it'd be wiser to stay put. Don't forget now what you're carrying, and I'm not referring to the trout – you're not listening to a word I'm saying, are you?'

'Nope,' said Oona, and she was out onto the roof. Oona turned and witnessed the last throes of Innislone: blaze mounting, reaching for whatever sparse stars, the noise and heat making her cringe. But around them were survivors, a fleet of other buildings pulling away. On other roofs many faces were watching, silent, their expressions flickering between lit and shadowed, pale and dark, distraught . . .

'Keep it going, men,' called Billy, but quietly as he could. He was crouched at the edge of the roof, the largest blade from his belt in his hand. Oona walked to the edge and kneeled beside. They weren't drifting at all – men in many currachs were rowing, dragging with tow-rope the buildings-now-boats, their oars entering the lough gently. Everything and everyone, Oona realised, was contriving towards quiet, as stealthy a leaving as they could manage. They were successful, so far – no gunfire, no Invaders. Not yet.

Oona wondered aloud, 'How long do we have before they know we're gone?'

'No time at all is the way to look at it,' said the Lough-Master. He stood, feet set, blade ready, looking back towards Innislone. 'Took us so long to build that town, so much hard work from so many men. It was home, and now it'll go down in no time.'

Oona didn't know what to say. But she knew how it felt, this kind of leaving. Knew what it was to see home changed. She knew what it was like to have no place to return to.

'Billy,' said Oona, thinking that if they were to have a chance at the world ahead, she needed to know all she could. 'Have you seen any Invaders taking anyone by on the way to the Divide? Any prisoners?'

Billy sighed and said, 'Dunno about prisoners, but I know you're not the only ones with a notion of going up into the North. Week ago – must've been about that – some of the Cause went through, recruited some of my men to go with them.'

'Fools,' said Merrigutt. 'Only boys playing with their father's guns, chasing echoes!'

'For once we're agreeing, old bird,' said O'Riley. 'They think they're going off to challenge this King – not a chance.'

'So what're you going to do then?' said Oona. 'Where will you go now?' Billy opened his mouth for some reply but –

'Lough-Master!'

123

A harsh whisper from one of the rowing-boats and a finger pointing towards shore. Oona looked – along the edge of the lough ran lamplight.

'Told you it wouldn't be long,' said Billy.

But it was less time than Oona thought before gunfire came.

'Quickly,' said O'Riley, and he suddenly had Oona lifted like she was nothing and carried her quickly to the edge of the roof. A boat no bigger than a coffin was waiting, bolted to the side of the building, and Billy lowered her in. He began to crank something at the stern.

'Listen now,' he told her. 'There's a town I've heard tell of, not far on from the Divide. But like all places up North, there's some strange chat about it – some have been and come back, called the place haunted. But might be a place to aim for. That's little enough, but it's all I know.'

Oona nodded, crouched in the boat, Merrigutt settled on the prow.

Billy looked at her, then let his eyes wander to the jackdaw.

'That's one stubborn creature you've bound yourself to,' said Billy, his voice lowering, leaning close to Oona. 'And I've heard stories about her kind, and not of the pleasant, hearthside kind. But one thing you can't do is go into the Black alone, so be glad you've got someone with you, no matter who it is. Hold tight now.'

He stood and swung the largest of large knives he had in his hand –

Rope cut, the boat dropped –

It struck water and as soon as it did what Billy had been winding tight was released – a wooden propeller began to whirr and Oona and Merrigutt were taken fast from the building, towards a shore not yet Invaded.

'Stay low now,' said the jackdaw.

Oona lay on her front and looked back towards Innislone. But so much smoke and steam was entwining that she could hardly see. And Billy himself? Already the Lough-Master was far behind. Too far for seeing.

'Do you still have the Loam Stone?' asked Merrigutt.

Oona's hand went to her cloak to check – the Stone was there, safe and cold.

'Aye,' she told the jackdaw.

Merrigutt said, 'Good. Maybe put it into that satchel he gave you, if you can find room.'

So Oona slipped the Stone in among the supplies Billy had given. But when her hand was retreating it found the final thing the Lough-Master had gifted. Oona decided to take a swift look – it was a pistol, fully loaded, wrapped in a length of faint lace. A box was packed beside and it contained plenty of bullets. And bringing it close (and not letting the jackdaw see) Oona managed to make out an inscription along the barrel, to feel out words with the slow wander of her fingertip: *For my very best niece, Bridget. Best with a gun I've ever seen! With such love, your Uncle Billy.*

28

Quickly from the currach and Oona and Merrigutt were grateful to be enfolded by dark – firelight and fire-lit lough were soon behind. Oona moved ahead without knowing the way ahead, every step taking her more into the uncertain. She had to say, 'Can hardly see!'

'Just keep on going,' said the jackdaw from her (becoming-permanent) perch on Oona's shoulder. 'Keep moving yourself.'

Oona's feet encountered a slope and she began, 'Is there no easier way to –?' Then a sudden fall into wet. Again – every bit of her soaked.

'Watch yourself,' said Merrigutt.

'Thanks for warning,' said Oona, feeling her way upright again, hands on the satchel, keeping it closest. At the top of the slope was no kind of view – the world looked unmade yet, undecided on anything but black.

'We can't go on in this,' said Merrigutt. 'You've no sight for seeing in the dark, like all South of the Divide. Wait here a wee minute.'

Then the jackdaw left, calling, 'You'll have to follow my voice! There's a sort of cottage here. It'll have to do for somewhere to stay till it gets a bit lighter.'

Oona moved. Her feet met the other side of the slope and she tried not to slip, keeping herself low with arms out and hands open in case she tumbled. At the bottom she stopped: the cottage was half-hid by a swell of dark ivy. A disjointed tree stripped of its leaves was sprouting from the roof, making a painful shape against the sky. An unwelcoming darkness – like the Big House of Drumbroken – was in place of a door.

'Hurry!' called Merrigutt.

Inside the cottage Oona saw only a vague furniture of broken rock, all clothed with web. There was that expected reek of things stale and damp. (Or maybe, Oona thought, that's just myself I'm sniffing?)

'Don't get fussy now,' said Merrigutt, flying past Oona and on, further into the cottage.

'You can't be choosy when we're out in the wilds like this.'

'It'll do,' said Oona. 'I've slept in worse. Me and Morris once found this cave and he told me a Hunched Hermit must live in it, so we –'

'Sounds like a great adventure,' said Merrigutt. 'But maybe another time – I'm bone-wrecked and exhausted! Freezing, too.'

'Fire then?' said Oona, looking to the cracked hearth at the centre of the room. 'Cook some food? Fish would go down well.' A smallish pause.

'Suppose it would,' said Merrigutt.

Oona saw the darkness around the jackdaw twitch and shiver; there was a groan of discomfort and the dark returned the sight of the old-woman-version of Merrigutt. She told Oona, 'Now don't get the idea that you can just demand me to change and do magic any time you feel like! It's not easy transforming all the time. It's a pain in the arse, if you're interested.'

Oona said nothing – if she knew anything, she knew when it was best to keep quiet.

No pan or griddle about, so the trout had to be skewered on sticks Oona snapped from the tree and then held over flames Merrigutt had brought into shivering being with a little of her scarlet powder. Oona wanted her fish well-cooked, so held it over the fire for as long as her hollow stomach could endure. She was gut-sore and drained enough herself, so didn't bother with speaking. She had enough to be thinking about. Innislone was large in her mind, and the discovery of her great-grandfather and the Big House and Bridget and Granny Kavanagh and the Loam Stone . . . but Oona's thoughts clung most to Morris. What dark was he in? Where out in the Black was he resting?

'Moping about that brother?' asked Merrigutt. Oona looked at her.

'How'd you know?' said Oona, then wanted to disagree: 'Not.'

'Fibbing,' said Merrigutt. The old woman turned the stick in her hands, trout getting an even blistering from the flames. 'I'd say you're definitely brooding about that brother.'

'He has a name,' said Oona. 'If you know a person's name then you should say it. It's an insult otherwise.'

'Right,' said Merrigutt. 'That a Kavanagh family rule, is it?'

'It's a decent person's rule,' said Oona.

Merrigutt said nothing. Did Oona hear the old woman chuckle to herself? Perhaps just the splutter and cackle of the fire. Anyway, Oona wasn't staying silent any more.

'You've something against the Kavanaghs.'

'Only some of them,' said Merrigutt.

'But you'd no problem talking to my great-grandfather, did you?'

'He's different.'

'How different? And how anyway do you even know him?'

For long moments, nothing. Then Merrigutt brought her mouth to meet fish and she took small bites, her words slipping out between: 'I knew him because I've seen a lot of this Isle. I might've started out in the back-end of nowhere much, beside the sea, but I've seen this Isle from shore to shore. From the Burren to bog, from the Marrim Meadows to the Scree, Beggar's Bluff to Helen's Falls – I've known many places. I've not lingered about in this life.'

'Then tell me things,' said Oona. 'Tell me about this King of the North.'

Oona could feel Merrigutt's reluctance, saw it shape her: the old woman's shoulders sank, her whole body sagging and leaning in towards the fire. Then Merrigutt's teeth tore tail from trout and she grunted, and she began to tell –

'This King – King of the North, King of the Echoes! He lives at the edge of the Black, beyond everything, beyond even the Burren. At the "edge of everything", people are fond of saying. Close enough to where I was reared.'

'When did he come?' asked Oona. 'How? I'd never heard of him till this past day or so.'

'Like this: quiet and sudden, like all bad things. Imagine now, my girl, your whole world shaking beneath you. Imagine time telling you it was dawn but the sky telling you different – so dark it might've been a winter's night. Imagine leaving your bed in bare feet and running outside and watching the sea itself being parted. And then this – something dark rising in the distance. A single peak, sharp as a Briar-Witch's claw.' Merrigutt paused, wetting her lips. 'The King's Mountain.'

Oona clung tight to what she had so little of – patience. But it didn't stay in her grip for long and she opened her mouth for a question, but Merrigutt said first –

'How do I know this? Because I saw it. I was there. I saw the waves rush in when that peak appeared and I saw the town destroyed around me. Whole chunks of coast taken away like bites from an apple!' Merrigutt paused, examining the trout. 'Sea could hardly be fished in after that. Everything that came out of it was too foul for eating, like it was all poisoned.'

'How long ago was this?' asked Oona.

'Long time,' said Merrigutt. 'And it was a long time silent, that mountain. Just there, just dark, quiet. And then the Invaders arrived.'

'Has no one tried to get to it?' asked Oona, thinking that if she and Morris had had a thing like that peak near, they'd be the first to take a boat and try.

'No one,' said Merrigutt, 'except the fools, and there's been plenty of them. Many a Northern man has gone out with his boat and his gun and his stubborn ways. Many's a one has rowed out, and not a single soul has come back. It is a place where no bird will settle, and where no man's foot has a chance of settling either. It is protected by a powerful magic. I heard some rumours there was a way to get to it. But only at night, only with the fullest moon in the sky.'

Oona wet her own lips and tried to still her own breathing to ask, 'And the King himself, he's living on that black peak?'

'Not a peak any more, and not black,' said Merrigutt. 'It's changing. Sometimes it's the colour of smoke, other times the colour of scorched stone. Sometimes just the same white as deep winter. And it's no longer a peak. On the coast they call it the City of Echoes.'

'"*City*"?' said Oona. 'But you said it was –'

'I said things change,' said Merrigutt. 'That's what you need to get into your head – nothing stays the same, especially in the North.'

'And that's where they're being taken,' said Oona. 'The boys, Morris – being taken to the King's City?'

Merrigutt nodded.

'But –' began Oona.

'Mind your fish doesn't burn there, my girl,' said Merrigutt.

Oona's concentration had been so much on talk that her trout had burned black.

'Here,' said Merrigutt, and she passed what remained of her own fish to Oona. 'Eat, then try for sleep. And try not to nightmare.'

But Oona had to throw one last question: '*Echoes* – my friend Bridget talked something about that. Why do they call it the "City of Echoes"?'

A last sigh from Merrigutt, the old woman settling, limbs all bunched close. And then she said, 'Because of the sound of the place. They say on the shore that if you listen hard enough at night, you can hear voices coming off the sea. *Echoes*. Words all frightened and pleading, drifting through the dark, all sounding from inside the walls of the King's City.'

29

Morning made Oona need to move. Soon as any light came to the cottage she said, 'We need to be going.' She was always up early in Drumbroken, but she had some sense of things following them here – knew they couldn't linger. And her own insistence felt matched by the Loam Stone: its impatience, its whisper: *It is close now. The Divide, the long dark – it isn't far. You need to move towards it.*

So through morning and so much mist Oona was wandering. On her shoulder, more of Merrigutt's moaning: 'Need to be more careful than you usually are, my girl. Need not to be just storming on, reckless as anything.'

'I'm not!' said Oona, and she was telling honest. She was determined, true enough, but not stupid: her steps went slow, and her eyes were sharp enough to any sight. The jackdaw was the only truly reckless thing – Merrigutt didn't know what to do with herself, one moment in the air and lifting so high she was nearly lost, and then falling back to Oona's shoulder and saying, 'And they say the Divide's much wider now. Grows wider all the time, probably wider today than it was even yesterday!'

'Aye,' said Oona.

'How are we gonna see it?' asked Merrigutt. 'Sure not even my eyes can see anything in all this mist!'

I can show you things.

Oona stopped.

'What?' asked Merrigutt.

'It'll show me,' said Oona. 'It'll let me see.'

'All right,' said Merrigutt. 'But be careful.'

Oona sent one damp hand to her satchel, letting it slither inside to tighten around the Loam Stone. She held it, and waited. And after not long and without need to shut her eyes, Oona was shown: houses she'd never seen the like of before arranged beside a river, wheels clinging to gable walls, churning, scooping clear water from the river and carrying it up and over. Laughter: children chasing one another through tangled gardens, hiding behind neat rows of broad beans and peas, their parents near by, chatting. Oona saw this perfect scene, sunlit, and she relished it for the moments she had. And then the Loam Stone showed its truth, the nightmare: the river began to drop, to drain into a widening gulf opening in its bed as the ground cracked and everything slipped, a swift dark unpicking the earth in a swift zig-zag and houses and children and parents and gardens all tumbling into the sudden Divide, any screams soon echoes –

Oona stopped herself. Her hand left the Stone.

'Well?' said Merrigutt. 'Did you see?'

'I saw,' said Oona. She swallowed, shivering. 'Not far now.' Oona walked – unsteady, awaiting.

And no more than minutes passed before they arrived.

The mist released them and Oona stopped and looked out onto the same dreamed-of dark. Same nightmare, same obscene chasm stretching away – the deep of the Divide. She was glad of the Loam Stone's warning – it had filled her with terror, but had prepared her, too.

'Sorrowful Lady preserve us!' said Merrigutt.

Oona said nothing. She stood, because what else was there to do when the world ends under your feet, gives up to be succeeded by dark? And beyond and beyond . . . in the distance mist shrugged its shoulders, stopping signs of the other side, giving no sight of the North. But it wasn't pale mist – it was black. On the brink Oona could feel – almost hear? – the will of the land, the strain and want of it to separate further. And at the same time such quiet, not unlike the hush brought by the Coach-A-Bower. She shifted her bare feet as if she needed to keep finding fresh purchase or fall. Oona felt drawn to the dark – it seemed to be inviting her, as though it was saying, *Want to see how far I go down? How deep and how dark? Well, come close and –*

'*Stop*!' called Merrigutt.

Oona stepped back, only realising then how close she'd come to toppling.

'How are we gonna –?' she started the question, and then spied inadequate answer: a rope-bridge with a blasted look, the planks all broken, or missing. All of it was battle-worn and bullied by the elements and drawn taut by the Divide.

'Well,' said Oona. 'I suppose there are no Invaders about, so that's something.'

'Doesn't need to be any Invaders,' said Merrigutt. 'You should be more worried when there are none – never a good sign, far as I've learnt. And why would they patrol here anyway? Sure only a fool would try to make a crossing on that excuse for a bridge!'

There's that word again, thought Oona. *Fool.*

'You're going to, aren't you?' said Merrigutt, and she leaned in so that there was hardly a hair's space between the jackdaw's eyes and Oona's own. 'You're actually standing there and weighing up and thinking of crossing that bridge, are you not?'

'I am,' said Oona. She didn't move – she wasn't ready, not yet.

'There's no return after this,' said Merrigutt. 'Once you cross, that's it. It's only on, my girl. Only on and into the Black. You understand?'

Oona said, 'Aye. I understand it.' She looked to the bridge – so many places to fall through. Too many!

'Some kind of North magic on the thing,' said Merrigutt.

'Then you need to help me,' said Oona. She heard the plea in her own voice. 'Will you?' Merrigutt did her shifting on Oona's shoulder.

'Start walking on,' said the jackdaw. 'And I hope the Sorrowful Lady Herself is watching over us!'

30

Oona tried for the fabled deep breath but couldn't get much air into herself. A gasp, bit of a rasp, and then she settled her hands on rope. And she may as well have taken hold of the bridge and shaken it for the way the thing suddenly swayed and shivered and under her fingers she felt more fibres give.

'Better say a prayer, my girl,' whispered Merrigutt.

Oona made another attempt at a deep breath – swift gasp-sigh-gasp. Then she said, 'All right: Sorrowful Lady, if you're any way real and not just some miserable-looking statue we like to have in the corner of the cottage, then some help would be bloody gratefully taken right now.'

'Suppose it's better than nothing,' said Merrigutt. And Oona took first steps.

'Wait!' said Merrigutt. 'Stay a minute.'

'Why?' said Oona. 'We've no time for waiting.'

'Did you know that if you fall into the Divide you fall forever? Ever hear that story? No? Well it's true, so just stay.'

The jackdaw left, circling and keeping her distance from the Divide. Then she came suddenly down and settled with wings still outstretched on a place where no plank was apparent.

136

And, strange thing – Merrigutt was held. Then away she went again, crying down to Oona, 'There's a place to stand there! Concealed by some sly magic, so it is!'

Some more words Oona said to herself: 'Sly magic. So there's somewhere to be standing where there doesn't look to be anywhere to stand. What does that say about where there does seem to be something to stand on?'

So what did it look like, this now altered way ahead? Oona had a dozen (now known as seeable) steps to follow, and then she would reach that first gap, the first place where Merrigutt had found something invisible to settle on.

'Right,' she said, and then walked. Took slow steps and soon reached that first opening in the bridge.

'Quickly!' called Merrigutt from somewhere above.

'I'll give you quick,' Oona muttered to herself. 'Bloody bird.'

She sucked in every breath and chewed on each lip. Then on. But it was the hardest thing to defy instinct, for Oona to move her foot to a place where there was nothing, with all her good senses screaming, *No*! But when she set her first foot on empty space, it held. She brought all her weight together, both feet: still held.

Oona breathed out. Then she did the worst thing – she looked down. Silence like it could suffocate her reached up and enveloped and all Oona's insides churned and she was suddenly snatching for any breath the way a spoon snatches at the bottom of an empty bowl. Oona wasn't afraid of heights – in Drumbroken she had taunts and mocking for anyone who was. But this wasn't height like she knew it: the worst that could happen if you fell from a tree was broken bones and shame, things a bit sore, but worst that could happen at the Divide was –

'Oona!' cried Merrigutt. 'Quick – look there behind you!'

Oona looked, but wished she hadn't – the first dozen planks she'd crossed were softening, were splinter and dust and then falling with a slow whisper and Oona shut her eyes and stayed, expecting to fall too. No prayers came into her head quick enough.

She didn't fall, though.

'Don't just stand there!' she heard Merrigutt shout.

Oona opened her eyes – the way ahead from feet to far distance was only four planks, places between promising nothing. But were there more invisible places to stand or not, concealed by magic maybe, or not? All sense had been dispelled.

Merrigutt returned to Oona's shoulder. The old bird sounded exhausted as she said, 'Thought something like this might happen.'

'Thanks for the warning,' said Oona.

'I did warn you!' said Merrigutt. 'I've been warning all the way from Drumbroken! The very worst of North magic, this is. We'll have to cross together, it's the only way now.'

Oona's next step was simple enough, she supposed: somewhere visible to walk. But she didn't move.

'Look,' said Merrigutt, some softness being attempted in her tone. 'This is as difficult as we make it. It's trying to make a fool out of you, make you too afraid to think right – don't be letting it.'

Oona Kavanagh didn't like the idea of being outsmarted by a bridge any more than Merrigutt did. So she nodded, and then moved on. But sure enough, something strong and spiteful was at work: the bridge wasn't getting its way so it went its own, swinging with sudden force and Oona was thrown from her feet and forwards – Merrigutt's cry: '*Oona*!'

Fell –

eyes shut –

middle of nothing and tumbling and then –

collided –

held what she could hold –

tight –

Her hearing sang shrill notes –

heart screaming, *Please*!

Pleading –

She breathed in –

throat dry –

breathed-out-breathed-in.

Cold tears stung each cheek.

She just breathed.

'You all right there, my girl?' Merrigutt asked. The jackdaw was still on her shoulder.

Oona didn't answer. No energy for speech – opening her eyes was enough effort. And when she did, everything she saw was sharpened by fear: the weave of the rope unravelling, the pattern of dog-roses on the sleeve of the dress she'd made at the hearthside at home. The familiar tangle and split of lines on her palm – the detail was all too much and made her stomach want to empty what little food it had in it. Oona swallowed – another simple thing, usually, but it was such an effort. And she wanted more than much else to be somewhere else.

Then she looked further –

Ahead was nothing but open space. Not a single piece of wood was left to stand on. Oona lay, held her satchel tight and said, 'Now what the (*swear*) am I gonna do now?'

31

'This is what it wanted,' said Merrigutt. 'It lures people out and then takes away all places to stand on, or seems to. Leaves you stranded. Most people probably just fling themselves off, too frightened to go on!'

Oona heard the jackdaw's words, but from a distance: she had too much in her own head to think of anything else. She swallowed, and said only to herself: I'm not flinging myself anywhere. And somehow Oona was on her feet again, all of her shivering but standing anyway.

Merrigutt dropped and settled on Oona's bare foot.

First thing – Oona's hands went to the rope on either side.

Merrigutt dipped her beak towards the dark – towards nothing but that malign silence – and touched something.

'Solid step, it seems like,' said Merrigutt.

Oona bid her hands to slide and her feet to lift and they complied, and she found somewhere to exist for a minute more.

And the next?

Merrigutt tried and found nothing there for standing on, but then there was something fresh to panic about –

'He said to check the bridge, said the girl might try to cross into the North!'

'Nah! Who'd be fool enough to do that?'

Again! thought Oona. Fool – and this time the word from a hooligan Invader!

But before Merrigutt could say a thing Oona breathed, 'I know – hurry and go quicker.'

On she went, faster in her testing and trying for somewhere to stand then shuffling forwards. But the voices of the Invaders, closer –

'Better check anyway! If we can find the thing in this mist and don't just fall in!'

'We need more time,' said Merrigutt. 'Whatever happens – keep going.'

Once more the jackdaw was off into the air. Oona watched Merrigutt turn towards the South and slip into the mist, gone. Oona listened – surely some shouts from the Invaders? Then certainly gunshots. But Oona had her way ahead – she faced the North, its wall of Black mist.

She watched her feet, moving them faster in many steps.

She looked up – she wasn't a bit closer to the other side. No nearer the end of it at all! How many paces had she taken and still she was where she was? Then Oona knew the true and proper trick of the bridge, and it was this: there was no way across. And if she tried to return to the South? She'd find it just as impossible to reach that end. No way over, no way back.

'Run on, Oona!'

Mist hurled Merrigutt back but behind were the Invaders, calling and gun-firing –

Only one thing left: Oona took the Loam Stone from her satchel and begged knowledge, craving nightmares. She shut her eyes, the Stone hot, and saw: others attempting the crossing, becoming stranded like herself then falling, surrendering . . .

Invaders –

'*There! She's on the bridge!*'

'*Don't shoot! We need to get her alive!*'

'*How? There's nothing to bloody walk on!*'

'*It's a Wander of Faith, they call it!*'

'*I can bloody well see why!*'

One last nightmare: man and wife on the bridge, wife running across with eyes shut and not falling until she felt land under her feet, landing on the other side. But the husband was too frightened to move. Even as his wife tried to coax him over, he stayed where he was.

Oona opened her eyes as Merrigutt fell heavy onto her shoulder. Oona said, 'I know what to do now. Hold on.'

The Loam Stone held high, her hands leaving the rope, Oona closed her eyes, breathing in, and ran, not thinking of anything except the wife on her way across, believing and needing and dreaming as the pointless shouting from an Invader went, 'Stop her! She's getting away!'

Then something snagged and Oona stumbled and fell . . . flat on her front onto something solid. She opened her eyes and saw dark: the Black of the North was beneath her. Looked up: Black mist around her. A moment, and then some laughter rose in her throat, low and breathless and relieved.

Merrigutt said, 'I don't know how you did that, but the tale can wait for later. Now let's get the hell away from this place!'

Agreed, thought Oona. And long before Merrigutt had finished with her hurry and demand for haste, Oona was on her way, running. And the Invaders – *the proper fools!* thought Oona – were soon left distant, all their pointless bellowing and threat dying quick on darkened air.

THIRD

'BEWARE THAT BLACK BENEATH YOUR FEET!'

32

It should've been day (and might've been somewhere), but the scene looked closer to dusk. Darkness pressed close, clinging to everywhere: palms and lips, sneaking under eyelids, fingernails and toenails. Oona looked for her feet and thought that if she stopped they'd slip invisible, no difference between their black and the ground they were walking. She had to move with care, the ground broken and uneven, gouged with dry gullies and parched trenches. She licked her lips – foul taste. Picked her nose and what she excavated made her stomach twist.

'When will it bloody end?' asked Oona. 'This black mist – just gonna go on and on?'

'Not mist,' said Merrigutt.

Oona began with a few words, 'What do you –?' but the rest was lost to a sharp and sudden cough, her whole body making a horror of the sound – a hack like a dull blade against wood.

Merrigutt said, 'Don't bother speaking. Not here. Keep the mouth closed. No mist I know chokes. Doesn't leave such darkness on you neither.' The jackdaw shook its wings and added more black to the air. 'No,' said Merrigutt. 'This is something else, my girl.'

Oona walked, lips bitten in, quietened.

Then came a sound like a thousand thunders, everything shaking and Oona staggering, so unprepared for anything but her slow onward walking. She fell, tumbled and tried to hold tight – to what? Coarse grass shorn low was all her fingers could find.

'What's happening?' Oona cried.

A low croak from the jackdaw: 'The remaking of the North.'

The ground beneath Oona began to rear and she recognised the same magic Merrigutt had used to summon their solitary soldier on the approach to Innislone. The jackdaw was in the air then, crying, 'It's not me doing this bit of magic! Run! Follow my flight!'

Oona's eyes went up: jackdaw in the sky to lead her, the ground was soon a slope to scramble up, and then suddenly there was nothing beneath Oona but a long and surely-to-the-Sorrowful-Lady fatal fall –

'Just jump!' Merrigutt called.

Oona leapt, and landed on colder and wetter and more barren ground, somersaulting, a smell like ashes clawing at her nostrils, filling her mouth. When she finally came to her stop she was shadowed. Oona looked up.

Like the bog-soldier, a figure towered high. But unlike the bog-soldier too: this one was taller than what Merrigutt had made, a height Oona couldn't compare with anything. Nothing in her life spent between the slopes of Drumbroken valley could have prepared her: to Oona, there, then, the figure was the tallest thing in existence.

Merrigutt returned close but stayed in flight to shout, 'Don't

150

just lie there – keep going!' Oona crept on palms and knees until she felt far enough away to return to her feet and run.

She couldn't stop a glance back – a raw abyss was left in the ground where the soldier had peeled itself free . . .

'I said hurry and stop gawping!' cried Merrigutt, and the jackdaw came closer to pluck at Oona's hand. But Oona had stopped. Ahead, as high as Black sky and in strides half a horizon wide, more figures summoned from the earth were wandering, staggering like things freed from unwanted graves. Arms hanging low, heads dipped, two rough wounds for their eyes shown by what little light was in the sky.

'Look out!' cried Merrigutt.

The figure Oona had leapt from came stalking up behind and Oona threw herself sideways to avoid it. It passed, with a thud for each step that made her heart tremble and eyes quiver.

'Muddgloggs,' said Merrigutt, alighting on Oona's shoulder.

'What?' said Oona. 'Aren't they the same things as you made at Innislone?'

'Not a bit of it!' said Merrigutt. 'This is a more powerful magic than I could ever summon. This is the King's dark work. He's using these Muddgloggs to remake the North. Changing things so much on the Isle that no one will know where they are any more.'

And this, Oona knew, these Muddgloggs – they were the cause of all the stirred-up Black.

She watched as one distant Muddglogg suddenly relented, and fell with the same thunder as Oona had heard minutes before, rejoining the earth. The impact made Oona cower. So what was the fallen Muddglogg then? New hill, new mount?

Part, anyway, of a newer landscape.

Merrigutt said, 'I've been in the North so much of my life, but I don't know how we're going to find our way anywhere now.'

'Let's keep going,' said Oona. 'First thing we need to find is that village Billy O'Riley talked about. Might be our only chance, or best chance anyway.'

'That's if it hasn't been carried off somewhere else,' said Merrigutt.

Oona was saved from reply – some other sound was surrounding them, approaching . . .

'What now?' said Merrigutt.

Oona listened. She said, 'It's singing.' Then listened more: a tune and words she knew too well. She told the jackdaw, 'It's *The Song of the Divided Isle*. It's the Cause.'

33

Their song went like this in the near silence –

'They came in with the tide and up with the dawn –
Conquered the North (that didn't take long)!
Put bullets in bones and blood in the ground –
Killed where they liked (and claimed all they found)!'

'This way,' said Oona. Maybe the Cause would know things, like what had happened to the prisoners taken from the South? The children being taken to the King? Maybe about Morris? Maybe. She listened. Then said, 'This way here,' and followed –

'So they began up North and burned it raw –
Eyes wept red (the Black all they saw)!
Wounded the earth and split the Isle –
A darkness Dividing (mile upon mile)!'

Her feet met a rise like something only newly dug, disturbed – where one of the Muddgloggs had collapsed, Oona was sure.

'Be careful now,' said Merrigutt.

Fighting against sinking feet, Oona reached the top of the rise, breathless, and looked down.

'Is this the White Road?' asked Oona.

'Used to be,' said Merrigutt.

White was Black – darker smear through dark enough.

'Won't be any good to follow anyway,' said Merrigutt. 'Not now with the King remaking so much of the place.'

But it looked like the Cause were for following it: Oona saw shadow and smoke stirred by their slow procession. Their faces were unclear, but Oona couldn't stop herself seeking Morris . . . no, still too far for spying. She considered the slope that led down to the White-now-Black Road, and wondered.

'No,' said Merrigutt, knowing well the girl whose shoulder she'd been perched on for many dark miles. 'You shouldn't go to them.'

'They might help,' said Oona. 'Might know.'

'No! Nothing we can't find out on our own, my girl.'

Oona looked again – the Cause were closer . . .

'Stay put for now,' said Merrigutt. 'I've got a feeling about this lot, and it's not a good one.' Then the Cause were so close they'd soon see Oona.

'All right then,' she said, and dropped flat to watch, to listen out –

'They had their plan to remake this Isle –
Shift it about (and laugh all the while)!'

And then at last she saw: the Cause were doing their marching on bare feet, hands holding tight to branches with crimson-coloured rags knotted near the top – the gaudy flags limp, hopeful of some triumphal breeze. Oona noticed that the hands that held the branches were cracked, scabbed, bleeding. But no wound, no worry at all, was going to silence their singing –

'Move about our mountains and rivers with a shout –
Bid the land to get up (and wander about)!'

Oona saw almost only or mostly just boys. And none looked like her Morris.

'Look at the state of them!' said Merrigutt. 'Awful, shameful crowd.'

True: like an amble of cattle with no one as guide, they were moving without much desire or hurry. Their singing sounding more like baying. And their feet were dragging, all cracked and scabbed and bloodied, same way as their hands. How long had they been walking? How many miles? Just following the Black Road, dumbly, numb, in endless circles? Then, a miracle! The Cause stopped as a small gust took one flag and opened it for moments and Oona had to hurry to read –

THE PERPETUAL PARADE TO THE BURREN!
IN HONOUR OF THE NOBLE DEAD!
THE MARCH THAT IS UNENDING FOR THOSE WHO
DIED SO THAT

There might've been more, but this was all Oona took before

the breeze left and the flag folded. The boys' heads slipped. In unison – they groaned. In unison – resumed *The Song of the Divided Isle* . . .

'And so we go North and we'll never quit –
Not till we win (and no sooner, not a bit)!
We'll fight to the death and sing loud our Song –
Honour our comrades (and carry them on)!'

Then passing by so close below, Oona knew more – on the back of each boy was another. Another body. And the one being carried did no singing, wasn't moving. Wasn't any longer living.

'By the Sorrowful Lady,' breathed Merrigutt.

'Dead,' said Oona. 'They're carrying the dead ones on their backs.'

'Why oh why,' said Merrigutt, 'do men devote such time to such ridiculous tasks? I swear to Herself, now I've seen it all!'

'We follow them?' said Oona.

'To the Burren?' said Merrigutt. 'To the farthest of the far North? No. We do no such thing. I'm making it my business to keep that Stone you're carrying safe, and it won't stay that way for long if we join this lot. And if you don't believe – keep watching.'

As the end of the Perpetual Parade passed, Oona's eyes landed on its last member – a boy who looked more burdened than any of the others. He was hunched lower, though his mouth was wider and his voice louder than any, fervent as anything in his singing. But he was sinking. He trailed a long cloak of coiling dust. And then he could bear weight no longer – the body he was carrying dropped to the Road with a desperate thud.

'What's happening to him?' asked Oona.

'Watch for the answer,' said Merrigutt. And Oona did –

The boy shouted the *Song* to his last shout but was soon silenced: slowly dispersing, vanishing, he joined the air as swarming dark, more like cinder and smoke than anything else. The last thing of him to go were words, sung loud –

'I'll honour my father and follow his might –
His belief and his memory (and history's fight)!'

Then nothing – the boy was gone. Was only –

'*Echoes,*' whispered Merrigutt.

34

Before Oona could ask a thing Merrigutt said louder, 'Look there now!' directing Oona's attention somewhere new. So little in the landscape moved at their level that anything that did demanded attention. A single figure was moving fast. Oona's only thought was – not one of the Cause. Too quick on the move, this one. In too much of a hurry somewhere.

'Invader?' asked Oona.

'Not at all,' said Merrigutt. 'That's a woman.'

'How do you know?' asked Oona.

'Because she's got the look of someone with a bit of purpose,' said Merrigutt.

The figure hastening had so much dark settled on (let's say *her*) shoulders, but (*she?*) was batting away at it – futile little jerks of the hand trying to keep (*herself*) cleaner. And she wasn't following the Black Road. She was devoted to a path only she knew. *Perhaps a former road*, Oona thought, *from before the remaking?*

Oona watched but the woman soon vanished into dark.

A fresh thunder pressed Oona closer to the ground and she was ready to run this time, ready for the ground to arise, but then something stunning in its ordinariness, so unexpected: it began to rain. Heavy and punishing and loud.

'Forgot!' said Merrigutt. 'As well as everything else, they get the worst weather up here!'

'Is that the King's work too?' said Oona. She had to shout, the downpour was so fierce.

'No,' said Merrigutt, 'it's always been this bad!'

'Maybe that woman is from the village Billy mentioned?' said Oona.

'Then you've got a choice, my girl,' said Merrigutt.

Oona looked for the Perpetual Parade – they were almost gone, made faint by the rain, continuing on their way North, to the place called the Burren. Would they lead to Morris and the other captured children? Would they even navigate the North at all with so much being remade? Would they survive, escape what had happened to the boy at the back – *the Echoes*?

The sound of their *Song* was soon drowned.

So Oona made her decision: 'We follow the woman.'

35

Oona was used to tracking in the forests of Drumbroken but there was no trail left by the woman, no footprint nor mark on the Black, no branch to be broken or trap to be tripped. Instead, Oona had to put her good listening to test. She was sure she heard footfalls falling on harder ground than where she stood. Perhaps on stone? So she followed.

Then Merrigutt, always first to see, saw and said, 'There's something – not far!' Oona looked, and she just about saw something too –

The land was flat and featureless, and then things formed: many things looming behind rain, tall and trembling and groaning like the trees of Drumbroken did in autumn storms. Oona thought, Forest! Must be! She kept fast-walking, her mother's cloak sodden and the satchel tight in her hands. But before any forest there was suddenly a road of stone underneath Oona's feet, and an archway of stone too – an entrance. The jackdaw left Oona's shoulder and with two hard wing-beats landed at the highest point on the arch. Oona looked up and squinted to read a wooden sign –

THE TOWNSHIP OF LOFTBOROUGH
POPULATION – ~~243~~ ~~156~~. 43

'Something in these numbers doesn't warm me,' said Merrigutt, leaning in to examine the sign. Oona didn't reply. She was still reading more. Another torn board, nailed slantways below the first, was telling them –

YOU BETTER BEWARE THAT BLACK BENEATH YOUR FEET!

One wing-beat and Merrigutt was back to Oona's shoulder, but before the jackdaw spoke Oona said, 'We've no choice! It's pissing down and anyway, if this is where Bridget's uncle was talking about then I believe him: it maybe won't be as bad here as everywhere else.'

'Lot of reasons there,' said Merrigutt. 'But still and all . . .'

They waited beneath the arch like they were awaiting welcome.

'To hell with it,' said Oona. 'Let's go.'

36

s
m
o
k
e slate
slate slate slate
slate slate slate slate slate
slate slate *Round Window* slate slate
slate slate slate slate slate slate slate slate
wood *Window* wood *Window* wood
wood wood *Window* wood wood
wood *Window* DOOR *Window* wood

L   L
O   E
N   G
G   S

Oona had to name so she could know. Those tall things looming – their groaning and trembling and teetering – *houses*?

'I'd say we take our chance out in the weather,' said Merrigutt.

'Quiet,' said Oona, but unthinking, only looking.

162

A rough street of hacked-at-and-packed-in-snug stone was flanked by houses on their high legs, two gangling rows doing a slow stagger off into Black and rain. A strong breeze came and every house swayed, easing close to the next as though keen to pass whispered comment on the new arrivals. Oona staggered backwards herself with the thought: How could anyone live in such a place? How could you ever feel safe, being shifted about so much?

Then suddenly at the nearest house instead of **DOOR** there was **PERSON**. A small woman, hair like a storm on her head.

'That's the one,' said Merrigutt. 'That's the woman we saw running.' Oona blinked back rain – the woman had a rifle.

But the woman hardly looked a bit interested. She'd noticed them, but her looks were for elsewhere – roaming the street of broken stone like she'd dropped something and needed to have it back in her hands. Eventually though, the woman shook her head, her rifle drooped, and she turned herself and went inside. She shut her front door and her whole house trembled from slate to wooden shins.

'What was that about?' whispered Oona, beginning to walk into Loftborough. Merrigutt told her, 'I don't know. I don't know at all what to make of this place.'

Oona said nothing. Especially didn't say that at her side, in her satchel, she could feel the Loam Stone burning so fierce she thought it could've burnt a livid hole right through her. The town of Loftborough was rife with nightmares.

Not too far and not too many steps and another door in another house opened up. But this time they were not just noticed but hailed –

163

'Here, you two! Bed and board?'

The voice brought fuss behind all windows – a fidget of curtains. Oona knew they were being watched, even if they couldn't see the watchers.

'Come quick!' called the voice. A woman's voice. 'I'll change me mind and shut this door, I'm not joking you!'

Oona and Merrigutt looked at one another.

'I'll give you no more time!' shouted the voice. 'I'll be shutting my door for the night and whatever happens to you can happen and I've no reason to be feeling any way responsible!'

Oona swallowed. Again she realised there was no choice, so she called back to the woman, 'Wait, missus! We want to come up!'

37

A stack of sticks bound with rope clattered down – a rope-ladder.

'Up!' came the order from above. 'It's almost proper dark and they'll not wait!'

Oona climbed. The rungs were damp and she was soaked, and the ladder was as uncertain as the bridge binding the Divide but as Oona realised how exhausted she was, how little energy was left in her, she thought: If I can do anything in this world – if I'm a Kavanagh at all – then I can climb better than any!

On she went, not quicker but more determined to be determined, wanting to be more like herself.

At the top Merrigutt hopped from Oona's shoulder onto a buckled strip of porch. The jackdaw looked about and took things in, as she liked to do: head jerking left and right and above and below, everywhere. But the most apparent thing, most important – a door had been left open for them, and within was light. Little of it, but enough to entice. And better, Oona thought, than the Black!

She dragged herself up to stand. The house lurched

underneath and she had to hold on. Oona noticed a wooden sign over her head: it was too paralysed with rust to do anything like swing and instead just ran with rain, but spelled out –

The Loyal Martyr Public House
(Maybe a few beds available – ask indoors!)

Some quick footsteps and a woman appeared in the doorway. Big woman. Big arms and hands and . . . big everything. Her eyes were wide and sleeves bundled back to above the elbow and her hair was as wild as a wind-bush and looked like it had never seen a wash. In her left hand she held tight to a rifle.

'In!' she told Oona.

Oona looked at Merrigutt. The jackdaw hopped over the threshold, so Oona followed on.

'Now,' said the woman of the house, using the word like it was a greeting. Then she settled the rifle to the wall, carefully flexed and cracked each finger and started the business of shutting the front door. Such an array of chains and locks and bolts were twisted and latched and snapped shut that Oona lost track, but in the last moment she registered just a small, final key snapped in a final lock, and this key was tucked by the woman into her brassiere. She gave the door a good tug, just to check – not a budge out of it.

'Now,' said the woman, again, and then lapsed into some absent-minded muttering of, 'More light, yes indeed. Makes things more homely. Yes. Now.'

She snatched the rifle from where it rested and marched off into dark. The flames kept a low enough profile in the fireplace.

166

Then Merrigutt was suddenly back on Oona's shoulder to say, 'I've had a quick look about. Doesn't seem to be anyone else here but us. Staircase near the back leading upstairs, but didn't get the chance to look up there so –'

'More light!'

The woman reappeared with a fistful of tapers, wicks all alight. Another meticulous routine then – each taper was given its own saucer, a few drops of wax to keep it upright, and when all were lit and stood firm, the woman found homes for them around the room. They allowed Oona to see more but still not much – so many chairs and tables crouched low like things all waiting, worried. Some things reflected flame – a beaten brass fender by the fireplace, a brass coal-scuttle, and on a shallow mantelpiece above were many small things, many shards of reflected firelight.

The woman – the landlady, Oona decided – declared: 'Better now!'

She slammed the rifle on something and Oona and Merrigutt both turned, shuddering. (Bit scared.) They saw the landlady only from the waist up. The dark had her lower half and Oona realised the woman was standing behind a counter. So no surprise when the question came: 'What can I get you in the way of the drink?' As soon as the question left her, the woman went to work cleaning: rag in hand, attacking the bar in wide arcs, far-reaching, trying to uncover a shine.

Oona cleared her throat and said, 'I think we're all right for the drink.'

'Now come on!' cried the woman, not looking up. And not severe, thought Oona, but probably not to be messed with either.

Oona decided to be honest and say, 'We've not a penny. We just wanted some room for the night. Somewhere out of the rain, nothing fancy or nothing.'

There was a small halt in the woman's wiping, then she went on, half to herself and half to the air: 'No money? But can't not be hospitable. If we lose that then we've nothing much left, do we? And she wouldn't be happy. No, she would've told me to do right by the guests.'

'She's a few stones short of a hearth,' whispered Merrigutt. But Oona said nothing, just waited.

Then the landlady straightened, tossing the rag from hand to loosening hand, eyes still sweeping, seeking something to have a swipe at.

'Well,' she said, with a big sigh, 'I can't turn you out on a night like this one, can I? You'll have a drink with me anyway!' Oona detected the smallest tinge of a plea in the woman's voice, and so she decided: 'Very kind of you, missus. I'll have some rushwater, if you have it.'

'And for the old one?' said the landlady.

Merrigutt spoke for herself, and from a suddenly human mouth –

'A tipple of Loftborough's finest brew!' she said, stepping up to the bar, an old woman once more, and weary. 'Make it the strongest you have! I need it after all we've seen, I tell you.'

Merrigutt gave Oona a wink.

'Good choice!' announced the landlady. 'Back in a tick!' She left.

'Quick now,' said Merrigutt, 'have a wee look at those photographs above the fireplace.' Oona hurried over. On the mantelpiece were a dozen or more small frames, all with the same face contained: young girl, all smiles. The landlady appeared in one or two, always cradling or cuddling the little girl. Always smiling. She looked less wild, much less worried. And they were surrounded by houses like Loftborough's, but not hoisted into the air.

The landlady's heavy tread could be heard returning, so Oona found two short pieces of firewood to add to the flames to make it look like she was there for good reason.

'That's it,' the landlady told her. 'Need to keep warm on nights like this.' She held a barrel high in her arms that she hefted onto the bar. A tap was found to puncture it, a small mallet to drive it in, and two glasses were wiped and readied.

'I'll enjoy this,' said Merrigutt, smacking her lips and rubbing her hands together. It was behaviour so unlike the usual Merrigutt, and Oona saw how much her companion was trying to slip into something else, transform into some other appearance – the jovial spirit. And Oona knew she should, and could, do just the same.

'The night we've had,' she said, struggling up onto the bar stool by Merrigutt. 'Looking forward to a good rest!'

The landlady of The Loyal Martyr said nothing. In the fireplace, the logs began to crackle and hiss. From the barrel she drew a fat, clouded pint for Merrigutt. Oona was given her pint of rushwater, and the landlady joined Merrigutt in the home brew.

'To hospitality when it's most needed!' said Merrigutt.

Then the clash of glasses, the three of them toasting like Oona had seen Drumbroken men do. She drank. She'd intended only a sip but soon had the glass emptied. And not much later there was the slam of glass on wood – Merrigutt and the landlady had drained their pints as well. Some silence, some satisfied sighs, and then the landlady asked, 'Have you come here to help us?'

Oona said nothing, Merrigutt neither.

And then without words the woman extended a hand towards Oona. Its surface was roughened by work, but it was tender as it touched Oona's cheek. It stayed there. And with only an edge of intention, Oona's own hand went to her satchel, to the Loam Stone.

Her gaze met the landlady's.

Some sharp jolt at the core of Oona's heart and she saw something, a flicker – a young girl running through rain, screaming, suddenly vanishing . . .

The landlady's hand left Oona and any nightmares went with it. Oona shivered as though she were still outside.

'I'll show you the place where you'll sleep and be safer,' said the landlady, taking up one of the saucers supporting a candle. She didn't look at them. 'You'll need rest now. You won't want to be awake, not on this night.'

38

'This here,' said the landlady, and Oona saw the woman's hand push against the dark, making it retreat with a creak, 'is the best room in the place.'

Oona was suddenly given the saucer and candle.

'You'll get something to eat in the morning,' said the landlady. 'But now sleep.'

Oona remembered to say 'Cheers' but the landlady had already left them. Oona looked to Merrigutt – still an old woman. They stepped over the threshold together and the door slammed shut on its own.

Oona had to wait to see what surrounded: like below, it was a small room spoiled with too much furniture. Just one wide bed dominated though, and would need to be shared.

'Not too bad,' said Oona, not liking Merrigutt's quiet; not liking the old woman's lack of complaint when usually she took any opportunity.

Eventually Merrigutt offered: 'Suppose not.'

Oona left her and forged a path towards the bed. She had to squeeze around two low chairs, a wardrobe with bulging doors, a trunk spilling clothes and another where delicate porcelain-faced dolls had been laid on a bed of felt and velvet. Oona stopped to rethink her journey and found a dressing-table to settle the saucer on. Candlelight showed a hairbrush, its handle patterned with daisies; then crept the length of a matching comb, then rounded the curved lid of a silver trinket box. Oona lifted her look and saw herself in an oval mirror, and what she saw in it didn't surprise: she looked like what she expected to look like. Like someone smudged, a darkened thing. Just like someone who'd walked through rain and dust and Black. She thought about caring, maybe washing and scrubbing and even picking out of her hair some of what clung. Thought about it, but didn't bother.

Oona faced the bed. And nothing could've made her feel farther from her own home than seeing a bed that wasn't hers: being shown an unfamiliar place and being expected to rest there.

Finally, Merrigutt spoke some more, sounding like she'd convinced herself (or was trying to): 'Sure it'll do for tonight.'

She had to shout it almost: the rain was louder where they were, the wind outside savage. And nothing wanted to stay still – the house tilted and Oona and Merrigutt had to reach out to steady themselves. Oona watched a wash-jug on the dressing-table slide towards the brink and she waited for the shatter and crash but just as it was about to fall, it stopped. Oona groped her way forwards, lifting the saucer with candle to investigate – candlelight showed her a single thread fastened to the handle of the jug, the other end bound to the mirror to keep it moored. The room made suddenly more sense.

'This landlady isn't as slow as she seems,' said Merrigutt.

Oona checked more things: on the bedside table was a vase with a clutch of limp cow-parsley, more thread looped around its base to stop any chance of toppling. And the wardrobe? Rope around its carven ankles. And the bed had all four posts secured with timber and plenty of nails.

'There's more going on here than we know,' said Merrigutt.

'And there are other things,' said Oona. 'In the pictures over the mantelpiece, there was a wee girl in nearly all of them. And I don't think Loftborough was always like it is now. Something happened here. Something's *still* happening.'

Again – a push from outside and everything changed.

Above the bed Oona found a candlestick to snatch for, to slot the taper into.

'You sleep in the bed there,' said Merrigutt. 'I'll find myself somewhere to perch.'

'Can you not just stay as you are?' asked Oona.

'Probably shouldn't even sleep,' said Merrigutt. 'Something tells me one of us should stay awake.'

'Then I'll not sleep either,' said Oona.

Both yawned, then both were beaten – once more the house was prodded by outside storm and the suddenness threw both of them to the bed.

In whispers, they told each other –

'Perhaps just a rest,' said Merrigutt, pulling her legs close. 'Get the energy and the wits back.'

'Just a short sleep,' said Oona, feet burrowing under blanket, looking for warmth. 'Just a wee while.'

Both sighed.

Then Merrigutt's last whisper: 'Try not to nightmare.'

But Oona had already decided: the last thing she did before slipping off into whatever awaited was to open her satchel, find the Loam Stone and force it beneath her pillow. And another thing before sleep – Oona needed to ask something, had been waiting for the moment since they'd seen the boy vanish from the rear of the Perpetual Parade.

'The Echoes,' she said. 'You said what we saw happen to that boy in the Cause was the Echoes.'

'I did,' said Merrigutt. The old woman kept her eyes shut.

'Then what is it?' asked Oona. 'You must know what the Echoes mean – *tell*.'

'I know them when I see them,' said Merrigutt. She sighed. 'I have seen so much of them, my girl. But that doesn't mean I know what they are or why they happen, or how to stop them.'

'How do you even know anything about them at all?' asked Oona.

But a moment and Merrigutt was apparently asleep, had already begun to snore.

39

Again Oona was walking through a dark and cold worse than any winter's night. Through shadow, and the same forest she'd seen before. But the trees were darker: as though they'd been seeded by a dispell and had grown with trunks cracked and yawning, had never had any expectation of leaves other than those they sent out – black, limp and damp as worn rags. It was a place content with its dark.

Then Oona saw other things. Among the branches, more things moving – eyes, crimson, and all watching. And then the voice she expected told her –

'You do not know what you carry. But you are learning – soon, you will command it. Soon, it will spill secrets and spill power that you cannot hope to control. It would be better to surrender it, but you are already in thrall to it. The Stone wants only to show you, and to let you see all nightmares. And you have such nightmares in you, don't you? Such things that you are hiding away in the dark.'

Oona answered, her own voice small but strong: 'I'm hiding nothing.'

'Oh, you are – we all are. But no nightmare can stay hidden.

No truth can be buried so deep that it can be ignored. Bury it, but still you shall smell the rot. Always, there are the Echoes.'

Then the forest floor churned, its black shifting like a Muddglogg waking. Or maybe –

'Briar-Witches?' asked Oona, and she looked to the trees like she might climb to keep safe, but none looked likely to support her.

'The creatures underground,' said the voice of the forest, *'are as vicious as any bad and buried memory, and as powerful as any hurt. They are what nightmares are made of. Nothing is secure now. Nothing in your world is certain. I am remaking what I wish, in whatever image I choose. I am making my own nightmares.'*

Oona's eyes stayed on the ground: pale things were emerging like fingers trying to fling off the dark and she had to look away. 'What are you? Are you the voice of the Stone, or something in my head?'

A pause, and then the voice said, *'I am both. I am as old as the Stone and older still. I am the dark on the horizon. I am what this Isle will become: it will be remade in my image. If you don't believe, then look – beware that black beneath your feet.'*

And Oona looked: the earth was churning not just with fingers but with faces desperate to rise.

'I am your ruler, Oona Kavanagh,' said the voice. *'I am the voice that will bid you, before the end. I am your lord. I am your King.'*

40

Some hour of night even the clocks don't wish to witness and Oona awoke: again upright and with eyes open like they'd been pinned and a throat like it had been scalded. And had she again been screaming? In her hand she held the Loam Stone, and it was slowly losing its heat, its small light.

Oona tried to breathe.

Nightmares lingered – things watching, things turning and dragging aside earth, so many small fingers and faces pushing through. And above all, that voice: a low whispering, an echo of something within her own bones. But if Oona tried to grasp it tight – hold the nightmare and examine and know it – then it was just as impatient to leave, weaving away, a flickering dissolving into dark.

She breathed, and looked about.

Their candle had burnt itself down to a stump. The only thing she could make out was Merrigutt beside, sleeping the way a child might sleep. Or, Oona thought, like how Morris used to.

Moments, and then more – moonlight showed a small circular window with a single length of something flimsy pinned across. Oona listened: she noticed then that it had stopped raining.

Noticed, because something had replaced it – a not-quite noise, not-quite silence. Outside, she was sure that something was happening.

Up from bed on tiptoe and to the window with the Loam Stone in her hand, with three Blackened fingers Oona peeled back the curtain. Loftborough was awake: on every porch and doorstep and at every window were women keeping watch. All had guns aimed at the ground. And their eyes too – all were focused on below.

Oona waited.

Then a sudden shudder everywhere as Oona saw something journeying beneath the street. Its progress was clear in the upset of stone and earth and it moved with such ease: like a child scrambling fast beneath a sheet. Oona saw the women point, try to aim. But then there was not only one thing burrowing but two, and then two more . . . and then too many more to continue counting. They were all converging on one house – the same woman Oona and Merrigutt had seen out wandering in the Black, the one they'd followed, was out on her excuse for a porch with her rifle, but she wasn't alone. A child held tight to her legs, a small girl. Her eyes too were watching the only thing in Loftborough that needed watching – the ground as it was ruined. Oona was sure without being certain that she could hear the small girl's sobbing.

Then things were silent. All stopped. The earth quit moving.

But Oona knew it was temporary, this seeming rest. She'd seen it before. She remembered the forest on the retreat from the River Torrid. Remembered the boys of the Cause, their capture. And Morris – saw him again in her mind.

She knew what next.

There were screams as something dark exploded from the ground, its exit flinging stone and dirt high and Oona watched it race – up the jointed legs of the house, a climbing-crawling-scrambling that was too quick, too swift to be seen let alone stopped. Oona blinked and it was on roof of the house. A breath and then it was on the front porch. A beat and the mother was struggling with it, fighting, her child wailing at her legs, the neighbouring women leaping the gaps between houses, rushing to help.

Slash of a claw and the woman fell back, hand to her cheek –

Breathe – the creature gone, dropping back into broken ground.

Oona still watched, and all of her shivered.

The child had been taken, the mother left alone. And as she realised her loss, the woman on her porch fell. Lucky that others were there to catch.

'This is the night they come.'

Oona turned to face the room: the landlady stood in the doorway. Her arms were outstretched, something laid lightly across. Oona thought for a moment of a small body. No, foolish thought – only a dress for someone small. Delicate, all lace and frill and dangling ribbon. Something for a child, a girl.

'They come,' the landlady, and the big woman's voice broke. 'They come, and they take.' Her eyes went to the dress. She pressed her face to the froth of lace at its collar and shook and shook where she stood, sobbing. 'You're not safe here. No matter how high we've put ourselves up or how much stone packed into the street, they'll find you out. They'll have you, too.'

'I won't let them,' said Oona, and felt foolish. She'd seen Briar-Witches snatch her brother and the other boys, seen children dragged into the White Road as blink-quick as she'd just witnessed. So how could she be different? How could she defy? She looked for answers – to Merrigutt, but the old woman still just slept.

'You can't stop them,' said the landlady, and she sounded relieved, in some way. 'I shouldn't think thoughts like getting my girl back. Shouldn't have been hoping.' She showed her face again but didn't look at Oona. Her eyes wandered the room instead. 'My Daisy couldn't fight them, and she was as strong as they come. Her room, this was. Tried to keep things just as they were. Same as from before she was taken.'

'I'm sorry,' said Oona. She didn't know what else to say so she turned back to the window. The women of Loftborough were gone, the town as almost empty-seeming as when she and Merrigutt had first arrived. Then Oona told her reflection in firm words, 'I won't let them take us. I won't just go like everyone else. And if I can, missus, I'll try to stop them taking any others, too.'

She turned to face the room again.

The landlady had gone, leaving the door wide and Oona wondering. And then promising – as a fresh breeze nudged The Loyal Martyr and everything inside slid, slammed, the door of their room snapping shut – she said to herself: 'I will be different. I won't fall into the dark, not like everyone else.'

41

Oona woke and the first thing she saw was Merrigutt on the windowsill, restored to her jackdaw guise. 'Looks like there was some disturbance last night,' said the bird, head doing a fierce amount of flick-flicking. 'The ground is all like something's been at it.'

'Listen,' said Oona. Sleep-softened, she struggled from the bed which sat at a severe slant, the Loam Stone still in her hand. 'I saw what happened. I was up. Woke and went to the window and was watching. There were I dunno how many –'

Interruption!

The landlady appeared, bedroom door arsed open as she reversed into the room, in her big hands a big enamel tray. Oona, on some instinct, hid the Loam Stone beneath her pillow.

'Something to eat, as promised!' said the landlady in a sprightly tone, not a bit of sorrow on show. She settled the tray on the dressing-table, clapped her hands together and told them, 'Now – it's not much, but it'll fill a hole.' The landlady hadn't looked at either of them. She'd spotted a spot of something on the oval mirror, whipped the rag from her waist and rubbed it away. 'Now,' said the landlady again, and was on her way to leaving but Oona wasn't going to let her.

'Wait!' said Oona, taking a step towards the landlady. 'Last night, what I saw and what went on – that's been happening for how long?'

The landlady still didn't have a look for either of them. Her eyes were on her hands, on the rag going from hand to open hand. 'Long time,' she admitted, eventually.

'When?' asked Oona, and she took another step forward.

'Since the Invaders came,' said the landlady. 'Ever since they went hoaking in the ground and woke those things.'

'Briar-Witches,' said Oona.

The landlady flinched. Her look strayed: from her own hands to the dressing-table laid with so many ornate things for an absent girl. Oona glanced at Merrigutt, the jackdaw still poised unmoving on the sill.

'Are there any children left in Loftborough?' Oona asked the landlady.

'I know of one child for definite,' she said. 'But others? If there are, it's not many.' The woman's gaze went wandering more – to bed, round window, beyond. 'Used to be all so close in this town. All of us as close-knit and together as anything. And now? Now all this.'

'Why not leave?' asked Oona.

The landlady looked at her, and looked as though she hardly knew how to answer. As though Oona had asked the unaskable, the unanswerable – the impossible! From somewhere strong, the landlady found these firm words: 'How can a person leave the place they're meant to be in?'

Some fierce movement came from Merrigutt then, like a

shudder, and Oona thought a transformation was about to happen, the old woman about to reappear. But then nothing. Merrigutt stayed just the same – as silent and still as two seconds before.

The landlady went to the door but Oona asked one more thing –

'The child, the one child you said you know for certain is still about – where are they?'

The landlady stopped by the door, one hand to the handle, and said with something like disgust, 'Lives at the edge of the town. In the direction of the marsh, in the Big House on top of Rotten Hill.'

'How?' said Merrigutt, snapping her beak. 'Can't be anyone there! Sure all the Big Houses are deserted!'

The jackdaw was all of a sudden impatient, but it was an impatience matched –

'I know they are!' the landlady snapped back. 'All except this one. Someone stayed, was left behind to keep it.'

Not to be beaten – never to be cowed or disagreed with – Merrigutt turned to the room full in one resolute hop and asked, 'And did the men and sons of Loftborough not come to help when it was needed? Or just stayed away, left you all to fight this battle on your own?'

'They went to fight,' said the landlady. 'Went on further North, to meet others at the Melancholy Mountains . . .'

'*Melancholy Mountains?*' said Merrigutt.

'Used to be to called Muckrook Mountains,' said the landlady. 'You know it if you're a Northerner at all: the quiet place where them Giants ponder their wild notions. Anyway. Then on to the Burren. All joined the Cause. Thought it best.'

'You thought it best,' said Merrigutt, 'or the men did? Or maybe –?' But Oona told the jackdaw, 'Just give over.'

Merrigutt shuffled on the sill, but said no more.

'I wouldn't expect understanding from the likes of you,' said the landlady, eyes narrowing, still focused on Merrigutt. 'Now I've things to do, so I'll leave you to your breakfast.'

But she didn't leave them, not yet. Oona knew the woman had more, and this was what she said –

'That Big House on its Rotten Hill – the child that's still there is only there because it's something those creatures don't want to take. Not like a child even – more like some other creature. And if I were you, I'd be as afraid of what's hiding in that Big House as I am of those BriarWitches.'

42

When the landlady went and bedroom door slammed itself, Oona looked to Merrigutt, and then to the tray on the dressing-table. No words: talking could be done later. Both moved fast to the tray the landlady had left and Oona found lots to look at and get watery-mouthed over: griddle-cakes, most of them singed and some probably dropped in the hearth when being baked but doused with enough sugar to make them do; drop scones that Oona took a knife to and opened, parting easily to show insides hot as hearth-stones, a soft chamber made for melting, for gooseberry jam and butter to be slopped into; small cakes dense with dried fruit that Oona gave a sniff, discovering a smell like almond. Then some kind of soft fruit in a jar Oona didn't recognise so had to dip a finger in – it was sour, made her tongue wriggle and eyes near water, but she doubted there was much on either side of the Divide more delicious. Tay was discovered in a chipped teapot (Oona unsurprised to see a faded pattern of daisies looping around its middle), and a matching milk jug and pair of cups beside.

'Check what's in there first,' said Merrigutt, tapping her beak on the teapot.

'Why?' asked Oona. 'It's only tay!'

'Could be anything,' said Merrigutt. 'Need to be careful.'

Oona removed the lid and got a face full of steam – inside she saw a parcel of leaves bound tightly, drifting. 'Smells like pennyroyal and thistle,' she said. 'So nothing like poison, that all right?'

'Suppose,' said Merrigutt. 'I'll have to take your word for it.'

Both began their eating in proper earnest.

'So,' said Merrigutt, her beak making small stabs at a scone, 'what's the plan? I'd be a fool, I've realised, if I assumed we'd be doing the sensible thing and taking the first foul breeze out of here?'

'Fool is right,' said Oona.

The jackdaw stopped, and glared.

Oona was busy doing a Bridget – cramming so much griddle-cake into her mouth that as many crumbs left her lips as words.

'Look,' she said, 'everyone says these Briar-Witches were brought down from the North, right? And Brid told me that she'd heard from her granda who'd heard from –'

'– the Sorrowful Lady herself?' finished Merrigutt. 'You're going to believe a game of whispers and gossip and take it as good Gospel?'

'Bridget told me!' said Oona. She swallowed what she had. 'And I believe her. And she said that the Witches had a nest someplace in the Black and that woman said that the children started being taken after the Invaders arrived, that they woke those creatures.'

'And?' said Merrigutt. 'How does that involve us?'

Oona lifted the teapot and filled a cup with the pennyroyal

186

and thistle brew. Merrigutt dipped her beak into it. She didn't keel over so kept on supping.

'I think if we could find a way to stop the Witches here,' said Oona, 'then it could only help all the people back home in the South.'

Merrigutt stopped drinking.

'And this child,' said Merrigutt, 'the one on the – what did she call it? *Rotten Hill?* Lady preserve us – *Melancholy Mountains, Rotten Hill?* The names they give these places!'

'I think we should go and see what's going on in that Big House. See what the child who lives there knows about it all.'

'Maybe not "child", remember? Maybe like herself said – maybe some other creature we'll have to be contending with.'

'Doesn't matter.'

Oona looked towards the window – to the woman at another window, another home, looking out onto Loftborough. The same woman who'd had her child taken the night before – one whose cheek had been opened by a sharp claw – was weeping.

And Oona said, 'Creature or not – if any child's been able to keep safe in this town and not be taken by those Briar-Witches, then I'm bloody well going to find them and get some answers.'

43

First bare foot on blessed stone! And Oona felt more secure – Briar-Witches or not, she'd decided that existing up in a house on legs wasn't for her. Not for Merrigutt either, it sounded like, on Oona's shoulder saying, 'Thank the Lady herself we're down from that place!'

'Well, you slept well enough in it,' said Oona. She couldn't stop herself: 'Even with all the noise going on out here you were like a dog just dozing in the – *ow*!'

Something sharp bit Oona's sole – a shard of broken stone. *Should've been more careful*, she thought.

'Should've been more careful,' said Merrigutt.

Oona pressed a palm to the leg of The Loyal Martyr, finding some meanwhile support, and lifted the stinging foot for looking at. Blood was rising there like an eager eye. *Not the best beginning to the day*, Oona thought, but she took some relief in the sight of crimson – something alive in such surrounding dead. Morning in Loftborough was scarcely brighter than night in Loftborough: the place existed in shades of ditchwater and dull.

'We go this way,' said Oona, nodding her head to the right,

settling her foot on the ground again. She winced a bit, then said, 'At the end of the town is the Big House, isn't that what the landlady said?'

'Suppose,' said Merrigutt. 'Though can I just say once more and strongly suggest that we –'

'*No*,' said Oona.

Merrigutt's reply was the usual shifting about on Oona's shoulder.

Oona began the walk, satchel on her shoulder with some supplies still in it, Loam Stone and knife and pistol hidden from sight.

Even without some storm to harass them, the houses of Loftborough still persisted with their constant creakings and groanings. Oona looked up and saw all the women outside. Some, Oona decided, were being busy for the sake of busy – they had that same way of spying and wiping down and swiping away dirt that the landlady of The Loyal Martyr had. Little or nothing else to do, they wanted distraction. But some were just sitting alone. Oona watched: discontent made the women's fingers drum and feet tap and heads twitch. As Oona passed, some of the women watched her with a look of slow, sad longing.

'Poor divils,' Oona whispered.

'No poorer than anyone else in the North,' said Merrigutt.

'Knew you'd be sympathetic,' said Oona.

A pause, then Merrigutt said, 'Listen, my girl: I'm trying to teach you that feeling sorry for yourself won't solve a thing. Won't help these women, and sympathy won't neither. Some grit, a bit of fight – that's what they need now!'

'Isn't that easy to find some fight when you've lost your child,' said Oona. Merrigutt had no response.

'And they tried,' said Oona. 'Last night, they had their guns and all. Did no good.'

'Why were you up anyway?' asked Merrigutt. 'What awakened you?'

Oona opened her mouth, ready to say . . . but something stuck. She felt some urge to keep things secret. Oona found herself saying instead, 'Just woke. Woke and then went to have a look.'

Merrigutt said nothing, Oona only walked. And the women continued to watch – Oona saw one cradling a portrait of a man.

'What did you mean about the men of Loftborough coming to help?' asked Oona.

'Things are different in the North,' said Merrigutt. 'Not like Drumbroken or anywhere in the South – up North, men don't live with the women. It was the same where I grew up, so not that unusual.'

Oona's instinct was to say, *No. That's not right. Can't be!* Then she remembered where she was, and how far from home.

'So no fathers or grandfathers,' she said, trying as she spoke to imagine it – their cottage in Drumbroken without her da or granda in it, or: 'No brothers?'

'Not one,' said Merrigutt. 'People get married still and have children, but then the men go off and live a few miles from the town – usually out on the land to work at it. They visit and all, sometimes. And if a child is born a boy, they get taken to live with the men. And if it's a girl, they stay with the women. So I'd bet all the children the Witches have taken in Loftborough were girls.' Oona was silent, still trying (failing) to imagine it all – attempting to see a life so different from her own. Then she asked, 'Did you ever see your father?'

Merrigutt said, 'Did. Once or twice. Wasn't bothered.'

And then, when they'd almost left Loftborough behind – the town of only women and their daughters – Merrigutt announced, 'Be ready, my girl. I can see something up ahead, and it doesn't look pretty.'

44

It was almost a minute before Oona had a sense of anything. Then some shape appeared, a dark space like grey sky had had a quick cut taken out of it, a scrap torn away by a rough hand: another new house for Oona to learn the shape of, and not like the cottages of Drumbroken nor the wooden huts of Innislone and not the long-legged houses of Loftborough, but instead this house was more in the family of Slopebridge Manor. Rotten Hill? More Rotten Heap. A nest even – a mound of earth where tree and briar and hedgerow were boss, mingling as they wished, untended, riddling and tangling, all coil and slither. And the Big House was bedded at the heart of it all – dark, leaning broken.

Oona had to stop as she met a drystone wall as high as her neck: only a crumbling thing, but fierce enough, a row of rusted iron arrows running along its rim. A sign near by was neatly written, and expansive in its saying –

KEEP OUT AND KEEP BACK OR ELSE!

'Very friendly,' said Merrigutt. 'And by the Lady – the stink of the place! Must be another dispell, the rankest kind.' She tried to hide her beak in Oona's hair. The jackdaw wasn't wrong. There was a reek so fierce it felt like even the air was urging: KEEP OUT AND KEEP BACK OR ELSE!

'You know what,' said Oona, bringing her cloak up to cover nose and mouth, 'people always go on and on about the Big Houses and all, but the ones I've seen so far are nothing much to be going on about.'

She let her eyes wander the surface of the building, edging up and up until she saw at the height of the house a tower, lopsided, with a single narrow window to look out from.

'Used to be called the snooping-window,' muttered Merrigutt, also seeing. 'So the landlords could keep watch over their estate.'

Snooping surely – Oona saw that someone was standing spying at the window. And Oona Kavanagh spied back. Then the someone spying saw Oona spying and quick as a snuffed-out flame the someone spying went.

'Right,' said Oona. 'Well if they think they're going to hide away up there, they've another thing coming.'

Oona took the iron bars and gave them a rattle, and found them a bit loose.

'You're not going to climb?' said Merrigutt.

'Any better notions?' said Oona, already up onto the wall. 'Unlike your good self, I can't fly. So unless you want to share some of that North magic with me?'

'I'm gonna have a wee look,' said Merrigutt. 'Wait a minute for me to come back and tell you what's what. And when I say wait I mean *wait*!'

A linger of a look, and then the jackdaw left Oona, vanishing off into the tangle of garden.

I'll give her just the minute, Oona told herself. But she wasn't someone who knew what the point of patience was: she'd counted only to twenty when she began her awkward scaling of the fence. Soon Oona was in this state: dress torn, each leg documenting each touch of the iron arrows with a neat scrape, hands reddened with rust. But she was soon near over, almost in.

No bother, Oona told herself. (She wished to ignore stings and bleeding.)

But bother came when she leapt in and landed – among all the detritus and decay she began to sink and kept sinking, soon past her ankles and up to the shins, and Oona held onto the iron fence to stop herself being swallowed. Then she stopped. It felt warm around her feet, and wet. Like standing tall in lukewarm porridge. And she couldn't ignore that smell! Oona moved only the littlest and the vapours – more coil and more slither – wove into her nostrils and down into her belly and settled, trying to make her retch.

Need to keep on moving, she decided.

Every step had to be a stagger and stumble, and when Oona reached for support whatever she touched prickled or oozed or stung or all at once – *hurt*. The more she walked, the more she felt like she was wading. The garden soon closed in around her waist.

'I told you to stay put!' cried Merrigutt.

The jackdaw arrived on a branch beside Oona.

'I just shouldn't bother any more, should I?' said the jackdaw.

'Should save my breath! Just you wait and see, my girl, there's coming a good day when you'll wander off and you'll need my help and you'll regret all this not listening!'

'Give it a rest,' said Oona. 'Sound like my granny.'

'Well luckily for you, it's not far. And there doesn't seem to be anything lurking or ready to take a bite out of you.'

Oona went on in a plunge, tramping down and snapping anything that tried to hold her. She found a stick, one she judged good for the job, and began to beat things back.

'See the statue there?' said Merrigutt, and added before Oona could look or reply, 'Just head for that.'

Oona didn't bother looking. She just kept her head down, battling harder, thinking of herself and Morris battling through Drumbroken forests when they were younger, all the scores of imaginary enemies they'd vanquished as they'd gone, the pair of them side by side, whacking rods at innocent-seeming undergrowth and –

'You can stop now, you maniac!' cried Merrigutt.

Oona stopped herself and looked up – Big House, Big Mess. She couldn't see any windows except the one at the very top in the tower, and no door, no way to get inside. House shut tight as a stone. And in case Oona was a doubter, a sign nailed near by said –

NO ENTRY IN AT ALL!

And then Oona saw the statue Merrigutt had mentioned.

In a stone fountain stood a stone girl. Naked, body outstretched, balancing on one foot, her legs heron-skinny

195

and stone arms up-reaching, hands open like she was waiting to catch. Her expression was blissful. Water seeped from the girl's scalp, coating her shoulders with a grey-greenish sheen and travelling on down her arms and ending in a stone bowl. Oona looked in – moss wavered like mermaid's tails over a bed of copper coins, a cache of cheapest wishes.

Merrigutt landed on the statue's head and started to sip water from the gurgling crown. Some voice spoke: 'Bloody cheek.'

'Did you just say something?' Oona asked Merrigutt.

'No,' said Merrigutt, but with a sudden stillness to match the statue. 'But I heard.'

'You'd better get out of here before I lose it completely! That's a warning there!' It was a shrill voice, sourceless.

Oona and Merrigutt looked at each other. And their looks shifted, in the same moment realising –

'That's it! Get off me, bird!'

Merrigutt was tossed into the air, complaining and *caw-cawing* as the statue of the girl in the fountain found life and leapt and beat her arms at the jackdaw. Then she went still again. Was blissful again, and expectant and peaceful and poised.

'What in Drumbroken's name just happened?' asked Oona.

Merrigutt came back to Oona's shoulder, whispering, 'I've never seen such magic. One thing to make the earth rise and walk, but to bring to life something that never had life in it? And with such spite and malice in its manner!'

'Who says I never lived? How dare you!'

It was the statue of the girl again, speaking. But Oona had been watching – nothing but the girl's stone lips had moved, and even then just with a small squirm as she'd spoken.

Merrigutt began to Oona, 'Look, I think we need to just –'

'– *leave*!' finished the statue. 'Get out and don't come back! You're trespassing here!'

Oona took a breath. *Now how* (she asked herself) *are we going to get around this?* She tried with, 'Please, we don't come to insult or nothing. I can understand, us just appearing like this in your . . .' Oona's hands swept through the air, attempting to encompass the –

'Dump of a garden,' whispered Merrigutt. The statue heard, scowled.

'Your *home*,' said Oona. 'And we'd be grateful enough if you could inform us of how we might get entry into the –'

'I'm not telling you the way in!' And for a moment the statue lost all serene aspect to stamp a small stone foot. 'You can get that notion outta your heads! The Master doesn't like to be disturbed. He likes to stay alone and do his thinking and watching and I will honour his wishes for always!'

Then she was still and restored again, her smile directed to dull sky as though it were flushed with summer.

'Madness,' was all Merrigutt said.

Oona half-turned and lowered her voice, trying to forge some privacy between herself and the jackdaw. 'All right,' she said. 'How do we get round her? No matter what, we need to get inside.'

'It's a fool's task,' Merrigutt told her. 'But I'll try anyway.'

Then in a voice so loud it made Oona cringe, Merrigutt declared: 'Statue! We wish to enter the Big House! And I believe as common citizens of this Isle – previously the Blessed Isle, now Divided these many years since the coming of the Invaders – we have a right to address whoever calls himself the Master of this area and the township known as Loftborough! On this firm basis, with this custom in mind, I request and implore you to obey!'

Replied the statue without hesitation: 'And I *request* and *implore* you to get lost!'

Replied Merrigutt: 'You cheeky little –!'

Oona tried not to listen. *Maybe*, she thought. *Perhaps* . . . her fingers went to her satchel, and then inside to find the Loam Stone. Perhaps and maybe, she might snatch some small knowledge.

Meanwhile, Merrigutt and the statue kept up their fierce bickering –

'If the man who lives in this Big House calls himself any kind of Master, as you say, then he'd be more than willing to receive guests, not just leave them to wander about in his excuse for a garden!'

'Go and get stuffed!'

'Some immature magic has brought you into being, I'm sure, with a tongue like that. Such words!'

'Here's two more words for you –'

The statue swore and Merrigutt loosed a furious call, somewhere between bird and old woman.

Oona kept silent, and waited. Her gaze was drawn again to that snooping-window in the tower. In the darkness behind glass, someone was crouched, but they couldn't stay hidden. Oona closed her eyes. The Stone warmed her palm, and then a nightmare was emblazoned on her mind –

Two children, a boy and girl crouching frightened, a

198

cold father standing close then closing something on them, shutting them in somewhere. Trapping them? Hiding them. The children were watching through small spaces – they saw other men arriving to take their father, not with fire or threat like Slopebridge, but here with firm requests, signed papers. And the man, the father, went without protest. The children were left on their own. The screams came later – other men came, in uniform, and the ground beneath the Big House was dug and dug and broken open and things were awoken in the dark that should have stayed sleeping and then sent off into Loftborough and –

'– and you're not getting in and that's the end of it!' said the statue.

'He's afraid,' said Oona. She opened her eyes. This time it took long moments – deep breaths – before the nightmare left her at all. But images were still keen to crowd, to show more, and the sound of screaming went on and on and on, tireless echo.

'What did you say?' asked the statue.

Oona thought some of the girl's snappishness had softened.

'He's afraid of what might come,' said Oona. 'Your Master, he's afraid of the Briar- Witches. Nightmares every night about them coming. He was left alone in the house. He's hiding, and he's afraid.'

Oona looked again to the tower, and what she saw there was a shadow small and fearful. The statue of the girl said nothing.

'We need to see him,' said Oona. 'We're here to help the people in Loftborough. All of them, your Master too.'

Merrigutt came back to Oona's shoulder to rest.

'Promise it?' said the statue of the girl. So different suddenly:

demure, almost obedient, like a child full of spite then scolded and trying to make amends. 'Do you promise you'll help him and not hurt him? Not like those things underground?'

'Promise,' said Oona.

'And her,' said the statue, prodding one stone finger in Merrigutt's direction. 'That old one on your shoulder isn't the politest. What's she going to do?'

'She's here to help, too,' said Oona, before Merrigutt said a thing. 'Don't worry about that.'

A silence.

Then the statue cleared her stone throat and said in words formal, rehearsed: 'Very well. In the name of the Master of this Big House, I shall admit you!' She left her fountain completely in a leap, and with two stone hands took hold of the stone bowl where she'd stood and twisted it like a stubborn wheel. 'My advice,' she said, no longer formal, sounding gleeful, 'is to keep your head down and your arms and legs tucked tight. Also eyes shut and nose pinched.'

Any asking there might've been from Oona of *Why?* or *What do you mean?* wasn't allowed. In the next moment the ground opened wide and Oona fell, Merrigutt clinging hard to her shoulder as the sight of wild garden and Big House and drab sky were left above, the stone girl's laughter the only thing to accompany as they plummeted into the earth.

45

Through plenty of dark and then dropped into more – Oona landed on her backside and stayed there. But Merrigutt stayed in the air, raging, sending echoes so loud and many that Oona thought all the jackdaws that had entered the Kavanagh cottage may as well have been back with her –

'Treacherous blood statue!' (Like the stone figure in the fountain could hear.) 'You've got some gall but I've more! Let me tell you, when I get a hold of you I'll make rubble out of you!'

Oona stood. She let her hands explore, checking she was all there and, most important, looking for the Loam Stone – still in her satchel, alongside their little leftover food, and the pistol.

Her raging in the air nearer done with, Merrigutt arrived on Oona's shoulder to complain:

'Fool of a statue! But me the bigger fool. Evelyn Merrigutt outwitted by a lump of stone – getting too soft for my own good. Well no more, I tell you. By the Sorrowful Lady, I say no more!'

'Would you be quiet!' said Oona. 'Hell's bells – sounded like my granny before and now you sound like my brother,

201

ranting and raving because someone got the better of you.'

Merrigutt surely had some retort to offer but hadn't time for it: instantly there was another loud voice speaking –

'Why have you been admitted here? No one is allowed entry to this house without some show of knowledge. Tell me – why have you come?'

It was a voice not unlike the statue's – high, demanding, almost petulant. And proud. Oona couldn't withhold an image of Morris, his way of standing and speaking when he needed to be listened to, agreed with.

'Do not speak!' the voice said. 'I shall pose the questions and you shall merely answer! I am the Master of this house and you shall do as I bid!'

Definitely a boy speaking, Oona decided.

'Do not tell me why you have arrived!' the boy said, though still neither Oona nor Merrigutt had attempted a word. 'I am going to guess . . .'

Oona waited.

Then a loud squeal from the boy of, 'I have it! Oh, I have it well! You are here because . . . *you want my help*!'

Merrigutt whispered, 'Quick on the uptake, isn't he?'

'*Silence!*'

So shrill a cry against the ears it made Oona cringe. She tried to see where the boy was standing, or maybe just sense him, but couldn't: felt as though she wasn't being allowed.

And again he announced, '*Silence!* I have not yet finished the full extent of my guessing! True knowledge takes time, don't you know?'

A pause from him. Some shallow breathing.

'I also deduce,' the voice of the boy went on, 'that you are here because you are on a journey. You have travelled far. And – yes, I know this is quite correct – you intend to keep travelling, to leave here and move on somewhere else. To travel, indeed, to the very edge of everything. Am I right?'

Oona thought it best to play, to agree: 'Yes, that's completely right. Well done, you. You have us all worked out. Now, we're wondering if –'

'Don't patronise me!' said the boy.

His voice was close, surely just beside, so Oona turned like he might suddenly appear. But then not. His voice shifted between near and further: a shout against her ear, and then like a distant call from across a valley –

'I do not need your flattery!'

Oona realised she didn't have a notion where the boy was, or where she was herself. Good thing she had Merrigutt and her knowing.

'Why are you making such a show of things, boy?' asked the jackdaw. 'And this trick of darkness and echoes so we can't see or find you – this is Briar-Witch magic. Why not show yourself without such veils and games?'

'I do not take orders!' said the boy, but not commanding – more snappy, stroppy. He cried, 'I am the Master of this house, how dare you venture in and – !'

Oona spoke up, saying, 'Look: we only want help! I'm from the county of Drumbroken, South and beyond the Divide, and we don't play tricks or fool each other where I come from. We say things out straight. And we were told that you're a child in Loftborough that the Briar-Witches can't touch, and we're only here because we want to know why!'

Some long moments in the dark. There was the sound of shallower breathing, and then the boy said from his undecided somewhere: 'You think you can defeat these creatures? You think you have that power?'

'I do,' said Oona. She reached into her satchel, felt for the Loam Stone and held it tight. And could she see him then? A figure standing near? Or an impression? Or perhaps only the vagueness of nightmare.

Merrigutt whispered, 'Get as close as you can, my girl. I'll do the rest.'

Oona took a small step, then another. And she did see someone – slight and with features too faint. She moved towards the boy, asking as she walked, 'How have you been able to keep the Witches out? Why haven't they taken you?'

Oona heard the boy's breathing – a rattle, the like you'd hear from someone older. Then some more speech from the boy: 'No one can defeat the Briar-Witches. Not now they are in the service of the King. And himself? Not any creature to be toyed with. The Echoes – they are everywhere now.'

Oona stopped. She tried the Loam Stone again, her affinity with it increasing all the time, hoping to squeeze something more, some small knowledge. But it wouldn't warm, gave her nothing. She found herself asking, 'You know what causes the Echoes?'

Sound of a giggle (but more a gurgle).

The boy said, '*Causes* it? No one even knows what brings it upon a person! It merely exists, without reason or neat rhyme. It merely takes, transforms and destroys. And that's what makes it so dangerous. Only the King of the North knows what the Echoes are truly composed of, and he is the –'

'*Enough!*' cried Merrigutt.

In one sudden move – the jackdaw left Oona's shoulder to transform and, as an old woman once more, Merrigutt tossed scarlet into the air. It diffused into the dark like freed and fiery swamp-flies, swirling as the Master of the Big House screamed, 'No! Stop it!' Oona's hearing sizzled and the air shuddered, the scattering of scarlet crowding into bright shivers, silent lightning strokes. Moments, and then the entire dark deserted them in a rush, flung back and fleeing into corners where it skulked, only small scraps.

It was fortunate that Oona found a wall for support – her senses felt singed, dazed.

'Apologies,' said Merrigutt, and she stood with one hand to the wall too, looking older than ever. But she was unwilling to show herself in such frail form – only a moment and Merrigutt was battling to become her jackdaw self. She managed it, and settled again on Oona's shoulder.

'Powerful magic,' said Merrigutt. She sighed. 'Took it out of me a bit there. Contrary child.'

'Why? Why did you have to do that?' The voice of the boy.

Oona looked down and at last settled her sight on the Master of this Big House. He'd been reduced to kneeling, had both hands over his face. He was whimpering, 'Why did you have to do that? Why be so cruel?'

'Why were you using Briar-Witch magic?' asked Merrigutt.

'Wasn't using it,' said the boy.

'He's telling the truth,' said Oona, knowledge spreading not from any nightmare, but from experience. 'It was a dispell – the Witches made the garden into that state and got rid of all ways into the house too, all doors and windows, all light kept out. They couldn't take him so they wanted to make it a hell to live here.'

'Why so worried about being seen, though?' asked Merrigutt.

A moment more, and they had their answers – as his hands slid from his face, Oona saw why the boy had been much happier in his dark, more content in concealment, why he would have done everything to remain hidden from the world.

46

Only half as high as me, if even that, thought Oona. *And age? Could be any. Fifteen, sixteen, or five or six or seven . . . or seven hundred!* All pointless guessing. The boy was split, body telling two stories, neither pleasant: his right side was a ruin of wrinkles and burst blood-vessel and blood-shot eye, and his left was more ruin – taken over by cracked stone, lichen-scabbed, chipped at the cheek.

'Like that statue outside,' said Merrigutt. 'Powerful magic. Nasty. A dispelling of flesh itself. Wouldn't wish it on a worst enemy.'

At this, the Master of the Big House cried, 'I didn't want to be seen so how dare you remove the dark! I can see the shame in your eyes, the two of you – the judgement as you look upon me! How dare you!'

He'd been so devastated, on his knees weeping, but suddenly the boy was up and standing proud, trying to arrange himself. His white-gloved hands rushed all over, along clothes faded and ripped and worn out, all of them old-fashioned: a jacket of grubby velvet, yellowed shirt with a collar that climbed high on his throat and was buttoned to just beneath his chin, and velvet trousers that stopped shy of the knee, socks tight over the shins. His tiny feet were bundled into tiny, infant-sized shoes.

Oona didn't know what to think. Like the houses of Loftborough, she'd never seen or imagined the like of him in her life.

'I am an oddness to you,' said the boy, lifting his head and trying – impossible task, him being so small – to look down on Oona. 'No need to tell me. But all things are odd to eyes so used to seeing only the normal and dull things.' Any words he spoke had to squirm free from the still-human side of his face. 'I may not have magic,' he continued, raising one gloved finger, 'but I assure you, I have such power at my command that I could make of you little more than dust if I wanted!'

'You've nothing,' said Merrigutt.

'I have the dark of this house!' he told them.

'Darkness isn't much of a power,' said Merrigutt. 'Happens every night in this world without need of magic.'

The boy's eyes widened, looking ready for renewed weeping, all other features on his divided face shifting aside to accommodate grief. Through sobs he said, 'You come here and bully myself and my sister. You come here unannounced and try to coerce me into helping you.'

Then Oona was revisited, for a blink, by the nightmare the Loam Stone had given her: two children, brother and sister, frightened. 'Twins,' she said. 'It's your twin sister, the statue in the garden.'

But the boy wasn't listening –

'I won't be forced to leave this house!' he shouted, and Oona saw that like his stone sister his mood could shift in

208

seconds. 'They took my father, drove him out, but I will stay and protect this Manor against all-comers! Whatever Witch or Wolf or Giant or any creature that attempts to take it, I shall see them off! It is what our father would have wished!'

'Fool,' said Merrigutt. 'I'd have left this house long ago and to hell with what your father would've wanted.'

'That's because you have no home you care for,' said the boy.

Oona waited for Merrigutt's response, but the jackdaw said nothing.

'This is my home,' said the boy, 'and no one is going to take it! Not those men in uniform, nor those things underground, nor either the –'

Oona said, 'The Briar-Witches – they have a nest beneath this house?'

'They do,' said the boy. Some pause, then he went on with, 'Such foul things. That's my opinion. Did you not heed the sign – *Beware that black beneath your feet!*'

'You wrote that?' said Oona.

'Of course,' said the boy. 'Not in person, but I have duties as the Master of the Big House.'

'You mean you were sending that statue to do your dirty work?' said Merrigutt. 'I'm starting to have some sympathy with her.'

The boy folded his arms and scowled as well as his statue sister could.

'Oona,' Merrigutt whispered. 'We need to keep moving. This is no task for us. And anyway, I thought this little quest was all in aid of finding your brother?'

'It is,' said Oona, and she didn't bother to whisper her

words. 'And he was taken by those Witches, and so were all these other children, all from this town.'

'So now we're setting out to save the world from any evil we come across?' said Merrigutt.

'If you're interested,' said the boy, 'the answer is yes: I believe there *is* a way to defeat these creatures, to banish them back to the ground for good. I have been watching them most closely.'

'How?' asked Oona. Then felt she should add (for Merrigutt's benefit), 'How can we trust you? And don't even think of lying to us or you'll not live long enough to regret it.'

'I am affronted!' said he. 'I have never lied in my life!'

'People who say things like that are the ones who lie the most,' said Merrigutt.

'I shall tell you such things,' said the boy of the Big House. 'Such secrets, such revelations! Such discoveries that only I have –'

Oona sighed and shut her eyes. In her mind, as vivid as those nightmares she was becoming accustomed to, she saw Morris – watched him dragged down, disappearing into the dark with his small stubborn hands still around their grandfather's gun.

'– and such observations I have made! Watching as –'

Oona opened her eyes and told the boy, 'Quiet! If you do know, if you are telling the truth, then don't just tell: I want you to show us.'

47

They rose through the dispell, through enforced dark, climbing high along the Big House's creaking innards in criss-cross and clamber and crawl. The staircases and (where staircases had given up) ladders and boards that took them were all as rotten as walls around and hill beneath. And only enough light was admitted through cracks to get a sense of things, not properly see. Oona passed places where windows might've once opened to let the world in – a rough puckering, a cinching in tight like shut and sewn mouths. She had to go carefully, slowly, and she didn't like it. Hated having to stop at gaps – or better described: *gapes* – and hop or leap, reaching and grabbing and taking splinters for her effort.

Of course, the Master of the Big House himself went on without trouble. He even had time to pause and straighten portraits on the walls, or wipe a surface with a gloved finger and *tut-tut* and *tsk* at the state of the place, but then move on in a hurry. He was half-ancient and half-stone, but he was well-practised, long-accustomed. Oona thought: *his house, his dark, and he knows well how to find his own way through it.* Merrigutt stayed on Oona's shoulder, this time not leaving to fly on ahead and see or check. Oona was grateful.

'Much further?' Oona asked, but with barely a breath for calling. Merrigutt shouted for her: 'Boy! Is it much more of this or what?'

'*Tis a far and hard journey to full enlightenment!*' the Master of the Big House called back.

'That's what my father used to say!'

'Your father sounds like an eejit,' said Merrigutt, mostly in a mutter. It might've made Oona laugh, if she'd had puff for it. She continued to climb. 'How can we trust this one anyway?' said Merrigutt.

'Don't know,' said Oona.

'Well, I'll be keeping my eyes on him,' said Merrigutt. 'People who've been on their own too long should always be watched. Does things to them.'

'Not his fault,' said Oona.

'You're too keen on understanding,' said Merrigutt.

'You're too keen on suspecting,' said Oona.

'I'm not saying the boy's at fault, but him and that statue, they –'

'*Sister*,' said Oona: felt it needing saying. 'His sister, not just *statue*. They're brother and sister. Twins.' What didn't need saying out loud: just like herself and Morris.

'All right,' said Merrigutt.

'I don't hear you following!' called the Master. '*It'll be a lot longer a journey if you don't move and motivate your feet!* My father said that one, too – very wise man!'

Criss, cross, clamber, crawl. And eventually a last ladder devoid of most of its rungs. Oona looked up and saw the boy scramble quickly and so easily up, dull thuds signalling the fall of his stone foot. He shouted down to them, sounding excited, 'Come on come on come on, too slow too slow too slow!'

'Just say the word and I'll peck him,' said Merrigutt.

Oona took to the ladder thinking, Just this now. Just this last climb.

When she rose it was into the crooked tower, pulling herself up and wishing she could sink to the floor, find some rest, even for a minute. She took a step forward and the floor groaned.

'Is this even safe up here?' she asked the dark.

Out of it, the boy called from somewhere, 'Safe as anywhere else in Loftborough!'

'Not much comfort,' said Oona, loud as she liked.

'I say just don't move,' Merrigutt told her. 'Just wait.'

A handful of moments, and then an announcement from the Master of the Big House: 'Now you shall see!'

There was a clatter and clash, a sound like a rusted wrangle of chains being dragged, and the dark on Oona's right began to rise: behind was the so-called snooping-window, same one Oona had seen from the garden, the pane grubby and near opaque with the dabble of fingerprints, of constant touching and watching.

'Very nice,' said Merrigutt. 'Lovely view onto that mess of a garden.'

'And now the other!' shouted the boy.

Quick footsteps, a dim glimpse of the Master of the Big House shuffling to the other side of the tower, and then the same sound of chains being hauled. And more reluctantly, the dark was lifted on Oona's left. She was shown a second window,

213

but this one circular, and without a single blemish. It was filled with another view – a forest under a sky of curdling cloud.

'Move closer to that window,' whispered Merrigutt.

'Why?' asked Oona.

'Just go,' said Merrigutt. She sounded breathless. 'Need to see. Go on.'

But as soon as Oona moved the boy said, 'Careful! They may be out, even if it is not their usual night! I've noticed them at other times – having a look, keeping an eye.'

'Ignore him,' said Merrigutt. 'Keep going.'

Oona walked on. As she reached the window Merrigutt breathed, 'Sorrowful Lady herself preserve us.'

Oona struggled to swallow. She sighed and misted the glass, then took a handful of cloak to clear it, to look –

Leafless, cheerless forest. But worse – it was more change, more of the remaking of the North, and of a childish-looking and brutal kind. The trees had been upended, all askew, a breeze making roots shake in feeble gesticulation skyward. Any part that might've once displayed leaf or berry or nut had been buried beneath. And the roots where boughs should've been had things hanging – children's clothes without their children. Blouses and jumpers and dresses with their arms bound to branches, torn stockings. Nothing moved. The clothes hung heavy, as though they still had small bodies inside. Oona saw a litter of shoes on the ground, like dropped seed that had failed to sprout.

'They were told to leave behind all traces,' said the boy.

The Master of the Big House appeared behind Oona. She let her attention shift enough from the forest to see his

214

reflection – he was half-stooped, head hanging low. He went on: 'They were told that in order to pass into the beneath, they had to remove everything they were given in the world above. And how they were tempted into doing it! Great prizes, they were promised. Such great feasts of milk and sugar and all the sweet things they could want. Treasure and toys, magical powers. Whatever they wanted, that's what the Briar-Witches told them they could have. All their dearest wishes and more, if they just followed down into the dark.'

Oona said, 'I wouldn't have gone.' She paused. 'Not ever. If one of those things came to me there's nothing they could've promised that would've made me go underground.' She said it strongly enough, but did she believe that she believed it? And suddenly, her fingers felt drawn to the Loam Stone, like it could give her certainty, decision. Instead, it gave her something new. For the first time it showed no nightmare of someone else or someplace near, but Oona herself: she was standing in the dark forest of her dark dreams, and before her was Morris. He spoke, and his voice was the voice she'd heard too in her nightmares, the tone of deep certainty that made her skin tingle: *'Follow me, Oona. Follow me – there's something you need to see. There's a nightmare I want to show you.'*

Oona's fingers fled as though stung. She was shaking. She shut her eyes and kept them the same. Merrigutt must've noticed – the jackdaw never missed a thing. But when Merrigutt spoke, covering Oona's silence, her voice was calm: 'Tell me this straight, boy – is there a way to defeat these creatures or not?'

'I have been watching,' said the boy, and he discovered another new mood: a whispering, morbid-sounding fascination.

215

'I have been observing their movements – very interesting. They appear at dusk, creeping from their nest slowly, waiting for the dark itself to empower them. Our only chance will be if –'

'We have to go down into the nest,' said Oona. She breathed, still hadn't opened her eyes.

'Indeed,' said the Master of the Big House.

'Oona, this is beyond us,' said Merrigutt. It was said in a whisper but the tower was too small for any plot to stay private.

'We have to try,' said Oona.

'They have such power,' said the jackdaw, and Oona felt the bird shiver on her shoulder. 'They are the ones who created all North magic. I don't know what we'll meet down there or how we'll get by it.'

'We have to try,' said Oona, again. 'And I know they have their weaknesses, like all things.'

Oona's hand went to her cloak. Her fingers closed around the thing she'd brought from home – from Kavanagh cottage in Drumbroken, across the Divide and into the Black, to the Big House on its Rotten Hill. She withdrew the kitchen knife and held it vertically. Oona opened her eyes, turned and faced the Master of the Big House. He swallowed, his sight on the knife, the bulge of his Adam's apple chugging under folds of flesh.

'I escaped from those creatures once,' said Oona. 'So I'd be a frighted fool or worse if I can't find a way to do it again.'

48

'This way now,' said the boy of the Big House. 'I'd advise not to make too much of a sound.'

Into upturned forest. And Oona felt such a lack, a chill of absence making the air colder: she walked among things abandoned, seeing more clearly and closely where children had once been. She saw clues: a stain on a flannel shirt, maybe a dribbled mouthful of a last meal? Muck on the leg of a torn stocking, from a last tumble? Dark spot on a sleeve – perhaps last blood. Or last struggle, last attempt at escape?

Oona kept her hands from the Loam Stone – some nightmares didn't need knowing. The Master of the Big House muttered low, '*Beware that black beneath your feet.*'

'We've heard that enough times,' said Merrigutt.

'Then you should listen to it,' said the boy.

Oona looked down – she saw raised mounds, depressions that went deep.

'Just keep moving, my girl,' said Merrigutt.

The jackdaw was a restless thing again, into the air and circling above and around Oona, then settling somewhere, then somewhere else new, on jointed root or barren ground, but always alert.

'Just at the top of this mound,' said the Master of the Big House.

Before they'd left, the boy had wrapped himself in a velvet cloak, but stone fingers weren't much use for doing up buttons. There was such a fuss to fasten them that Oona had felt time rushing away too quickly and said, 'Here, let me help.' She'd gotten as far as reaching when the boy had pulled away and told her, 'I can do it myself! This was Father's favourite and best cloak, only right that I should adorn myself with it. Don't need another's help.' Then he'd spent many minutes more fumbling. The cloak dragged far behind him, and Oona had to mind not stepping on it.

They reached a sudden rise, one Oona felt had no business even being there – to Oona Kavanagh from Drumbroken, things like trees and rivers and mountains were fixed, to be worked around, not shifted. But in the North all had been changed as the King desired. And on this solitary rise was a single tree left leaning, roots raised to the sky.

'This is our way in,' said the boy. The upended trunk of the tree had a narrow cat's-eye split for an opening.

Merrigutt arrived back on Oona's shoulder.

'You all right?' Merrigutt asked her. 'Been quieter since you looked out at all this from that tower. Since you touched the Stone. What did you see?'

Oona closed her eyes, and awaiting her was the same image: Morris. Same words: '*Follow. Follow me, Oona . . .*'

'I'm fine,' she said, opening her eyes again. She could've told Merrigutt. Could've confessed to the jackdaw what she'd seen the night before, what she'd heard – the voice, the blackened

218

forest with its crimson-eyed watching and floor churning. But she didn't. Oona had an instinct to keep these things to herself: her nightmares were her own. So she said again, 'I'm fine.'

'There'll be more dispells below,' said Merrigutt. 'All kinds to try to stop us. Need to be strong-willed down there.'

'I know,' said Oona.

'Don't be afraid,' said Merrigutt. 'Fear is no good to us, my girl.'

'I'm not,' said Oona. Another lie! And she liked to tell herself that she didn't like lying.

'Well I may as well be honest,' said Merrigutt. 'Don't tell that boy this, but I'm bloody terrified.'

'Good,' said Oona.   Her knife was just inside her mother's cloak, a hand's snatch away.

'Because I'm afraid, too.'

49

Oona peered into a passage that delved
  deep

                down

                            dark . . .

. . . not too steep but she knew that on all-fours was the only
way. Merrigutt moved in a hop just behind Oona, the tunnel
too low for perching on a shoulder. Further behind followed
the drag of the boy's long velvet cloak.

Oona went slowly. Anything she touched crumbled. She
imagined one kick bringing the tunnel down with the three
of them buried. Then thought to herself, *Why do I imagine
these things?* She tried to unthink it, and failed. She thought
then – *the Loam Stone is doing this, must be divulging these
nightmares, thoughts I don't want.*

'How far to the nest?' whispered Oona, trying to distract
herself from herself.

'Always concerned with how far,' said the boy.

'He doesn't know,' said Merrigutt. 'No point in asking.'

'I'd be more wary of the magic than any distance or depth
of a physical nature,' said the boy.

'My theory is that they'll try to separate us. Try to isolate – then they'll find us easier to defeat.'

Oona said, 'We won't get lost if we go one way all together.'

'There is only one way,' said the boy. 'This is a labyrinth – one path, no choices or diversions. She'll have other ways to make us lose one another.'

'*She?*' asked Oona.

'The Mother,' said the boy. 'The one they all follow faithfully – their Queen.'

'Quiet now,' said Merrigutt. 'One thing that won't help is chatting on, they'll hear that a mile off.'

Merrigutt kept to the place between Oona's creeping hands and told her, 'Just stay close.'

Then

down

and

suddenly steeper

d

o

w

n . . .

. . . everything not crumbling but clinging, everything wet. Oona's hands were sinking, mud clogging her toes and fingers. She slowed, and any notion of outside – comfort or ease, daylight or open air – was leaving her. Was it some magic already insinuating itself into her mind? Some dispell, ridding her of any hope?

Oona stopped and said, 'Just need to rest a minute. Need to think.'

She looked down at Merrigutt. But the jackdaw continued, beak moving, Oona suddenly not hearing. She looked back, towards the boy – he'd stopped, too, mouth moving but giving no sound.

Oona spoke: 'What's happening?'

But she couldn't hear her own voice. She closed her eyes.

Then a final thing, a whisper so distant, as far off as the soft memory of any Drumbroken dawn: 'Stay close, my girl. Don't lose your way.'

Oona opened her eyes, and she knew what she'd find. Or who she'd not find: no Merrigutt, no boy of the Big House. They'd lost one another. She was alone.

50

Then Oona overheard –

'Not the best one, that girl!'

'No, too much gristle! Too much fat and fidgeting!'

'Too much of those second-skins on her, those . . . what do you call thems?'

'Clothes.'

'Aye!'

'Should've left her. We're meant to be keeping anyway, not eating.'

'We're grand – boys meant for the King, not the girls.'

'But no sense now in taking any more, not with what we've got on its way!'

'We'll soon be well above that sort, if the ones from across the sea keep their promise!'

'They will if they know what's good for them: you don't make a Mud-and-Blood Oath with a Briar-Witch and then break it!'

'True. Break the Oath and we'll break yer neck!'

Such laughter: wet and dry, crackle and gurgle and crunch. It made Oona think of bones and blisters and she put a hand to her mouth to stop any retching. To mask her breathing, too.

And, not caring what nightmare might come, what she might be shown, Oona took the Loam Stone from her satchel as some protection, or comfort. But it was cold, dark, so quiet.

Somehow she breathed, somehow crawled on.

A little ahead: brittle roots were corkscrewing from above, intent on concealing, and Oona was certain the Witches' nest was hidden just beyond. She listened again for their prattle –

'The ones from across the sea are due with our prizes this night, aren't they? All fresh as chicks taken out of their eggs, they promised and said so!'

'And what about the one in charge? The Faceless one?'

'He'll be there too, no doubting. And that Changeling.'

In their tone she heard something close enough to fright. Oona waited. *But can't wait just here forever*, she thought. Without Merrigutt though, without even the Master of the Big House, how could she try to –?

'Are you here to help us?'

Another voice from somewhere close, and not Witch. In a whisper –

'Girl – please tell me you're here to take me home.'

Oona searched but saw nothing except wet. But her imagination willed her towards something, the Loam Stone warming a little and urging her to recognise: she saw a face on the wall beside. Face of a child, a girl, but with no flesh or blood left in it. It spoke and its lips crumbled, cheeks caving – it blinked and clay fell from its eyes, a solid stutter of tears. Oona heard it whisper once more: 'Please tell me you're here to take me home to my mammy.'

Then not one but many faces, more captured girls forming

224

in the walls, more whispers –

'Please help us.'

'Take me home to my mother, I miss her.'

'I want to go back above, I never wanted to come down here.'

'I'm sorry I ran away from home, I should never have trusted those creatures.'

'*Quiet out there or we'll do worse to you!*'

Oona shrunk tight, stilled. The whispers of the children dwindled. Oona looked for but could no longer discern any face. A shout of a Briar-Witch: '*That's the good girls! Behave yourselves or we'll have to go and tell your mammies that you've been bold and not done as you should!*'

More damp laughter.

Surrounded by nightmares, no escape, Oona wondered, *How could I have lived so long and not known the like of this nastiness? Not known nightmares at all, not had such desperate sights?*

The thought of the children, of the Witches and their merciless taking – it all pushed Oona lower, and she was certain as certain that a dispell was winding its cold web around her heart. A sure banishment of hope, and a thriving of misery pouring into its place. But she'd seen such hopelessness before. She'd seen her grandmother trapped by it, and Oona was determined to be different. She'd promised herself she'd fight and this was the time to.

But then a sharper voice spoke, and all other Witches were quietened –

'*My daughters.*'

Oona remembered words from the Boy of the Big House: *the Mother, their Queen*. She listened, and the same sharp voice continued, like the slow scratch of a fingernail along stone –

'*We waste time with such games when there are more pressing matters, don't you agree?*'

An agreement in silence, no reply came.

'*I trust that you are aware of the presence of another close by?*'

Nothing in Oona moved.

'*Someone of great interest just beyond our nest?*'

Oona tried to make herself ready for what might come but all she had for encouragement was her own wilful and contrary heart, and a final whisper by her ear, one of the girls in the wall returning to say, 'Now she'll take you and toy with you but listen – the only way to stop her is the claw. If you can take the claw off her altogether that'll kill her, and then the other ones won't know what to do. They say whoever holds the claw of the Mother of the Briar-Witches controls the whole lot of them.'

'*Bring her to me.*'

Oona had no time for reply, no time to nod or thank the trapped child as the rattle of roots sounded over the entrance to the nest like an agitation of old bones. The ground churned beneath and Oona's hands went fumbling for a weapon, thoughts skipping – knife, pistol, Stone? Fight or slash or shoot or –?

Claws around her ankles –

Oona knew purest panic – earth in her eyes and mouth and throat, thickening on her tongue and no seeing and nothing heard as she was dragged down into dark.

51

When air came again it was clammy and sour – spiked with the same kind of stench as in the garden of the Big House. But worse. Oona was released, spat and dragged dirt from her eyes and spat more. She realised her hand didn't hold the Loam Stone. And her satchel? Couldn't find it. What about her knife? She didn't try for it. And dragging more earth from her eyes made her wish away sight: surrounding were so many lips peeled back from so many mouths, blank spaces all adding to the reek with impatient blasts of putrescence.

Then the sharper voice said –

'Such a skinny thing! Just a collection of bones with skin like a bag thrown over and another foul, fake skin over that. Hasn't eaten much in days, I'd say. Small breakfast this morning maybe? Bring her closer, my daughters.'

Oona saw the mouths mass, pressing forwards. Then claws, then clubbed hands – one hand went to the back of her neck and a sharp spur settled at the soft hollow of her throat. Again Oona was dragged, over broken earth and discarded bone to a whorl of snapped stick and reed. Something dark and glistening had been smeared to bind it together, and the sharp voice of the Mother was speaking from this tangle: *'Why have you come here, child?'*

Oona said nothing. Sweat covered every bit of her. She watched, but didn't see anything until the Mother moved. A scalp sprouting rushes stirred, and Oona discerned a face – a stiff mask of encrusted earth that cracked and split as the Mother of the Briar-Witches spoke:

'Why would you come here? Why venture down when you know well the stories? Why seek us out? You think you have something you can accomplish?'

Oona was seeking but didn't see eyes. She saw the Mother's claws twitch – one almost human, nails long and thick and curling, the other rough and misshapen, bloated, its spur longer and thicker and sharper than the others Oona had seen, felt. Still, Oona said not a thing. She couldn't reach for her knife, had no gun near, no Stone – no notion of what to do.

'And I see you are not unaware of my daughters. You have encountered them before.'

The Mother of the Briar-Witches ran a long finger over the wound on Oona's hand – her touch was the coldest thing, and at this slow caress the pain in Oona awoke, a memory of the hurt returning to bite. It made her wish to scream, but she wouldn't. *Can't!* thought Oona. *Mustn't show more weakness.*

'You escaped before?' said the Mother.

'I did,' said Oona.

'It has made you bold. You think if you found escape once, you can find it again?'

'Yes,' said Oona. She swallowed. 'I will.'

Outrage from the other Witches – hissing and spitting,

phlegm and venom spilling.

'*Silence*,' said their Mother, and the Witches were quietened. '*Only a childish arrogance, thinking you can change a world already so changed. There is nothing you can do now to stop the ones from across the sea. The King of the North, of the Echoes – he commands all things. You will, in the end, bow to him. Or you will be destroyed.*'

'Then I'd rather be destroyed,' said Oona.

'See – she is a stubbornly proud one, this girl.'

A new voice, and Oona recognised it immediately. The Briar-Witches shifted, and Oona was allowed to see: Master of the Big House, huddled in his father's cloak in a corner. He was cowering, but at the same time nothing about him said 'prisoner'.

'I think you'll agree I've brought you a good one,' the boy said. His mood at that moment: mixture of haughty, proud, but not without fear. His gloved fingers fiddled with the brass buttons on his cloak. Fiddled and fiddled. And he spoke only to the Mother of the Briar-Witches, throwing her looks and then looking away but anyway beseeching: 'You promised that if I brought you every child in Loftborough or told you where they were then you'd restore my sister! You said that you'd make her human again and lift the dispells on us and on our home!'

'*I did promise*,' said the Mother. '*Did indeed. And you have been useful.*'

Oona saw the human side of the boy begin to shake and she wished she could take hold and do more than shake him, the two-faced fool! Then, from behind him came briars snaking, closing slowly around his ankles, creeping around his

229

wrists and across his neck –

'No!' he cried. 'No! I did as you asked!'

'*My promise was this,*' the Mother told him, her voice too calm. '*If you had stopped your yapping and listened properly, this is what I promised: that once all the children of this town were ours, I would release you and your sister. But there are many types of release, boy. So your release will come now, as will that of this girl that you've brought. And I assure and promise you this – your sister will have her release soon enough, too.*'

Oona was suddenly thrown from the Mother's grasp like something foul, falling, and she was quickly encircled by salivating Witches. Their Mother spoke, slow and delicate and sly: '*My daughters – you may now satisfy yourselves on the final two children of the town of Loftborough.*'

52

Briars went for Oona boasting thorns two fingers long and she scrambled back. Her hand went for her knife – wasn't there. She looked but could discover nothing for protection – no weapon at all to save her. Then unlikely help came – from faces in the walls, the girls who'd been snatched and trapped were emerging, swarming to one point and all shouting, 'Over here! It's here!'

Oona looked again – below where the faces showed was her satchel. She crawled for it, claws at her feet all grabbing, and she was kicking – anything that touched she fought against. Then her fingers found leather and they hunted: whatever came to her hand first she was determined to use. It was the Loam Stone. Oona turned and wielded it –

'Stop!' she cried. The Stone's light was small, unwilling. 'I have power you don't! I can see what haunts you all, what nightmares you have, and I'll use them against you and don't think I won't!'

The Briar-Witches stalled, so many eyes and claws and mouths around her. Then they looked to their Mother for guidance.

'What is this?' said the Mother. 'Nothing less than legend and rumour and whisper made real! Can it really be the Stone? The Darkness and the Seeing?'

'It is,' said Oona. 'And I've learned how to use it, so stay back!'

Then the worst laughter from the Mother of the Briar-Witches, and implacable words: 'That Stone can have no effect on me or my daughters. How can we nightmare? We are made of such nightmares.'

Every word spoken by the Mother was true, and Oona knew it. And knew nothing else, the Stone cold and empty in her hands.

'Take her!'

Briars bound Oona's body, squeezing and wanting to strangle, tendrils itching towards her throat, and she had only one thought, one wish, one image in her mind – for Merrigutt to find her, as jackdaw or old woman or any way she chose to appear, and in answer the Loam Stone blazed against Oona's hand, so hot she was certain she'd have to release it . . .

Something dark dropped to the ground and a voice told Oona –

'Didn't I say, my girl? Didn't I say there'd come a time when you'd wish you'd not gone wandering off!'

It was a jackdaw.

The scream of the Mother: 'Grab that bird!'

A precise plucking of her beak and Merrigutt discovered Oona's knife and lifted into the air, swooping and dropping the blade by Oona's hand as the Mother screamed again –

'Stop her! Woman of the North transformed, shame to her family and exile – stop her!'

All the Mother's attention was on the jackdaw flying and evading claws and teeth. So no one noticed Oona cutting herself free, slipping the Loam Stone back into the satchel. No one saw her inch closer to the Mother, readying herself for the strike. No one but one: just feet from the Mother and hands came to Oona's ankles to anchor her – one hand flesh and the other stone . . .

'Please don't!' the boy of the Big House said. 'I want my sister back and this is the only way! Don't kill her!'

And Oona took such pleasure this time in kicking, her heel catching him on the aged side of his face. The boy of the Big House released her but –

'*I have her now!*'

Merrigutt was caught in the Mother's long-fingered hand and Oona watched the Mother's mouth widen to a fathomless dark, ready to drop the jackdaw inside.

The girls' faces appeared again in the walls, a chorus of support for Oona –

'Get her! Stop her!'

'Do it now! Strike the Mother!'

'The claw! Remove the claw!'

So Oona stood and lunged – first slash of the knife was to the hand that held Merrigutt, releasing her, the Mother shrieking.

Merrigutt added her voice to the din: 'Do it now, my girl!'

And Oona slammed the blade against the Mother's clubbed claw. It left the wrist, fell heavy to twitch and squirm and weep black and half-scratch at the ground. But the scream that exploded from the Mother of the Briar-Witches sent Oona flailing onto her back. Everything scuttled and roared, every

233

Briar-Witch opened her mouth as wide with the same pain.

'*Vermin!*' was the scream and the echo. '*Plague! Pest!*'

And screams and echoes to match the Witches: from the children in the walls, all rushing to surround a darker place in the nest and telling, 'Here! There's a way out! Over here!'

Merrigutt swooped and snatched up the claw, shouting to Oona, 'Quickly! Follow!' and then she vanished through the dark in the wall.

The nest was collapsing, Witches being buried –

Oona grabbed her satchel and slung it over her head, knife still in one hand. And with the other hand she took the boy of the Big House by the hair, telling him, 'Come on, you two-faced get, or I'll leave you down here with them!'

Oona whispered thanks to those faces, those girls overarching the way to escape, and then she crawled on into the dark. And up. A climb through a passage near vertical that crumbled at every scratch, fingers and toes working hard, Oona feeling like she was having to burrow. And still the screaming behind them, the ceaseless rage and roar of the Mother –

'*Follow them, my daughters! To the ends of the North, to the edge of everything – stop them!*'

53

Oona arrived at a rim of earth and sank the knife into somewhere above, using it to heave herself free. She emerged into a different dark, and such welcome cold. Stars were starting. What surrounded looked like night. But Oona was beginning to realise that in the Black there could be no firm naming of things like 'night' or 'day'. They were in a place of constant gloaming – a ceaseless desire always towards Black.

There was no sight of the Big House or its Rotten Hill. Then Oona heard once more the almighty creak and complaint of Loftborough: across the Black, she saw houses long-legged and lurching in the wind.

'So what do we do now?' said Merrigutt, almost lost, only two yellow eyes seen hovering near the ground. Beside the jackdaw, Oona saw the severed claw from the Mother of the Briar-Witches. Oona took a step towards and the claw shifted – still the slow opening and closing of its fingers, like an enduring wish to strangle.

'Would you kindly now release me?' asked the Master of the Big House.

Oona still held two things tight – knife, and the boy's hair.

She relieved herself of one but kept hold of the other: the blade went back into her cloak so she could use both hands to clutch the boy and shout, 'Why did you lead us into that? You should've just told us what was happening and we would've helped!'

But the boy said nothing. Mood? Contrite, humble, whimpering and lamenting, the aged side of his face gathering tight for tears. And this angered Oona all the more, made her shake him and shake him as though he might shed the answers she wanted. But Merrigutt came to Oona's shoulder and said, 'Just leave him. Not worth bothering with.'

So Oona stopped. She released the boy, letting him slump onto Black.

'Thank you,' he said. 'And I offer my humblest apologies for –'

'Oh, give over!' Merrigutt told him. 'You're an insufferable dose and spoilt rotten! And don't even think about mustering any more of those hearthside-tale-tears, for you'll get no sympathy from either of us! Treacherous brat.'

'I deserved that,' he said. He didn't weep. 'You are quite right and I accept it. I won't be long left in this world anyway, at least not in the form I'm accustomed to.' And he unbuttoned his father's cloak to show: the arm that had been flesh was darkening, being seized by stone, a greyish crust creeping down from the shoulder. Soon he'd be the same as his sister.

Oona felt she should ask Merrigutt, 'Is there nothing we can do?'

'No,' said the jackdaw. 'There's no reversing of it. It's the kind of magic that –'

Then the boy said, 'Wait! Quiet! Do you hear that?'

Oona listened. The fall of boot and hoof on stone? The call of male voices? She heard, saw: a mass of firelight was marching, on horseback invading. Arriving, just as the Briar-Witches had said.

'The Invaders,' said the boy. 'They've come to –'

'Wait,' said Oona. 'Quiet. Do you hear that other thing?'

They listened, and heard this sound: the rattle of collected metal. And then hardly a sound at all, like the end of hearing: a deepening hush, a silence like the place after a man's last breath. Oona looked at Merrigutt, and both knew: it was the prompt arrival of a funeral coach; pulled by a silent stallion, driven by a figure of shadow, and summoned by the promise of death.

54

'We make haste back to my home,' said the boy of the Big House. 'And quick – it's the only place safe now.'

But Merrigutt and Oona agreed: 'Nowhere safe.' The call of an Invader made them all recoil –

'Search every rickety place in this dump! Don't stop until you find that child!'

Oona thought of the Briar-Witches, their words: 'prizes' is what they'd spoken of, children being brought to them. Then more orders from the Invader's voice, a shouting of, 'And make sure she has that object our King described!'

'They're looking for you,' said the boy of the Big House, and with more than half of him stone he had to limp and drag towards Oona. 'That Stone – it is what they want. They know that you have it.'

'If you even think about betraying us again,' said Merrigutt, and she threw herself at the boy, wings batting his face with furious dark. 'If I even see a hint of a notion coming into your eyes about giving us over to the Invaders then I'll –'

'I'm not going to do anything of the sort!' said the boy.

'What now?' Merrigutt asked, back on Oona's shoulder.

'What are you going to decide?' Oona didn't speak: she was thinking things almost hopeful, things she wasn't ready to say.

'They'll burn the whole place to cinders,' said the boy. 'They won't care! They're remaking the North anyway so –'

'Quiet!' snapped the jackdaw, and she asked again of Oona, 'Are you going to speak or not? We can't stay here watching. If you want my opinion, we've done all we can and more than enough. You did well – that Mother of the Briar-Witches is likely dead now after losing her claw, so the other ones won't know what to do without being told.'

'I beg to differ,' said the boy. 'It won't stop the daughters from attacking. The Briar- Witches may no longer be organised, true, but that doesn't make them peaceful. If anything, I'd venture that makes the more dangerous – they'll be feral now.'

'No one asked for your opinion,' said Merrigutt. 'Isn't there a fountain for you to go and stand in?'

And they argued, voices shrunken by that hush – the quiet brought close by the Coach-A-Bower. And at last, Oona decided, but with no need for words – she quickly plucked the claw of the Mother of the Briar-Witches from the ground and added it to her satchel, and then ran back towards Loftborough.

Merrigutt was in the air, flying close to follow, demanding, 'What the blazes are you doing?'

'Something,' Oona told her.

'Well, you might want to slow or himself is going to end up as a fence-post in a field!'

Oona half-glanced back – the boy could only lag, might as well have been dragging a millstone. But Oona didn't slow. Not till she arrived at the long limbs of Loftborough's houses. She crept and kept low. And then she saw her hopeful thoughts made visible –

'*Children*,' she breathed.

A single carriage was stopped in the street. Only one, though. What about the dozen from Drumbroken? Where was the rest of the procession? Oona examined and saw so much bewilderment in the children's faces trapped inside: their pale peering-out soft, incurious. Just a pair of Invaders on horseback were doing the guarding, the rest elsewhere with their shouts to the women of Loftborough, 'Drop your ladder down! We are here to search your home in the name of the King!' But no ladder or anything like it came tumbling. There was no light in any of the houses.

'Maybe they left,' whispered Merrigutt. 'Saw the Invaders coming and just deserted, like we should be on our way to doing.'

Oona didn't answer – she was examining the carriage, seeking just one face and one set of eyes, certain that she'd recognise them even in such cram and dark. And like it might even bring him into existence, to her attention, Oona murmured, 'Morris? Morris?'

Merrigutt said, 'Stay put. I'll go investigate. *Stay*.'

The jackdaw left. She went high to circle then suddenly down, landing lightly on the carriage. One Invader standing close gave the jackdaw a glance, but only that: wasn't bothered.

Oona saw Merrigutt's head dip between bars. What was she asking? Was she getting a response? Oona waited but didn't want to, more anticipation bubbling in her belly than she could bear, her breathing shortened, hands holding tight to the leg of the house.

Then Merrigutt soared, circling so no one would watch or care where she went, then finally down to resettle on Oona's shoulder. She said, 'Isn't there. They don't know of him.'

'Might still be in there,' said Oona, needing to believe. 'Maybe they just don't know his name. Or maybe –'

'No,' said Merrigutt. 'Can't be – all the children in that carriage are girls.'

Oona said nothing. She closed her eyes. And there again, indelible – the image like a mockery of Morris whispering, *'Follow me, Oona. Follow . . .'*

And Oona wouldn't rest, wouldn't relent – she opened her eyes and all energy and agitation she switched to another mission.

'Right,' she said. 'I'm still not letting any of these girls be fed to the Briar-Witches. I won't let that happen.'

'I'm glad to hear it.'

Oona turned.

The landlady of The Loyal Martyr stood close, and around her stood the answer for the lack of light in Loftborough: all women were waiting, all with rifles in hand and looking more than ready.

'We're here to help,' said one.

'Time to put an end to this,' said another.

'I won't let any more young girls be taken,' said the landlady. 'Not a chance of it.' And every head gave a slow, solemn nod.

'Good,' said Oona. 'Then we fight.'

'Oona,' Merrigutt began, 'listen to me, I think we –'

'Don't tell me what to do,' said Oona. 'It's decided now.'

The jackdaw persisted, her tone hardly troubling with whisper: 'Oona, these women can't fight. They can't even –'

'Go then,' said Oona. 'You don't have to stay. Leave if that's what best for you, but I'm staying to help. I'm helping these girls. Morris might not be with them but I'm not gonna let them be fed to those things underground.'

No more words from the jackdaw. But Oona pictured – perhaps nightmared – Merrigutt lifting once more, not circling or wheeling, and not returning. Making her decision: leaving.

'We have to do this,' Oona told her. 'No choice.'

Still no words from Merrigutt.

Oona thought she knew what to say to soften the old bird –

'Look: it's these women against all those Invaders, all men. We can't leave them to it. You wanted some fight out of them and now we're gonna get it.'

The jackdaw flexed its wings. Twitched and spasmed and Evelyn Merrigutt appeared as an old woman and said, 'Right, but on one condition: I'm in charge of them. Because if we're going to have any chance at all against Invaders and Funeral-Makers and Briar-Witches, we'll need more than rifles. We'll be needing some strong North magic of our own.'

55

'All right, my girl,' said Merrigutt, returning to Oona's shoulder, 'now the magic's been sown, let's see what shape it takes.'

Oona had watched Merrigutt pinch some scarlet powder from that useful supply in her clothing, enough to bury by the legs of two opposing Loftborough houses – two volunteered by the two most willing of the women, a Mrs Molloy and a Mrs Hanlon.

Then Oona, Merrigutt, the Loftborough women and the beleaguered boy of the Big House all waited. And slowly, things began –

'Stand back,' said Merrigutt, speaking more to the women of Loftborough than Oona. The long legs of the nearest house began to tremble, Merrigutt's magic making them wake. And then the legs of the other on the opposite side of the street, the same – started to shudder in a way unrelated to any element. The two guarding Invaders were noticing because their horses were noticing – tossing their heads, spooked. So the soldiers began to debate, but stupid against stupid –

'What's going on there with them houses?'

'It's nothing! That's the way these houses are, they shift about!'

243

'Nah. Something else.'

'I said it's nothing, so stop your –'

Then they couldn't deny it –

Terrified and excited at the sight, Oona saw the houses tear themselves free: like men fresh out of The Loyal Martyr and full of the drink, they staggered towards each other, windows fracturing, glass as fine as splinter falling, slate slipping from roofs and legs crunching almost buckling –

One Invader cried 'Look out!' and the other echoed and they both drove heels into their horses to make them fly one way together, abandoning the single carriage of the Coach-A-Bower and captured children –

'Ready yourself,' Merrigutt told Oona.

And then the collision: Mrs Molloy and Mrs Hanlon's houses slammed into one another, rebounded and – as the Oona and Merrigutt had planned and hoped it – toppled to the street on either side of the carriage.

Oona said it to herself: 'Now.'

She took the Master of the Big House by the sleeve and led him. Merrigutt stayed, ready with the women to fight, to cast magic on any other house that needed it.

Oona had to scramble over the fallen legs of Mrs Molloy's home, the boy from the Big House doing his best to follow, but doubting: 'You sure this is the best possible plan?'

'Yes,' she told him, though really she was thinking, It's all the plan we have! 'Keep moving – you've got some making up to do so you better do as I say!' Both over and then low.

Oona looked to the dark figure that sat at the front of the carriage – the coachman hadn't moved, his whip remained limp, looking threatless. Oona went slower though. Faces inside the carriage saw her and might've stirred a bit, but not in any way lively. Oona knew it would take a lot to get them moving. Luckily enough, just one large lock kept them in. Locks were easy – Oona had seen plenty and knew the knack. She took her knife from her cloak and slipped it into the keyhole, letting the blade do the work, feeling, and letting those subtle feelings travel into her fingers.

Then a volley of Invaders' shouts –

'What's happened here!'

'Keep an eye on them children! That's the most important thing!'

'Them Witches won't be happy if we don't have any fodder for them!'

But the lock wasn't for opening at all so Oona said, 'Bloody thing.'

Then a voice inside the carriage asked, 'It's not Oona Kavanagh, is it? I must really be dreaming here.'

Oona stopped her work with the lock – the face of Bridget O'Reily was peering out at her. They looked at each another, saying nothing. Bridget's eyes were dark, had almost entirely misplaced life. And then Oona went to work harder, grinding the blade, trying just to crack the insides, any subtlety done with –

Invader: 'Coachman! Keep an eye on those children!'

Bridget whispered, 'Hurry!'

'Trying,' said Oona. She grabbed the stone arm of the Master of the Big House, lifted it and (small apology to him: 'Sorry') slammed it down on the lock. The lock came apart like shattered

245

porcelain, breaking into many small pieces. But before any freedom for anyone –

'Behind you,' said Bridget.

Oona dropped, crawling under the carriage, boy of the Big House beside. She watched feet make a slow approach, then stop: dark, see-through, and a whip that idled like a cat's tail. Oona held any breath, and reached into her satchel and found another weapon: the pistol intended for Bridget. She held it as ready as she could.

'No use,' the boy told her. 'No bullet nor blade will hurt these creatures.'

No bullet or blade (thought Oona, one of each in either hand), then what'll work? How do we win this?

'Well,' whispered the boy from the Big House, 'perhaps I can make some amends now.' And he took a breath and rolled out from beneath the cart, squirming to his feet and calling to the Coachman, 'Here! I'm here and I've escaped!'

Oona saw the dark figure turn, then drift with such painful slowness towards the boy.

'Good man,' said Oona, and she rolled back out, stood and threw wide the carriage door. Out streamed girls – dirty, ragged, like they'd been dragged across the North and not carried, and first was Bridget who threw herself on Oona.

'I knew,' said Bridget, holding tight. 'I dunno how I knew but I knew, I said to myself and everyone – if anyone's gonna come and rescue us, then it'll be my mate Oona Kavanagh! And I just knew that –'

Then many cries –

From one Invader: 'They're escaping! Get them!'

From Merrigutt, passing overhead: 'Oona – any time for chat is later! Move it!' And from the boy of the Big House, cornered by the Coachman: 'Help! Help me!'

Oona freed herself from Bridget's arms and stood, pistol ready to be aimed at whatever target. But there was no problem a bullet could solve. The boy of the Big House dodged the Coachman's calm outstretched hand, and limped a return to Oona's side.

'Now what?' he asked.

Oona had no answer.

Then falling fire – Invaders with their torches, hurling them. And the fallen houses – whether slate or wood, round window or long legs – were quick to burn, to let flame race across and Oona and the others were soon encircled by their blaze.

'Now what?' the boy asked Oona, again.

She looked, trying to see something, a way free. Oona couldn't see the Coachman, his dark indistinguishable from smoke and shadow. Her eyes settled finally on the only thing – the carriage.

'Everyone!' she called to the girls. 'Get behind the carriage and push!' At her order, the girls all moved quick, keen.

'Now push like you've got the strength of any man in you!' she told them, but they didn't need much telling – already they had heads down and hands pressed to wherever they could. And slowly, as painfully snail-paced as the walk of the Coachman, the carriage was pushed towards the flames. Oona kept an eye and then cried, 'Stop! That's close enough. Now up top!'

Taller girls helped smaller, and a good few had to help to get the weight of the boy of the Big House up. Bridget and

Oona stayed on the ground till they were the only two left.

'Right,' said Bridget, 'you go now, Oona.'

Oona returned her knife to her cloak but kept the pistol in hand, settling one foot on a carriage-wheel and finding hands ready to take her, pulling her up. She turned for Bridget to offer the same help, but then a sound shook her – a crack like bone between a dog's teeth and she saw the whip of the Coachman lashing out of the dark, enclosing Bridget's ankles. Bridget was dragged back.

'No!' cried Oona.

But it was pointless – the Coachman already had one hand around Bridget's arm. Had already claimed her. From the roof of the carriage Oona still called like it might change things, like it might not be too late: 'Don't touch him! Shake him off, Brid!' And she would've leapt, would've gone to save her friend if she hadn't seen: Bridget wasn't moving, was only fading, the darkest parts of her spreading, shadows like slow smoke enclosing her. It took less than little time, and Bridget was nothing, was soon nowhere to be rediscovered in the dark.

56

Oona stood. Shaking, shaken. Her heart felt as though it was ending. Tears came that she had to ignore because she had to aim, to direct the pistol that had been destined for Bridget's hand. And she felt she had to fire – the first bullet struck earth, passing through the shadow and silence of the Coachmen. She fired again, and again and again, but her anger was so deep it couldn't be drained and as ever on her journey, Merrigutt arrived on Oona's shoulder to talk sense: 'My girl, no gun in this world and no amount of shooting it will do anything to that creature. You have to move.'

Oona saw flames laying themselves against the carriage to further blacken.

'You have to jump!' Merrigutt told her.

Oona heard the sound of the girls coughing, throats swallowing smoke. Choking. She did her best to banish tears with a fumbling pair of fingers and then told them in a scream, 'Go!'

Such bravery, Oona saw: some of the girls went alone but most hand-in-hand, leaping together from the roof of the carriage, clearing the flames and landing in the awaiting arms of Loftborough women. Soon, only Oona and the boy of the Big House were left.

'I'm not cut out for this,' he told her, and she took his sleeve.

'Me neither,' said Oona.

They ran what little they could run – no more than a trio of tripping steps – and then hurled themselves forward . . . but the boy's weight in stone was enough to drag them down and falling into fire was a certain thing, Merrigutt on Oona's shoulder holding tight and flapping. They fell, rolled, Oona's hair shortened by the singe and the boy landing with flame clinging to his back. He was able to extinguish himself, one-armed. Oona breathed again when he showed what was beneath burnt-away clothes – stone, flesh almost completely dispelled.

Pain then – Oona was taken by the little hair she had left and lifted by an Invader.

'Oh no you don't!' came a cry.

And Mrs Hanlon was there too, some dull instrument in her hands to drive into the back of the Invader's legs. He released Oona and buckled at the knees like Mrs Hanlon's home. She gave him another whack on the skull to floor him.

'Hooligan!' she cried.

And through the creep of smoke and steady fire, Oona saw the women of Loftborough fighting: some still on the ground, some in their houses, firing on Invaders or, if they had no rifle, attacking with rake or spade or shovel or strong words. But the Invaders had the better preparation – those uniforms, skins reaped from Acre-Changelings, allowed them to mirror flame and any whim of shadow, keeping them hidden. And then more allies of the Invaders: racing underground then bursting through full, leaping on the Loftborough women, spurs ready to tear what they wanted – Briar-Witches. Fiercer than ever they attacked, just as the boy of the Big House had predicted.

'Run!' Merrigutt cried, entering the sky to shout. 'All up into the houses!'

'I'd say that is a bloody good idea,' said the Master of the Big House, and this time it was him that led Oona. They joined the rush of girls. Rope-ladders had been dropped from the remaining homes and the girls were climbing quick, not needing to be told. Oona's choice was The Loyal Martyr.

'Go,' Oona told the boy of the Big House. (Slowest, so he needs to go first, she thought.)

Then Oona felt the tremble. Against her soles the ground shivered and knew without looking what was approaching so she leapt as high as she could and grabbed, hanging from the rope-ladder. But the Briar-Witch was snatching – long-fingered hand and claw both burst through stone to tear at Oona's feet and she saw what could be shot this time. Oona half-turned and shut one eye, gave herself just a moment, and then fired. The Witch fell to the ground; into it – the creature returning to its own forged dark.

'Where did you get that gun?' asked Merrigutt. 'Who from?'

'Doesn't matter,' said Oona. 'It was made for Bridget, so it's only right I use it now.'

A call from the landlady, dragging the Master of the Big House into the pub: 'Hurry!' Oona climbed quicker –

Gunfire rattled against wood, Invaders seeing, firing –

She reached the top and crawled into the pub, head down.

'That's it!' the landlady told her, helping her up by the scruff and then pointing her rifle down and firing two shots, and then adding like there'd been no break in the chat, 'You've lost a bit of hair there, girl, but that never hurt anybody.'

Oona stood and saw only one small girl in the pub. She stood close to the empty fireplace as though it might still confer some warmth.

'That gun won't do any good,' Merrigutt told Oona. 'May as well be rid of it, my girl.'

But Oona paid no attention – she'd approached the girl. Slow approach, not wanting to frighten: careful, delicate, because she wanted one answer. She thought there was only one thing that might ease the loss of Bridget.

'Please,' she said. 'There were other carriages carrying boys, taking them North – can you tell me where they are?'

The girl didn't look ready to give answers. Oona settled a hand on the girl's arm.

'Please tell me,' she said again. No good at softness, she wanted to shake answers from the girl. 'You have to tell me – where are the others?'

Slowly, the girl raised her head, pale tongue emerging from dark face to wet Blackened lips. She didn't look at Oona, but said, 'They weren't for here. The boys were all for the King. They went on, towards the Muckrook Mountains.'

'*Melancholy* Mountains,' the landlady corrected.

'Quiet,' Merrigutt told her.

The small girl finished: 'He said that the King wanted all the boys for himself.'

'*He*?' repeated Oona.

252

'The one,' said the girl, and she shuddered, 'with no face.'

Suddenly, gunfire ceased like sound had been shut off. Only one sound was permitted, a single shout heard –

'Weak-minded women of Loftborough – let's have none of this needless waste now! Let me say just this and make it simple, ladies: you've got as long as it takes for my men to reload before we destroy your town entirely!'

'Sounds a bit more well to-do than a common Invader,' said the boy of the Big House.

'It's him,' said Merrigutt. She was looking at Oona. 'Faceless Invader, Carrion Changeling on his shoulder doing the talking: the King's Captain.'

'Very well then!' came the voice of the Faceless. 'We have given ample opportunity!'

'What do we do now?' Oona asked Merrigutt.

'Now you need to be going,' said the landlady, hands pushing, willing Oona away. 'Me and the other ladies, we'll take it from here. You go upstairs and left, end of the hall and then out, onto the window and across to Mrs Donnelly next door. I'll hold them back as long as I can. And I'll look after the wee girl here too.' And the look she gave the girl was so fond, so full of affection – it made Oona happier, feeling that maybe the fight had been worth something.

'Thanks for your help, missus,' said Oona.

'No bother at all,' said the landlady. 'Now go on!'

So away then, Oona up the stairs with the jackdaw on her shoulder, boy of the Big House thumping along behind, calling, 'Wait for me!'

Long hallway – Oona ran left like she'd been told, ceiling

and floor sharp-sloped, whole place shaking. Something struck the house and made it pitch and Oona was jostled by walls. She kept going though, pistol still in her hand, and at the end reached a circular window. Stubborn thing, it had to be elbowed open and across the gap she saw a woman waiting – must've been Mrs Donnelly.

'Come on!' the neighbour shouted over. 'Be quick!'

Oona climbed onto the sill. It was only feet between The Loyal Martyr and Mrs Donnelly's but if things changed, if either house moved, then – ?

'Jump now!' said Merrigutt. Oona didn't think, just leapt– Mrs Donnelly caught and held Oona tight, helping her in through the window. They turned together and watched the boy of the Big House make his leap – he managed it better than any one of them would've thought. Oona and Mrs Donnelly both grabbed for him and hauled him in.

'Here,' said Mrs Donnelly, and she opened Oona's satchel and added things. 'Some food and that. Take it and go – all the way to the end there, past me mother's ugly oul vase with the green faces of the Wee Folk on it, then right, and then out. Mrs O'Keefe – she'll be there to help you next.'

A nod from Oona, and on into another corridor. Another storm of gunfire from outside felt like it was following – had some Invaders seen them leave The Loyal Martyr? Then Oona saw the vase: green faces all grinning, figures shrunken and ugly as Sorrowful sin, and she went right. Another circular window and then –

No, thought Oona. Too much of a gap to the next house, too much to be cleared in a leap!

But Mrs O'Keefe was there and ready – from the window next door she was pushing a ladder, giving them something to clamber across on.

'No other choice,' said Merrigutt, still on Oona's shoulder.

Oona climbed out. She preferred to stand, balancing with arms out. She went fast as she could across, praying to herself as she went, as gunfire and falling fire and smoke all boiled around her – *Sorrowful Lady, protect us. Sorrowful Lady, don't let me fall* . . .

'You'd be best to drop that gun and you'd move quicker!' Merrigutt told her.

But over safely anyway, and as soon as Oona arrived Mrs O'Keefe said, 'Here – take this.' Oona felt more food stuffed into her bag.

'It's Innislone all over again,' said Merrigutt. 'Forgot how keen the Northerners are to feed people.'

The boy from the Big House arrived with them and Mrs O'Keefe said, 'Now Mrs McSooth will help you, but her place is too far over. You'll need to climb up into the attic and along, out the end window. Tight squeeze but it's the only way now.' And by her knees Mrs O'Keefe stooped and opened a low door. Behind hid a steep staircase.

Oona crouched and whispered to no one, 'Tight squeeze is right.'

She crawled in, and as soon as the boy of the Big House followed and was through, Mrs O'Keefe shut the door. Oona heard a key turned in the lock. She had to clamber up steep steps and when the attic was reached it was too low for standing so Oona had to stay crouched.

Merrigutt left her to circle for some seconds and then shouted, 'Over here!'

The jackdaw was at the end, perched at another circular window. Oona travelled in a hunch across the attic to see – true enough, the last house was far. Just too far, like Mrs O'Keefe had said.

'Up onto the roof,' said Merrigutt. 'Either that or nothing.'

'How do we get out though?' asked Oona.

'This is how, ladies!' said the boy. He'd found a wooden step-ladder. He shook it out and settled it on the floor. All his criss-cross and clambering ways in the Big House had been a help – he was up it quick and opening a skylight to squirm through.

Oona followed, calling, 'Don't call us ladies!'

Out onto the roof, and Oona saw all of Loftborough, all of what was becoming –

Some women still on the street but most were at their windows firing down on Invaders and Briar-Witches, or throwing what furniture or kitchenware they could, dropping boiled water or bags of flour that ignited blue when they met flame. But the battle wasn't a battle – fire was travelling too easily, houses shifting and passing flame to one another. Loftborough would defeat itself soon, would be destroyed by its own whims.

'Over here, youse ones!'

Oona turned at the call of another Loftborough woman, and saw what must've been Mrs McSooth.

'Quick!' Mrs Next-Door was calling. 'Not much time now!'

But how could they cross? Crazy! Could the woman not see it was too far?

And like blown blades in a meadow, the houses drifted away from one another and Oona lost footing, falling and rolling and almost dropping, but Merrigutt was there to save her with sharp claws, the boy of the Big House too, grabbing, dragging her back onto the roof. But they'd been seen –

'That house near the end of the street! I see people on the roof!'

Oona stood. She watched – one of the women on the ground was being held by an Invader, and another arrived to jab her in the belly with his rifle-butt. There was laughter, from men and from Briar-Witches. And Oona discovered her own hands moving, without much thought: tucking the pistol into her cloak, the hand going suddenly to her satchel, to snatch for the Loam Stone.

'Oona,' said Merrigutt, 'what're you doing now?'

Oona held the Stone tight: its heat felt like it could scorch, so ferocious she thought it was ready to flower into bright flame. And Oona was shown her way to revenge. The Stone had called, made claims and boasted – telling Oona what it could do if she willed it – she needed to test. So she lifted the Stone high and held it, all thoughts swirling around Bridget . . . and then anger made her act. She swung her arm as though the gesture could flatten all in sight with one sweep and flame was dragged like wire from rooftops, falling and settling among Invaders and Briar-Witches. And the night was made raw – torn open by their screaming.

But no sound for Oona. Like the hush that the Coach-A-Bower brought into a place, she heard nothing but the certainty of her own thoughts: all that existed was the rightness of her anger.

Spurred by her own sense of command, Oona whipped her arm upwards and flame reached high, a funnel that she dreamed wider, brighter . . . and then let fall, spanning the stone street of Loftborough. And did she feel better, watching Invaders and Witches transformed to cinder? Did she feel herself not someone to be captured or ruled, but a person who could have what she dreamed, desired?

A voice answered, one heard in the darkest of forests, dimmest of nightmares: *'Now you know. Now you realise, Oona Kavanagh. Now you see.'*

Oona felt one sure emotion besides anger: understanding. She knew as she stood on that rooftop and flooded with the fullness of the Loam Stone's power, why the King of the North desired it so desperately.

57

'Enough,' said Merrigutt. Oona met the jackdaw's eye – there she saw stillness, a bewilderment, as though she was looking on someone new. 'Enough,' she said again.

'I have an idea!' cried the boy of the Big House, suddenly. 'Just wait . . .'

And he shifted his weight only a little, in the smallest way, but it started a tipping of the house, a moving closer to next door, one chance shown to Oona as she ran, grabbing the Master of the Big House and throwing herself forwards, Merrigutt clutching tight to her shoulder –

Moments in the air, flung and falling –

Then the roof of Mrs McSooth's house slammed against Oona's chest. She held on. An impact beside said that the boy from the Big House had made it too.

'Good girl,' said Mrs McSooth, there to help them up. 'Now follow.'

They didn't go down into the house but across the roof, having to scamper sideways along its narrow spine. A rope was waiting at the far end.

'Here,' said Mrs McSooth, 'you'll need food for the journey

ahead.' She produced a substantial parcel of goods.

'Don't even think about taking that!' Merrigutt told Oona.

More explosions, gunshots, Oona and the others on the roof the only target –

'Quick!' said the jackdaw.

Oona slid the length of the rope to the ground, Loam Stone still in hand, the boy close behind, Mrs McSooth herself soon after. The fire dreamed by Oona still remained – barrier across the street to keep Invaders well enclosed, and keeping Oona and the rest safe for a little longer. Perhaps long enough for escape.

'Do you have a horse or something, Missus?' asked Oona. 'Something we can leave on?'

'I've got better than any oul horse!' said Mrs McSooth, grinning, and the woman went into a delirious kind of jig – she clapped her hands three times quick and then stamped her right foot twice. And out of the dark loped something large: a creature flecked with filth and reeking of the wild, that Oona thought might've been born with a coat coloured somewhere between grey-white and moon but had been stained with so much, marred by long travel through the Black. It had no eyes, no way of seeing that Oona could make out.

'A Whereabouts Wolf,' said Merrigutt.

'Last one left here in Loftborough,' Mrs McSooth told them, and she approached the creature, laying one hand between its tall, hooded ears. 'Used to be a whole pack of them but the men took them when they headed off with the Cause. She'll take you anywhere you need going, this one. Just whisper and she'll know it – I guarantee.'

Oona moved towards the Whereabouts. She saw short legs

and paws splayed and a snout as long as her arm dripping with wet, nostrils opening and shutting like a heart in alarm. She touched it – muddied coat was soft at first, and then each hair was suddenly as stiff-standing as the fibres on a hearth-brush. Oona watched the Wolf's coat ripple – an intricate undulation in small circles, as though frisked by unseen palms.

'Thank you,' said Oona, though any words at all felt too little.

'No, you're the one to be thanked,' said Mrs McSooth and the firelight showed tears coming to the woman's eyes. 'For taking this stand. We'll not forget it. You'll need to go North now. My husband, Eugene, he went North to fight. To the Burren is where the Cause is all gathering to fight this King. Head for the Melancholy Mountains pass, and then you'll –'

'Oona,' said Merrigutt.

One word, and not the beginning of a command to hurry nor a telling-off. The tone of the jackdaw was something else, made Oona colder. She turned to see –

An Invader was standing few feet away. A figure with no face. And stationed on his shoulder, watching, was a small bird with crimson eyes.

261

58

Nothing spoke but near by fire. Then Mrs McSooth cried, '*Go!*' She snatched a pitchfork from the ground and ran at the Faceless Invader. He knocked her to the ground, a dismissal in one single blow. He advanced on them.

'Get on that Wolf, my girl!' cried Merrigutt.

Oona took handfuls of the Whereabout's hair and pulled herself up onto its back, her eyes never leaving the Faceless. The figure stopped. The bird, the Carrion Changeling, spoke –

'You have something, child. Something you do not understand.'

'I understand it,' said Oona, no lie in the words. She held the Loam Stone close to her heart. 'I know it well enough!'

'But you are not its rightful owner,' said the bird. 'It is no burden for a child to carry, for a young and foolish girl to have to bear.'

Oona thought fire, thought of her own fury, the pure nightmares of the Stone still in her power . . . but she didn't will it, didn't act.

'Let us take the Stone to its rightful owner,' said the bird. 'To the King of the North, soon to be the King of all this Isle! You know him already, do you not? He has been walking those dark lonely paths inside your mind. He knows you well, knows what to expect from you.'

'He does,' said Oona. A moment then of waiting – as though she was considering – and then Oona took Bridget's pistol from her cloak and said, 'But I'm a Kavanagh, and Kavanaghs don't do as expected.'

She fired a single shot. But like the Coachman, it had no effect on the Faceless.

A sudden scream from the crimson-eyed bird –

Shock made Oona drop the pistol –

So small then suddenly large, changing in flight – size of a sparrow then size of a hawk, the Changeling left the Faceless Invader's shoulder and swooped towards Oona, and at the same moment Merrigutt launched herself. Claw and beak and feather battled in the air as the Faceless continued towards Oona, arm outstretching –

'Stop!' cried the boy of the Big House, and he positioned himself in front of Oona, in front of the Whereabouts. 'Like my father before me, I am Master in this town and I say no further!'

He found some weapon to wield – like Mrs McSooth, something dull and practical and blunt and he ran at the Faceless. But too like Mrs McSooth – an easy blow from the Faceless and the boy was batted aside.

'Do something!' Oona told the Whereabouts, but the Wolf only quivered, hungering only for direction, to go. And hope left Oona, left her weak as she saw Merrigutt pinned to the ground by the Changeling.

'Surrender the Stone,' said the crimson-eyed hawk, one massive claw enclosing the jackdaw's skull, tightening, 'or I shall break her.'

'Just go, my girl!' the jackdaw told Oona. 'Don't wait! Whisper to the Whereabouts where you want to go and it'll take you there!'

Oona looked to the hand of the Faceless: reaching, there to receive –

'Take the Stone from her!' cried the Changeling.

Then something new charging into their midst – in shadow and shiver of firelight Oona tried to see. Small figure? Something like a small child with a shrill cry of –

'Get away from my brother!'

'Sally!' shouted the boy of the Big House.

The statue of his twin sister was enough of a force to push the Faceless Invader aside and aim a kick at the hawk. The Changeling lifted, eyes like wildest wildfire as both birds cried –

Hawk: 'Stop them!'

Merrigutt: 'Just go! I'll find you, my girl! No matter where in this Black, I'll discover you!'

And Oona whispered to the Whereabouts the first words she thought: 'Take us to the middle of nowhere.'

The Wolf bolted, Oona almost falling and then holding tighter, turning to look – so far on from the town in only a blink, Loftborough was a livid scar shrinking on dark, wreathed with smoke. She saw brother and sister of the Big House crouched together, transformed, a pair of stone statues clinging close. But less glad sightings: no Merrigutt, and the Faceless Invader standing with a stillness to match any statue, the Changeling on his shoulder watching, following with crimson eyes as Oona made swift escape.

THE PONDEROUS PASS OF GIANTS

59

So swift so cold that Oona had to keep eyes shut. Arms laced around the Whereabouts Wolf's neck and face pressed into the animal's soft-then-stiffening hair, she still held tight to the Loam Stone. And what waited for Oona in her mind, in the black behind her eyes? That darkest forest, that voice speaking from somewhere in her own deep self: *'You cannot outrun me. You cannot escape what you have become. Like all things in this Black North, you are changing. Soon you will see. Soon you will know.'*

Oona knew this: she could relieve herself of the Stone, add it to cloak or satchel and have quiet in her mind. But Oona needed to know, to hear. The Stone had burned a place inside her, dark and hungering: she couldn't close herself to the promise of knowledge.

'You flee, but nowhere can be sanctuary for you now.'

Oona whispered to the Whereabouts, 'Faster. Please – take us faster on!'

And the Wolf found more energy to move them; tireless, sightless thing thundering through Black, across empty wastes peopled only with trees looking like lone travellers lost. But despite their speed, Oona wondered how she could be safe wherever she went. Somewhere or nowhere or middle of nothing, what did it matter? The Faceless had seen the Loam Stone and there'd be no rest in him till he and that Changeling had it . . .

The voice promised Oona: '*I will have it. You will bring the Nightmare Stone to me.*'

Enough, thought Oona, and she returned the Stone to her satchel, holding tighter to the Wolf and telling, 'Keep going now! Please don't stop for nothing!'

As they sped, Oona's thoughts settled on Merrigutt –

She'll find us, decided Oona. She said she would so she must.

But any decision was quickly contradicted, and Oona didn't know whether it was her own mind saying words, or something else –

'*But what if she was captured? And if not captured, then maybe lost? How will she ever discover anything in so much nothing, so much changed and so Black?*'

Maybe seeing would bring some sense: Oona opened her eyes, and had to wipe them clear of unwanted weeping. And once more dominating the world: Muddgloggs. Wandering, staggering, falling. Forging fresh valleys, beginning new hills, their limbs stacked high for fresh mountains – fallen length forming the ripple of blank horizons. Oona knew their heads would open and chests would part and throats split and all run wet with the altered course of old rivers. They would reshape the world on the whims of a King. And on the shoulders of the Muddgloggs, did she see a glimmering? The lights of houses, whole towns being carried? She imagined the townsfolk having

270

gone to their beds, mothers tucking children in tight, families closing their eyes for prayer and then welcoming in dreams. And then tomorrow, imagine their surprise – waking to discover themselves somewhere new, home no longer home, all familiar things changed.

'What if nothing's the same at all?' Oona asked herself – perhaps the Wolf too – in a voice so small she could scarcely hear the sound. 'If they've changed so much we won't be able to find the right way to the Burren.'

But the Whereabouts didn't answer.

More weight, more worry on Oona then: would the Wolf beneath her know these new ways? Could it truly lead her to anywhere with so much of their map in motion? Oona began to drift, but just before sleep enfolded, she let her fingers find once more the Stone, and she half-dreamed half-hoped a voice, one that complained and soothed in unequal measure: '*Didn't I tell you I'd find you, my girl? Didn't I say? Well, that'll show you something: that I'll never leave your side, I am coming for you – wherever you are in the dark, I will find you.*'

60

Oona awoke, and her first knowledge: she was no longer being moved. She shifted and all muscles itched and all joints creaked. She had an effort to make to open her eyes, a battle to lift her head and see – she'd bidden the Whereabouts Wolf to take them to the middle of nowhere, and that's where Oona found herself. Stranded in marshland, a landscape drowned, more light below than above, ground gifted with pools of cold luminescence. Oona couldn't see far – mist, familiar foe, had reappeared to obscure things. She blinked back moisture. Already her hair and cheeks and eyelids and lips were cold and dripping.

Oona cleared her throat and said to the Whereabouts, 'On North. Take me now to that place they call the Burren.'

But the Wolf moved slowly, paws sinking with each step, damp coat constantly bristling, each fibre of hair shivering and nose a ceaseless twitch – extraordinary senses all straining to discern a right way ahead. But it didn't seem to know which way the Burren was. And Oona thought, Well, how can it know? Mist-clogged or clear, who knows where is where in this Black? Oona tried anyway for a sharper tone like it might help, saying, 'Look: I said to you just keep heading on North and to the Burren, to the Cause. Now go!'

But the creature didn't run, wouldn't bolt like it had done to take them free of Loftborough. And Oona realised late that they were lost.

Then sound: a single loud, hollow note.

And suddenly Oona felt horribly surrounded by things –tall darknesses cut sharp, angled like ships that had strayed too far inland and become marooned in the marsh. It took minutes for Oona to understand, then she thought: *Worshipping Houses.* Then remembered what Merrigutt had said: '*Invaders have been doing the same up North – dragging all into the marsh and dumping them there, leaving them to sink.*'

So many! Oona tried to count . . . but only countless, some Worshipping Houses sunk to their steeple but others struggling more, only the tip of their spire still visible. Any move they made was sluggish, like they had some notion of trying to shift themselves from the marsh but couldn't. And it was the bells in their small towers that struck another hopeless note – some summons no Worshipper was going to answer.

Instinct made Oona look to the space above her shoulder, expecting to see a jackdaw perched there and to feel the clutch of claws and simple words she could follow, or disagree with. She felt a sob rise in her chest but told herself, Come on now! You're a Kavanagh, are you not? And Kavanaghs don't just sit and cry. I've been lost ever since I've left home – since I left Drumbroken I've not known any right way ahead. And that hasn't stopped me yet.

So once more Oona whispered to the Wolf, trying for that

softness she wasn't used to: 'We have to keep on going. I dunno how we're gonna get to where we want but we'll not get anywhere if we don't keep moving and moving fast! Please now.'

A moment of worry as the Whereabouts paused in its walking, then stopped completely. It tilted its head upwards. And then, appearing to take some notice of Oona's tone and resolve, the Wolf began: a quick trot first and then running proper, not as fast as before but better than plodding. And Oona felt herself sitting taller, pleased she'd managed to spur the creature on. She felt that same way – pleased, almost proud – until she realised there were other reasons for the Wolf's running. She realised this: they weren't alone.

On either side, Oona noticed things moving fast, hurtling – pale things leaping the Worshipping Houses or landing brief on roofs and walls and spires and then on. Then something else new, a fresh sound: her Whereabouts Wolf began to whimper, and Oona knew what things were bypassing them –

Another Wolf passed close by, seen suddenly and then gone. And then another, and more besides: Whereabouts Wolves countless as Worshipping Houses and everywhere, all on their way somewhere.

Oona leaned close to her own Wolf and whispered fierce, 'Follow them!'

61

Middle of nothing and nowhere and then freed – mist released them, graveyard of Worshipping Houses behind. Oona's Wolf suddenly stopped. Ahead was a broad plain of Black. Oona judged: maybe a half dozen miles? And beyond, the same Blackness reared: a row of mountains sliced the horizon, barring darkly the way ahead, each pinnacle relieved only by a pale and fraying collar: receding frills of old snow. The sight of the mountains made Oona colder, somehow sadder.

'*Melancholy Mountains,*' she said to herself.

Oona watched, dreamed: imagined that like so much in the North the mountains would soon stir, would be up and abandoning foundations however ancient, however deep, in favour of wandering. She waited. But this darkness stayed stubborn.

Across the expanse between her and the mountains were rushing the other Whereabouts Wolves – so many separate packs emerging from the dark to join, hundreds fast-flowing towards the space between peaks to disappear into deep shadow.

The Whereabouts Wolf beneath her trembled, whimpering louder and with such longing to be on its way and join its fellows. But it wouldn't move until Oona said.

Then from behind, in the mist – did Oona hear the pound of horses, call of Invaders? Oona said to her Wolf: 'Follow them into the mountains!'

And the Whereabouts raced.

No more than a minute and Oona was enclosed by mountain: sheer dark on either side and in front as they followed the other Wolves into a narrow pass. Then up – a slope of unstable-seeming stone that the Whereabouts attacked, finding the narrowest ledge to climb as up and up and up . . . up until Oona was afraid to look down, every fall of a paw sending a cascade of stone down into the dark. She held tighter, till her knuckles twinged. Clung closer to her Wolf till she was stiff with exhaustion.

Oona saw a chasm ahead and she almost screamed out for caution –

But they were across before she could start – a swift light leaping and they were on the other side and on, continuing. And hardly a sound – nothing beyond Oona's own shallow breathing and the faintest pant of Wolves and the whisper of cold over their coats.

Then the ledge they followed opened out, the pass widening: on a small platform, the Whereabouts Wolves paused to peer down. They began to whimper, near howl. The full moon had set itself sentry low in the sky, showing Oona a valley narrower than Drumbroken. It looked like a battle had been lost within it: a scatter of massive hunks of rock, most broken, some so tall they looked stacked. She saw the clear run of a river coming down from the mountains, slithering through.

'What happened here?' asked Oona.

A breeze stirred her hair, and brought her something – a snapping and billowing sound she couldn't attribute to anything. But as the Wolves resumed their descent – so fast they looked as though they were burrowing, a torrent of meltwater cleaving – Oona soon saw the source of sound: a crowd of tents being crack-snapped taut by the wind, and flags too being stirred. Did she imagine the flags were crimson? Closer still she saw the grey-white blemish of cinder where fires had been lit and let fail. And (almost there) Oona saw things she didn't know she was expecting till she saw them: dark figures, men standing as though awaiting her arrival. All unmoving, silent. And on their backs were strapped other men – fallen company that had been carried who-knew how many miles across the Black.

62

As soon as the Wolves arrived among strewn stone at the bottom of the valley, they dropped. Limbs folding neat, heads bowing and nuzzling close to one another for comfort, their muddied sides heaving with fatigue. Oona slipped from her own Wolf's back. Quick pat of her palm on its snout, and the animal collapsed. Their whimpering didn't falter though, and Oona thought that if the Whereabouts pack could grieve – could feel alone and isolated and lost – then this was their lament for a land so altered. The sound plucked at something in Oona, some similar strain of sadness, and she longed to lie down among them and rest. But then she saw the figures standing, others strapped to their backs – surely the Cause – and the old Kavanagh resolve returned.

'My name's Oona Kavanagh!' she called. 'From a good and decent family in the valley of Drumbroken! Me and my brother were both in the Cause back in the South, both fighting but when the Invaders came he –'

She stopped only feet from the nearest man – he hadn't moved.

'Hello?' she asked. Her voice sounded suddenly too loud, too weak – too desperate. And still no answer. For encouragement she sought the Stone: it was already lukewarm, but the shred of light at its centre was shrunken, reduced to almost nothing. And it had a new feeling in her hand: it had things it was desperate to impart, if she'd let it.

Oona cleared her throat and shouted, 'Who's standing there? *Tell!*'

The echo of her words went on and on, but still nothing from the unmoving Cause. The tents continued to snap, straining at pegs as though they wanted to flee. Oona noticed: the men all had rifles in hand and mouths opened wide as though roaring, triumph or celebration making them wild but making no sound.

Oona had to know. She reached out, and instantly the figure she'd only brushed began to dissolve – scalp collapsing into skull into neck into chest into torso into legs . . . and then he was only dust toiling in the air. Oona looked to the others, and then remembered: the boy on the Black Road at the end of the Perpetual Parade, what he had become. Oona spoke aloud to herself: '*The Echoes.*'

The Whereabouts Wolves sounded a louder howl, gently tearing open the silence – they'd come back to these men who were going to take them North to the Burren, to battle, but now no further. The creatures didn't know where to go, what to be, who in the Black to serve.

Oona addressed the dark: 'What's happened? What are these Echoes?' The Stone warmed Oona's hand. It said –

'*I will show you and I shall tell. You must sleep now, Oona Kavanagh. Sleep, and you shall see.*'

Helpless with longing, Oona lowered herself and was soon

279

lying among the warmth and press and low howl of the Wolves. Arms hugging her satchel tight and Loam Stone scorching her palms, Oona shut her eyes for sleep. She welcomed the dark, awaiting whatever answers.

63

'Follow me, Oona! Follow me now, sister dearest, and you shall see!'

Oona was hurrying, knowing that she was near to the heart of the blackened forest – she sensed secrets ready to be discovered. And it was Morris leading her. Almost just out of sight always, his heel seen and then vanishing, his fingers were lingering to curl with beckoning: *'Follow me, Oona! Follow quick!'*

Those watching eyes were ripening in branches. Widening, dark crimson. Oona ran on.

And finally she was somewhere, the place she'd been moving towards ever since she'd first held the Loam Stone in hand and heard the King's voice, his promise: she saw home, Kavanagh cottage, Morris standing by the window on tiptoe to look in, his back to her. Oona heard him whisper, *'Come see, sister! Come see!'*

Like they were younger, like a game.

Oona ran soft and reached the cottage and on tiptoe beside strained to see in. But the pane was misted, couldn't be seen through or wiped clear by any hand.

'Wait,' whispered the voice of her brother. But his voice

was less like himself, closer to that of Oona's nightmares – the King of the North speaking. And still he kept his face hidden as he said, *'Just listen now and watch – things will become clearer.'*

And then a shout from inside the cottage that Oona knew instantly as their da's voice. He was demanding –

'What the hell is happening to me, Mammy?'

Oona remembered only then how fond the man had been of raising his voice. She heard some soft reply but then her father shouted louder –

'Shut up you! Don't know what you're talking about! One of you hurry up and do something to fix it! It's creeping up the arm more by the minute! What are all your potions and bits for if you can't fix things like this?'

Another voice that she recognised in the first syllable as her Granny Kavanagh said, 'I don't know what this is, son. Never seen the like of it. Some North magic and I don't know how to –'

'Get away from me!' cried Oona's father. 'Bloody useless. And she's not much good either, is she? Sitting there, doing her pictures!'

Again: same soft reply.

'What was that? Speak up, woman!'

Oona heard Granny Kavanagh say, 'Leave her be, son. She'll be no use – she's a dreamer, that one. I told you that when you married her.'

'Do you hear that? Me own mother didn't want me to take you!'

Oona wanted so badly to see but still the window wouldn't clear. Then the voice of the King through the mouth of Morris told her, *'Accept what you are hearing, and then you will see.'*

Oona thought, Accept what? Mother and father arguing? Granny goading, not helping?

But as she thought it – dreamed it, same way she'd dreamed fire on the rooftop in Loftborough – the window began to allow her: like frost shrinking to show what was beneath, slow thaw, and Oona saw into the Kavanagh cottage. Saw this scene, twilit –

Mother seated at the family table, a sheet between her elbows, head lowered and hair fallen, paintbrush poised. Oona angled her head to see more. The painting was almost complete: picture of that unlikely land that rolled, emerald-coloured, scattered with thin trees of silver and small stone cottages. Oona's father stood close to her mother, leaning in but not in a way that meant love. He was breathless, all of him damp with sweat and shivering, one hand held delicately against his chest as though injured. And then he roared –

'*Speak, woman!*'

And father struck mother with his injured hand.

'No,' said Oona. She recoiled, almost toppled. The window began to cloud and she murmured, 'No. This is made up – nightmare, not real.'

'*The Stone tells no lies,*' said the voice of the King. '*Some might call it the Nightmare Stone, or the Darkness and the Seeing, but it tells only truth.*'

'Liar,' said Oona. She swallowed, pressing both palms to her face and roaring as loud as her father, 'You're lying!'

'*Some view the truth as nightmare,*' said the voice of the King, '*because they cannot bear to know it. But you must look. You must know – there is more to be seen.*'

Oona looked – the window remained opaque. No, she

thought. I want to see. Need to.

And things began to clear, slowly. And Oona heard – Father: 'Look at me now! What the hell's happening?'

Granny: 'I said I don't know, son, but calm down! Doing no good getting upset.'

Oona saw her father weeping frustrated tears.

'Some filthy magic them Invaders have put on me!' he shouted. 'Pray for me! Pray for it to stop!'

Then he held his hand to the shrine for the Sorrowful Lady: the hand was grey, like he'd rubbed it with cinder. Not just the hand but all the way to the elbow and crumbling, one finger already missing.

'Like it's rotting away,' Oona heard her father say. 'Turning to dust! Sorrowful Lady help me!'

Oona thought, *The Echoes.*

'And you!' her father shouted, returning suddenly to Oona's mother. 'What have you got to say?'

Oona's mother remained: same position, unmoving, as though nothing was happening.

'You think I'm stupid and don't realise?' her father said, teeth gritted, spittle flying. 'But I know things, woman. I'm not so slow! It was you that brought this North magic into this place, isn't it? It's you that's doing this because you want rid of me, isn't it? So you can go back to that filthy North? Back to that woman you were so friendly with? That's the answer. See – I'm not so slow!'

'Son,' said Oona's grandmother. 'Leave her be – she's no use to man or beast, that one.'

But the attention of Oona's father – the anger – was all for

284

Oona's mother: 'Why are you still painting that place? *Tell!*'

A long time of nothing. And then Oona heard her mother say in the lowest whisper: 'Because it is home, and soon it will be gone. Like everywhere in this Isle – it will change. Like you – it will Blacken, and rot.'

A breath, and Oona saw her father lift his hand to strike –

'Now you see,' said the voice of the King. *'Now you know.'*

Oona looked to Morris – at last he showed his face, and it was the face of their father.

'There is no escaping, ' whispered the mouth of her father, *'No denying this truth.'*

And same scene inside the cottage as out: hands raised to strike and Oona feeling the blow as it fell on her own back, in the same nightmared moment the same pain breaking on mother and daughter. In the same moment, same scream.

64

Some nightmares know no end. Oona opened her eyes, yet every dark thing remained. She felt a festering inside her, and waking did nothing to soothe it: she couldn't escape new knowledge. She had to move. She reached out but discovered nothing – the press of Whereabouts Wolves was gone. They'd left her. Again, Oona was alone.

No, the Loam Stone told her. It felt like the rawest wound on her palm. *Not ever alone, not now.*

And what Oona had seen she saw anew: Kavanagh cottage, Morris at the window peering in, father with his hand rotting and mother and grandmother and then –

'Ach look – she's awake now! Sure isn't she just the most delicate wee mite!'

Oona struggled to make sense of the world. She was being shadowed. What she'd taken for all those stacked stones, were they all leaning close?

'Must have had a bad dream, the look of her! Now don't go too close, ladies. We don't want to go and crush the poor dear. But let's look after her, surely. Cuddle her and keep her safe, should we not?'

And then a dark hand came reaching and grabbing and Oona was up, scrambling back with satchel thudding against her side, voices from everywhere saying –

'What's wrong with her? Skittish wee thing – like she's scared of us old beings! Maybe she's never seen a creature going through the Change?'

Oona tried to see more clearly –

Thickset pillars of stone, but did she imagine them like legs? Smooth bulges of stone – bellies? Great hunks with dark spaces that squirmed – surely eyes and mouths and nostrils? And – heart still a thundering thing wracked with pain – Oona was struck by a notion, a word: *Giants*.

Indeed, the Loam Stone told her.

'What she needs is a good looking after and that's the truth!' said the Giants, their flabby heads turning on stone shoulders; what must be hair crackling like straw and swinging like frost-stiffened rope. Each moment things made more sense: the Giants could move their arms, hands, but little else, too much of them covered in stone. Some didn't move at all, as though they'd transformed long before.

Oona said again, 'The Echoes?'

'What this one needs is a good family to cuddle and comfort her and that's that!' the Giants announced.

And again came hands reaching and Oona felt a scream suddenly build in her throat that needed to be released: 'Just get back and don't touch me! Leave me alone! I'm sick of this damn Black North and all the filthy things in it so stay away! If you touch me I'll cut your bloody fingers off and don't think I won't!'

And again her words echoed and echoed on, in her hand the Loam Stone blazing bright. Quiet. And then the Giants all said, whole lot crying loud –

'Bless and save us! In the name of the Hollow Mountain and all that's holy – the wee creature has the Nightmare Stone! That damnable plague of ages, surely to goodness! Enduring dark!

287

Worst dreams of the world and she has them in her wee hands!'

All? Whole lot? To Oona's ears it had sounded like the Giants spoke all together, but not in clamour – their voices rose and fell in unison, a low rumble forming words, collaborating on same sentences.

'We can't let her leave! Take her now!'

So many hands came snatching for Oona but they were futile – she was too fast, and the Giants too anchored by stone to shift themselves. She hardly had to dodge or duck to evade as they wailed on: 'Get her! Capture her or else!'

And then one voice spoke alone –

'You have nothing to fear from us, child, as you can see. No more reason to feel terror at the sight or sound of us than you do from the clouds in the sky! We are undergoing the Change. Like all in this Isle – we are not what we once were.'

Oona looked for the source of this speaking: to the highest tumble of stone. But not stone at all. Oona knew better than to judge quick so waited, and then sure enough saw: like a memory of a face, a ridge of sharp stone for a nose and above it two dark openings for eyes with somewhere darker below to speak from.

'Who are you?' asked Oona.

The other Giants chorused a reply –

'The Aged One, so she is! More ancient than any! And she'll know what to do for the best, oh aye. She'll tell us all what to be doing! But she doesn't have long left for chat, not long at all!'

Oona watched the high tumble of stone. Saw it shift, and the voice of the Aged One said –

'Such a burden to carry for such a delicate little thing as

288

yourself. That Stone: you do not know what power it commands, what terror could be wreaked in the wrong hands if you do not –'

'Look: I'm not *delicate* or nothing like it so stop calling me that!' Oona had heard enough and let anger again rouse her: 'And I know what this thing is! I know what it can do! I'm no fool.'

A fresh glimpse, cold needle driven into the heart: cottage, father, mother, grandmother . . .

'No,' said the ancient Giant, 'indeed you are no fool.'

Oona saw swathes of dark moss covering the Aged – like sleeves on stone arms, like a bodice across the chest, like a crown encircling a head that was neither skin nor stone. There was no separating what might've once been flesh and what was no longer.

'This Change you're going through,' said Oona. 'Is it the Echoes?'

The Giants all around groaned, moved as much as they could, but the Aged One said –

'No. The Change is something that our kind have gone through always. It is no shame, no cause for weeping: all things must know the Change, in the end. As the rain falls and freezes, the woods rise and fall and mountains turn to dust – all things transform. But these Echoes – they are not a change, but an ending. Like the horror of the remaking that is taking place all around us, the Echoes lead to nothing except destruction.'

And Oona thought: if the Cause are suffering from it, what might be happening to Morris?

'The only place safe now is here,' said the Aged. 'Only these Melancholy Mountains can be a haven for you, child.'

'No,' said Oona. 'I have to keep going. I need to warn people.'

'It cannot be halted,' said the Aged One. 'Our husbands in the Hollow Mountain have spent years trying to unravel the mystery of the Echoes, to discover its source or secret. But they have failed. And even our husbands – wise and well-read! – are not destined for long life in this remade world, longing only to sleep.'

'But we need to –' began Oona.

'The King is destroying so that he can raise his new Kingdom,' said the Aged One, words unstoppable. 'Smell the air – foul and dank with decay! Nothing is the same – the very foundations of things, the natural ways are being disrupted! How long has it been night? How long has the moon been full? How long will winter cling to the world? There is no stopping him.'

'There has to be,' said Oona. She held the Loam Stone tight, as thought she could squeeze answers from it.

'As long as the King of the North exists,' the Aged One told her, each word fading, the Change soon t o seize her completely. 'As long as that creature lives, then so will these Echoes. But know this too: so long as men have evil in their hearts, so long as this Cause persists so thoughtlessly, then the King of the North cannot be defeated. That Stone in your hand, child – if you cannot master the nightmares within, cannot take what truth it offers – then it will mean the end of everything.'

65

'There she is! Get her!'

Oona slipped the Loam Stone into her satchel, instinct hiding it. She watched: Invaders in hundreds were entering the valley, their cries loud and vicious –

'Don't let her go! Do whatever you have to do to get that Stone!'

Oona stood surrounded, Giants silent and not wanting to be seen. She didn't know what to do, not till she heard another voice calling –

'Oona! Hurry now – follow me!'

Familiar voice? Oona looked for it, and first saw only a face. But it was one she recognised as well as she'd know her own: she saw her own self there, and shades too of her father and grandparents. And mother, in smaller ways. Oona spoke what she saw, and the word nearly snagged in her throat: 'Morris?'

'Oona!' the face of her brother called back. He was standing not far, almost hidden behind stone. 'Quick! They'll be here soon – follow!'

And Oona had to obey.

She moved and Morris moved and they were soon running

among Giants fully Changed.

'Quick!' she heard Morris calling. 'Follow or they'll catch you!'

The cries of the Invaders were still heard, but Oona couldn't hear words. She kept running, following. She rounded a final stack of stone and saw the river running so clear, bright mirror for moonlight. And crouching beside, hidden behind a final stack of stone – her brother.

'Come closer!' he told her. 'Quick!'

Oona ran to him, falling beside and pulling her legs close, asking again, 'Is it really you?'

'It is,' he told her.

'Morris,' said Oona, and then again, 'Morris – I've seen so much. I've seen things. I –'

'I know,' he said. 'I know. Quiet now.'

Oona wanted to embrace him – not something she'd ever done, but felt she needed to. But –

'We've no time for that, dear sister,' he said.

'But,' said Oona, and was ashamed at the sob that rose to her lips. She swallowed, and could only repeat, saying again, 'I've seen things. Mammy – I think that . . .' And there stopped.

'What have you been shown?' asked Morris

Oona looked at him: his eyes were wide, dark despite the moon. She whispered: 'I've seen what them Invaders are doing to the North, what they've done already. The South could be in as bad a state by now. Everyone who wants to fight is going on North to some place called the Burren, so that's where we should go too. Us two together, just like back in Drumbroken.'

'Yes,' said Morris, sighing. The thinnest smile appeared on

his face, the neatest tear. 'You have been a good girl, Oona. But tell me this: I'd say you have something that could be used as a weapon against the Invaders. It is something they are seeking for their noble King and it was bequeathed to you, was it not? An object of immense power. Please tell me – do you still have it with you?'

Oona nodded. The river made a racket. She could hardly think her own thoughts let alone hear if any Invaders were near so she said, 'We should move on, Morris. Shouldn't wait here.'

Again – Morris was all sighs and small smiles.

'I am so very glad to hear you still have the Stone,' he said. 'Now – give it to me, will you dear sister?'

Oona half-stood, slowly, asking, 'How did you even know about it anyway? And since when did you start talking all fancy?'

Morris's face still just smiled that bland smile.

'Don't be difficult now,' he told her. 'Has that meddlesome creature – that filthy jackdaw – polluted your mind?'

'How do you – ?'

'I know more than you can imagine. And I swear to you now – you will give me the Nightmare Stone.'

Oona swallowed, stepping back and back until her feet met mortal cold in the river. Then she said, 'And I'd swear something too – on the Sorrowful Lady's head, you're not one bit my brother!'

Only then did Morris's smile slip: one side of his face began to collapse, all features avalanching, and in their wake was left white, only a cold blank. A face that was no face at all. And the being that Oona had taken for her brother, had wanted so much to be Morris, returned, was rising – limbs stretching and clothes falling away to show a uniform underneath. A small bird with crimson eyes alighted on the Faceless Invader's shoulder and in a small voice that burned with malice it said, 'Take her!'

66

Oona turned, ran. But hopeless –

Hands appeared, reaching out of nothing and grabbing and holding her: Invaders, unseen and patient among the dark, cloaked by Changeling skin. But Oona bit and kicked and screamed at them, 'Let me go, you pack of animals!' And in the scuffle they tore her mother's cloak from her body, ripped the satchel from her grasp to search it. 'That's mine! Give it back you fools! Give it back or else I'll –'

'Else nothing,' said the bird on the Faceless Invader's shoulder. 'Quiet now. No need for all this fuss – this is a solemn place, after all.'

'Here, I found it!' called one of the Invaders, suddenly. He held the Loam Stone in one hand and Oona's satchel in the other. He couldn't have looked happier.

'Give it to me!' said the bird, lifting its wings and shaking them, a sharp crackle, peevish impatience. The Faceless extended one arm – its reach snaked all the way to the Invader and snatched the Stone from him.

'We have it now,' said the Changeling, shifting on the Invader's shoulder. 'The most powerful object in this world, and now it belongs to the most powerful being – the great King of the North!'

'And this too,' said the Invader who still held Oona's satchel. On the barrel of his rifle he'd hooked a half-closed claw, bruised, bloodied – what Oona had stolen from the Mother of the Briar-Witches.

'And that too could be useful,' said the Faceless.

The Invader – not so happy at so gruesome a sight – returned the claw to Oona's satchel.

'You don't know what to do with that Stone!' Oona told the Faceless. 'It's mine by right – been in the Kavanagh family for years! I'm the only one that can –'

'I said quiet!' cried the bird, breathless, eyes still on the Stone. 'You are to be afforded a great honour, child: we shall escort you North, and first you shall be of great use in gaining some information of us from the remaining Giants. You shall witness the fall of the last members of the Cause as we destroy their haven at the Burren. And finally – to the edge of everything, to the City of Echoes, to meet your King. You will show him what power this Stone possesses, and you shall show him how to make his nightmares a reality.'

Oona loosed a final call: 'Like hell I will!'

And in answer – in support, Oona was sure – the Loam Stone blazed brightest white.

Then a flood of grey-white-silver mud: the clearing where Oona and the Invaders stood was engulfed by Whereabouts Wolves. They charged, knocking Invaders aside as Oona kicked and slapped and bit on the hands that held her.

She was dropped so ran –

But Oona wasn't far before gunshots sounded –

Grey-white-silver-mud, then red: the Wolves falling, broken.

'Get her!' cried an Invader.

'She's escaping!' shouted another.

'No she isn't,' Oona heard the Faceless say. 'She will not leave – she will not be allowed to.' And Oona knew this truth: the Loam Stone wouldn't let her leave. It wouldn't be abandoned.

She wasn't far into her fleeing before she was stopped – her heart or someplace near it was seized.

She felt as though she might retch. Then Oona only wilted, falling against stone.

Next thing felt – a cold hand enclosing her waist, lifting her. Through tear-soaked eyes she saw the bird on the Faceless Invader's shoulder spread its wings and throw its head back and cry an appalling cry. An answer came in no more than heartbeat – descending hush, a quiet that laid itself with the softness of snow as one of the carriages of the Coach-A-Bower swept into their midst and stopped. Its insides were empty, dark, and awaiting a new passenger.

'No,' murmured Oona, but barely a protest. 'No.'

Ropes were knotted around her wrists, a sack slung over her head and tightened and another dragged up to enclose her squirming body. And Oona's only feeling then was of slipping – into cold, desperation as she was added, a lost soul, to the carriage of the Coach-A-Bower.

The Faceless Invader stepped into the carriage beside, perhaps impervious to any feeling. And Oona heard the order of the Carrion Changeling: 'Coachman – we have the Nightmare Stone! Take us now to the blazing heart of the new Kingdom – to the Hollow Mountain!'

67

A kind of movement that mortals rarely know: the travel of dreams, miles conquered in moments and acres overcome in the space of a shallow breath, seasons crossed like narrow streams. This was the travel of the Coach-A-Bower. It made a mockery of time and distance, and death. And Oona was imprisoned inside, unmoving, felt encased in the blackest of black ice. Only one thought kept Oona's mind from slipping whole into the dark, one dreamed-of thing: Merrigutt. And a hope: that somehow the jackdaw would find her.

And suddenly they were no longer moving. The carriage stopped, door eased open, and Oona felt herself being lifted, carried with such care. She felt she should struggle, give some protest somehow, but she didn't. Instead Oona put all her concentration on listening . . . a few moments more and she heard a *whisper-hiss-hush*: sound of rushing water. Then she struggled.

The Faceless, carrying her, soothed, 'Settle now, child. No need at all for protest. Have I not said how very important you are? No harm will come whilst I am with you. I will keep you to the ends of the earth. Further than that – to my King's city at the edge of everything.'

And then Oona was laid down with such delicacy.

A hollow knock – elbows and knees against wood. Oona writhed and found what was beneath her willing to shift, almost drift, but she had little room for moving – a small boat, she guessed. It shifted under the arrival of another, the Faceless Invader joining. More sound to be interpreted – she guessed at the soft touch of a paddle on water, and then they were moving on once more, fast.

'Oh, just wait until you see it,' she heard the Changeling say. The voice of the bird was low, a sound barely above the scurry and splash of water. 'You will marvel at it! It is just the beginning of the new Kingdom. It will be the King's greatest outpost, where I shall oversee things as his Captain!'

Oona said nothing, too busy thinking: What about escape? Throw myself from the boat into water, but how deep?

'No one can save you now, child,' the bird assured her in the same soft whisper. 'Do not contemplate anything foolish. And why miss the chance to see things that you have never seen before? Such marvels! Just wait . . . just wait . . .'

Minutes more of dark and her own fruitless thoughts, and then the sack was suddenly torn from Oona's head. She was content to breathe as a beginning, welcoming air like that moment of blessed emergence from the nest of the Briar-Witches. Cold bit – no cloak of her mother's to protect her. Then she looked, and saw first a former-forest on either side of the river. Another miserable sight of destruction – only sawed stumps where trees had once been. But among them moved things. Figures? People, Oona decided. But all silent.

'We had to put the men and women of the North to some good use,' said the Changeling. 'And they are hard workers, no doubt. Very keen in their wanting to serve their King.'

Men and women, of course no children. But whether male or female – mother or father or grandparent – Oona couldn't have told. There was too much Black on the people, their movements so slow and selfsame that there was no telling anyone apart. Made blank and anonymous by the dark, they were attacking any remaining tree with hatchets, snapping and stacking boughs.

Then the bird on the Faceless Invader's shoulder cried out with a reverence Oona thought ridiculous: 'Behold!'

Oona had to twist herself to see . . .

Not so far off that it could be called beyond – a singular dark, final peak of the Melancholy Mountains soaring sharp against night-sky. It was scattered with enough white light to make Oona's eyes cringe and weep, scattered too with enough crawling dark to make her wonder. But for all that was striking about the sight, the most disquieting thing was this: the slopes had been eaten- in and torn out, most of the remaining mountain bulging above and below. Hour-glass-shaped, impossible-seeming. No, thought Oona. Possible, but only with some powerful magic to bolster it.

'The Hollow Mountain,' said the bird on the Faceless Invader's shoulder. 'Palace of the Ponderous Giants. Or I should say – formerly the Palace of the Ponderous Giants.'

Closer then, Oona could watch what darkness wandered, working on the surface – many Muddgloggs were helping to dismantle the Hollow Mountain, earth remaking earth. And again closer – nearer and almost there – Oona saw Muddgloggs embedding narrow towers on the mountainside, great cylinders of granite that were already lit from within. The acrid taste of smoke settled on Oona's tongue, darkness streaming from the mountain to collect in the sky.

River narrowing, the mountain admitting them into an echoing dark, a sudden roar sounded that Oona's imagination took for the Hollow Mountain itself – furious protest at its own transformation.

'Ah,' said the Changeling. 'It sounds as though the Ponderous Giants are ready to speak.'

68

Oona had only a dim sense of activity ahead . . . and then suddenly such glare and din and industry from all sides. An enormous cavern opened around her, a space bounding with so many echoes of echoes of echoes that she couldn't know where they began, where the first stroke fell or first mouth hollered or first spark spawned a flame. And so much fire: in the hands of Invaders heating metal and hammering, in furnaces overfed with felled trees, and in the hold too of countless soldiers hanging from ropes, working at openings that awaited the arrival of more lit Towers. The heat and stench was colossal, stung – so much smoke hopelessly seeking places to escape through. And some stranger activity – a tearing out, ripping of many helpless things. *Books*, Oona realised. Huge volumes as high as a man, their many pages being given a cursory glance then torn loose and added to the nearest fire.

'Two caverns were revealed when we started our work!' the small bird on the shoulder of the Faceless had to shout. 'Two chambers, one beneath the other! So it made perfect sense to sculpt the Hollow Mountain into something more impressive, something more beautiful! This lower cavern will be a military base and the upper shall be my seat of command!'

The river threaded on, carrying Oona into the midst of everything, commands flying –

'Fast over here with that gunpowder, lads!'

'Need more ballast for this, boys! Keep it moving, keep it steady!'

'Gimme a hand with this, quick! Right men – all hands to this and *lift*!'

And the results: rifles and pistols stacked, knives bound in leather and packed, cannons rolled, ammunition stockpiled . . . all the blunt and unforgiving instruments of battle being formed.

'As I think you'll agree,' said the Faceless, 'we have more than adequate resources to defeat any Cause that might seek to oppose us.'

Oona couldn't disagree. She felt a single tear trace a cold track down her cheek. She thought: *war*. Everywhere she looked the word screamed its promise.

Another sound: bone-quivering and world-shuddering and, to Oona at least, heartbreaking. She heard the Changeling say, in a tone trying for softness, 'Now what are they doing to those Giants? Why can't they just leave the poor creatures alone?'

Oona saw a large group of Invaders clustered close to the wall of the cavern, and above them, and taller than any twenty of the Invaders if they'd stood on each other's shoulders: the male Giants of the Hollow Mountain. A dozen, all bald and brute-ugly and huddled tight together and bound around the ankles with iron and leather. But not much like the women Oona'd seen – these men looked more like infants overgrown, skin all bloated and in places blackened, naked but for rags knotted loose around their waists. And they were weeping. They were, Oona knew, the source of the terrible roaring. She heard words from the cluster of gathered Invaders, teasing –

'You think you're powerful just cos you're big, do you?'

'Think we're scared of you?'

'Big helpless babies, that's all you are!'

More roars. And roars of laughter too from the mob as the Giants tried for escape, attempting to scale the wall but with large, blunt, cumbersome fingers – no relief, no way free. And the Invaders continued to revel, prodding the male Giants with torches and crude brands, singeing skin so that the whole place shook with a Giant anguish.

Then the Faceless Invader added his own roar to the cavern –

'Cease this at once! Get away from those creatures!'

As though scalded the rabble fell back, most dropping their fire and trying to distance themselves. Surprise, some shame, but Oona noticed some keeping close their conviction. The leaders who'd led the humiliation, who didn't see a bit of harm in it – they refused to be cowed.

The boat that had brought Oona and the Faceless at last reached rock. Invaders were swift in their stumbling forwards to help – a rope thrown and caught, slipped through an iron ring fixed into one of the largest rocks and the Faceless left the boat in one long stride. To Oona's eyes he appeared to grow taller as he stalked up the slope towards the group of Invaders. Without forewarning he stopped and struck one of the soldiers, knocking them backwards – a blow with as much ease in it as Oona had seen in Loftborough. The soldier didn't get up. And

304

that crimson-eyed bird spoke with an anger Oona would've attributed to a creature much larger: 'So you bully and torment these creatures as though you were back in the playground? Do you not remember that this was their mountain before it was our own? We should show them respect!'

Alone in the boat Oona made small moves, testing the ropes that held her, squirming free of the sack that enclosed her bottom half, seeing how possible escape might be. But one Invader on the shore saw and aimed his gun like he was going to shoot. She stopped.

'That's a good girl,' said the Invader. He tried a sarcastic smile. 'And if you think you're going to be going anywhere without my say-so, then you're a bigger fool than you look.'

So Oona stayed, silently cursing, raging. She listened –

'A report please, Corporal,' said the Faceless, and an Invader stumbled forwards, a branch of fire still snarling in his hand. 'Tell me: how goes the interrogation?'

'Sir,' said the Corporal, hardly knowing where to look, not sure whether to direct speech to the Faceless face or the bird on its shoulder. 'Sir, we've been trying to get them to tell us about how to reach the Burren, but they ain't talking. And we've looked through all their scrappy books but we can hardly read the writing in half of them, let alone understand any of it!' He looked to the fire in his hand, cleared his throat. 'So we thought more forceful methods were needed to get them answering.'

'*Forceful*?' said the Faceless. He took the torch from the Invader's hands and closed one large hand over the flames to snuff them. 'Or *barbaric*? We do not want to lower ourselves

305

to the levels of the others who live on this Isle, do we?'

'No sir,' said the Corporal.

The Faceless took a step towards the Giants and their whimpering rose once more and they pressed themselves closer to the wall, to one another's comfort, fingers fumbling at toothless mouths.

'We have been patient with you,' said the Changeling. 'We have treated you, I believe, with the utmost of respect. However, now my patience has been worn to its thinnest. I am going to ask you questions, and you are going to answer. Do we understand each other?'

But the Giants their had ready words, a way of talking that sounded to Oona like the oldest rhetoric, querulous: 'What right do you have to come here and disturb our quiet contemplation inside the Hollow Mountain? You being a creature born of broken earth and wicked magic. A being plucked like a weed by that creature on your shoulder, who you have bent to your will, that speaks for you? You, who has no soul but only a bitter will! You, who has known no love nor affection but only hate! You have come and you have broken! You have destroyed and opened these sacred caverns to the whims of a cruel world! What right do you have to commit such a crime? What authority do you have over us?'

The Giants had all spoken more bravely than Oona would've reckoned. And like their wives: spoke so closely together that it sounded almost like rough song. The Giants went on: 'You serve the creature that came across the sea! That King who is not Kingly, not meek nor mild! Oh King of un-Kingliness! No righter of wrongs! No doer of nobler deeds!

306

No writer of wondrous –'

'Quiet!' shouted the Changeling. 'Cease this lamenting, I've had enough of it!'

The bird abandoned the Faceless Invader's shoulder to circle, then return. And as in Loftborough – it had become something larger, darker, eyes both blistering.

'Answer me this now,' it said. 'The place a dozen miles North from here, the place the river flows towards and you barbarians call the Burren: how do I locate it, and how do we enter?'

The Giant's reply, in delicate harmony: 'Why do you wish to know the way into a place of such safety, of such healing? Why would you seek such solitude as it provides, that place of oldest North magic, where contemplation is prized and –'

'I said *enough*!' shouted the bird, and everything shook, everything stopped. All work within the Hollow Mountain ceased, every eye and all attention drawn to this confrontation. But Oona knew – no matter how much questioning, how much demand or threat, these Giants wouldn't tell. Wouldn't, maybe couldn't: perhaps the answers were so buried so deep they wouldn't rise, couldn't be spoken. And some other had the very same thought –

'Maybe they don't even know, sir,' said one of the Invaders. 'They're that old, maybe they can't remember?'

'How dare you!' cried the Giants, and Oona saw them begin to rise. 'We know all stories and tales and ways of this Isle! All legend that we have recorded and you now see fit to burn! Have we not sat in the dark within this mountain for generations, turning over all mysteries, poring over all notions large and small? Have we not – ?'

'*Enough,*' said the Faceless one, interrupting once more. The Giants shrank. A pause, and the darkest colour seeped into the bird's feather, into its voice: 'Whether you wish to remember or not, I will have the information I need. Perhaps barbaric methods are indeed necessary.' The Changeling turned crimson eyes on Oona, and said, 'It is time to test the truth of legend: we shall see now how powerful and persuasive this Nightmare Stone can be.'

69

'I'll bring her,' said the Invader who'd been keeping keen watch on Oona, and he was as careless and as rough as he could manage in retrieving: by the hair or arm or wherever, dragging. But Oona refused to make any sound or scream, didn't want to satisfy him. He dropped her by the Faceless Invader's feet.

'Untie her,' said the Changeling.

Some hesitation, but the same Invader yanked the knife from his belt. He gave Oona a long look as though he could do what he liked with the blade, with her. A jerk of his hand and he'd cut her bonds. Oona rose, watching the Faceless take the Loam Stone from its tunic: it was utterly devoid of light. But at the appearance of the Stone the Giants began to shiver and a low and wordless moan rose in their flabby throats.

The Changeling told Oona, 'Your task is simple, Oona Kavanagh: you are going to use this Stone to extract the truth I need from these Giants. And you are then going to tell me that information. Do you understand?'

Oona didn't offer answer. She didn't want to touch the Stone. In truth was afraid of the thing and what new disgrace it might show. So she cleared her throat to say, 'I can't use it like that.'

'Silly girl,' said the bird. 'How can you know, if you haven't yet tried?' The Faceless offered the Stone.

And all Oona had seen and wished she could unsee squirmed to the surface of her mind as the shred of light squirmed wild within the Loam Stone. She shut her eyes, but no solace. No choice, she knew: the Stone was her possession whether she wished it or not.

So Oona opened her eyes, and stepped forwards to reclaim it.

Instantly: as though their separation had been a trauma and it had so many things it was anxious to share, the Stone showed Oona too much. Images all swift as light glancing on grey water –

Cold fire –

Shattered sea –

Broken moon –

Echoes –

Screaming –

Clawing shadow –

Dust –

Everywhere and everyone dust –

Isle ending –

And as with the landlady in Loftborough, Oona locked eyes with the Invader who'd taken her from the boat and was shown nightmares: he was powerless and cowering in a forest with Blackened trees, tangled boughs bearing flame but burning with a chill, soundless fire . . .

Oona forced herself to withdraw. And she saw the Invader anew: whether he held rifle or blade or both, he was terrified. Was doing what he was doing because he was scared of what would happen if he didn't.

Oona looked quick to another Invader and (strange – somehow not a surprise) she saw the same nightmare in his mind: Black forest writhing with the same white flame. And fast, Stone growing hotter in her hands, she focused on another Invader, and then the next, and next, and another. And all were harbouring the same nightmare, all besotted by an identical fear.

'Ask them now!' cried the Changeling, and Oona was forced to return fully. She looked up, eyes drawn to the crimson gaze of the bird. What nightmares waited there, Oona wondered? But no matter how long she looked, she saw nothing. Their crimson held no more than surface: no truth, no nightmare. And to Oona this was more terrifying than anything.

'Ask them!' the bird shrieked, wings extending, trembling.

Oona shifted her feet and faced the Giants. She took a breath, then looked –

Such nightmares were seething in the Giants! So many that she couldn't discern any single thing, their worst imaginings engulfing her like sudden tide, collective fear, worry, remorse and mystification rushing. The only thing Oona did know: all their nightmares were of destruction and ending and plague and withering. All, she realised, were symptoms of the same: the destruction of their cherished Isle.

'Well?'

The voice of the bird came from far off, could almost have been ignored, but the grip that enclosed Oona's arm couldn't.

'What did you see?' the Changeling asked. 'Did they show you the Burren? Did they tell how to enter it? How to tear through the old magic that surrounds the place?'

Oona didn't know what the Burren looked like, but she did

311

know one thing. Unexpected, simple – how she was going to escape.

'I did see something like that,' said (lied) Oona. 'I need to try again though. Their thoughts are all over the place, nothing clear enough for me to see.'

Slowly, he released her.

'Very well,' said the Faceless. 'Look only once more. And this time, you will find the truth I need. Or we may have to revert to the use of those methods more appropriate to the barbaric kind of this Isle.'

Oona felt the shuffle and smile of the surrounding Invaders – she didn't doubt their willingness, the eager and terrified torturer slumbering in all.

So Oona looked once more –

Again the same press and onslaught of Giant nightmares: rising fire and ocean, earth cracking open as it had already done at the Divide, dust and echoes and suffocating quiet . . . but this time Oona had decided not just to watch, but to dream. If I could dream fire in Loftborough, she thought, and command that, then maybe I can do more? She knew what the Giants feared, so knew what darker things would inflame. The Stone boiled in her hand, sending fierce encouragement everywhere, power trickling into limb and head and frantic heart, and Oona gave the Giants fire: wavering sheets like she'd seen in Innislone. And then water: as Merrigutt had told, the sea sent storming over land when the King's City had first risen. And then earth: land rising and walking, so much tearing that the ground was a mire of dark places to fall. And then the worst truth: the Hollow Mountain itself, the dark eating in, the end of knowledge as books were torn and burned. And this last was the spark that started everything –

The Giants roared, '*Stop!*' and its force sent Oona staggering backwards, falling, but she didn't release the Loam Stone. Oona looked up, held the Stone high and persisted with nightmares, showing the Giants a North swept clear of every tree and township, every roaming or squirming or foraging thing lost, destroyed, the whimper of the Whereabouts Wolves rising on dark-choked air and their wives, the Giants in the pass, nothing but dust –

The cries of the Invaders –

'Hold them back!'

'Shoot them!'

'Use the fire! Stop them!'

But the Giants were rising. So small and sobbing one moment, fit for nothing, and then an alarming height: from crouch to stand, any fold of flesh stretching taunt, muscles thickening beneath. The Invaders scattered, hurling what fire they had but seeing it deflected, dying. And the Giants roared a rumble of such words: 'You shall not destroy nor decimate all that has been here for centuries, all that history has woven! We shall not sit and watch this land reduced to ash and cinder! To bid the land to rise, for generations to be exhumed and defiled when they wish to lie dead – such a crime!' And they had only to move their feet to rip themselves free of bonds, had only to reach to tear hunks of dark rock from the walls and hurl them into the air – their aim precise, their power peerless, they struck Invader weapons on the farthest side of the cavern, shattering cannons and firearms and sending soldiers into a scatter.

Oona decided she'd better move herself – in a crawl she went, eyes on narrow river, small boat, thoughts fixed on escape.

She heard the bird on the Faceless Invader's shoulder screaming, 'Shoot them! Bring them down!'

Perhaps some gunshots, but not enough to slow the Giants: skin so tough, hardening almost to stone like their wives, deflecting any bullet.

Then the bird's screech of wondering: 'The girl, where is she? Do not let her escape with the Stone!'

Oona ran.

She heard Invaders throw the call to one another to stop her, and Oona was snatched at, but when any Invader came near she held her defence high, Loam Stone bringing to their minds the shared nightmare she knew terrorised them. They cringed like uncared-for children, all uncomprehending.

Oona reached the river and leapt into the boat she'd been brought in. But of course one –

'Didn't you listen to me earlier on, girl? I said you weren't going to be going anywhere!'

Same Invader who'd taken her from the boat took her once more, same fashion – hair and arm and whatever he could grab and Oona squirmed and bit and in the struggle she dropped the Stone, hearing its hard clatter in the bottom of the boat. She formed a fist and caught the Invader on the side of the skull with it. He cursed her up and down and Oona had a moment's release to reach for the Stone.

'You're going nowhere,' the Invader told her, taking her by the ankle. 'If we're all gonna die in this mountain, then so will you!'

But no giving in for Oona Kavanagh: she had a last surge of

strength and kicked out and feeling the Invader's grip loosen she reached for the Stone, laying a touch on it with only tips of her fingertips. She'd no other thought or command or wish in her head, only this dream: *Evelyn Merrigutt and all the jackdaw women – save me.*

'No escape!' said the Invader, flipping Oona on to her back and pressing a knee to her chest, blade to her throat. 'You've got nothing to save you now, my girl!'

'I wouldn't be so certain about that, young lad.'

A single jackdaw alighted on the rock that did the job of mooring the boat. Jackdaw, then old woman – a blink and the black and grey of the jackdaw was replaced by the black and grey of Evelyn Merrigutt who plucked a handful of that scarlet powder from her clothes and tossed it into the Invader's face. He screamed, holding both hands tight to his eyes as he lunged blind, blade slashing air as Merrigutt stood aside, calm as anything, and let the Invader topple scalp-over-soles into the river.

Oona and the old woman looked at one another.

A moment, and then the rest: dozens of jackdaws stormed through the cavern, attacking the Invaders and crying –

'Ruin our North, will you? Monsters!'

'Ruffians and thieves and pillagers and nothing else!'

'Foolish and proud and ridiculous men remaking the world!'

And the attention of the Invaders was split between birds and Giants, not knowing what to aim for or where best to fight, but then one screech outdid all: 'Stop the girl!'

The Invaders closest ran for Oona but Merrigutt tossed more scarlet powder –

Up soared flame from the ground, keeping the soldiers back.

'Not just as good as you are with the fire,' said Merrigutt, looking at Oona, 'but it'll have to do. Now, my girl – I say we get the hell out of here!'

Both into the boat then, Merrigutt flicking (what looked like last) supplies of scarlet powder at the rope that held them to the shore. It sizzled, snapped, and Oona found the paddle to push them off as rock fell everywhere, exploding on water, soaking them. Oona struggled, setting sight on the way out – a dark tunnel she fought towards.

'Such an easy escape? Surely you didn't think it so?'

The bird with blazing eyes landed on the stern, leaving the Faceless Invader standing on the shore. It said, 'You think you can defeat the King with mere powders and tricks?'

'No,' said Merrigutt, 'but I know very well how to deal with an old bird.' And she snatched up the sack that had been used for covering Oona's head and enclosed the bird in it, tightening its top and hurling it into the air. It went high, landing on the opposite shore. Oona watched for the Faceless, worried: without the bird, what was it? Only this: a puppet with its strings cut, powerless. Arms scarecrow-stiff, the Faceless collapsed backwards.

'Keep going,' said Merrigutt. She laid a hand on Oona'a shoulder. 'Almost there.'

Oona drove the paddle into the river, pulling them towards the tunnel. Almost at it, close to almost free –

But gunfire –

And so many jackdaws falling, transforming into women as they struck stone –

And Giants in a storm of smashing rock –

An Invader shouted, 'There! Stop that boat!' Another ordered, 'Blow it up!'

A fizzle of fuse and seconds later a cannon-blast collided with rock: above the tunnel, everything began to fall.

Invader: 'We've got them!'

Another: 'Kill the old one, we need the girl alive – King's orders!'

The tunnel was blocked by tumbling stone, the prow of the boat arriving to bump pointlessly against. Trapped, Merrigutt chose this time to say, 'I've none of my powders left and no other trick up my sleeve. It's up to you now, my girl – show me proper what power you've learned from that Stone.'

70

'I dunno if I can,' said Oona, looking to the Stone still lying by her feet. 'What I've seen – too much. It showed me –'

'It's shown you all the very worst I bet,' said Merrigutt, speaking over. She took Oona's hand. 'Things you didn't want to see. But I'll tell you one thing – if you can use it to bring me from another place to this place just by dreaming, then you can keep going and not let us just get killed or captured by this shower of fools.' Merrigutt took Oona's face in her hands. 'Don't let this be the end of it. Not after all the Black we've ran and walked and crawled through.'

More jackdaws were dropping, not returning to the air –

More Giants cowering under the assault –

An Invader close by called, 'We're not letting you go, girl! But old woman or whatever you are – you better say your goodbyes now!'

And then Oona saw with sudden clarity – the Invader's finger tightened around the trigger. Oona snatched up the Stone and snatched too at any dream and a limb of compacted earth with tree and bush and briar sprouting like brittle whiskers along its length suddenly thrust itself through a gap in the mountain. It swept the Invader aside and any gunshot went astray.

The arm of a Muddglogg waited. Awaited instruction, Oona realised.

And she saw in the eyes of all the Invaders the same thought: Is our own magic turning on us?

'Now this is more like it, my girl!' cried Merrigutt, and she gave Oona such a smile.

And Oona only had to imagine it and more Muddglogg arms came reaching, snatching and sweeping through the air to send Invaders tumbling as the Giants called, 'The girl has the Nightmare Stone! She has learned how to use it! Protect her!' Then one of the Giants crouched close, slipped massive hands beneath the boat and lifted it clear from the river. He huddled it close to his massive chest to shield Oona and Merrigutt.

But still there was Invader gunfire – made the Giant shudder, groan, stumble.

Oona said nothing, only imagined: the arm of the first Muddglogg she'd brought began to move towards them –

Another cannon-blast made everything shake and the Giant that held them was hit –

'That's one's got the girl!' shouted an Invader. 'Load that cannon and fire again!'

'Hold tight!' Oona told Merrigutt, the Giant doing its best to lift them high as the Muddglogg was there to take, securing a hand beneath the boat. And as the boat left the hold of the Giant, Oona heard their collective voice rumble with words: 'Remember this, inheritor of the Stone – in the end it is not nightmares that prevail, but instead dreams that defeat the dark.'

'*Fire!*'

A final cannon-blast struck the Giant hard over its heart. A sound like shattering rock, and he toppled. And the sight of the Giant splayed – of its body shrinking small once more – made Oona stronger. Before they were withdrawn on the hand of the Muddglogg, Oona whipped her arm upwards and willed the river into a rise that swamped the Invaders who began to flee through whatever discoverable opening would let them, on their way still harried by claw and beak of the jackdaws. And then, almost free of the Hollow Mountain, Oona heard such echoes: a voice so close but coming from a City across the sea, a screaming from the edge of everything –

'You will regret this, Oona Kavanagh! Soon I will show you such dark, such secrets, and you will wish you had never been born! You think you are close to the end now, close to triumph? I promise you this – your nightmares have not yet even begun.'

71

From among stars, on the palm of a Muddglogg, Oona could see the mountain itself beginning to end. All magic was deserting: like Innislone burning, she knew the peak's time was short, would soon be nothing.

'Need to get away from here,' said Merrigutt.

So Oona directed the Muddglogg in a shout: 'Take us to the river!'

It obeyed with long strides, Oona feeling as though they were crossing not just the miserable Black of below any more but the exhilarating black of the sky. She looked to Merrigutt – the old woman's grip was tight on the edge of the boat. Oona said, 'Now you've got to admit it – this is just a wee bit amazing.'

'I never knew,' said Merrigutt suddenly, slowly. 'Never knew proper till I saw you on that rooftop in Loftborough how powerful that Stone is. Never knew such things could be done in the world.'

The look the old woman gave Oona: same as in Loftborough, an expression of awe, fearful wonder. And like possession and onus of the Stone, it was something Oona didn't think she deserved. All the while, the Loam Stone stayed hot in her hand. But she could bear it, its heat indistinguishable from the heat and hammer of her own heart.

'Is that the end of them?' asked Oona. 'The Invaders?'

'Not a bit,' said Merrigutt. 'They're hell-bent on getting to the Burren.'

'The Giants didn't tell them how to get in,' said Oona.

'They'll not need that knowledge,' said Merrigutt. 'My guess is the magic around the Burren won't be for lasting. It's an ancient place, but too much has changed – the protection around will be fading.'

Their obedient Muddglogg stopped suddenly, one leg planted on either side of the river. It sank, lowering their boat and laying it with such gentleness on the surface of the river. Straightaway the current took: around one bend tight as a crook, swift, and then in among trees untouched.

'You cannot escape what you have seen, Oona Kavanagh. The sight of it will tear you apart.'

No, Oona told the King: not saying, just thinking. I won't let it kill me like it's done to others. And I'll destroy this Stone before I'd let you have it.

'Fool! It cannot be destroyed. It is a thing that thrives on nightmares, so how can it end? There is enough dark in a person to sustain the Stone for a lifetime: it shall endure, survive even as you slowly are destroyed.'

Oona said nothing more. Only let herself sink, finally. At last let the Loam Stone slip from her fingers to tumble into the bottom of the boat. She shut her eyes.

'You'll be fine enough now,' said Merrigutt. One of the old woman's hands went to Oona's shoulder, and the other she

322

laid on Oona's forehead. 'You're flushed as anything – you need to calm yourself.'

Oona wet her lips, wanting to speak. But she didn't know which words.

Merrigutt told her, 'Aye, just rest yourself. There's not so much to worry about now, my girl.'

'He's been speaking to me,' Oona confessed. 'The King of the North – I've been hearing him in nightmares. It's been like he's been calling to me, leading me. He wanted me to see things.'

'Quiet now,' said Merrigutt. 'These are words for later.'

But Oona was shivering all over like sudden disease had taken. And with sorrow she realised this: without the Stone in hand, she was worse. She needed it, had to have knowledge, and perhaps power. Without it she felt almost lost. But Oona resisted, instead holding tighter to Merrigutt and talking aloud all secrets she needed to tell –

'I've seen things. From my family. Horrible things. I don't know whether to believe them.' She wanted to be contradicted, craving disagreement from the dependably disagreeable old woman, but –

'I believe you,' said Merrigutt. She sighed. 'There's some things we learn and we wish we hadn't, my girl. And it changes you, but there's nothing we can do about that. And if we're in the mood for airing things, I should say that I've not been the most honest with you that I could've been.'

Oona opened her eyes. The old woman was looking off into the gloom. Oona didn't know if she could endure any more harsh truths. Instead she asked, 'What am I now? I'm a Kavanagh still, but . . .' Oona tried to feel the familiar comfort of the name, that sure sense of somewhere belonging. 'I'm a Kavanagh. And I –'

'I'll tell you what you are, my girl,' Merrigutt interrupted. 'You're just you now. Not this or that other thing or whatever name you have. This is the North, and Black as it is and miserable and ruined as it's become, there's one thing we say up here that's about right: *You are whatever you wake as in the morning. But if by evening prayers you're something else entirely, then be happy. Don't weep nor worry: it's no sin at all to become something today which yesterday you did not dream of being.*'

72

'Waken up now, my girl. We're far enough on from things, but I'd bet not far enough from harm.'

Oona had found sleep, and imagined herself near home. Dreamed herself and Morris: back in Drumbroken, scrambling up trees in a race to pilfer eggs from a kite's ragged nest, then fleeing the vengeful mother when it returned. Then Oona challenging her brother, 'Race you to the Torrid!' And through forest and leaping into the river whatever season and splashing and diving down to disturb eels and search for imaginary treasure or snaring mayflies and using them as bait. And then after – dozing, damp to their souls, only waking when the first chill of dark descended. With eyes closed, it was easy for Oona to imagine this. And to dream the Kavanagh cottage closer – that she could just up and hurry to it. And home would be warm and secure and subdued, her grandmother whimpering with those worrisome dreams Oona understood well. And Oona would wake her slowly, whispering, 'I'm here, Granny. I was away but now I'm home again. Don't worry. You're safe.'

Then Oona heard Merrigutt's voice once more and all imagining had to be left behind: 'Up now and have a look.

It's a better day about you, and another new place to look at.'

So Oona left dreams to look.

Unexpected day, unexpected daze – full of bluster, the sky shifting like an old skirt, its whites grubby and fast-moving, its blue wane but bright. Sunlight was scattered on the surface of the swollen river, and Oona could tell they'd travelled far – clear water, small shoals of minnow and stickleback. The idea of the North and its Black shrank almost to nothing in Oona's mind. She noticed the Loam Stone still lying in the bottom of the boat. Despite the day's light, the Stone kept its dark.

'Where are we?' Oona asked.

'We –' said Merrigutt. She stopped. She had the paddle in her hands and hadn't returned to her jackdaw form. And Oona thought: Such brightness is a good thing to wake to, but it can be cruel enough too, showing up every wrinkle and crease and tiredness in the old woman. Merrigutt found words to finish: 'We're almost there. This here is a part of the North the King hasn't paid much attention to. Not since he first arrived anyway.'

No current hastened them. Their progress had to be at Merrigutt's discretion, and to Oona the old woman looked intent on slowness, on careful and delicate appreciation of everything. When Merrigutt allowed paddle to touch water it was only momentary, barely moving them on.

And then Oona said, 'This place is where you came from.'

Merrigutt said, 'Is indeed.' She suddenly half-rose from sitting and said in words so slow they had to be sighed, 'Here. I suppose we'll leave the river here.'

The boat eased towards the bank, to a wooden set of steps hanging.

Oona half-stood, then thought of her possessions, then realised – all she had left was the Loam Stone. No cloak of her mother's making, no satchel, no food packed inside, no knife. She found the other sack that'd been used to hold her body, plucked the Loam Stone from the bottom of the boat and dropped it in.

Slowly, the pair of them helped each other from the boat.

Oona climbed the short steep bank and was stopped, caught sudden by a coupling of anguish and happiness: the touch of grass beneath her feet was a joy she hadn't realised she missed, so used to it in her Drumbroken life. She found herself smiling.

'Keep going there,' Merrigutt told her.

At the top of the bank Oona looked out over a portion of land not flattened and not Blackened but torn across by wind. Low hills were lurking, a shallow rippling still holding some shade of green. She saw trees with pale bark and slim trunks and skinny boughs, tender leaves casting a flurry of turquoise shadows. What she saw was familiar, so she said: 'My mother was here sometime. Must've been. I know this place from a painting she did.'

Oona turned for Merrigutt, but the old woman was already a little ahead.

'This way here,' she called to Oona.

They followed a path that feet might've walked along in the past, but was almost concealed, so overgrown. Its meander took them between low rise and hollow. Oona saw no houses at all, not a person about, but enough modest life anyway to cheer: a patch of damp snowdrops, flags of winter sun like stepping stones across grass, and then a simple sight that warmed – a single swallow scissoring across sky. They walked. And walked the path all the way to a taste of salt on the tongue, to the sound of distant sounds – a strong sigh in every other moment.

'The sea,' said Merrigutt, and she stopped for a moment. Then she continued.

Only a minute more of walking and Oona saw a small cottage settled in a hollow. It was one-windowed, walls white-washed, and had a tough roof on it of what looked like driftwood. Not grand but neat, and simple. And simple was good enough for Oona after all the homes she'd endured in the North. It had a dark door, and some signal was offered of life inside: pale scrolls of smoke straying from a narrow chimney.

Merrigutt said, 'Let's go,' and started to walk down the slope.

'Who lives here?' asked Oona.

'Someone who might help,' said Merrigutt. Her feet slowed, each step held hovering by uncertainty. 'Someone who I once relied on more than anything.'

When they reached the cottage, Merrigutt was again full of pause, and when she eventually knocked it was with knuckles so gentle they could hardly have wanted an answer. It took a long time for anything inside to respond. When someone did appear it was two someones – an old woman leaning on a rough driftwood cane, eyes in her head of no colour at all that had to squint and search out her guests, and a young girl.

Oona was suddenly very aware of herself – standing in just her thin dress, hair damp and face mucky, bare-footed, sack hanging from her hand that held the Loam Stone. Her shame increased the more this old woman and young girl looked and looked. Then the old woman's mouth worked hard to expel a word: '*What?*'

'It's me,' said Merrigutt, her voice small.

'I know it's you!' said the old woman in the doorway, and her jaw shook like a tray seeking spare change. 'I'm not that far gone! And what do you want coming back here like this, disturbing us?'

Merrigutt had no answer.

The young girl stayed silent, half-hidden behind the old woman.

'We aren't asking for much,' said Merrigutt, voice still soft. 'Just some food, somewhere to stay even. Bit of rest.'

Silence, and then Oona's stomach took its chance to growl. They all looked at her.

'Sorry,' said Oona. 'Bloody starving!'

The young girl gasped and slapped a hand to her mouth. It annoyed Oona, this attitude. Irritated her, the whole situation of them standing on the doorstep, so she said, 'Look: you heard Merrigutt, can we come in or not?'

All heads but Oona's went into an embarrassed bow.

'Don't leave the door open or you'll let the heat out,' said the old woman, suddenly, mouth snapping shut on each word. She turned and took herself away from Oona and Merrigutt, followed so close by the young girl.

Oona looked to Merrigutt and asked, 'Is that us being asked in?'

'It's the best we'll get,' said Merrigutt.

'Who are these people anyway?' asked Oona.

'The woman,' whispered Merrigutt, settling one foot on the threshold, 'is my mother. And the young girl trying to hide herself is my daughter.'

73

One room, and it hadn't much to make it worthy of the word 'home'. Only the essential things were in sight: Oona saw two chairs sitting at a scrubbed table, and a tall dresser. A third chair, bit softer, was backed into a corner on its own. Nothing on display, except a large and lurid-looking shrine for the Sorrowful Lady. The flames in their hearth had to make do with a single twist of driftwood to cling to.

Oona held tight to the sack with the Loam Stone in it, and took one of the two chairs going at the table. Everyone gave her a look.

'I'm tired,' she said, but it was no attempt at apology.

'There's a bit of bread about I suppose,' said the old woman, sinking onto the soft seat in the corner and turning to face the wall. 'And the kettle's only just boiled.'

Merrigutt was the one who went to find food, leaving the room, leaving Oona feeling alone. The young girl stood by the dresser, the old woman kept her face to the wall. Neither spoke. And this was supposed to be Evelyn Merrigutt's mother and daughter? These two quiet creatures? Mischief made Oona look to the young girl and ask, 'So you're not gonna say hello?'

'*Oona*,' said Merrigutt, returning. It was all she said – the look she gave was enough. Oona sighed, and sat silent too.

Merrigutt poured tay the colour of vinegar from a stone crock, and had found a solid loaf of black bread and a earthen dish of butter. Oona wanted something to do (something to eat): she stood and sliced the bread, buttered it thick and was the first to start eating. She'd have liked something more – something heartier and warm – but it would have to do. Roughened wanderer she'd become, Oona crammed as much into her mouth as it would hold, only half-heartedly holding a hand under her mouth to catch any crumb.

Merrigutt gave her mother a small plate with a heel of bread, a tumbler of tay, and asked, 'Any Invaders, Mammy? Been any trouble?'

'No,' said her mother. The old woman took her bread between two fingers and took a large wet mouthful, made wetter by slurps of tea. 'Not that I've got the sight to see anything any more! I've not long left, you know. Like the Isle itself – I might not live to see tomorrow!'

'What about you?' Oona asked the young girl. 'Seen any Invaders?'

The girl shook her head, then nodded, then didn't seem to know what she knew. They ate on in silence.

'We'll rest now,' said Merrigutt, after a while. Oona almost marvelled: so outspoken at all other times, and here was Evelyn Merrigutt shuffling about with head bowed and saying with a horrible sense of sorry, 'We'll just have a sleep and then be on our way.'

Merrigutt twitched her head towards the door, and Oona

understood it was time to leave the room. But Oona couldn't stop herself from asking the old woman, 'Do you not care that your daughter's back to see you, missus? Do you not care that the whole Isle is going to blazes and she's doing something to help stop it?'

The old woman turned her old head, colourless eyes quivering on Oona.

'You don't know,' she said. Her mouth went in for another sloppy bite of butter and black bread, tucking it all into the left side of her face to fill out a hollow cheek. 'You don't know what my daughter did, do you?'

'Let's go,' said Merrigutt, hand on Oona's shoulder, moving her towards the door. 'Please, just leave it all be.'

'Should be ashamed!' called the old woman from her soft chair. 'Should be ashamed coming back here!'

Oona wanted to ask more, but Merrigutt was so keen to steer her from the room. Shoulder to shoulder they walked a short, bare, narrow hall.

'What's going on?' asked Oona. 'Why's your own mam treating you like you've turned up and flung dirt at her door?'

Merrigutt said nothing.

(Not yet, thought Oona. Not just now).

Short hall ended in another short room: barren but for a tiny window showing green, a narrow bed draped with a quilted bedspread, narrower wardrobe, and a rush-mat on the floor. When the door was shut Oona said again, 'What's going on?' Then she somehow felt the right question would've been: *What happened here?*

Merrigutt sank onto the bed.

'She's not had it easy,' said Merrigutt. 'You shouldn't be too hard on her.'

'You sound like me when I was saying about my granny,' said Oona. She stood by the wall, arms folded, sack containing the Loam Stone hanging from a hand. 'And you know what else you said to me then – that people have a choice how to be behaving, no excuse for anything. Remember?'

'Did I say that?' said Merrigutt. Her hands held tight to the edge of the bed, like it might suddenly try to tip her off. 'Sorrowful Lady – don't I talk some amount of rubbish sometimes?'

'No,' said Oona. She sat down on the bed by Merrigutt. 'You were saying the truth. Now do the same for me – *tell*.'

Merrigutt nodded, and then asked something Oona couldn't have expected: 'You said the Stone was showing things to do with your mother?'

'Yes,' said Oona. 'But why do you – ?'

'Do you remember your mother well?' asked Merrigutt. She'd turned to face the window. After a moment Oona said, 'A wee bit, but not much.' She didn't say that any memories of her mother had been almost eclipsed by what she'd seen in the Stone.

'And was she a happy enough woman, or sad?' asked Merrigutt.

Oona opened her mouth, then realised she had no swift answer, no certainty. So she said, 'Don't know. A bit of both. She never did much about the house – that was Granny, and there were rows about it. Bad arguments.' Oona thought more, and then said, 'I never even spoke to her much. I was out in

333

the forest with Morris most of the time. It was like . . . like she was hardly even there.'

Then Merrigutt turned – she was crying.

'Please,' said Oona, and her own voice quivered. 'Tell me what you know.'

'No,' said Merrigutt, 'I'll not tell you, my girl: I'll show.'

74

Merrigutt settled a hand on Oona's and said, 'Now: see all the nightmares I have in me.'

Slowly, Oona took the Loam Stone from the sack. The warmth of it was a low throb – steady heartbeat, deep breathing. Oona allowed a moment, and then let herself see –

In her mind she saw Merrigutt: girl about to become a woman, standing in the same living room they'd left minutes earlier. Merrigutt's mother was there too – younger, brighter, smiling. The pair of them were pacing. Barefoot, they wandered the room together. From their fingers fell scarlet – powder being sown slowly like bright seed on every surface. And magic made flowers sprout, sudden spring – daffodil and tulip and rose and crocus, brightest colours bursting from tabletop and floor and dresser and sill and hearth . . .

Merrigutt and her mother stopped – such smiles, such laughter, no bitter silence.

Oona heard Merrigutt's mother say, 'You see now, my girl – see what wonders we can do. We don't need your father or any other man.' She linked an arm with Merrigutt, clung to her. 'So let them stay where they are at the Burren, and we'll be happy enough here. We'll always have home as long as we have each other.'

Things began to fade, colour draining from the scene. Merrigutt's mother was lost. Not gone, if Oona looked close enough, but not as clear as she was. The mother was, Oona understood, suddenly less important. And what grew clearer, what meant more: a boy standing in the living-room. Tall, pale, dark curls, dark-eyed. He was holding Merrigutt's hand. And Oona felt for the first time that she shouldn't be seeing, wasn't decent to be watching . . . there might've been only these two in the world, in this one bright room. So close, they were passing words in whispers that Oona couldn't hear. Then some sound, some low song from someone approaching on the same path Oona had walked with Merrigutt. Was it Merrigutt's mother returning? Quickly from his belt the boy plucked a single snowdrop and slipped it into Merrigutt's hair. Oona heard words this time. He said soft, 'I would do anything at all for you, Evelyn. Would you do the same?'

Merrigutt nodded.

'Good,' said he. 'Then meet me by the river at dark. Make sure you come just yourself.'

Merrigutt nodded again.

More sound closer, and the boy's lips pressed a soft kiss to Merrigutt's cheek and then he was gone.

Oona waited.

The scene in the living room shivered, changed, darkened. Oona heard words familiar, same cry and same kind of pleading she'd heard from her father but from Merrigutt's mouth –

'What's happening to me, Mammy? How can we stop this?'

336

New sight, same living room: white easing through black outside the window, delicate shreds of snow. Spring was long-gone, a lost season. And Merrigutt was standing, staring down at her mother who was in her softer seat in the corner, facing the wall. Merrigutt was showing her mother her arm, sleeve folded back to the elbow – a grey-whiteness was creeping upwards, ashen stain, fingers as though they could fall away if shown a strong enough breeze.

'Please!' said Merrigutt. 'Do something to stop this, Mammy!'

'I can't,' said Merrigutt's mother, and still she didn't look at her daughter. 'It's sin that's made this come upon you. And serves you right! Deceiving me the way you did and getting yourself into this mess. Trust you to let something like this happen, and a grandchild on the way too.'

I'm so slow, thought Oona. So slow to see things clearly.

'It's not sin,' said Merrigutt, and her unaffected hand went to the bold curve of her belly. 'Not just me. Same thing is happening to all the girls. We're all changing, even girls married and decent and with daughters of their own. They say it's that thing out to sea – that darkness as sharp as a Briar-Witch's claw.'

'Nonsense,' said Merrigutt's mother, but with little passion, little care.

'I'll not just let this happen,' said Merrigutt, and Oona heard some shade of the Evelyn Merrigutt she knew: 'I won't just stay and let this change keep coming. Not me and not the other girls either.'

Then Merrigutt's mother said, 'You've no choice – this is home, my girl. And there's no getting away from the place you belong to.'

A darkening and no sight, only sound: a screaming, agony that was black and blood-red and weeping crimson. Silence, and then a single voice – Merrigutt's mother saying, 'It's a girl. And let's pray to the Sorrowful Lady that she's nothing like her mother.'

Another change, new truth: not the living room then but the sight of Merrigutt alone in darkness. Look closer – on the coast, but the sea showing no white and making no sound. Oona could tell that Merrigutt was waiting. And it wasn't long before another figure stepped into sight: she wore a hood, was breathless and was quick to take Merrigutt's hands and said, 'You got away all right?'

'Did,' said Merrigutt. 'You? Anyone see?'

'No,' said this other girl. 'How's the child?'

'Well,' was all Merrigutt said.

'Why'd you ask me here, Evelyn?' said the woman.

'Say nothing,' said Merrigutt. 'Just listen.'

They stopped. And in their silence Oona heard – whispers, words that she couldn't recognise but drifting in host from across the sea. Both Merrigutt and her companion stood hand-in-hand for long minutes.

Then Merrigutt said, 'The Echoes.'

'You think that's doing it?' asked the woman. 'That whispering is the reason we're all going the way we are? All changing?'

Merrigutt nodded, then said, 'We have to leave. We have to get away or else we'll change completely.'

'Your little one,' said the woman. 'She –'

'Won't have a mother anyway if I stay,' said Merrigutt.

No warning, and the other woman whipped her hand from

338

Merrigutt's and Oona thought the gesture meant disagreement. But it was only so the woman could drag her hood from her face, show how far her transformation had gone. And even in such dark Oona could tell two things quick: that the woman had been almost overcome by the Echoes, and that this woman was her mother.

'Almost gone,' said Oona's mother. Her face was almost covered with the same ashen mark as Oona had seen on her father's arm, on Merrigutt. 'Almost taken me. I'll be nearly nothing now soon.'

'Caithleen,' said Merrigutt, and she settled a hand on the cheek of Oona's mother. 'It must be tonight, or Sorrowful-Lady-knows I don't think I'll wake in the morning at all. We'll be only dust. We have to be telling the others, and quick.'

Oona's mother nodded.

Then together, some magic to move things: Merrigutt and Caithleen delved into their cloaks and scarlet powder was found and sown in the shape of men on the dark hillside. And as Oona had seen it so many times in the North, figures tore themselves free, smaller than the women but a strong dozen that awaited instruction.

'Go!' Merrigutt told them. 'Find the other girls who've been poisoned by these Echoes and bring them to the river! Hurry!'

So the summoned men moved off.

And then a shift in the scene that Oona knew was final, and last sight –

Her mother holding Merrigutt's hand as they hurried to the river, other girls around them running, trying not to stumble. Full moon was watching and shouts were following, a torment of echoes –

'Stop them!'

'Come back!'

'You're not going to abandon your mothers and children!'

'If you leave then just you wait and see what'll happen!'

'By the Sorrowful Lady, you'll regret it all!'

But the women wouldn't wait – to the river and lowering themselves into boats, ropes undone and paddles found and Merrigutt calling, 'Head South! Quickly!'

And the women had to fight to leave – thrash of paddles, no current to take them and on the riverbank shadows arrived to shout such abuse, such curses and swearing and promises of retribution thrown –

'Abandoning your children and leaving your mothers – shame on you!'

'You are now exiled! Let none of you ever darken our doors again!'

'You'll regret this! Just wait and see – you'll regret ever leaving!'

But Merrigutt and Oona's mother and the other women only moved off into the dark.

'Keep going!' Merrigutt told the small fleet. 'Keep paddling – we're almost free!'

And already Oona could see the women hopeful – checking themselves, running hands and slow fingertips over their bodies, faces. Hope rewarded: the Echoes looked to be leaving them, skin softening, pale, restored. There were smiles, low shouts, some weeping: such happiness! Oona saw her mother and Merrigutt embrace.

But beneath all, Oona felt the Loam Stone telling otherwise –
*No, this is not the end. This is not being free. Watch, wait for
the nightmare* . . .

Only minutes, and then –

'What's happening to me?'

Cry of one woman, then more, then all: the women gasped
and grabbed at their bellies, groaning, seized by sudden agony.
Oona could hardly watch. Her mother was making such an
effort to take only a breath, finding it impossible to stay upright.
Merrigutt was holding Caithleen's hand and whispering, 'It's
all right. It's all right – we're free now.' But Merrigutt herself
was in the same state as the others.

And from far off, the firm words of their mothers –

'You cannot leave the place you belong to! You've no home
now! And if you've no home then such a change will happen
to you – worse than the Echoes! A dispell of the flesh! You'll
not know yourself and there's no way back!'

And then screams of the same kind as Merrigutt had made
in childbirth.

Oona forced herself to witness: flesh and hair became feather,
limbs darkening to grubby and ragged things, bodies shrinking
tight, feet sharpening to claws and mouths speaking not with
screams any more but sharp *caws*. A sound like skin being
stripped: mouths not mouths but beaks snapping.

Oona heard Merrigutt's distant voice say, 'Now you know,
my girl. Now you've seen.'

Oona's final sight: flurry of dark entering the night-sky, a
flock of jackdaws screaming as the Loam Stone, satisfied, let
Merrigutt's nightmare melt from Oona's mind.

75

Oona sat, saying nothing. Any sound came from elsewhere – cup being settled in its saucer, another stick added to the fire, clearing of a throat wearied by a long winter. The creak of a board outside the bedroom?

Finally, Merrigutt ended the silence –

'You can think what you need to think.' She took her hand from Oona, eyes shut as though reliving all past pain. 'I wouldn't blame you anyway if you hated me, thought me the worst in the world.'

'I don't think that,' said Oona. She didn't know what she thought about many things – anything any more – but she was certain of this. 'I don't hate.'

'I left my daughter,' said Merrigutt.

'Yes,' said Oona.

'Never came back and never set eyes on her till today.'

'I know. I saw.'

'Then you should think bad of me, my girl.'

'I won't.'

Merrigutt opened her eyes. And Oona wondered: Does the old woman look younger? Are the eyes less clouded, face less worn, hair darker?

Then Oona said, 'You did what you thought better than anything else. So did my own mother.'

A moment, and then Merrigutt said, 'I don't regret it. Even seeing her after fifteen years, I don't think I did the wrong thing. If I'd stayed – I wouldn't have stayed. Couldn't have survived, wouldn't be here at all. The Echoes would've taken me, and she'd have even less than what she has now.'

Moments transforming into minutes: a long while of saying nothing, and Oona had to think, and understand all the silence of the house, all the bitterness.

'What happened after you left?'

'Went anywhere we could,' said Merrigutt. 'Everywhere across the Isle, but never back here. Never home.'

'You were all transformed,' said Oona. 'How can you be like this now? How come my mother was able to stay human?'

'Because,' said Merrigutt, 'like I told in your cottage back in Drumbroken: a dispell can only thrive where there's little enough hope, where it's let in and let settle. And we fought against it. But it was an old and poisonous magic, so potent it couldn't be undone. Best we could all comfortably do was make ourselves look like old women. None of us could shift it, except your mother. She fought harder than any.'

Merrigutt paused, and for once Oona found the patience to wait for more words.

'I saw it happen,' said Merrigutt. 'We were in a forest together in a small and quiet county in the South. A valley, a near-silent place. That's where she first laid eyes on your father. She was in human form when he saw her, and that was it – she was

343

free, never changed back. She was restored to the girl she'd been before we'd abandoned home.'

'How?' asked Oona.

'Hope?' said Merrigutt. 'Or love too, I suppose? Who knows for certain. But I'll say this – she was free, I think, because she found home. She saw your father and saw a place she could properly belong.'

Oona looked to the Loam Stone.

'That can't be right,' said Oona. 'The Stone showed me the two of them. Showed me what he was like with her. How can she have been any way happy with him?'

Merrigutt sighed once more.

'Don't know,' she said. 'These things aren't simple to work out. You can't know everything, even with that Stone in your hand.'

Both were quiet then.

They felt each other's breathing, felt each other's memories like something shared in that small space. Oona didn't need to touch the Stone to feel Merrigutt's grief – it was the same as her own.

'Rest yourself now,' said Merrigutt.

'Stay with me?' said Oona.

A moment, and Merrigutt nodded. They lay down beside each other on the bed.

But Oona couldn't let sleep come without saying, 'I'm not like them. Don't want to be like my father or Morris or –'

'No choice there,' said Merrigutt, and her tone returned to that commanding way she had, to the same dogged insistence, but softer. 'Listen to me now and don't disagree: there's no escaping family. There'll be a time when you're speaking and you realise you're using the same words your own mother used, you'll half-hear yourself sounding just like her. Or you'll be walking along as happy as anything and catch yourself in some mirror and see your own father glaring back. There's no getting away. More you try, more you'll know there's not a bit of use in bothering.'

'Then what do I do?' said Oona. 'No home to go back to, no home I want.'

'Then wait,' said Merrigutt. She settled a hand on Oona's cheek. 'In the end – if you're lucky and like your mother – you'll find your own. You'll find a way home.'

76

'Open up in the name of the King!'

Oona awoke, sat up, Loam Stone still in her hand. She heard fists against a door – not the bedroom door but somewhere close. She shook Merrigutt awake.

'I said open this door now or we'll kick it down!' Invaders.

And then the bedroom door was thrown wide –

Merrigutt's mother was in the room, Merrigutt's daughter beside. The mother kicked at the rush-mat and showed an iron handle in the boards. She kneeled and tugged on it: a trapdoor, a square of cold dark. Nothing needed saying. Merrigutt and Oona were both on their feet as two gifts came from Merrigutt's mother and daughter: from the young girl Oona was given a fresh fur cloak, and Merrigutt's palm was blessed by her mother with something small and almost-silver.

'Just break the door down!'

The sound of boots beating and it was Merrigutt's daughter who spoke, strong words for her mother: 'Go, Mammy. I heard all last night. I know now.'

The sound of the dark front door surrendering –

'Go,' said Merrigutt's daughter.

346

And Merrigutt moved, crouching by the hatch as Oona hunkered beside and they both leapt, adding themselves to the space beneath the room. The trapdoor was dropped shut.

'Follow,' was all Merrigutt said, and Oona saw her move off.

Some light accompanied them – dawn in thin strips showing through boards, slicing them into light and shadow. The sound of things falling followed. And then the sound of someone screaming. Merrigutt slowed, then said aloud, 'No, this is more important,' and moved on faster.

The passage took them far, farther. And when they reached its end it surprised Oona – it was open to the world like anyone could've found it. But the place it left them was uncertain: once more they were stranded in cold mist that looked solid. Oona couldn't see anything except some of herself, some of Merrigutt. Could see tears trembling new on the old woman's face.

'She'll be all right,' said Oona.

Merrigutt twitched as though pinched, then said, 'No time for that worrying now. We're close to the Burren.' She wet her lips and breathed in. 'On now – this way.'

Oona shook out the cloak that Merrigutt's daughter had given: a dark and well-made thing, the hood lined with stoat fur. She flung it around her shoulders and instantly felt warmer. She hurried after Merrigutt, and still the sounds persisted on the air – screams, things falling, things coming for them? And other sounds – an immense smashing- crashing that Oona imagined was the sea. She still had the Loam Stone in her hand and she focused on it, wanting knowledge, but was pierced by a single image: a legion of Invaders in pursuit, and Muddgloggs and Briar-Witches and Coach-A-Bower and fire and smoke and shadow their weapons . . . such potent North magic in their service! And at their lead marched the Faceless, the Changeling with its crimson eyes . . .

'No,' said Merrigutt. She snatched at Oona's hand. 'Not now. Almost there, my girl. Keep going. Stay close.'

Only then did Oona notice the thing Merrigutt had been given in the last moments by her mother, the only close-to bright thing in sight – a rough coin. Merrigutt held it tight and high, like its modest shine might lead them.

More noise from behind them, louder. They moved faster.

Through the nothing, a nowhere like everywhere else in the North . . . and then something formed. In the mist stood an archway. Tall, tapering to a sharp point, crumbling. Oona saw no walls on either side – no Worshipping House or cottage or anything else for the arch to be part of. In the archway was something that Oona described to herself as a door – a single sheet of bark stripped whole and settled there.

They stopped.

Oona was certain she could hear the sibilant rush and retreat of the sea. She thought, This is it – the entrance to the Burren.

But Merrigutt wasn't looking at door or arch but down, so Oona did the same –

Someone was slumped at the foot of the archway. He looked like he was asleep, but looked too like wakening wasn't something he often bothered with. Oona watched, and then saw some sign of life – in the man's right hand he held an empty enamel cup, and he started to shake it.

'Gate-Keeper,' whispered Merrigutt for Oona. 'He's been

here longer than anyone can remember.'

'Is he dead or –?' asked Oona.

'No closer to death than he is to life,' said Merrigutt. 'But here anyway to keep people out. And to let others with the right means in.'

Merrigutt obliged with payment – dropped her silver coin into the cup and the sound it made was loud enough to make the old man shift, for his legs to kick and body begin to rise. It looked to Oona more like magic than proper life, the man being tugged and teased into action. Whatever mystery moved him made his left arm twitch and his left hand shudder, and his fingers went to do some searching in his waistcoat. What they came back with was a key that looked closer to a gnarled twig.

About-twitch and sharp turn and the old man faced the sheet of bark inside the arch. He lifted the key and began to draw shapes. Slow and deliberate, the sound like something being split: branch of a tree being torn, hard earth being tilled in winter, throes of a fast river against broken stone. He dragged and drew in long patterns for the longest minutes and Oona worried about how close the Invaders were, thinking they'd be on them soon if they didn't hurry.

Then the old man stopped his sketching and spoke, voice a low crackle –

'I have drawn the map of the place I once knew. I have shown my knowledge of the Blessed Isle, as it was. I have declared my dedication to the place I was born and the place I shall die in.' A moment more of waiting, and then the door opened.

Beyond, Oona saw a stretch – perhaps only two steps' worth – of stone to walk on, and then more mist. But was it perhaps lighter, brighter? Touched by some trace of sun?

'Many thanks to you,' said Merrigutt. She stepped through the archway, telling Oona, 'Quick. Follow.'

Oona didn't hesitate – stepped through and then turned, but there was nothing at all to see. As the sound of following footfalls and shouts almost reached them, the mist softly conspired, and stole the archway from sight.

77

'Almost there now, my girl.' Merrigutt's refrain. 'Not far. Keep going. Stay close.'

But Oona felt some strangeness in the air she had to struggle against, something wanting to hold them back. Like a soundless gale – some stubborn magic didn't want them there.

'Pig-headed protection!' cried Merrigutt, and Oona heard the same battle in the old woman's voice, saw it in her jaw tensed and eyes crushed tight. 'Trying to keep the women out! But it's failing! Weaker than usual, not able to –'

Oona heard nothing more: her hearing was twisted towards a single shrill note and it was suddenly too much to fight on. She wanted to crumple, retreat . . . but Merrigutt was there, gabbing fast and contrary, mouth moving though no sound was heard, taking Oona's hand and pulling her on further into the press of noise.

A few words reached Oona's ears, Merrigutt saying: 'Just a wee bit further . . .'

Then sudden release: Oona felt as though she'd surfaced, gasping for each shallow breath, eyes streaming, hair flung wild by a breeze.

Oona heard sound: explosions of unseen sea smashing unseen shore.

Sight: a landscape like an ancient palm under strong sun, the whitest stone riven and cracked and worked flat by weather. A darkness wounded it, splitting its surface in narrow veins. Nothing was vertical but Oona and Merrigutt. Nothing moved. Mist encircled the space like a barricade.

Such quiet.

Oona felt she should whisper, 'Where is everyone? Anyone?'

Then some flicker: from broken ground something upped like it was budding, and then retracted.

'What was that?' asked Oona.

'That,' said Merrigutt with a snap, 'was the Cause. Watching us and just hiding.'

'Maybe they'll be able to help,' said Oona. 'Might know where the children were taken to, where Morris is.'

She heard Merrigutt sigh.

'All right,' said the old woman. 'For your sake only, my girl – I'll try my best to be all helpful and polite to this crowd.'

Oona watched.

Then once more and only for a moment – an appearance and disappearance. But this time Oona registered eyes and a face half-obscured by crimson: flag of the Cause tied across a mouth.

'We should call out,' said Oona. 'Shout maybe so they know that we –'

Then cold steel was pressed tight to Oona's neck and she heard a muffled voice behind her threaten, 'Don't move or I'll put a bullet in you. You even breathe in a way I don't like and in the name of the Cause I'll shoot you dead and don't think I won't! Now give me answers: why're you two here, how'd you enter the Burren and what's your business? *Tell!*'

With a groan of deepest agony, Merrigutt managed to become her jackdaw self once more. She worked hard to lift herself high, fast, calling loud, 'We're here to warn you, members of the Cause! The Invaders are on your threshold and the magic that surrounds the Burren is failing!'

Then a louder shout from someone hidden: 'Lies! There's some dark magic in that bird – bring it down!'

The gun left Oona's neck to aim and at the same time she screamed, '*No!*'

Single shot.

Merrigutt jerked in the air, wings turning suddenly inward. The jackdaw fell, a slow spiral through sunlight. The unendurable echo and echo and echo. Oona didn't move. And then she was only movement – she ran, voices calling, *Stop!* Hands reaching and wanting to grab. But she didn't let herself slow. With each slam of her soles on rock she felt she was shedding small pieces, losing little and little more of herself along the way. Thought by the time she reached that small scrap of dark there'd be nothing of Oona Kavanagh left at all.

When she arrived she sank, settling the Loam Stone on the surface of the Burren.

Merrigutt was no longer a jackdaw, but not an old woman either. Instead a girl, and not much older than Oona. She was pale, and calm, and beautiful. She was restored, surely returned to the same person she'd been when she'd left home years before.

Oona took this Merrigutt in her arms. No words.

Then Oona wanted so badly to blame herself: 'I should've just been up and left last night. Left you at home with your mother and daughter and just gone on by myself.'

And then Merrigutt found strength to lift one hand, to settle it against Oona's cheek. To whisper: 'Then I would've been alone. And I would've followed you – to the edge of everything, to the end of all things. You see what you've done for me, my girl? The dispell has left me. Like your mother – I found my place to belong. It was with you. You showed me home.'

Oona closed her eyes and gathered her friend close.

She heard Merrigutt's last sigh: 'My girl.'

And Oona waited. Held what little she could hold, and remained. But what she held closest was hope, this most futile kind of longing – that it was all a nightmare, and that soon she would awake, and things would be different.

Then someone shattered her silence, another shout across the desolation –

'Good shot, boy Kavanagh!'

Oona looked up.

There was shadow on her, a coldness: the figure who'd fired. Oona watched fingers creep slowly to a mouth to tug crimson away, to reveal a face. Only a boy beneath. Only her brother, Morris. And the look he looked down on her with was so like their father. And in his grip he struggled still with that same rifle that had belonged to their granda.

Oona had a familiar, draining thought: Too heavy for him, that weapon. Still too much of a burden to be carried by such small hands.

FIFTH

BATTLE ON THE BURREN

78

Oona stood and punched her brother in the heart. It hardly moved him. So she thumped, pounded – both fists. He hardly reacted. And again and again and with eyes shut, Oona hit and cursed him, beat and battered, fists becoming feeble, flattening into open palms that surely stung her more than himself. All this, but near blinded: she saw nothing through eyes too scalded with tears. All this until Oona felt arms take her – from behind she was grabbed and dragged back, held too tight. She saw more shadows, a small crowd of boys surrounding. Less to this Cause than she'd imagined there would be: two dozen would've been kind, and some of them looking as young as seven.

Oona heard the click of rifles, a cold barrel pressed again to her neck.

And she thought: Now do it – end things. Because if I had the Loam Stone in my hand and could dream it and make it happen then I would. I would wish it.

Then Morris shouted at her –

'Why are you even here? Why did you follow me?'

Oona said nothing. She could hardly stand.

'I asked you a question, so speak!' roared Morris. '*Tell!*'

'I followed you . . .' said Oona, and stopped. Because I'm a fool, she thought. A fool I am, true enough.

'Why?' said Morris. Then some slow realisation in his slow eyes. 'You think I needed saving, is that it?'

Some laughter from the lads of the Cause.

'For true?' asked Morris, and his own mouth showed a neat smile so like the counterfeit smile of the Faceless. 'You thought Morris Kavanagh of all people needed saving? And by a girl?'

Such laughter!

'The last I saw,' said Oona, 'was you being taken by one of those Briar-Witches.'

'Those Witches aren't anything to be frighted of,' said Morris.

'I know,' said Oona.

'We escaped from them ages ago,' said Morris. 'Got free of them and the Funeral-Makers and had to travel by ourselves a good dozen miles before we got here.'

The boys cheered, so pleased – with themselves, with their efforts, with each other.

Oona looked to the Loam Stone – so dark. And to Merrigutt. And still to Merrigutt. Didn't want to look, couldn't stop looking, but –

'I came farther than you,' said Oona.

'Shouldn't have bothered,' said Morris. 'You should go home.'

'I can't now,' said Oona.

'You came all this way on your own so you can go home on your own,' said Morris.

'I wasn't alone,' said Oona. But to herself – Morris had already turned away.

He was shouting to his boys, 'Come on now – we need to

360

make preparations! We'll march on the Hollow Mountain at –'

Dull explosions but not the sea – like thunder-strokes, or vast things, collapsing.

Oona looked – around the Burren, the wall of mist was thinning, slowly lifting.

The boys' mouths all rounded with surprise, a stammer of questions half-formed –

'What the – ?'

'How can they – ?'

'There's no way they can –'

'They can,' said Oona. Everyone looked at her. She continued: 'The magic is going around this place. Everything in the Isle is changing quick – I've seen it.'

'You know nothing,' said Morris.

And Oona's voice built suddenly into a shout: 'You've no clue about anything, Morris! I've seen the worst things and not you! I saw our cottage in Drumbroken fall in with Granny Kavanagh inside! I saw children all dragged down into the dirt by those Briar-Witches! And it was me that went down into their nest and chopped the hand off their Mother! I've been to Innislone! I've been to the Hollow Mountain you're talking about! I've seen the Giants in the Melancholy Mountains and I've ridden a Whereabouts Wolf! I've seen Muddgloggs! I've been captured and taken by the Faceless and travelled across the Black in the carriage of a Funeral-Maker! I did all that, not you!'

Silence. Oona watched her brother's face – it didn't know what expression to wear.

'I believe her,' said a small voice.

Oona turned and saw another hand tug crimson from another face. Beneath was Eamon O'Riley. And Oona nearly wept – saw so much of Bridget in him, heard her voice almost as he asked, 'Are them Invaders are on their way? Is that right?'

'Yes,' said Oona.

'And what magic do they have?' asked Eamon. 'Things more powerful than our fathers' guns?'

'Aye,' said Oona. She swallowed. 'They've everything you can imagine and even worse.' She felt the arms that held her weaken, grow loose. Saw boys of the Cause look to their battered rifles, to pistols dented and crawling with rust. And then to each other. Last of all, to Morris.

'There's nothing we can do to change where the Invaders are,' he said. 'We keep to the plan we've been making – Hollow Mountain is where we need to strike.'

'Too late for that,' said Oona.

Morris shifted from foot to foot, then found something to cling to: '*Kavanaghs don't do as expected!*'

'Kavanaghs are fools,' said Oona.

The boys released Oona, backing away. Brother and sister faced each another. Oona didn't move. Morris's hand strayed to a dull-looking blade at his belt.

'You won't win,' said Oona. 'You won't stand a chance in hell of beating these Invaders.'

'Is that right?' said Morris. 'Then what's your great plan, sister dearest?'

He didn't await any answer, just jerked his head, drew his Cause closer, and started to whisper orders.

Oona looked to the Loam Stone. And as her eyes met it – as

she began to wonder, to imagine – it began its blaze. Looked further, to the body still lying alone on the Burren. She heard words, and couldn't know whether they were her own thoughts or not, the words of the King or her own worry: *Such nightmares, such darkness still ahead. And no chance of beating it.*

But Oona replied, 'No: nothing ahead now darker than what's behind. I've seen the worst, so whatever happens can happen. I've nothing to be afraid of any more.'

79

'Oona,' said Eamon, settling a hand on her shoulder.

Oona flinched away. Eamon's hand was ashen, crumbling, near broken. She looked farther – Morris going on, telling the boys what to do, but struggling more than before with their grandfather's rifle? She saw: his hand too was greying, withering. And the other boys – no crimson flag worn whatever way could conceal it, not only their hands or fingers but faces blighted by the Echoes.

Oona swallowed, wanting to say so much but managing to say nothing. Not yet. She knew they wouldn't listen.

'Just wanted to ask,' said Eamon, 'if you'd like me to help.'

Oona nodded, and they moved together towards Merrigutt.

Only a moment before Eamon asked the thing Oona was expecting –

'Bridget – do you know is she all right?'

Oona said nothing, and Eamon O'Riley was no fool.

'She'd have died fighting,' he said. 'I know that much.'

'She did,' said Oona. 'She did braver things than I ever could.'

They arrived. Sun was strong, too bright – Oona felt as though the whole world should've darkened itself, fallen into instant grief at the fall of her friend. She knelt – first for the Loam Stone. And as soon as her fingertips were reunited with it, she felt better. Not warmer nor a bit happier, but not so alone: perhaps bolder.

'What is that thing?' asked Eamon.

'The thing that's going to save us,' said Oona. 'Or else destroy us.'

She stood and held the Stone on her palm, allowing Eamon to see, allowing it to blaze. Not long, and he had to look away.

'I'll lift her sure,' said Eamon, leaning down for Merrigutt. But Oona said, 'No. I'll carry her.'

The young girl Merrigutt had become once more was hardly any weight at all. Oona carried her easily, held her close.

'Where?' was all Oona asked, craving purpose.

'Follow me,' said Eamon.

They walked to one of the splits in the surface of the Burren, found shallow steps hacked from the stone and Oona descended. A narrow place, walls so close, like the space between two trees in a neglected forest. But it was cooler, darker, so quiet. And when they reached the bottom they walked a slip of ground between high stone, and Oona remembered the roar of the Giants in the Hollow Mountain: *Why do you wish to know the way into a place of such safety, of such healing? Why would you seek such solitude as it provides, that place of oldest North magic . . .*' And in quietness – this solitude and safety – Oona did feel a slow healing: a calming, any anger ebbing, and any hurt and heartache draining away. But still she had her burden, and was grateful for it – Merrigutt unmoving in her arms.

Moment by moment, she found she could force herself to

keep moving, to exist.

'Here's the place,' said Eamon.

They'd reached an opening, an alcove carved, and within was a tall shrine for the Sorrowful Lady hewn in the wall. There were no candles gathered, not one meagre offering on display. An empty space, simple. And for the first time Oona felt the softness of the Lady – her placid gaze softened more of the pain, soothed it, because Oona knew Merrigutt would've appreciated this place.

So Oona laid her friend gratefully on the ground.

'Will we say a wee prayer?' asked Eamon.

'No,' said Oona. 'No need for prayers – this is enough. Thank you.'

A last thing – Oona tugged the cloak from her shoulders that Merrigutt's daughter had given, must've made, and laid it over the body.

Last words –

'I wish I was more,' said Oona. 'I should have dreams strong enough in me to wake you. But I don't. If I could dream you back to life then I would. I'd not wait – I'd imagine you in the world again.'

Oona looked to the pale, impassive face of Herself.

'But I'll keep going,' said Oona. 'I'll not stop till this is done. I swear it on this Sorrowful Lady.'

The Loam Stone grew hotter in her hand, a searing hurt. But, Oona thought, it's only pain. And only on flesh, so how much did it matter?

She would not allow herself to weep.

And when an explosion sounded – a thousand thunders!

– from somewhere above, she didn't scream, didn't shudder. Instead it was Morris who made most noise, calling for her –

'They're here! This is it – things are about to begin!'

80

Burren stained by the sinking of the sun: red and looking raw, and the twins were looking out over, saying –

'That sound is the magic being torn open, Morris. We don't have long.'

'Rubbish. Can't be! Safest place in the Isle, this.'

'No more. Nowhere safe. Not now.'

'Look: we need to get ready. I need to rally the lads.'

'It'll do no good, Morris.'

'Course it will – we need to fight!'

'You can fight all you like but it'll not stop them.'

'I'll put a bullet in any Invader who comes near!'

'You might and all, but these Invaders aren't the ones to worry about.'

'Sister dearest, you don't know what you're –'

'Show me your hand.'

Nothing, for a moment. Then –

'No, Oona. I dunno where you've got your ideas from but I –'

'That thing that's happening to your hand is what needs worrying about.'

'Shut up.'

'And happening to the others too.'

'Be quiet!'

'There's only one way to save things – to stop the King of the North.'

Another moment of nothing, then –

'And how will you be doing that, sister dearest?'

'With this.'

And Oona showed the Loam Stone – it shred of light was shivering, awaiting.

'Let me see your hand,' said Oona.

And Morris showed, slowly – two fingers already lost, hardly able to hold his granda's rifle.

'Soon there'll be nothing left of you or any of the Cause,' Oona told him. 'Trust me – I've seen it.'

And then another impact –

Mist almost a memory, any protection threadbare, failing –

Final thing: everything trembled, and a call came from a voice Oona recognised –

'Members of the Cause – this is the King's Captain addressing you! Surrender the Burren, surrender yourselves, and perhaps we will decide to show you some mercy!'

Oona saw a line lengthening along on the horizon, a heavy darkness like the spread of spilled ink. It was masked only faintly by the linger of mist, then things were revealed to make the heart quake: a mass of soldiers, hundreds on horseback and well readied with rifles and cannons and mortar all waiting to be unleashed. And behind them moved more massive darkness – an army of Muddgloggs.

'As you no doubt see,' the Faceless called,' we have more

power at our disposal than you can possible conceive of! We have too the magic of the Briar-Witches, who have worked to shred the last of your magical fortifications! We have the shadows of the Coach-A-Bower! We have the very earth itself at our disposal! Your own precious Isle has risen against you! And the Cause has this – in simple words for your barbaric minds, no hope at all!'

Oona felt the gaze of every member of the Cause settle on her. She heard one boy say, 'What now?'

Another ask another, 'What can we do against all that?'

A final wondering, thrown at Morris: 'What do we have? What power that can match them?'

Silence, and then a softer voice: beside Oona, Eamon whispered to her –

'Show them what we have.'

Oona stood. And her cry wasn't just for the boys of the Cause, not just for the Faceless and the army of Invaders of creatures they'd recruited, but for Merrigutt –

'We have this!'

She lifted the Loam Stone high and its light brightened as though it sought to blind, bleaching the already white Burren whiter and sending everyone into a cower, shielding their eyes. And even distance couldn't stop Oona seeing: the Invaders too were lowered by the sight, shrinking from the Stone's power, menaced by their own nightmares.

It was Morris who regained himself first. 'You see! We've got more magic than you and we've got more fight! And we've got something on our side too that you can't ever come and claim – the blood and bone and history of this Blessed Isle!'

And the cheer that erupted from the Cause was enough to cheer Oona: she felt an unexpected enough (near unwanted) rush of warmth for her brother, wondering where he'd found such words.

They looked at one another.

'If all we have left of the Kavanaghs is us two,' said Morris, 'then we might as well work together. Like back in Drumbroken?'

'Aye,' said Oona. 'I'd say that's a plan.'

'Very well!' called the Faceless. 'You have made your decision, and now in the name of your King – you shall die by it!'

81

Oona saw so much strength in the lads of the Cause as they formed their own line, kneeling, crumbling hands fumbling with old rifles and crooked pistols. It was the same kind of attitude she'd seen on her journey: in Innislone and Loftborough, in the Hollow Mountain, from men and women and jackdaws and Giants, prepared to fight even if victory couldn't be predicted.

They could never be ready, Oona realised. Not now, not against this.

But Morris was there, calling, 'That's it, boys! That's the spirit! We'll be fit to fight them, won't we? Send them back across the sea to whatever hole they crawled out from!'

A roar of agreement from the Cause.

'What's that sound?' Eamon O'Riley asked Oona.

'I hear nothing,' said Morris, rejoining them. 'You must be just –'

'Quiet,' said Oona. 'I hear it too.'

She asked the Loam Stone for sight and saw this: the Faceless holding a half-closed claw, at his feet the remaining Briar-Witches, their bloated claws beating the surface of the Burren at the same time as the long nails clattered and scratched on

372

stone as though trying to discover a rhythm. What else? Oona looked closer: from the place the Witches were making noise they were making magic: briars were surfacing, then snaking, splitting. They were coming for the Cause.

'Briar-Witches,' said Oona.

'No bother,' said Morris. 'They can't burrow here, not through this stone. We'll not let them get close even.'

'They don't need to burrow,' said Oona for reply. 'They're not coming themselves. Not yet.'

Eamon understood: 'Fire burns any briar better than anything. Used have the things in our scatter-garden back home. Me and Bridget used to get rid of them with a bit of singe-moss and bracken. Two stones smashed together to make a wee spark and away you go! We could try that?'

'Bit short on bracken and moss here,' said Morris.

'Lay a trail of gunpowder?' said Eamon. Morris looked to Oona.

'Didn't I always say an O'Riley would come in useful,' he said.

'Just do it,' said Oona.

'What about the fire?' asked Morris. 'We've no time for smashing stones together.'

'Leave that to me,' said Oona.

So Morris issued the order. Rifles and pistols were opened and gunpowder emptied – boys of the Cause back-walking and letting it leave the same way Merrigutt had laid her scarlet powder over the surface of Ballyboglin, summoning her solitary soldier. Or in the Hollow Mountain or at home in the Kavanagh cottage, same powder used to summon flame. And it was these

373

bright memories, Oona knew, that would give her enough to dream fire when the time came –

'Look!' came the cry of the one of the Cause.

A time already with her –

Oona saw the slither of briars stretching wide over stone. They were crimson, as though they carried blood inside – bright veins on dark, covering the narrow splits on the surface of the Burren. And when their thorns burst through they were black, sharpening in seconds, swelling and –

'Oona!' called Morris. 'Ready when you, sister dearest, but I'd say you better do it now!'

Oona shut her eyes: saw Merrigutt flinging scarlet powder at the feet of Invaders –

Morris: 'Oona, now!'

Opened her eyes and sliced her arm through the air as she'd done on the rooftop in Loftborough –

The line of gunpowder ignited. Flames blue-green sprang towards the sky – high as Oona desired and sizzling with the arrival of briars. Oona's head felt lighter, limbs near weightless: she felt flooded with so much power.

'Get your heads down!' called Morris.

So much smoke – Oona and Morris and Eamon and the other boys had to hide low.

'Can't see,' Oona heard Morris say. 'Stopped the briars but can't see a bloody thing, Oona!' But Oona knew it wouldn't last. Gunpowder would be soon spent. And then?

'It didn't work!' cried one of the Cause.

'Shut up!' Morris told him. 'Worked well enough! Was never going to be that easy!'

374

Sooner than Oona'd thought: smoke departed, and a blackened and smouldering tangle lay on the Burren. Burning briars, but more would follow, wouldn't stop.

'That was good,' said Eamon, 'but what now?'

Oona didn't answer. The Stone was growing colder in her hands, felt so fragile, weakened. Morris allowed barely a moment before he demanded the same: 'What now? What else can you do with that Stone, Oona?'

But another voice was addressing Oona, one that had been too quiet for too long –

'You have nothing, Oona Kavanagh. No power. Nothing but these simple, childlike, colourless dreams. You should have learned by now – nightmares are the most potent thing. You have not mastered your own, but I have so many. I have a multitude awaiting you, in my City across the sea.'

Oona had an image, a sight seen and then slipping away quick: moonlight laid on dark water, a path of rippling silver that stretched towards the edge of everything . . .

'You have so much you still need to know, Oona Kavanagh. So many Echoes you need to hear.'

'Oona!' said Morris, and he suddenly had hands on her shoulders, was almost shaking her.

'What's wrong with you? You can't stay daydreaming! What do we now? *Tell!*'

The sun had almost sunk, would soon leave: magical protection gone, the world around the Burren was lapsing into the same dark that covered the rest of the North.

Oona turned to her brother and said, 'Which way is the quickest to the sea?'

82

'They're coming!'

A call from one of the Cause but may as well have been all –

Oona saw every boy stand, saw the line of darkness in the distance no longer distant but drawing closer: soldiers, Muddgloggs, Coach-A-Bower and –

'Briar-Witches!'

Scratch and scuttle of claw on stone was the nearest thing, the Witches crossing the Burren so swift –

'Which way is it to the sea?' Oona asked her brother again.

'Can't leave,' said Morris. 'Not abandoning the Cause, not these lads.'

'We have to,' said Oona, harsh whisper. 'Listen: you can shoot as many Witches and Invaders as you like but as long as that King lives then nothing will stop this. Nothing's gonna stop the change in this Isle.' She looked to her brother's crumbling hand. 'It'll all be dust and Black before long, you and all your boys of the Cause too, and that's the truth.'

A flinch from Morris. The rifle slipped in his hand.

'It's the Echoes,' Oona told him. 'They're poisoning all of you. I don't know why they start on a person or why you and not me, but we need to find out. And only that King has answers.'

Sound of the Briar-Witch claw closer, almost with them –

'Morris,' said Eamon, coming near. 'What do we do for the best?' The twins looked at one another, hearts fairly hammering.

'Whatever we do,' said Morris, eyes on his own hand, 'we need to do it all together. We took an oath – *Stick together till the end, or else die of the shame of deserting.*'

'Morris,' said Oona, Loam Stone burning, a hungering thing in her hand. 'We have to –'

'Go,' said Eamon. 'It's decided: you too run and we'll stay and fight and distract them.'

'No,' said Morris. 'I'm not dodging the fight now that it's here.'

'And you're not,' said Eamon. 'I believe Oona – the real fight isn't here, it's the one you'll be going to. This King is the one to be stopped. The Isle needs saving or else what'll we have left?'

A moment more, and then first gunfire from the Cause – the decision was taken from them.

'Go on, you stubborn fool!' shouted Eamon, pushing Morris on his way and calling to the Cause. 'Protect Morris and Oona! Don't let a single damnable thing touch them!'

And the Cause were all kneeling, firing, gun smoke adding to smoke from the earlier fire as Briar-Witches leapt, fell, faltering –

And finally –

'East is the way to the sea,' said Morris.

'Then let's go,' said Oona.

They ran right, staying behind the line formed by the Cause but they were hardly far before –

'Look out!'

A glimpse of Briar-Witch – dark and ragged and filthy and bounding and about to descend on them . . .

Stopped by a gunshot.

Oona turned for the source and saw Eamon, rifle releasing a ribbon of smoke.

'Don't stand gawking at me!' he called to the twins, and on they ran.

But too many Witches were attacking and Morris and Oona fought as they went –

She: Stone swung through the air and still thinking fire, flame exploding upwards from the Burren to scorch Briar-Witches, keeping them back.

He: quick rifle-shots, rarely missing.

'Still a quicker eye for all this than you,' said Oona.

'Aye,' said Morris. 'Keep dreaming.'

A seething skein of briars was covering every scrap of the Burren's stone. Morris took the blunt knife from his belt and had to slice rough lumps out of anything that reached for them. He took care of the close, Oona the ahead – but how far to edge of the Burren, to the sea? She couldn't see any end. But what she did see stopped her – the line of dark had severed, Invaders splitting so one group could move north, towards the sea, and the other still heading for the remaining members of the Cause.

'How far?' asked Oona.

'Maybe a mile or two,' said Morris. 'Why?' Then he looked.

'They're gonna get there before us,' said Oona. 'There's too many and we –'

Against her soles Oona felt a tremble. Then a shudder, like stone itself was ready to tear itself free. She knew without needing to imagine: Muddgloggs.

'Can you hear that?' said Morris. 'Or feel it?'

Oona could hear, feel: a deepening hush, a silence, the Coach-A-Bower nearing too.

When Morris spoke she could hardly hear him say, 'We're not enough. They've all this magic gathered and we've nothing. We're from this Isle and they're not and we're the ones with nothing!'

It set Oona wondering – flame was one thing but wasn't good enough. But she'd seen things, met more of the Divided Isle than her brother. And hadn't she brought Merrigutt and the jackdaws to the Hollow Mountain with a desperate wish, so maybe –

'Oona,' said Morris, taking her by the arm. 'We need to decide: go back or keep going on our own. So which now?'

Oona looked to the Loam Stone.

'We keep going on,' she said. 'But if I can manage it, we'll not be alone.'

83

Oona shut her eyes and clutched the Loam Stone so close to her chest she might've been wishing to press it into her heart.

The tremble and shudder was stronger –

Hush deepening, as though she was slipping underwater –

She felt Morris close, his anguished breath against her face. He was waiting, same as Oona: she was waiting to see faces, detail, to remember the way things were, to pluck enough images from memory to summon things . . . but like trying to sketch on a blank page with a numb and unwilling hand, it was almost too much. Fear made itself a distraction as she stood and willed herself –

'Oona!' cried Morris, and he grabbed her arm to drag her away –

She opened her eyes, but didn't move –

A Muddglogg above, towering monstrous, a thing Oona couldn't hope to control. Its body was hedgerow and dispelled forest, cottage and farmhouse and field, shards of gravestone studding its scalp like a grim crown. Oona imagined generations buried safe being ripped from the earth – so many settled bones now disturbed, secreted somewhere within its massive body.

And then came a memory for Oona, enough of a kindling for her imagination, the Giants and their condemnation: '*To bid the land to rise, for generations to be exhumed and defiled when they wish to lie dead – such a crime!*'

Morris shouted, '*Run!*'

But still Oona wouldn't move herself.

'Oona, for the Sorrowful Lady's sake!' said Morris, shaking her.

'No,' she said. 'Wait . . . wait . . . I almost have it . . .'

The Muddglogg raised one dark foot above them –

And Oona dreamed Giants, the Loam Stone flaring into its pure white self –

They heard: 'There! The girl who has mastered the Nightmare Stone – protect her! Stop that unholy creature!'

A trio of Giants came striding then sprinting across the Burren and throwing themselves on the Muddglogg. Even straining to their tallest height, the Giants only had half a hope of being almost half as high as the Muddglogg, but their weight was enough to make the creature stagger, fall back.

'Now let's go,' said Oona.

'Oona,' said Morris, breathless but not from running, 'are you gonna tell me what in the Sorrowful Lady's name is happening?'

'Something,' said Oona, and smiled.

'Well if you can do that,' said Morris, 'could you not think a way of us to beat those Invaders to the sea?'

But in the same moment two darknesses dropped – dusk, and the Coach-A-Bower sweeping to a stop in front of them.

Oona and Morris stopped where they stood.

The heard the queasy clash of metal against metal, saw the

stallions with their off-milky eyes watching. But it was too dark to see the Coachmen.

'Stay behind me,' said Oona, remembering Loftborough, remembering Bridget.

Morris cocked his rifle.

'Won't do a bit of good,' Oona told him. 'No bullet or blade will stop these things.'

'How do you – ?' began Morris,

'I know,' said Oona. 'I know too well.'

'Well, we can't just stand here and –'

A crack like bone between teeth and a whip lashed out of the dark and closed around Morris's throat. He fell, was dragged, feet kicking but not relinquishing his grandfather's rifle – Oona took the blade from his hand and slammed it down on the whip. It didn't snap. She tried again – same nothing. Gave it a third time go and this time saw in her mind the Mother of the Briar-Witches in her nest, heard again the scream as Oona had separated the creature from its claw . . . and for a moment in her mind there was no *then* or *now*, only the act: the blade went down and the whip was severed, the rest of it retreating into the gloom and Morris left released.

'Don't move,' said Oona, pulling Morris to his feet. 'They could be standing around us.' They stood back to back, Oona still with the blade in her hand, Morris still with his rifle, the pair of them with eyes sweeping the sudden night.

'We're near blind in this dark,' said Morris. 'Could do with some more that fire right now, what you think, sister dearest?'

But Oona's hearing had snagged on one word: *blind*.

She had barely begun to think it before a fresh sound tore

382

open the hush. A single howl sounded, then more – a myriad as so many hurtling bodies coloured grey-white-silver-mud arrived, Whereabouts Wolves storming from nowhere as they had down into the pass of the Melancholy Mountains. And just like Oona had first seen them, they were leaping high – over the carriages of the Coach-A-Bower or, if she wished it, colliding with and toppling them.

Morris's mouth hung open.

Oona did her best imitation of the same jig Mrs McSooth had done in Loftborough – clapped her hands three times quick and stamped the right foot twice – and one Wolf stopped beside her. She knew it was her very own Whereabouts, same one that had carried her across Black, and without a pause Oona took handfuls of its hair and pulled herself up to straddle its spine.

She looked at Morris.

'Are you serious?' he asked.

'Just get on,' Oona told him. 'She'll not bite.'

Morris pulled himself up, awkward as anything, to sit behind his sister.

The coat of the Whereabouts Wolf went as stiff as wire – such a yearning for somewhere to go, and Oona had only to lean close and whisper into one of its hooded ears: 'Take us to the edge of everything.'

84

Oona with her arms around the Whereabouts Wolf's neck and Morris with his arms around her waist, and they were a tireless thing bounding across Black, towards more awaiting dark – the line of Invaders massing, looking as much like one animal as the twins and their Wolf.

Beside them ran the other Whereabouts, as countless as they'd been in the Black and all hurling themselves forward with such speed it made Oona giddy to witness. She held on tighter, and looked ahead –

More Muddgloggs were stationed behind the Invaders, and in front was the squirm of dark scraps, more Briar-Witches making their magic. Oona felt terrified, but only for a moment: she had her Stone, after all, and her ideas, and herself.

'Faster,' she told their Wolf.

'Nearly there now,' said Morris, readying his rifle.

And sure enough there was sound – the sea not far, Oona imagining it shrugging restless against the shore.

The first gunshot that came was from the Invaders – Morris returned fire –

And Oona felt as though she only blinked and then suddenly

could see the eyes of the soldiers, their rifle-barrels aiming and uniforms still adhering to their surroundings so perfectly as Morris told her, 'Head down!' His hands left her waist and Oona ducked so he could fire over her head and keep firing.

She whispered to the Whereabouts, 'Keep going. Keep going as long as you can!'

But they were deep into the thicket of briars and Oona felt them reach for her, the Wolf slowing as it was ensnared. The rest of the Whereabouts pack powered on and threw themselves on the Invaders, knocking some from their horses but most only falling, broken on the Burren.

A sudden tightening around Oona's arm, the one that held the Stone – a briar that had her, then pulled her bodily from the Wolf, any cry for help lost to the air and Morris being carried on, still shooting at the Invaders.

Oona was slammed against stone and instantly encircled, and no matter how much she tried with the blade to beat the briars back they had the better of her – around ankles and chest and neck and she thought of the Briar-Witch nest and herself and the boy of the Big House almost strangled . . .

'I spy her over there, Sally! Go and help her, quick! She's trapped in those fouls things!'

Had Oona even thought it? Dreamed it fully? Whether she had or not she had help in the next moment – a stone girl liberated from her fountain sprang into the scene and started to rip and tear at the briars that held Oona, swearing and cursing and shouting as she tore one squirming limb after another, 'Leave her be, you filthy weeds! Let her go! I'll show you some strength!'

'That's it,' said a voice, 'keep at them, sister!'

And the boy – liberated from his Big House – was beside Oona, his stone hands too doing their best to free her. Not as strong as his sister, but he was as decided on helping and soon Oona was free, abandoning the blade, holding only to the Loam Stone.

'Very well done, Sally,' said the boy of the Big House.

'Not so shoddy yourself,' said his sister.

The three of them moved closer together, but it was a reunion short-lived –

'There she is! Don't let her escape! Get the Stone!'

Cry of an Invader – the Faceless? She could hardly tell – and Oona felt the earth shake beneath her as soldiers on horseback and Briar-Witches and Muddgloggs all made her their target –

'Oh dear,' said the boy of the Big House.

'Oh dear indeed,' said Oona.

'Stop with your oh-dear-dears!' Sally told them. 'You've got that Stone, girl – use it!' But what else or who? From where?

'Look out!' shouted the Master of the Big House, pointing upwards. Oona registered crimson eyes, dark feather, claws ready to snatch –

A volley of images and wishes and hopes shot through her –

A knife thrown into the air sent the Changeling wheeling at the last moment –

'You lose that gun I gave you?' said Billy O'Riley. 'Prefer these anyway.'

He stood with another blade in his hand, and many more at his belt. Then more detail, the more Oona remembered him: arms tattooed to the elbows, hair and clothes singed, just as she'd seen him last, as though no time had passed between the night of Innislone's burning and there on the Burren.

'Are you even real?' she had to wonder aloud. She realised she was asking herself. Realised it didn't matter a bit.

And behind Billy were more of the men of Innislone, all with knives ready. But not only men, thought Oona. She decided: we need more.

'We're ready and willing as ever,' said another voice, a woman's voice.

Out of the black stepped the landlady of The Loyal Martyr. And behind her all the loyal women of Loftborough – Mrs McSooth and Mrs Molloy and Mrs Donnelly and Mrs O'Keefe and more, all with rake and shovel and spade and whatever weapon in hand.

'Are these women up to this fight?' asked Billy, looking them over.

'We're better able than you, sonny jim!' the landlady told him.

'Now this is an army!' cried the boy of the Big House, knocking his stone hands together. Gunshots from the Invaders, and a roar went up, not from the men of Innislone but from the stone statue of Sally: 'Attack!'

As one, they raced ahead: Oona between the children of the Big House and Billy and his men and the Loftborough women behind. And behind Oona sensed the trio of Giants she'd summoned following too, ready for the fight. Whatever Whereabouts Wolves that still remained threading by them. One Wolf ran up alongside, and from its back someone called –

'Get on!'

Morris took Oona's free hand and hauled her onto the Wolf's back.

'Now quickly,' he told the Whereabouts. 'Straight ahead now!'

Oona saw the line of Invaders and Muddgloggs and Briar-Witches –

'Now leap!' Morris ordered, and the Wolf rose high, vaulting over the army –

Moment like weightlessness, hovering in the dark –

And then down, and then on.

'I could get used to having one of these,' said Morris.

'Is it far?' asked Oona, seeing nothing.

'Not far at all,' said Morris.

'How do you know?'

'Because we're already there.'

85

They stopped at the end, the edge – a cliff that dropped deep and sheer and Oona looked out over her first sea. It spoke in small whispers of cold and loneliness and danger. She looked with a kind of longing towards the battle.

'No,' said Morris. 'They're all back there fighting so we can do this, remember?'

'Yes,' said Oona, but still she had to fight to tear her gaze away: from friends, from those she'd brought from miles away to fight the Invaders. The Loam Stone grew hot in her hand. She heard that voice say: '*Do not pretend that what lies behind is what you are craving, Oona Kavanagh. The dark of what lies ahead is what draws you now.*'

'You're right,' she said, and Oona slipped from the Whereabouts.

'He's a handy one to have,' said Morris, laying a hand on the Wolf's snout. It shook him off – so docile and suddenly so violent.

'What's wrong with it?' asked Morris.

'It's not a *he*,' said Oona.

'Sorry,' said Morris.

But the Whereabouts was gone – pale thing streaking off into the dark, back towards the battle.

'Here,' said Morris, kneeling by the edge of the Burren.

Oona saw a shallow steps trickling down the cliffside. Near-vertical, not a bit of support. It was all they had as a way down.

'Let's go,' she said, and began.

As soon as she settled her first foot on the step, the weather began to harass them: wind plucking and rain beginning, driving cold into their bones. It reminded Oona of the contrary magic that controlled the rope-bridge spanning the Divide – something wanted to stop them.

'We're gonna be blown clean off this!' cried Morris.

'No!' Oona told him. 'I'll not be beaten by a bunch of bewitched steps!'

The tumult from the Burren was lost – there was no point in thinking of what was happening there, Oona knew. The King of the North was right – there was only the way ahead, the way down into the dark.

Soon they had to move in a crouch or risk falling, and holding hands, and shuffling.

'How did you learn to use that thing?' asked Morris, suddenly.

'Don't know,' said Oona, not being able to remember exactly when, exactly how she had come to understand the Stone. 'Our great-grandfather Aedan explained first to me about it.'

'Great-grandfather?' said Morris. 'You mean one that's dead?'

'Yes,' said Oona.

'Sounds true enough,' said Morris.

'It is true!' said Oona.

'Sounds like you were dreaming,' said Morris. Oona didn't

390

bother with anything more.

And not too soon or any way unwelcome – their feet touched rock together. Shattered rock, everything broken, ruined shore, and Oona remembered: what Merrigutt had described when the King's City had first surfaced, the wave it had sent crashing over land destroying, removing so much of the coast.

'What the – ?' said the Morris.

Oona saw a desperate litter of thousands, fish all stranded on sand and stone, bodies darkened and bloodied. Poisoned, just like Merrigutt had said. And she glimpsed other things too: stone that might've been a wall once, driftwood that might've been a roof. All homes, all destroyed.

'We need to keep going,' said Oona.

Clamber, crawl – Oona's feet were grazed, elbows becoming bloodied, the rattle of Morris's rifle one of the few sounds. Her brother didn't ask where they were going exactly, or how far or how they'd get there even. And Oona was grateful – in the image she'd been given there'd been the full moon laying light across the sea, but no moon was above, the sky too overcome with cloud.

Morris slipped, swore.

'Can't see a thing!' he said. 'Anything could be hiding here and we'd not know!'

So much shadow. Oona stopped: she remembered the cellar of the Big House, the boy she'd since come to know so keen to remain concealed within it. And remembered Merrigutt's magic –

'Don't move,' said Oona.

She held the Loam Stone high and saw in her mind those

silent lightning strokes, bright shivers, and the black above them was rent by a single streak of scarlet. The clouds were thrown back and the face of the moon was unveiled. So bright, so full it looked overflowing. It poured a long trail of silver on the surface of the sea – a causeway stretching from broken shore, but towards where? What unknown elsewhere at the edge of the world?

'This way now,' said Oona, stepping down to the sea.

'Where are you going?' asked Morris. 'Have you lost it completely?'

Oona settled one foot on moonlight. Cold raced into every bit of her, as though the surface had frozen solid beneath her soles. She stood for a long time, wondering if she could bear it, breathless.

'*You have endured worse, Oona Kavanagh. What is the simple pain of the flesh, after what you have witnessed?*'

And Oona found she could suffer it.

'Quick,' she told Morris. 'We don't have long left. He's waiting for us.' And Oona settled sight on the horizon, and started to walk across the sea.

FINAL

THE CITY
OF CITIES

86

Last time: see Oona, in a place not near broken shore but nearer to where she must go. On her journey she had walked many roads: White, Blackened, and now Silver. A moonlit way leading to the edge of the everything. In her hands she held the Loam Stone, its single shred of white light unmoving. Dark sea was spread calm on either side, a surface so cold she had to go along on tip toe. But not alone – see Morris, walking two-steps-and-a-bit behind.

Together, the twins were crossing the sea.

And not for the first (or second or even umpteenth) time, Morris in shivering words asked her, 'How far now?'

'Not much longer,' said Oona.

'How do you know?' asked Morris.

'Just do,' said Oona, truthfully.

Not a minute had passed and as though Oona's certainty had summoned it, she saw something pale against the sky, like frost clinging with brittle fingers to the dark in the distance. Oona felt the Loam Stone warm her hand for a moment – acknowledgement, or warning?

She paused and pointed ahead, breathing, 'The City of

Echoes.' Morris swore under his breath.

They watched, and the City spread, wanting to encompass the whole horizon. It was crowned with sharp needles of rock. But Oona blinked and the needles appeared softer, rounder, announcing a place more grand – elegant turrets and spires, soaring towers of cold white.

'You are almost here,' the voice of the King told Oona. *'So far, so much pain in your mind. But you have not yet seen the worst.'*

'Ready?' asked Morris. Oona nodded, then began again. The twins hadn't walked far when they reached out in the same moment, wordless, and took each other's hand.

Oona kept her eyes on the City, unable to ignore the rising warmth of the Stone . . . and as she watched, she saw the City rise further, widening. Too soon it was all she could see. Too soon, they were there.

'Which way is the way in?' asked Morris.

Oona searched but didn't see any place to enter: the City's surface was pock-marked, so many dark places where things could be lost. And for a moment it looked to Oona like somewhere unspeakably ancient: sunken and then hauled to the surface, broken and rebuilt, enduring. But then not: another moment, another blink, and things looked better – not wounds at all but narrow windows, sculpted arches, broad balconies . . .

Oona was glad to hear Morris say, 'It changes.'

Oona nodded and said, 'Wants to fool us. Wants us in.'

'But where do we – ?' began Morris.

Summoned by their asking – the City allowed a new dark to form, only feet from the twins: their wished-for entrance.

They looked at one another, tried for a deep breath each,

and in they walked.

Narrow passage, no part of it even. Oona had the same sense of unknown nightmares and pernicious magic as on her journey down into the Briar-Witch nest. Same feeling: this was a place they were't meant to be, and they were moving towards something that shouldn't ever be seen.

'Move faster, Oona Kavanagh.'

And the walls twitched. And the twins hurried on, still hand-in-hand, Morris ahead and at the end both of them stumbled and fell onto their knees as the entrance squeezed shut behind them.

Oona was first on her feet, asking Morris, 'You all right?'

'Fine,' he said, but stayed where he was. He was watching the slow crumble of his own hand.

'You're not all right,' she said. 'It's the Echoes. You're starting to –'

'Don't bloody fuss,' he said, and summoned the effort to stand, eyes shut tight. 'Need to keep going. Don't worry about me.'

Oona said nothing more as they moved on. But they'd taken hardly a shuffling step each before they were stopped by a sight, and both swore to themselves –

A city made of cities – a magpie place, ruins gathered and stacked, so many palaces and temples and Worshipping Houses and mansions and cottages and all homes gathered in hoard, and all broken and shattered, teetering or already toppled. Oona saw pillars reaching high and others only stumps; archways that reminded her of the entrance to the Burren, some the right size for a child to wander through and others tall enough for a Muddglogg to pass comfortably beneath; staircases spiralling high, to nowhere sensible, and then stopping . . . And it was black. After the pale exterior (the lie, Oona realised) of the City, and everything inside was burned, decimated. And so cold. And something else – everywhere around them stood dark statues.

Morris leaned close and whispered, 'They look just like people.'

Oona knew he was right. Not statues at all. And more than this – she knew why they had come to be that way.

'Do you hear them, Oona? Do you hear the desperation of Echoes?'

'I do,' said Oona, aloud.

Morris looked at her.

'Listen,' she told him.

And the air was filled with low whisper – *the Echoes.*

The twins were drawn onwards, hearing –

'I will not give in, not ever! My father was a great man and I was his son!'

'I'll not let my family down by relenting! I was born in this Isle and I'll die here!'

'I'd rather be turned to dust than die with dishonour! I will not surrender!'

Hundreds (or thousands!) of figures populated the King's City, but Oona knew if she'd decided to look and examine each, she wouldn't have discovered one that wasn't a boy. Like the men of the Cause she'd encountered in the Melancholy Mountains, she saw so many frozen attitudes – of fright, of defiance, but all open-mouthed, hands lingering in half-raised poses. And still their fervent whispers, the abiding echoes –

'We'll fight on till the end!'

'We'll do our fathers proud!'

'Nothing better than an honourable death!'

'For country and not for King – we'll fight till the end!'

'Come on,' said Morris. 'We'll not end up like these ones. We'll not fail.'

Oona's eyes went to her brother's hand, to the grey canker that had gotten rid of two fingers already. It was still managing to hold their grandfather's rifle.

'Come on,' he said again. 'We need to find the centre of things. That's where this King will be hiding.'

And Oona only nodded.

Such a distance they wandered through – felt like lost miles, long years, generations wasted. And everywhere the black. Or, thought Oona, Black? Things more made sense – this was the King's home, and he wished to have everywhere look like it. She remembered from what seemed like another time: *'I am what this Isle will become: it will be remade in my image.'*

But finally Morris pointed with his rifle and said, 'Look there.'

A forest. Familiar sight, almost comforting – as though it had been chosen just for them. But not – it was the forest Oona recognised from her nightmares, and from the nightmare of every Invader.

'This is it,' said Oona. She held the Stone tighter.

On Oona's eyelashes and toes – against lips and fingertips – she felt a wintry feather-brush, like slow snowfall. Ash. The forest was slowly burning, soundlessly, silent white fire devouring.

They stopped on the fringes and waited for entry.

'Don't be afraid,' Morris told her.

'Too late for that,' said Oona.

'Good,' said Morris. 'Because I'm bloody terrified.'

And with sickening sounds of crunch and snap and groan – and the Echoes of the boys growing to such a cacophony of vow and assurance and affirmation that Oona couldn't think her own thoughts – the trees parted, and the Kavanagh twins stepped into the forest.

Only in, and the trees knotted closed behind. The whispers died. They were surrounded by silence, standing in a clearing with a floor of scorched stone.

'Where is he?' asked Morris.

All around the forest continued to burn without protest.

'Hiding probably,' said Morris.

Something moved. Or perhaps everything: branches were squirming, roots leaving the ground to waver and crackle and Morris pointed his rifle high and low, higher, Oona holding the Loam Stone close, both turning on the spot, spine-to-spine, watching.

'See anything?' asked Morris.

'No,' said Oona. And then she whispered, 'He won't let us see him. Not till he wants it.' And standing there in the centre of the King's City, Oona felt so closely examined. As though she was being stripped of her tougher self and left like a fluid denied its jar: the longer she stood, the more vulnerable she became.

Then the voice that Oona knew well decided to speak, but not only for her –

'You come to confront me, Kavanagh twins? Or have you come to learn?'

Not a moment and Morris shouted back, 'We've come to destroy you! Same way as you've been destroying our Blessed Isle!'

A sound like breathing.

'Come out and fight, you bloody coward!' shouted Morris.

And as her brother's words died, Oona saw the Echoes take stronger hold of Morris – his hand crumbling, the rifle slipping no matter how strong he tried to hold it.

'You have come to confront your King?' said the voice of the forest.

Morris opened his mouth but Oona took his hand, whispering, 'Don't say anything. Look at your hand – you're making it worse.'

But he pulled himself free, telling her in a hiss: 'We have to stop him! And I'd rather die anyway than let this creature take our Isle! Da and Granda wouldn't have allowed it if they were here!'

'A boy of large ambition,' said the King. 'Who wishes only to walk the footsteps of his father and grandfather, to speak their rotten words. But so simple a child too, so base – like so many I have met on this Isle, you have nothing in your head but Echoes.'

'Don't play games with me!' called Morris, breathless. 'Show yourself!' More silence.

Oona watched the slow squirm of branches, the waver of white fire.

'Your brother,' said the King, addressing Oona, 'will soon

be no more. He sees the rot, the thing that is destroying him, but yet he cannot resist it.'

'If I have to be destroyed then I will be!' shouted Morris. 'I'll happily go the same way as this Isle that you've Blackened!'

'I have done nothing more than what is natural,' said the voice of the King, from beside them, from above: from everywhere, even inside their own heads. 'What is more inevitable than destruction? What else does a forest long for than to burn? Or a mountain to fall? Or a heart to be broken?'

'Shut up!' called Morris. 'Stop trying to fool us and bloody-well show yourself!' A pause. And then the King spoke: 'Very well.'

Oona's eyes were drawn at once to a single tree – its trunk massive, dark, starting to shudder.

'Stay behind me,' said Morris, trying to position himself in front of his sister.

'No,' said Oona. 'Side-by-side.' So together they faced things.

The tree split. The bark began to flake, peeling away like the tenderest skin against flame. And within was an uneasy darkness. It breathed, shivered, wheezed, and Oona had the sense of something as ancient as the City that surrounded them.

'Be ready,' Morris whispered to Oona. 'Don't think – just fight.'

'Thoughtless boy,' spoke the King, spoke the dark within the tree. 'It is what will be your undoing.'

A final pause.

Then the Loam Stone burned so hot in Oona's hand she would've any other time released it.

'You cannot see what dark you move towards,' said the King.

404

'Now – see me.' And the forest gave up the King of the North –

A figure as tall as any tree surrounding. Looking sculpted from the same charred and pitted wood too, the King trailed leaves still alight – a mantel of white fire. He took small steps forward and the twins took larger steps back. Oona saw what she decided was a head – rough block bitten with faint features, hollows gouged for eyes, a rough gash for a mouth. Long needle-sharp splinters were the King's soaring crown. As the King moved, stumbled, one gnarled hand was held close and one leg trailed long after like a withered root.

'He's nothing,' said Morris, almost smiling. 'Nothing powerful at all. Too old.'

And with any similar sight, Oona might've felt pity. But Morris wouldn't ever have been prepared to relent –

'In the name of the noble Cause,' he said, raising the Kavanagh rifle, finger sneaking around the trigger, 'and for the people of Drumbroken and for my father and grandfather and all in this Blessed Isle that you've destroyed, I will –'

'Will not,' said the King, and the hollows of his eyes burned with the same white fire that covered the forest.

And Morris couldn't pull the trigger. His remaining fingers were softening, slowly falling.

Not only his hand but whole arm was transforming, transforming to dust and blackened earth and he roared with frustration, 'I will kill you! I'm stronger than you are! You won't take this Isle! I will be the one to –'

No more words: only a stream of dark earth was expelled from between Morris's jaws.

'Stop it!' said Oona. She stepped in front of her brother,

Loam Stone held high. 'I can do anything I like with this Stone, so don't think I won't!'

'It is not for me to stop anything,' said the King. 'He has brought this magic onto himself.'

'You were the one who brought the Echoes!' said Oona.

'No,' said the King. He began to move towards Oona, cape a pale slither behind. 'The Echoes were here long before I came – you know this, Oona Kavanagh. You have seen those nightmares.'

And the Stone gave her fast these sights – father with his hand crumbling, men of the Cause only dust and dropping, boy on the Black road dispersing on darkened air . . .

'If you can dream whatever you wish,' said the King, 'then why don't you save your brother? You hold the truth in your hand – can make your wishes a reality, so why not help him?'

A pause. Oona knew the answer before the King provided it –

'Because you cannot bring yourself to dream it.'

Oona wanted to contradict. Looked to her brother and thought of him as he should be: bone and flesh with blood whirling beneath, not the slowly decaying thing she saw. But still he continued to change: feet hardening, a slow grey climbing his legs, still unable to speak.

'Why did you come here?' asked the King, still slowly approaching, still dragging his cape of quiet fire. 'Why did you need to face me?'

'Because I needed to know things,' said Oona. 'I had to find out. What are you?'

'I have wandered this world for countless generations,' said the King. 'I have feasted on cities and peoples, on children.

406

Drawn sustenance from their dreams – from all the wild and wondrous wishes of humankind. And I came to your Isle seeking such riches. But instead I have found not dreams in the children here – not ambition nor adventure nor inspiration nor anything that could be called new – but only Echoes.'

'You only took boys,' said Oona.

A pause, and the King said: 'I doubt I'd find anything more nourishing in any other child.'

'What are the Echoes?' asked Oona, stepping back and back but at the same time wanting to stay close to Morris, and at the same time needing to know. *'Tell!'*

'You have been listening to them your whole life,' said the King. 'I did not bring them to this Isle – I only used magic to make them manifest. They are the words and ways that endure without thought, without question: the hatreds and traditions that trickle from one generation to the next, poured like a poison from the mouth of a father into the innocent ear of a son. From a thoughtless mother to an unknowing daughter. They are the opposite of the Stone you hold in your hand – they are the enemy of dreaming, of all imagination, of the kind of hope that takes a person beyond their own horizon, as your own hope and ambition took you.'

Somehow, each word was expected by Oona. It was already known. It was what she'd seen, heard, had nightmared on her journey North: her father and his fight to follow his own father, and her brother and his fight to follow them both. And Merrigutt and the other women – their fight to be free of what was expected of them, what their mothers had been doing for generations . . . only they had resisted, and succeeded in escaping the Echoes. And –

'The Cause.'

Another voice.

Oona turned – the Faceless stood behind, scarlet-eyed bird on his shoulder.

'The Cause that embodies all these things,' said the Changeling.

'The Cause resists you too,' said Oona. 'It's not all bad – at least they're fighting!'

'What is a fight worth,' said the King, moving towards her, 'if it is so heedless?'

'So pointless,' said the crimson-eyed bird, Faceless closing in.

'Stay back!' shouted Oona.

'You have no power to dictate anything here,' said the Changeling. 'You have done well to get this far, but no further now. You have no one to save you, nothing to help.' The bird was growing, claws lengthening. 'The command is simple, Oona Kavanagh – give us the Nightmare Stone.'

Oona looked to the object her grandmother had given her, the thing that had plagued the women of the Kavanagh family for generations. Then she looked to the King.

'You need this,' she said. 'You need this Stone to survive, to give you dreams enough to keep going?'

'Yes,' said the King of the North. 'You have seen so much pain, Oona. Surely you wish, now to surrender it. To be free of its darkness?'

Oona closed her eyes, and she saw again the things she wished she'd never seen: her family with all secrets and hurt uncovered . . .

'It has driven many in your family mad,' she heard the King say, sounding so close, voice like the slow dying of a forest at the hands of fire. 'You see, you cannot fully know yourself – it is the hardest thing, child. The Stone will show you such horrors, such truth that you will be ripped asunder by the knowledge. Give me the Stone, Oona, before it destroys you completely.'

Oona opened her eyes, and she saw again the worst thing as though it was being reenacted before her: Merrigutt entering a bright sky, ready to help, hopeful, and then shot down, falling through sunlight . . .

'You're wrong,' said Oona. 'I've seen the worst already, and I've survived it. And by the Sorrowful Lady – I will not surrender this Stone.'

A moment, and then the cry of the King: 'Take her!'

Hands of the Faceless outstretched, Changeling shrieking –

Oona swiped the Stone through the air and the first thing that came were jackdaws – dropping as they'd done on the White Road and attacking the Changeling, so much feather and blood and noise –

'Give it to me!' cried the King, reaching for her.

Another swipe: Oona bid white fire to leap from the trees and lunge at the King –

Shrunken and decrepit he was, but powerless he wasn't: his own dreams leeched from countless minds, the King waved a creaking hand and willed the pale fire to become mist, to drop and enshroud Oona. And she was suddenly lost. Couldn't see Morris, couldn't see herself.

Silence, and then the voice of the King –

'You have not seen the worst, Oona Kavanagh. There is one

final nightmare. One thing you need to see – I promised you it would be shown, and now you shall know it.'

And the Loam Stone blazed bright in Oona's hand, shaping a scene on the mist –

She saw Morris. Not the Morris of that moment, nor the one before; not even the same boy she'd seen taken by the Briar-Witches so many miles since. It was Morris as a boy, standing on tip toe, peering in through the window of the Kavanagh cottage.

Oona heard her mother's soft voice from inside: *'Like everywhere in this Isle – it will change. Like you – it will Blacken, and rot.'*

And then the blow from her father.

Then nothing. For a long time, no sound. Their father appeared suddenly in the doorway, spying Morris and grabbing him and asking, 'Where's your sister? Where's she hiding?'

'Not here,' was all Morris said. And then he asked, in a small voice: 'Mammy fell. Why isn't she getting up?'

Their father said nothing, not at first. But lies came easy: 'She's with the Sorrowful Lady now. Let's go in and get her laid out, like you saw with your granda, just the same as that. And Morris' (he leaned close to his son) 'don't tell your sister what you saw. Keep it between us and your granny, yes? Just our secret. We're the men of this house, and that means taking care of things, okay?'

Morris nodded, and let himself be led indoors.

'He knew?' said Oona.

'Yes,' said the King. 'Knew, and tried so unsuccessfully to bury it.'

410

'No,' said Oona, but her protest was nothing. And never had the Loam Stone felt so fragile, so reduced, so dim. As Oona watched, it looked to liquefy in her hand; to melt until she could've been holding in her cupped palm only a dark puddle of blood.

'Now you know,' said the King. 'Now you must surrender it.'

But Oona knew something else. Something learned, something remembered: *'It cannot be destroyed. It thrives on nightmares, and there is enough of those to sustain it for a lifetime. It shall endure even as you slowly are destroyed.'*

'It can be broken,' said Oona. She swallowed. 'It's done the worst it can, it has nothing now – no more nightmares to torment me with, no more truth. It's mine, and I can destroy it.'

Suddenly the mist deserted and Oona saw: the forest had closed in, Morris standing closer – He forced out a cry: 'Oona, behind you!'

Oona turned: the Faceless was rushing towards her, Changeling on his shoulder, and she snatched her grandfather's rifle from Morris's hands, more words resounding in her memory: *'The bird does the talking, the thinking, all things – the bird is the thing you need to worry about.'*

And she aimed and she fired. Bullet struck the bird –

Nothing, only the Faceless stopping dead.

And then a final scream, the Changeling flickering between so many desperate forms – small or large or sleek or ragged but always dark. And then no more, the Faceless only an empty thing without its manipulator sinking beside.

'Oona.'

A single word from Morris, so faint. And then he fell too.

411

Oona dropped the rifle and rushed to catch, kneeled and held him as she'd held too many. Watched him as she'd had to watch others leave. One arm was gone, had been eaten away by the Echoes. And the rest of him – no more substantial than the straw men the pair of them had made back in Drumbroken for the Loughleagh Fires. And when he spoke, it was from behind a mask of ash, words just whispers –

'I'm sorry,' he said. 'I should've told. Should've said what our father was. We should've run away. Just left.'

'We couldn't have done that,' said Oona. 'Left Drumbroken just like that? Left home?'

'You did,' said Morris.

Oona looked for the King but couldn't see him, couldn't tell him apart from the trees surrounding.

'It's not too late now,' said Oona, but didn't know whether she believed it. The Loam Stone was slipping from her hand, so keen to leave her: it knew that if it found no fresh nightmares to feed on soon, it would end.

Morris throat twitched, forcing final words out. He said, 'I wish I wasn't a Kavanagh.' Oona closed her eyes, and told her brother, 'You're not. You're just you now.'

And she waited for what felt decided, all the while dreaming of herself and Morris and back in Drumbroken together, as they'd been before, memories returning she didn't know still lived in her mind . . . She felt a hand touch her cheek. Opened her eyes: her brother's face was clearing, the Echoes retreating as swiftly as they'd left Merrigutt and the other women of Loftborough as they'd escaped home.

'You're doing it,' said Morris. 'You're making them go away.'

But there was no time for more –

White flame an inferno around them –

Trees shriveling like scorched ribbon –

And the King reappeared, bearing down on the twins.

Oona knew she had less than a breath, time only for one last dream: scarlet powder in her hand that she flung into the ruined face of the King. Fire swept over him, consuming him, but still he was reaching for the Stone as Oona cried, 'Now the end of all this!'

She slammed the Loam Stone against the ground –

It came apart so easily, ending as though in relief –

A crack shook everything, a breach zig-zagging across the ground –

Oona made weak: she fell beside her brother as though she'd taken a blow to the stomach –

And the ground split, and the remains of the King of the North fell into the opening dark.

'You didn't do too bad,' said Morris, all the time strengthening, trying to rise. 'Not bad at all, sister dearest.'

But Oona wasn't rising: she wanted to weep, to curl in on herself and remain, a grief so heavy on her it was like losing Merrigutt all over again, and worse. In her palm, she held the smallest possible shard of Loam Stone.

'Morris,' she said. 'What now?'

'No,' Morris told her, 'you're not giving up now, not a bit. Not after you dragged me all the way here.'

The ground began to tilt, pitch. The ruins of cities of countless ages all crumbling – the City of Echoes was collapsing.

'I say we escape,' said Morris. 'And live to fight another day.'

And he lifted Oona to her feet.

What else then? They ran, feeling everything around them folding, crashing and trembling – Kingdom without its King destroying itself. And on their way they heard the boys who had been taken by the King whispering new words –

'*Go! Escape! Build a better place than we left behind!*'

'*Don't make the same mistakes we did!*'

'*Run!*'

'*This way!*'

'*Here! Over here!*'

Not just calling but pointing then, willing their ancient arms of ash and dust to shift, directing the twins towards the way out –

'*Hurry! You don't have long!*'

Avoiding the fall of those mammoth arches, of cascading cities, Oona stayed close to her brother, half-leaning against him. And no passageway, no walls – they were suddenly out and into an erstwhile-light, an almost day. But no way back – their path across the sea had thawed.

'Dream it!' shouted Morris, the sound of the city's collapse so loud. 'Imagine you're back on the shore!'

'I don't know if I can,' said Oona, trying only to breathe.

'You can,' he said. 'You must.'

Oona looked up – stone was falling towards them, a spike as sharp as the King's crown –

'Please,' said Morris.

Oona shut her eyes, squeezing the shard of Loam Stone until she felt her skin tear and her mind tear too with the effort of dreaming, a scream leaving her lungs and –

Nothing, nowhere –

No breathing, no words. Not until Oona heard something: a crashing of water, but from far off. Until she felt something: her brother's breathing, and his hand in hers.

'Open your eyes,' he told her. 'Don't be frighted.'

Oona looked – they were back. The broken shore was scattered around them, and it was just as dismal as sight.

'Not there,' Morris told her. 'Look up.'

She saw a sky that might've just discovered colour – so much blue and purple and pink. And on the horizon there was no lingering dark, no threat – only the blazing promise of a new day.

Finally, Oona sank to the ground, Morris dropping beside her.

'Where is it?' he asked. 'The last bit of the Stone?'

Oona lifted her hand to show: only a splinter, and it had worked its way into her palm; something so small there was no hope of it being unpicked. But it glowed, faintly, like a fresh bruise – a crimson-darkness just beneath the skin. She found herself thinking of her great- grandfather in the Big House, trapped by the act that had killed him. His warning, and her promise: that she would be different from all the Kavanagh women that had gone before.

'It's nothing that can hurt anybody now,' she said, and closed her eyes.

A breeze smoothed the sea, made silence.

'Where now?' Morris asked. 'Where will we go?'

'Don't know,' said Oona. 'Maybe anywhere.'

She felt the splinter of Stone shiver inside her palm. Only small jolts, like the last kicks of life, and not nightmares shown but surely dreams – like her mother's paintings, Oona saw places made by her own imagination . . . scenes beautiful, full of colour, improbable, maybe possible . . .

'Or everywhere,' said Oona. And suddenly she was standing, was taking her brother's hand and dragging him to his feet and telling him, 'To some new place. Somewhere we've not seen. Somewhere maybe that'll show us home.'

Nigel McDowell

Nigel grew up in County Fermanagh, rural Northern Ireland, and as a child spent most of his time battling boredom, looking for adventure – crawling through ditches, climbing trees, devising games to play with his brother and sister, and reading. His favourite book as a child was *The Witches* by Roald Dahl.

After graduating with a degree in English (and having no clue what to do with it!), he decided to go off on another adventure, spending almost two years living and working in Australia and New Zealand.

Nigel now lives in London. He has written articles on film and literature for a number of websites. He is always on the hunt for books about folklore and fairytale.

Nigel's debut novel, *Tall Tales from Pitch End*, was published in June 2013.

Follow Nigel on Twitter: @NMcDowellAuthor
www.nigelmcdowellauthor.com

Thank you for choosing a Hot Key book.

If you want to know more about our authors
and what we publish, you can find us online.

You can start at our website

www.hotkeybooks.com

And you can also find us on:

We hope to see you soon!